I0730168

A VISION OF VIOLENCE

Also by Nichelle Seely:

Audrey Lake Investigations
A Memory of Murder
A Vision of Violence

A VISION OF VIOLENCE

Nichelle Seely

*For my mother, Norma Seely, and my sister, Elia Seely,
fellow writers on the journey.*

A Note About Mental Illness

The protagonist of this novel, Audrey Lake, suffers from mental illness. She has Post-Traumatic Stress Injury brought on by her time as a homicide detective. At times, she is borderline psychotic, with a fragmented identity.

Audrey downplays her own mental illness as a defense mechanism, and uses self-deprecation of her condition as a coping strategy. She derides her symptoms as "craziness." It isn't meant to be offensive. Audrey doesn't direct this attitude to anyone but herself. Her sarcasm is a kind of gallows humor, used to deflect emotion so she can function. This is common among law enforcement and the military.

It isn't my intent to injure anyone. My inclusion and portrayal of PTSI isn't uninformed or thoughtless. In creating Audrey's character, I have spoken to folks who suffer from PTSI brought on by various causes. People struggling with mental illness are all along the emotional spectrum, and deal with it in a myriad of ways. I've tried to make my character realistic. Audrey isn't particularly emotionally healthy, and that is part of her character arc as she learns to feel and face the trauma of her past.

Audrey Lake is a fictional character. She isn't modeled on any particular person. Her thoughts and feelings and attitudes are not necessarily those of the author.

OCTOBER 18 - DAY 0

1

MY NAME IS Audrey Lake. I'm a former cop, now a private investigator. And sometimes, I can see into the past. But only when it involves violence and death. Except when it's my own past. That's got some fuzzy spots. Especially around violence and death.

Yeah, I'm kind of messed up. So what the hell am I doing here, standing on the sidewalk long after sunset, hood pulled up against the rain? The cloud cover makes the night pitch black, except for the murky glow of a halogen street lamp. The puddles tremble under the drizzle, and fallen leaves have turned into a mushy carpet. The smell of damp is so heavy I can taste it. In other words, a typical fall evening on the Oregon coast.

In front of me is a rambling Queen Anne mansion, complete with a corner tower. My mother, the architect, would love it. Me, I see a repair and maintenance nightmare. Several of the windows glow with light, and indistinct silhouettes of people move about on the second floor. A faint snatch of laughter comes from inside. It seems pleasant; people enjoying themselves, sheltered from the weather. I've been invited, but haven't decided whether or not to cross the threshold.

A movement catches the corner of my eye, and my cop instincts kick in. I reach for my weapon, but the Glock in the shoulder holster is absent—I don't usually bring it to social occasions. I turn to see a dark figure a block away, walking hunched against the rain. I relax. Just another person on their own in the dark.

I must be really desperate. Or really lonely. Or both. Why else would I have left my own house, on a rainy October night, to join a group of strangers who think they have psychic powers? But in our last therapy session, Phoebe urged me to get out and meet more people. She said being social would be good for me, get me out of my head. She said it would help with my PTSI. And I do want to get better. Be normal.

Like that's ever going to happen.

And here we go with the craziness. Say hello to Zoe, the alternate identity I used when I was working undercover. Only she didn't depart when the mission was over, after everything went to hell. I didn't go back to completely being me, Audrey Lake. Some splinter of Zoe remained behind, manifesting as a strident voice intruding on my thoughts.

I resent that remark.

In the law enforcement business, you soon discover that people are the most unfathomable of all the variables—you can do your best to save them, protect them, warn them about their danger, but in the end you can't control what they do, or who they choose to be. Lovers will love, lawyers will argue, creators will create—

And murderers will murder.

Yeah, that got dark real fast.

I shake my head, and the rasp of my hood fills my ears. You can dress for the weather, you can turn on a light to push back the dark, but dealing with people is never so straightforward. And my mental health issues don't help. Maybe I should just go back home.

You're getting awfully good at running away.

I refuse to let Zoe be right, so I make myself walk up to the shelter of the covered porch. The wood smells damp, and a stale whiff of smoke wafts from a potted plant where someone has crushed a cigarette. The big house has been subdivided into apartments, and it takes me a few seconds to find the name of my host on the intercom and press the bell next to it. A staticky, masculine voice comes from the speaker as the entry buzzes open.

"Come on upstairs. First door on the left. It's unlocked."

I obey instructions and walk through the door. Because sometimes, in order to move forward, we have to do things we don't want to do. Because sometimes, the only way out is through.

2

BERNIE'S APARTMENT FEELS packed with people. Lamps and candles yield a warm glow, and I'm moderately anxious that the house is going to catch fire with all these open flames. The place smells like cinnamon and incense. I hang my dripping jacket on a hook with other damp coats and make my way to a squishy armchair in the living room. A Rider-Waite Tarot deck graces the end table beside the chair alongside a pink crystal on a metal stand. Bernie is the balding man with a red Van Dyke beard sitting over on the sofa. All around are some other members of what he calls 'the seeker community.' Everyone is white and middle-aged, like ninety-five percent of the people in Astoria. They look surprisingly conventional, given the circumstances.

Hey, even you *seem normal in a mirror. Not to mention white and middle-aged.*

Right. No one can tell by looking that I've got an acerbic alter ego who can't keep her mouth shut.

I originally met Bernie through my therapist, Phoebe Rutherford. When I first came to Astoria, I was a basket case, and she helped me work through some of the PTSI left over from my career as a homicide detective in Colorado. I had stopped taking my meds and was having hallucinations that I was convinced were a symptom of psychosis.

Unlike the shrinks in the Denver psych ward, Phoebe didn't make that diagnosis; instead, she called in another expert on the powers of the mind: Doctor Bernard Flowers. He helped define what was going on: that I had an ability to tap into scenes from the past which had been imprinted onto the surrounding environment, like a hologram. According to him, the more intense the emotion of the event, the more likely it was to create a lasting impression, discernible by someone with a sensitivity to such things. Someone like myself, apparently.

I wasn't quite convinced at the time—I'm still not, to be honest—but a good detective follows all the leads, even the ones that seem ridiculous on the surface. My own attitude toward self-proclaimed psychics is mixed. They crawl out of the woodwork in murder investigations. Some are well-meaning, some are outright scam artists. I tend to fall on the side of skepticism. But here I am, hobnobbing with the local sensitives.

Bernie leans forward and lights a stick of incense in a burner on the coffee table. The scent of jasmine drifts through the air. "Welcome, everyone. Thanks for coming. Gather round."

I wonder if he's going to build a campfire next?

Maybe we'll tell some ghost stories.

When everyone has clustered together, he says, "Why don't we all tell our names, and what our superpower is? I'll start."

Superpower. Argh. I wrap a strand of hair around my finger and tug until it hurts. At least that's pain I can control.

"I'm Dr. Bernard Flowers, but everyone calls me Bernie." His smile is wide and friendly, and his ruddy cheeks bunch up and obscure his eyes. "I'm a psychologist, and I'm interested in the mind and its latent abilities. I've done a lot of research and experimentation, but haven't discovered any abilities of my own yet. So I'm the coach, not the athlete. And I want everyone here to feel good about their differences, and not be afraid to share." He looks to another man to his right. "Bruce, would you go next?"

Bruce mumbles something inaudible, making no eye contact—quite a feat when there's this many people in the room. I've interrogated enough perps in my time to recognize his obvious discomfort. Unlike those situations, this time I have sympathy for the man in the hot seat.

"Don't be shy," says Bernie. "Everyone, Bruce here has the ability to see the future."

Bruce turns red and looks like he wants to exit stage left. I feel even more sympathy, especially as I shift position and realize I've chosen the wrong chair. It's too soft for me to get up and make a rapid retreat.

Introductions continue. There's a medium. An object-reader. A pet whisperer. And now it's my turn. I've never talked about my visions to strangers, or even outside the psychiatrist's office. But I'll be more conspicuous if I refuse to speak. So I paste a smile on my face and say, "Hello everyone. My name is Audrey Lake. I'm a private investigator. And I can see the past. Sometimes. I mean, other people's pasts. Not just my own. Once I even saw a murder."

My words are greeted with silence and a few raised eyebrows.

And your other power is being a buzzkill.

I'm sure as hell not introducing Zoe. She gets too much airtime as it is. But she's right. Everyone is looking at me. And I realize I'm still pulling my hair. So I stop, and pretend to be adjusting my coiffure. Which might be more convincing if my hair were actually styled instead of just flopping over my head.

The medium—dressed in jeans and an Icelandic sweater—inclines her head. "Retrocognition. Interesting. I've always wondered what it must be like to visit a past that's not your own."

The introductions continue around the circle. Then Bernie clears his throat and steeples his fingers. "The object of this gathering is to form a support group for folks who are trying to develop their personal powers. To that end, I'd like to establish regular activities where we explore our abilities." He stands. "But for now, let's get to know each other better. There's snacks and drinks in the dining room. Let's make this less like a meeting and more like a party. Follow me."

I'm the last to leave the room, due to the gravitational suck of the armchair. But I quickly catch up to Bruce, who is hovering in the doorway of the dining room, watching the guests fill plates with finger food. He smiles at me in a desperate manner, a bare twitching of his lips.

"Audrey, right? Hello. So you're a private investigator? That's exciting. Your power must really help you in your work."

If he only knew how wrong he is. "Hi Bruce. Can you really see the future?"

Bruce runs a hand through thinning, gray-streaked hair. "I wish he hadn't said that. Mostly, I do object-based divination. Tarot, runes, I Ching. You know the things. But occasionally, I get a flash. A hunch. A feeling that stands out. About something that is going to happen. And it always comes true."

"Always? Can you give me an example?"

He shifts from foot to foot, eyeing the rest of the group. "Well, it's usually little things like knowing someone is about to call me, or what commercial is going to play on TV, or what my wife is going to fix for dinner. But once, I knew what the Megabucks numbers were going to be, and I was right."

Practical magic indeed. I'm impressed despite myself. "So, did you buy a lottery ticket?"

He shakes his head, shoulders slumping. "No. At the time, I didn't believe me."

I resist the urge to pat his shoulder.

Or smack him upside the head.

He continues. "But I'm working on that. Bernie has me doing exercises to improve my ability. Meditations, visualizations, and—"

My eyes begin to glaze. "Really? How interesting. Let's get some cheese."

At the table, I find myself standing next to the medium. She's short, barely to my shoulder, and I think of that old joke, 'small medium at large.' Her smile is bright and sharp, her blue eyes dreamy as she looks over my right shoulder.

"Excuse me," she says, "but do you have a relative or friend who has passed over? Someone close to you?"

A frisson of alarm raises the hair on my forearms. I wonder if that's Zoe she's seeing. "Do they look like a broken-down, middle-aged sex worker?"

Who's broken-down?

The medium laughs. "It's not that distinct. Just a fuzzy presence behind you."

I've never thought of Zoe as fuzzy. More like a cactus, in fact. But I resolve to try out some small talk. "How long have you been a medium?"

"All my life. It's not like an occupation, it's more of a calling."

"So you've always talked to the spirits?" I can't keep the disbelief out of my voice.

I bet I could talk to some Jack Daniels if I tried.

But she's nodding. "Yes. I didn't always know what it was, but I've always heard their voices."

There's a lot of that going around. At least my voices are limited to one.

Underachiever.

"I'm sorry, I didn't get your name. I'm Meg." She shifts her plate to her left hand and extends her right.

"Hi Meg. I'm Audrey." As I shake her hand, I note her grasp is firm without squeezing and her palm is dry. She's not nervous or uncomfortable. Unlike myself.

"You seem skeptical, Audrey. You're here, and you've said you have your own ability, so can I ask what makes you doubt my own?"

"Why do you think that?" I ask carefully, neither confirming nor denying her assessment. I've learned something from therapy, at any rate.

She laughs again, and rolls her eyes. "Please. I can see it a mile away. But I'm not offended. The spirits are real, whether or not you believe, but it does make me curious as to why you're here."

I try to pick my way through this minefield. "I'm afraid in my job I have to depend on physical evidence. And not all my experiences with psychics have been positive. But I try to keep an open mind."

"That's laudable, considering you've got your own intuitive gifts. Retrocognition, wasn't it? The ability to see the deep past. We should collaborate sometime, seeing as how our gifts are aligned. Information I get from the spirits is always secondhand, but you can witness directly."

She hands me a business card. I take it and she smiles and nods before drifting over to talk to the pet whisperer. I can't tell if she was being serious, or ironic. So I take my plate of little toasted breads and smoked provolone and walk over to Bernie. I'm going to ask him for directions to the bathroom and then I'm going to hide there for an hour. It was a mistake to come here. I'm not like these people, not one bit. I don't want to have a power. I don't want to encourage other folks' delusions. And I *really* don't want strangers to peer into my unfortunate past. Or to imagine the ghosts that surround me. Especially when it's only thirteen days to Halloween.

I munch on my snack, the smooth and smoky taste of the cheese is enhanced by the sharp flavor of toasted rye. I'm waiting for Bernie to finish chatting with one of the other guests. But before I can get a word in, someone bangs three times on the apartment door. Bernie glances at us apologetically and answers the knock.

On the threshold is a middle-aged man dressed in jeans and a gray sweatshirt with the words "Gonzaga University" emblazoned across the chest.

The visitor clears his throat. "Dr. Flowers, as you know, I live in the apartment below and I'm sorry to say, you're making too much noise. Again."

"I apologize, Father Mike. We'll try to keep it down. I'll ask my guests to remove their shoes."

The priest's gaze sweeps the room. "You know I dislike this kind of thing. As long as we share this building, you have no right to pollute the atmosphere with objectionable practices." He sniffs. "Not to mention smoke and incense."

Hear, hear.

"I'm sorry it bothers you, but I have every right to have people over. Perhaps you'd like to join us?" Bernie steps back and opens the door wider. "I'm sure most of the folks here are interested in spirituality."

The priest shakes his head, his expression shifting from annoyance to sadness. "I don't think we're on the same wavelength. But," he raises his voice, "if anyone wishes to visit St. Mary's, the church is always open, and we welcome newcomers."

"I always encourage my patients and associates to attend to their spiritual needs. Are you sure you won't come in?"

"No, thank you. Please, just keep it down." Father Mike puts a hand on Bernie's shoulder. "Someone less understanding than I might call the police before having the courtesy to speak to you face to face." He nods once, and turns to walk away.

Bernie shrugs, shuts the door, and goes back to the gathering. Talk has died down, and people look at him inquisitively. "Sorry folks, there's always someone who misunderstands what we're doing here. Don't let him bother you. Bruce, would you like to give some readings? The cards are on the end table."

I get my coat and sidle toward the door. I've only been here half an hour, but the visit from a priest has put the nail in the coffin. I feel like an outsider all over again. I'm not a believer in religion, either, but this place isn't for me. I'm not comfortable around folks who think they can see ghosts, or believe they have superpowers. It reminds me of the horrors of addiction and psychosis, things I encountered too much of when I was a cop.

Maybe I'm *your superpower.*

Not a chance, Zoe. Not. A. Chance.

OCTOBER 19 - DAY 1

3

Plink.

Plink.

It's started again. The sound of dripping water.

Plink.

I roll over on my cot and reach down to the floor for my phone. Push the bangs out of my eyes and check the weather app. Drizzle, for the foreseeable future. My arm is bare, and goose pimples cause the hair to rise. I put the phone down and pull my arm back under the sleeping bag I use for a duvet and press it against my chest, closing my eyes. Last night was busy, and I didn't sleep very well. All the socializing with the seeker community exhausted my few shreds of extroversion. Not to mention the run-in with a priest.

Plink.

Somewhere, the roof is leaking. Individual drops seeping slowly into the house. Through the protective shingles and into the vulnerable wood structure of the roof and attic. My stomach hollows with dismay, but I can't say I'm surprised. The asphalt shingles on my inherited 1915 bungalow are old and black and curling at the edges, with tufts of moss growing between the joints. I personally think the extra green fuzziness makes the house look picturesque, but I've been told that moss on the roof is not a good thing. Holds water like a sponge as tiny rootlets dig into the substrate, making the surface permanently damp and increasing the chance of rot. Time to tear off the old and put on the new.

Except, you know, money. A new roof is going to cost thousands upon thousands of dollars, and I haven't had a case for weeks. Did okay for a while after the Harkness murder, which was six months ago, but clients soon petered out. There's not a lot of activity that needs a private investigator, especially since most folks can do their own stalking on the internet. Had a few skip traces, a couple of wandering spouses. One lost dog. I'm not exactly making my fortune here. In fact, I'm digging myself into a hole, maxing out my cards to keep food on the table.

Plink.

Plus, Detective Olafson with the Astoria Police Department doesn't like me. He thinks I'm an interloper, a big city cop throwing my weight around. If he only knew. But it's a small town, and his word carries a lot of force. I'm sure he's been slowly and methodically discrediting me with possible clients: business leaders, city officials, the local monied crowd. Such as they are in a town whose population barely scrapes ten thousand, and that's only if you count the outlying rural area.

Let's slash his tires. Show him he can't push us around.

If I'd known Zoe was going to become something more than an undercover identity made up by myself and my handler, I'd never have taken the assignment in the Baxter Building. If not for that fiasco, I might still be a Denver detective, stacking up time until retirement. But. What's done is done. What can't be cured must be endured. Even if it's just not fair.

Any more clichés for the folks at home?

How about you and me getting a divorce? Or maybe separation surgery, so I can escape my alter ego like a conjoined twin.

Plink.

I put my head under the covers, because at this particular moment, warm darkness is better than the cold light of day and harsh reality. But then the phone rings, the sound muffled and faint. I emerge from my cocoon for a second time to snag the phone. Don't recognize the number, but it's local. So I pick it up. Clear my throat. "Lake Investigations."

"Good morning, Ms. Lake. Karthik Biswas, calling from the Clatsop County public defenders' office." His East Indian accent is immediately identifiable. I met him when I was working on the Harkness murder, after my friend Claire had been wrongfully accused of killing her husband.

"Good morning, Mr. Biswas." I try to make my voice brisk and competent, as though I've been up for ages chasing wrongdoers instead of lying in bed in my pajamas.

"Ms. Lake, are you able to come to my office this morning? I would like to hire you to take on an investigation around a new client."

An actual job, fallen straight into my lap. Trying to keep my excitement in check, I confirm the appointment for ten o'clock. I like the idea of working with an actual professional, instead of an emotional member of the general public. He might actually pay me on time. I pull on some clothes and run a comb through my hair before heading for the stairs.

Plink.

Downstairs, I open the curtains, turn on the electric kettle, and fill the French press with four scoops of dark roast. Just the smell gets the neurons in my brain to fire, and I begin to hum a little song. Outside, the drizzle is accompanied by a thick wall of fog, and I can barely see my downhill neighbor, let alone the docks or the Columbia River. It's a day for a sweater and my raincoat.

While the kettle boils, I think about Biswas. He's a transplanted East Indian with an expensive education. I'm not keen on lawyers as a rule, especially defense lawyers. Intellectually, I get that everyone deserves to be defended, innocent until proven guilty, all the checks and balances of the system. But emotionally, if I'm honest, when some dude in a fancy suit sits there and picks holes in the evidence painstakingly gathered by hard-working cops who put their safety on the line, it seems like a betrayal. And never a regret when some lowlife is put back on the streets.

But. Beggars can't be choosers. And I'm grateful for the opportunity. As I pour water into the press and wait for the requisite four minutes of brewing time, I wonder what he wants me to do. Follow someone who's claiming disability but can still lift boxes and ride motorcycles? Check out the security system of an office where a theft occurred? Some follow-up of the police work, maybe. That'll endear me even further to the local cops.

But Biswas works for Clatsop County, not just Astoria, so I'm hopeful the case is in Warrenton, or Seaside, or even Cannon Beach, and I'll be checking up on a different cop shop. Spread the love.

I fill an insulated cup with coffee and put on my boots.

Traitor.

Oh, pipe down. I don't notice you coming up with any money-making ideas. And maybe this will lead to other things. Give me a professional reference.

Sad to see you've fallen far enough to join the other side.

We're all on the same side. Justice. It's how the system works. Isn't that what they say?

Yeah, keep telling yourself that.

And I do, all the way downtown, because I've already decided to say yes.

4

THE PUBLIC DEFENDERS' office is located on Duane Street in a two-story concrete building, painted institutional beige with molded art-deco details around the parapet. It's across from a historic building which houses city hall, the courthouse, and other assorted offices. In the lobby, Juanita is at the front desk as per usual. She's a brown woman in her forties with long black hair interwoven with gray, which she wears in a single braid, and big gold hoops in her ears. She calls Biswas on the intercom before ushering me into the conference room.

The inset lights scattered across the ceiling illuminate the fingerprints around the border of the glass-topped table, and I wonder how many would pop up on AFIS—the Automated Fingerprint Identification System—if I ran them.

I snag a yellow legal pad from a stack on the table and jot the date and time on the top. I'm beginning a doodle of my weapon, the Glock nestled in my shoulder holster, when Biswas walks in. He's dressed in a dark blue suit and a psychedelic yellow and orange flowered tie. He's also about forty, a few threads of gray in his dark hair. His black mustache looks like he trims each individual whisker with manicure scissors and a laser level.

I nod, stand to shake hands. "Good morning, Mr. Biswas. Thanks for giving me a chance to help you." My gut feels like there's a little animal with claws running around down there, and I take a big drink of coffee to quell my nerves. Because despite my reservations, I really need this job.

"Good morning, Ms. Lake." He gestures back to the chairs and we sit. He has a bulging three-ring binder under his arm which he lays on the table.

Trying for some friendliness, I say, "Nice tie."

He looks down at it, bemused. "A gift. From my sister in Mumbai. I find a spot of color is a welcome thing under these gray skies."

"Ah." My supply of small talk is drying up like the Great Salt Lake.

He folds his hands on the table top. "Ms. Lake, I understand that you are a licensed private investigator, correct?"

"Yes." Just barely.

"And I understand that you formerly worked as a police detective."

I nod. "Twenty years in the Denver Police Department."

"May I ask what sort of cases you specialized in?"

Murder and mayhem.

I clear my throat to drown out Zoe's snide remarks. "I mostly worked with the Homicide/Robbery Unit in the Major Crimes Division. We were called in whenever there was a death that wasn't traffic related, or whenever property was taken from someone by force. We also covered weapons violations by juveniles." The canned description rolls easily off my tongue. "And I participated in some undercover ops." One, anyway. When I was thinking of joining the narc squad.

Biswas nods. I've apparently passed muster, because he says, "I'm defending a man who has recently been arrested. I'd like you to look through his case file and see if you can identify any circumstance which may help to exonerate him. I have my own ideas, but before we discuss them, I would appreciate another viewpoint, from someone with police experience." He clears his own throat, and I wonder if it's contagious. "You may, perhaps, see something I missed."

I shrug. So far, the gig sounds easy enough. "Okay, Mr. Biswas. What's your client been charged with?"

"Aggravated murder."

The atmosphere of the room seems to ripple with that word. Outside, a foghorn sounds three times as a freighter moves along the river. A vehicle in need of muffler repair cruises down the street outside, and a spat of rain hits the window. In other words, foreboding.

I guess I assumed the case would be something more like a misdemeanor. Theft, or property damage, or fraud. Low stakes. I'm honestly not sure how I feel about helping Biswas to defend a murderer. Someone who intentionally took another person's life—the ultimate crime.

Except when you do it yourself.

Oh, shut up! You were there—it was different circumstances.

Are you sure? Because we both know you don't really remember.

My palms start to sweat, and the skin beneath my holster dampens. The scar under my collarbone begins to itch.

Get a grip, Lake, I tell myself sternly. Focus on the present. You are *not* going to lose it here in the public defenders' office. I bite the inside of my lip and fixate on the pain.

The lawyer is saying, "Before we go much further, I need to know whether you will contract with this office as an investigator, and adhere to our rules of confidentiality. And your assurance that you will help to the best of your ability. I need to know of possible holes in the investigation, things that call the witnesses or evidence into question, other possible suspects, anything that creates a reasonable doubt."

"You want me to see if there's something you can use to get your guy off." My tone is accusatory, but I can't help it.

"I am the attorney in charge of this office. It is I who decides on procedures and caseloads. I want to defend him to the best of my ability. As I would have defended your friend, Claire Chandler, had it been necessary." His voice is calm, civil. And very pointed.

I wince inside. He's got me. Made it feel like a 'pay it forward' or maybe 'pay it back' kind of moment. I came to him in a time of desperation, with no one else to turn to and half-crazy besides, and he's just caught me in a noose with my own rope.

I think of the leaky roof, my ongoing need for groceries and gas. I don't actually have much choice. And if the police did their job, there shouldn't be a problem, right? Except it's always easy to question something later, play the armchair quarterback. Undermine the efforts of someone doing their best in a difficult situation. I'll just have to trust that the cops were on their game.

"Ms. Lake? Your answer?"

Remember. Food. Shelter. Transportation. I swallow past my reluctance, pushing through the barrier of past loyalties. "I'm willing to sign on with you, and I've never done anything less than my best."

Sure about that, are you?

He nods. "Good. Juanita will go through the contractual paperwork and the scope of work with you. Here's the case file." He pushes the binder across the table. "Why don't you get back to me tomorrow, after you've read it. Once you've done your analysis, we'll decide what angles to pursue."

I take the binder. "Is this all?" Cases I've worked on fill up box after box of interview records and files and notes. I wonder how thorough the investigation was.

"This is what they gave us." He shrugs. "I hope I don't need to tell you that time is of the essence. And that a man's life and freedom may depend on this."

What about the murder victim's life, I wonder, but restrain myself from saying it out loud as he escorts me back to the lobby.

"Oh, I should inform you," he says, looking over his shoulder as he turns to leave. "The grand jury hearing is on October 29th. We need to complete the investigation before then. So why don't you go out there, nose around and see what you can come up with, and get back to me in two days, on the 20th."

And with that little bombshell, he walks away.

Damn lawyers.

5

As I GET out of the car in front of my house, my phone starts to vibrate in my pocket. I have the binder under my arm and am digging for my house keys so I can't answer it right now. Plus, the drizzle is collecting in a puddle on the sidewalk at the top of the stairs. I know it will eventually drip down the outside stairs and make a lake at the base of the covered porch. Astoria is built on a hillside, and this is the disadvantage of living on the downhill side of the street.

While walking down the stairs I feel a twitch of vertigo. For some reason, the fog seems to be getting thicker. It ripples and twists, and now I can barely see the house.

When I reach the covered porch, I see a trail of wet footprints on the painted boards. They weren't there when I left—I'm obsessive about these things. They go to the door, over to the window, and back to the walkway to mingle with the general wetness.

My heart rate ratchets. Someone has been here.

Lots of explanations for that, I tell myself. Package delivery. Mail carrier. Neighbor. But I haven't ordered anything, and the mailbox is up by the street. The tracks are big, probably male. Maybe my next-door neighbor has paid me a visit. But he's a judge—I don't think he'd be peeking in the window.

Maybe they got inside.

I take my Glock from the shoulder holster. The cross hatching on the grip is pressed tight against my palm. I check the windows, tugging at the lower pane to see if it will rise. Still locked. The door is shut tight, rattling softly against the latch. I lay the binder on the doormat where it won't get wet and begin my perimeter walk: east, street side elevation, check. Go down the exterior stairs on the south side in the narrow alley between my place and the empty house next door. The rainfall is heavier and beats against my jacket. At the base of these stairs is a broken concrete landing with weeds poking up through the cracks and the walkout basement door. Can't tell if someone's been at it, but the door is still shut and locked.

Keep going, along the west side. I'm two stories below the street level now, and the ground is slick with moisture. I see a rough trail across the yard where something or someone has recently walked, crossing toward the alley on the other side of the Rutherfords. But it could be a deer or neighborhood cat, even a loose dog. My yard isn't fenced and I get all kinds of animal visitors. The windows on this side are at head level. An intruder would need a stepladder or a trampoline to get in. The ground is bare at the base of the foundation, and I don't see any footprints in the damp clay.

Up the hill on the north side. There's no stairs over here and the grass is slippery. Windows are low but inoperable, and look intact. Some of my anxiety dissipates. As near as I can tell, there's been no intrusion. I glance over at the Rutherford's house, ghostly in the swirling fog, but the windows are dark. It looks like no one is home.

Back on the front porch, it occurs to me that I should have taken a picture of the prints. They are now hopelessly smeared by my own, and there's no evidence anyone but myself was ever here.

Paranoid much?

If I am, Zoe, you of all people should understand why.

I pause on the porch, listening to the rain patter on the roof and drip from the eaves. Who would be trying to break into my house? Realistically, no one. But I can't help but think about the gang I came up against in Denver, the Junkyard Dogs. Sonny, and Blue, and the rest. Sociopaths, every last one of them. But how could they know where I live, thousands of miles and multiple states away from Colorado?

Chill out, Lake. You're overreacting.

Zoe is right. It's impossible. Much more likely to be someone local. I had antagonized a few individuals during the Harkness case. Or maybe it really is just a nosy neighbor.

Taking a deep breath, I unlock the door, then push it open with gun in hand. Do a quick clear on each floor. It's easy since I don't have any furniture beyond the cot, camp chair and card table. My house is empty, and quiet, and cold.

My hand is shaking a little with tension as I holster my weapon and retrieve the binder from the porch. Back inside, I turn the deadbolt and sit in the camp chair with the file on my lap. Look out at the falling rain and wait for my heart to resume its normal cadence. When it does, I make a hot cup of tea.

Finally I open the binder. Because I've got a job to do and I signed a contract, and I promised I would give it my best. But every now and then I stand up and look down into the fog-shrouded yard, and wonder if there's someone outside looking in.

6

IN THEORY, THE case file contains all the information gathered by the police in the course of their investigation leading up to the arrest of…I check the form for the name of the accused: James "Jim" Horne, formerly a resident of Anchorage, Alaska, but now homeless.

In reality, I know there's a lot missing from the documentation—the dead ends, the trails that went nowhere, thoughts and ideas and speculation. There's probably boxes back at the station. But it's a start, and I begin to go through the contents and develop a picture of the case. For those of us who remember such things, it's like waving a Polaroid photograph in the air and watching the image emerge.

On September 6, at approximately 3:15 a.m., just over five weeks ago, the body of Jack Reynolds was found floating in the water beside his crabbing boat (the *Beatrice*) where it was docked at the Warrenton Marina. The finder was his crewman, Charles Joseph "Charlie" Phelps. Phelps was reporting for work. Was in fact running a little late. The two of them were going out early to set some crab rings. When Phelps arrived at the boat at around three a.m., he didn't see any activity, so he got on board and started a cigarette while he waited for his employer. He saw no one else during that time. He finished his smoke and went to throw it over the stern into the water, and that's when he saw the body, floating face down.

Phelps called 911 on his cell, and waited until the police came. The detective on the scene was a man named Judd Daily. He and another officer fished Reynolds out of the water and determined that he was dead. According to the autopsy report, Captain Reynolds had been conked on the back of the head with a blunt object, possibly a hammer, and his throat had been cut from behind. There were no defensive wounds, no hesitation cuts; in fact, there were no other injuries at all. The killing wound had been deep and long, the weapon sharp and thin, probably a knife.

An image of a gleaming blade appears before my eyes. There's a face beyond, a glint of teeth, but all I can focus on is the knife.

"You can die, pig."

And the cold metal slides into my chest, just beneath my collar bone.

The sound of the binder hitting the floor jolts me back to reality. I'm shivering and sweating both. A flashback. That's all it was. Sonny isn't here. The pop of bullets isn't echoing in the hall. My hand where it presses against my chest isn't covered with blood, but I can feel the raised line of the scar.

I'm fine. Everything's fine. I'm alone. There's no one here. And I'm freezing cold.

Screw the gas bill. I lurch to my feet and jab the button on the thermostat until warm air roars from the wrought iron registers. Then I kneel to collect the papers from where they've sprung loose from the rings and scattered across the painted boards. The old wood is hard under my knees. The papers crinkle in my too-tight grasp.

Wait. Was that a noise on the porch? A footstep? I cross the living room, press against the wall next to the window and peer out beneath the edge of the blinds. Nothing.

Holy cats, Lake. Get a grip. Stop being so paranoid.

I make sure the windows are locked and return to the card table, sit down and re-open the binder, engage my jittering brain with the autopsy report. Fish scales had been found in the neck wound, but it was unclear whether they came from the weapon or from the water. Reynolds' toxicology screens were clear, no drugs or alcohol in his system. Time of death was estimated between ten p.m. and two a.m.

While the crime scene was being processed, a man appeared on the deck of the neighboring vessel, an abandoned sailboat. He called out to the officers and asked what was going on. Detective Daily investigated and discovered this man was apparently camping on the sailboat. The squatter's name was Jim Horne. He did not own the vessel, nor did he know who did.

There's a copy of Horne's Alaska driver's license in the file. Crewman Phelps later identified Horne as someone who had recently applied for a job with Jack Reynolds as a deckhand. Reynolds hadn't wanted to take him on, and according to Phelps, Horne had been 'royally pissed,' yelling and uttering threats. Horne's account was that he had met Reynolds up in Alaska a few months before, and Reynolds had offered him a job at that time, if Horne wanted to come down to Oregon. Horne had taken Reynolds at his word, and had come looking for employment after hitchhiking down the Alaska Highway.

According to Horne, when he arrived at the port, Reynolds rescinded the job offer. Horne was angry, but left without doing anything about it. Later, he noticed that the sailboat in the slip next to the *Beatrice* appeared to be abandoned. The registration on the prow was expired and the boat looked as though it hadn't been used in a long time. He didn't have any money to stay in a motel, and decided to shelter in the derelict until he convinced Reynolds to take him on or until he found another job.

A knife was discovered in Horne's possession. It fit the profile of the murder weapon, and traces of blood were found on it. But the scene was very clean: no blood on Reynolds' boat, none on the sailboat or any of Horne's possessions.

The police searched for witnesses but there were none. Other fishing boats had been moving about within the harbor but no one had come forward to the general plea for help, made through the harbormaster. Interviews had been conducted with Reynolds' ex-wife and his associates who confirmed that offering a job and then revoking it might be something Reynolds would do. Also, he was behind on his alimony payments.

He sounds like a prince of a guy.

I thumb through more documents, taking it all in, imagining the scene and subsequent investigation. My interest sharpens when I see that Reynolds had recently been cited for stealing another man's crab rings. When the rings were recovered, the charges were dropped. He had also been caught crabbing on the marine reserve off Cape Falcon. He'd claimed he didn't know he'd strayed onto the reserve and agreed to pay a fine. There's a copy of a receipt for a cash payment of five hundred dollars.

Horne, the accused, also has paper: an assault charge in Kodiak, and a car theft in Anchorage. Drunk and disorderly also in Anchorage, and resisting arrest. Not a man with a whole lot of impulse control.

There's other stuff in the file, but I close it for now. On the face of it, Horne checks the boxes. Motive. Means. Opportunity. A history of violence. Plus the knife. And he was observed threatening the victim. I can see why the detective zeroed in on him. Still, Reynolds wasn't exactly an upstanding citizen. There could be something in his past, some enemy who came out of the woodwork.

I lever myself out of the camp chair and stretch my back before retreating to the kitchen to prepare another cup of tea. I want to check the front door again, make sure it's locked, but I refuse to add OCD to my list of mental abnormalities.

Speaking of, maybe you can conjure up a psychic vision.

Maybe you can go jump in the lake.

I'm already in the Lake. Get it? Audrey Lake?

I'm doing this one straight. Footwork. Logic. Deduction. No magic tricks. So there.

I stand in the kitchen sipping my tea, pretending that I'm not talking to myself, and think about what I've read.

Biswas, lawyer that he is, is going to be digging into the police procedure to see whether Horne's rights were violated. He wants me to come up with something that causes a reasonable doubt. The best way to do that is to see if there's anyone else out there who wanted to kill Jack Reynolds. Discounting Horne, who had motive, means, and opportunity, my go-to suspects are the ex-wife, the guy who got his crab rings stolen, and maybe the crewman Charlie Phelps. Wouldn't be the first murder committed by a disgruntled employee. Phelps could have gotten there earlier, offed his boss, and then waited around to report the body.

I'd also like to talk to the detective, Judd Daily, and see what didn't make it into the file, but that's a bit of a 'don't tread on me' zone. Daily isn't going to want some outsider to come in and question his work. On the other hand, I feel I owe it to him as a fellow cop. When you're hired onto the force, you take an oath to protect and to serve. And an unspoken promise to support your colleagues.

Still, I know first hand that not all cops are clean, or even competent. They're like anybody else—some are heroes, some are assholes, and most fall somewhere in between. I figure, the best I can do is to dig into the case just like the investigating detective would. If there's a hole, I'll find it. If there's not, then just by confirming that, I'll have done Daily a service.

At least I'll be dealing with the Warrenton police and not Astoria.

It's already mid-afternoon—I've been engrossed in the case file for hours, and my stomach is growling. I know there's nothing in the cupboards, so I get online and order a pizza, Canadian bacon and black olives, from the Astoria branch of Fultano's. I hold my breath waiting for the card to go through; when it does, I sigh in relief. A family size pizza will last me three days if I'm not greedy.

While I'm waiting for the delivery, I draft a proposed plan of action to Biswas. Let him know I want to re-interview some of the people surrounding Reynolds, and also that I want to speak to both Detective Judd Daily and the suspect, Jim Horne. Send it off in an email.

A loud knock makes me leap to my feet, gun in hand. I'm in full defense mode before remembering that I asked for this. I verify that it is indeed the delivery guy. I open the door, grab the box, and hand the man a couple of bucks as a tip before shutting the door and engaging the deadbolt.

As I sink my teeth into the melted cheesy goodness, I think it's no wonder my jeans are getting snug. But it's a small con against the pros of immediate comfort and warmth. I promise myself to exercise tomorrow. And also to stop being so paranoid.

OCTOBER 20 - DAY 2

7

THE NEXT MORNING, after a night of non-sleep, I call Biswas, to see if he's looked at my message. He has, and agrees to my plan of identifying people I think might work as alternate suspects. But he puts his foot down about talking to Detective Daily.

His voice is matter-of-fact. "I don't want the police or the prosecution to know we're digging in before the grand jury. They expect me to wait until after the indictment. But if I can gather enough evidence for reasonable doubt, and present that to the district attorney, we may be able to avoid a trial all together. Or plea bargain down to manslaughter or assault."

Huh. Well, I'm not a lawyer or well-versed in all their wily tricks, so whatever. I've got enough to do without talking to Judd Daily. But it puts me in a bad position if the Warrenton cops find out about my investigation, and I resent it. Like that means anything to Biswas.

Serial killers notwithstanding, most murders are not stranger-on-stranger crimes. Statistically, people are much more likely to be killed by someone they know. Since Jack Reynolds isn't alive to tell me about his enemies, I decide to talk to the next most likely person: his ex-wife.

Or at least, that's the plan. But as I climb the outside stairs to the street, I see my neighbor out walking her dog. Not a big deal, except my neighbor is also my therapist.

"Hi, Phoebe," I say, and stretch a hand to her pit bull, Delilah, who positions herself for a head scratch. Who's really the dominant species here?

"Good morning, Audrey." Phoebe nods, her silver hair beaded with moisture from the mist. "You didn't return my call."

"What call?" Belatedly, I remember the phone buzzing yesterday morning, before I was distracted by the trespasser. I take it out and look, see a voice mail from Phoebe Rutherford. "Sorry, Phoebe. I've got a job. A case that needs looking into. I promise I'll call you later."

Delilah nudges my leg and I resume scratching. "Who's a good girl, then?" I croon. What a love sponge.

Phoebe smiles fondly at her dog before resuming her lecture. "It's not about me, it's about you. The appointments are for your benefit. And it's been a few weeks."

"I know, I know."

She cocks her head. "Is Zoe still bothering you?"

None of your business, lady.

It's bad form to lie to your therapist, so I hedge my bets and temporize. "Uh…sometimes? But it's fine, really."

"When did you hear from her last?"

Tell her to get lost—you've got a deadline, here.

Phoebe smiles slightly. "Is she talking to you now?"

Damn. How does she know? Caught in the cognitive dissonance, I simply can't think of a response.

Phoebe nods. "Uh-huh, I thought so. Listen, Audrey, you've made a lot of progress, but it's easy to let that progress slip away. If you're serious about working through your PTSI, or integrating your… visions…you should resume your therapy schedule. I have an opening tomorrow."

"I'll call you later, okay?" Because I need to get on with the work of the day.

Oh, great. I'm so looking forward to an afternoon of navel gazing.

Delilah will be there.

Well, that's something, at least.

"I'll be expecting it, Audrey." Phoebe's voice is firm. "And meanwhile, try not to engage with Zoe. It will only make the problem worse."

Eff you, lady. I was here first.

Hoo boy. "I'll be back tonight, truly. Now I really have to go." I give Delilah a final pat, pull a handful of mail from the mailbox, and get into my car. Then I remember the footprints and lower the window. "Hey, Phoebe?"

"Yes?"

"Did Linc or you happen to come over to my place yesterday?"

She shakes her head. "No. Linc's not here—he's taking over for a recused judge down in Gold Beach. He'll be gone a few days. Why?"

"Just wondering. Thanks. See you tomorrow." My voice is slightly too high. I close the window and give her a jaunty wave. As I head down the hill, a glance in my rear view mirror shows Phoebe looking after me, hands on her hips, and Delilah wagging her tail.

8

ACCORDING TO THE file, the victim's ex-wife, Alicia Reynolds, lives in a trailer house out on Lewis and Clark Road. My map app indicates it's about twenty minutes away, and as I drop down the hill to Marine Drive along the shore of Youngs Bay, I observe that the tide is out. The mudflats are exposed, much to the joy of local herons and egrets who are out in force, searching for prey. To the east, a thin mist drapes the lumpy spine of the Coast Range, and the eponymous crest of Saddle Mountain is barely visible. One of these days, I'm going to go hiking up there.

What, you mean get some actual exercise?

La, la, la, not engaging.

To occupy my thoughts, I mentally review what I know of Alicia from the file. She works from home, has an online storefront for various handicrafts that she makes. She and Jack Reynolds had one child, a boy with Down Syndrome named Christopher. He lives full time with his mother. I wonder if the pressure of having a special-needs child is what caused them to divorce. The interview notes indicate that she didn't know of any enemies, but that her husband sometimes sailed a little close to the wind, meaning, I take it, that he drifted across legal lines a time or two. As I told Biswas, my intention is to evaluate the probability of her being a suspect.

My wheels rumble over the metal grate on the Old Bay Bridge. I follow my phone's directions up a winding gravel road to a sky-blue single-wide. There's a battered orange pickup in the driveway, and the decomposing remains of an old seventies-era sedan off to the side, with blackberry brambles curling out from under the hood.

I really hope I can do this. It's been awhile since I've done an actual homicide investigation. Interviewed suspects. Tried to winnow out the truth from a blanket of lies. I hope I haven't lost my edge.

I take a moment to activate the recording function on my phone before tucking it into my breast pocket. The curtain in the front window twitches as I get out of the car. As I approach the dwelling, the door opens and a heavyset woman dressed in jeans and a loose-knit cardigan sweater steps outside. Her dark blonde hair is pulled back in a ponytail, revealing an inch of gray at her scalp.

She folds her arms and leans against the door frame. "Who are you? If you're with the electric company, the check is in the mail."

The wooden porch steps sag a little underfoot as I mount the porch and extend my hand."My name is Audrey Lake. I'm a private investigator. I'd like to ask you some questions about your ex-husband."

She ignores my hand, tucking hers under her armpits. "He's dead." Her affect is flat, as is her tone.

"Yes, I know. I'm following up on the police investigation."

She pulls her hair out of the knitted scrunchy that holds her ponytail, puts it back. Shivers a little and sighs, to let me know my visit is taking up her valuable time. "You'd better come in."

I follow her inside. The front room is a factory in miniature, with a sewing machine, tubs of fabric and yarn, and three half-finished knitting projects on the sofa. Piles of multicolored hats and mittens and socks are stacked against the baseboard. Every wall surface is covered with hand-painted pictures on paper, done in a childish style. There are so many it looks more like a collage than an attempt at display. She pauses to scan the cluttered room, then sits down at the kitchen table, a small round affair of retro orange with matching chrome chairs. The cushions are split and stained.

She rests her chin on her fist, exuding weariness. "So, what about Jack?"

"I'm following up on the police interview, and I just want to confirm what you told them."

"God, more questions. He's more trouble dead than alive." She waves a weary hand. "Go ahead."

I hope she's as compliant as this all the way through. "First, let me say I'm sorry for your loss."

She blinks. "Jack, you mean? Yeah, I didn't mean what I said earlier. He wasn't perfect, but he didn't deserve what happened to him." She sounds like she's talking about a mutual acquaintance. I gather she's not heartbroken. Interesting.

"What can you tell me about him? What kind of guy was he?"

She takes her ponytail out of the scrunchie again, puts it back in. "Well, he couldn't hold down a job for shit. One of those guys who talks a good game, but doesn't have any follow-through, you know? When he said he was going to buy a boat, that's when I bailed. He'd had other get-rich-quick schemes that didn't pay off. And I didn't want to be on the hook for a big-ass loan. Besides, he'd been so flaky for so long I was just done, you know? He never kept his promises, and finally I was just, like, enough."

I nod sympathetically, as though I've dealt with my share of unreliable men. "So, he took out a loan to buy his boat? He owed money on it?"

"That's what I said." Alicia shrugs. "Maybe he didn't pay on time and the bankers sent a goon to collect."

Sounds like she's been binge-watching "The Sopranos." "Do you know who the loan was through?"

"Nah."

Something Biswas can follow up on. "Anyone else have a reason to hurt him?"

She sighs again, long-suffering. "Like I already told the police, I don't know. Doesn't mean there wasn't, though."

"Are there others he owed money to?"

She snorts. "Probably. He was always asking *me* for cash."

"But no one you know for sure?"

"I try to keep out of his life. He comes—came—around every now and then to visit with Christopher—that's our son—but that's all. He's too disruptive, and I didn't really want him around, to be honest. He loved Chris, but he got too impatient with him. That's another reason it didn't work out between us." Her gaze strays to the painted pictures on the walls.

In an effort to reclaim her attention, I make an arm gesture. "I understand that he took someone's crab rings?"

She rolls her eyes. "Yeah, what an idiot. Plus, that's just wrong, you know? I mean, take a guy's equipment, how's he supposed to make a living? But that's Jack for you, all short-term benefits and no long-term consequences."

"Can you tell me more about that?"

"Jack took the rings from my cousin Keith. Keith Larson, owns the *Georgia Peach*. He'd gone crabbing with him a few times, learned how to do it, and then went off with Keith's rings to do it on his own. But then what's poor Keith supposed to do, with his rings gone AWOL?"

"How did your cousin feel about that?"

"He was really pissed. I mean, Keith doesn't get upset at too much, but he hit the roof over this. Well, he didn't know who'd done it at first, but then when they caught Jack on the reserve and were going to confiscate his rings, and then they saw the rings had Keith's boat's name on them, that unravelled pretty quick."

While I'm trying to make sense of all this, we are interrupted by a young man coming into the kitchen. He has short white-blond hair, wire-rimmed glasses, and the characteristic facial features of someone with Down Syndrome.

"Hi, Mom! I made another picture!" He holds out a crinkled piece of paper, painted dark blue with a birds-eye view of what I think is a boat surrounded by black circles.

"Thanks, Boo. I like the colors. See if you can find a place to hang it up."

The young man comes to me with hand outstretched. "Hello, I'm Christopher."

He's got better manners than Alicia.

I shake his hand. His grip is firm and slightly damp. "Hi Christopher, I'm Audrey." He's taller than me, definitely not a child.

He proffers the paper. "Would you like a picture?"

"Uh, sure. Thanks." I lay the painting face down next to my phone.

He grins before retreating to the living room. Alicia's gaze follows him, a small smile on her face. Her whole expression is transformed. "He's such a great kid. The best thing to come out of our relationship."

"Not a kid, though, is he?" I take in the heavy thighs and shoulders. He looks strong, like a wrestler.

"No, he's twenty-two. I just think of him as a kid. Jack loved him to pieces, you know? My ex wasn't much for child support after the divorce, but he did give me some money last summer—God knows where he got it—to send Chris to a special arts program. That's where he learned how to paint. And he's been doing it ever since, as you can see." She makes a gesture that takes in the walls and their covering of pictures. "He's discovering his gifts. I tried to teach him to knit, but that was a disaster. But painting, it gives him a way to really express himself. We should all be so lucky."

We talk about her son, and about the program: two weeks of intensive creativity geared towards individuals with special needs, a day camp that included instruction, supervision, and three meals a day.

"Sounds expensive," I say.

"It was. Really out of my reach. But for once, Jack came through." She shakes her head. "I mean, except for occasionally taking Chris out on the boat, he didn't spend much time with him. And Chris really wanted to hang out with his dad. God knows why. Probably all Jack wanted was some free labor."

We continue chatting, me trying to see if she harbors residual rage or satisfaction or some other indication that she might be a murderer. But she's good at deflection, and I get the sense that she's moved on. After an hour, I'm feeling a bit weary from trying to keep the conversation on track, and I now know enough about Etsy to start selling my own potholders and paint-by-numbers. Despite her professed independence, and her devotion to Christopher, I get the idea that Alicia is a lonely person. But she seems to be doing all right otherwise.

See? You don't need friends. They're just a distraction.

I thank Alicia for her time and click off the voice recording. Then I walk over to examine the pictures.

Dozens of paintings flutter haphazardly against the walls. Images of the trailer, the woods, the ocean. Boats, and crabs, and fish. I'm no art critic, but there's a vibrancy to the colors and style. Despite, or maybe because of, the lack of polish and skill.

"I like these," I say, as I return to the table to gather up my phone and Christopher's gift. "I'll hang on to this."

Alicia smiles at me for the first time. "Thanks for that. Chris will be thrilled to think someone besides me wants one."

As I leave the trailer, I note the vegetable garden in back with neat rows of lettuce and carrots. The trailer isn't a mansion, but I feel like Alicia and Christopher have constructed a nice life for themselves out here, despite being mostly on their own. It seems as if the ex-wife has moved beyond rancor or bitterness. Is that because she's established her independence from Jack Reynolds, or because she got her revenge?

9

My next step is to talk to Charlie Phelps, the guy who discovered the body and who also worked for Reynolds. I know from the police file that he is twenty-nine and has a new job stocking shelves at Englund Marine and Industrial Supply. The store is near Pier Three at the Astoria port, and the parking lot is full of pick-up trucks and utility vans.

I track down Phelps inside the store, stocking shelves with coils of rope from a plastic crate. He's got a ruddy, wind-burned complexion that makes him look older than he is. His shock of dirty blond hair is tousled, and his pale blue eyes are bracketed by the beginnings of crows' feet, probably from squinting into the sun.

I give him the spiel I gave to Alicia, about following up on the police report. He puts down his crate and tells the man at the cash register he's going on a smoke break.

"What, again?" The man's expression is annoyed.

Phelps ignores that, and leads me through the racks of wet weather gear and outside to the loading dock. It's stopped raining for the moment. A chill wind is blowing in off the water, but I resist zipping my coat up. Because if I do, I can't get to my weapon right away if I need it. Although Phelps isn't very big, he's got a wiry strength which I observed as he handled the crate.

Paranoid much?

We've been attacked before, remember? Situational awareness is a good thing, Zoe. Especially when you're alone in an isolated place with some dude.

Let me know when that awareness kicks in.

Crap, I've engaged. What Phoebe told me not to do. And I'm letting Zoe distract me from my job. He's been waiting for me to begin, lighting up a Marlboro with his back to the wind. I start with things we both know, ask him to walk me through how he found the body. He does that, more or less following the account I've already read in the file. He doesn't seem particularly upset, but he's keeping his mouth clamped around his cigarette and not giving much away. So I go off-topic, and ask him what he thinks about Jim Horne, the man currently in custody for the murder of his boss.

Phelps scoffs. "That weirdo? Surprised he'd flip out like that. But you never know what guys will do. He was kind of a loner type. Survivalist."

"A survivalist? You mean like, a prepper?"

He scowls. "What's that?"

"Someone actively preparing for the end of the world."

Phelps removes his cigarette and spits off the side of the loading dock. "Nah. I mean, he hitchhiked down from Alaska with no money, and then just set up camp in a random boat. Ready to do whatever it takes in the moment, right?" He shrugs, uninterested. Scratches his scalp like he's chasing something down. Looks back at the employee entrance.

I ask another question to keep him talking. "Were you there when Horne talked to your boss?"

He inhales, and the ash on his cigarette magically elongates by a quarter inch. "Yeah."

I wait for him to elaborate. When he doesn't, I ask him what happened.

"We were hosing off the deck of the *Beatrice* when this guy walks up, says he's looking for Reynolds. Jack went down on the dock to talk to him. I was still hosing but heard Horne say he was there for the job. Surprised me, didn't know Jack was looking for another hand. You'd think he'd say something, if he was planning to replace me. Bad enough that he uses that kid of his for free labor."

"His kid? You mean Christopher?"

"If he has another, I don't know about it."

"What did he have Chris do?" Alicia had mentioned that Chris went out on the boat, but I hadn't thought that meant actually working.

"Doesn't take much brains to pull in the pots. I'll say one thing for him, that kid is strong."

Interesting. "Did Chris work on the boat much?"

Phelps gives me a look I can't interpret, a kind of knowing sneer. "Enough. So it's not likely he'd need *another* guy."

It's a good segue back to the topic I came here to ask him about. I can find out more about Chris later, if I need to. "Did that piss you off? Reynolds talking to Horne, I mean?"

Phelps frowns. "You said you're a cop?"

"Nope. Just following up on the police interview."

"So you're not a cop?"

"No."

He lifts a hand to scratch his head again, and the tail of his sweater lifts to reveal a small utility knife in a sheath on his belt.

I'm distracted by the sight of the knife. I remind myself that a lot of innocent guys carry knives. It's just a tool.

He notices me noticing, his brow furrows, and he tugs his sweater down. "You seem like a cop. Asking questions and all."

"Well, I'm not." Technically. But I used to be a cop, and his persistence on the topic is interesting. I wouldn't be surprised if he has sidestepped the law himself on occasion. I think about saying I'm working for the defense lawyer, but something tells me he wouldn't like that either. So I leave it hanging. Go on to the next thing, which should be a softball.

"Was the work on the boat all getting done? Did you think Reynolds needed more help?"

"I did everything. All the time. More than he did, even. Definitely more than his dumb kid."

His dissing of Christopher is irritating, but I force a laugh. "Ain't that always the way? Worker bee does the whole job, boss just leans back and rakes in the profit."

He frowns, but doesn't reply. Takes his smoke out and looks at it, then throws it off the loading dock.

Maybe I was a bit heavy-handed. Crap. My interview skills have gotten rusty. "So, Reynolds was just into crabbing, right? I mean, he didn't do fishing, correct?"

"That's right."

"I understand he was caught with stolen crab rings on the marine reserve."

He takes one step away. Jams his hands into his pockets. "Don't know anything about that."

"You weren't with him at the time? Even though you do most of the work?"

He's looking at me. Not answering.

"Look," I say. "I'm really not trying to get you in trouble here. None of this is about you, it's about Jack Reynolds, and Jim Horne. But Reynolds is dead, and Horne is in custody. So you're the guy I've got to talk to. Did Reynolds take Horne out on the boat? Did they go onto the reserve? Or did Reynolds just kick Horne to the curb?"

I can see the wheels turning behind his eyes. He's thinking about lying, maybe throwing Horne under the bus somehow.

I keep pushing. "Did you go out on the reserve with Jack?"

"He was the one driving the boat. I went where he did."

"Did you know you were on the reserve? Did you know it was illegal?"

His eyes narrow. "It's not like we're the only ones out there."

"What do you mean?"

"I mean, other people fish on the reserve. Jack just happened to get caught."

"Know that first-hand, do you?"

"Yeah, I do."

So, that's interesting. Maybe. Or just classic deflection. Dangling a shiny object in front of me. Bait.

Well, he is a crabber. What do you expect?

I resist the bait, get back on track. Because I'm not interested in other people's infractions.

"Just to confirm, Reynolds never hired Horne?"

"That's what I said."

"So when Horne came looking for a job, Reynolds told him to talk to the hand?"

Phelps is shaking his head. "Nah. Just said sorry, he didn't have a job open."

At last, a straight answer. "What did Horne do then? Just go off quietly?"

"Guy tried to argue. Said he'd talked to Jack up in Kodiak, Jack told him he'd have a job."

"Was Horne mad?"

"Yeah, he was steamed. Said he'd come a long way, all the way down the Alaska Highway. That Jack owed him."

"What do you think about that?"

Phelps shrugs. "Was me, I'd be mad. But I wouldn't go crossing the country without a sure thing, either."

I nod. "Right, you'd be smarter about it."

"Yeah, I would."

"Do you think Horne killed Reynolds?"

"The cops arrested him, so he must be guilty." He looks right at me, strong eye contact. "Now, I gotta get back to work." He turns and walks back into the store. I'm left wondering if he's hiding something.

10

AFTER TALKING TO Phelps, I head over the New Bay Bridge to Warrenton. It feels like I'm zigzagging all over the county, but I've got some errands to run, and all the big box stores are on the south side of Youngs Bay. By the time I'm done with all that, it's getting dark. And it just so happens that the Warrenton wharf isn't far away, just past the mouth of the Skipanon River, a tiny tributary of the Columbia.

Thinking of busting into a crime scene? Last time you did that, a building burned down.

That was not my fault. Besides, I like looking at boats.

Oh, we're going sightseeing? Tell me another.

Dammit. Zoe catches me off guard, and I have to consciously not react. But it's like not responding to your own thoughts. And in a way, they actually *are* my own thoughts, right?

Biswas didn't specifically say I couldn't look at the crime scene. He just wanted me to stay away from the cops or do anything that might alert them.

And seriously, there *is* something very, I don't know, *satisfying* about looking at boats. It hints at another life, a free life untouched by land-based problems. Of course, I know that's all nonsense. Romanticizing. But. I still feel it. #LifeAtSea.

OMG. Stop trying to be cooler than you are.

Stop texting in my subconscious.

#DefensiveMuch?

#ShutUp.

After yet another brief scrimmage with Zoe, I wander along the dock, listening to the melancholy squawk of the seagulls and looking at fishing boats. Crabbing boats. Pleasure boats. Then I see one with a scrap of fluttering yellow tape and the name on the prow: *Beatrice*.

Jack Reynolds' vessel.

The *Beatrice* seems smaller than some of the other commercial craft. The hull is white, the cabin is black, as is the deck. It looks worn. There's a wooden access way between the slips, and I walk out on it, feeling the sway of the water and the slight movement of the boards under my feet. From where I'm standing, I see spots of grime and reddish brown rust on the sides of the *Beatrice*. At least, I think it's rust. And there is also a fair amount of bird poop. Then I glance down to the narrow channel of water between the hull and the dock. There's a headless fish floating there, a string of entrails emerging from its body. The flesh is torn, perhaps by seagulls or other scavengers.

I shudder in revulsion. Me, a seasoned homicide detective who's seen more corpses than most people ever will, who's watched autopsies and witnessed scenes of violence and pain and the aftermath of grotesque crimes. I'm not sure why the fish affects me this way.

Predators and scavengers are everywhere.

I tear my eyes off the fish and concentrate on my mission. The body was found here, floating in the water at the stern of the *Beatrice*. There's plenty of traffic, even at twilight; I see people walking, and boats motoring slowly up the estuary toward the docks. Seems hard to believe that someone could be killed right here without being seen, but maybe there's less activity at night.

I'd like to get on the boat, to see if I can conjure a vision, but I hesitate just to clamber aboard. Maybe there's another way. Looking around, I don't see anyone nearby to wonder what I'm doing. And I'm pretty well screened by the vessels on either side of the walkway.

Maybe rethink how someone could hide a murder.

Yeah, that brings a nice optimistic note to the proceedings. Feeling like an idiot, I close my eyes. Think about being here at night, the slap of the water, the cool and clammy air. Feel the gentle rock of the tidal current. Smell the dankness of the river. I imagine that I'm standing on the deck of the crabbing boat, maybe waiting for someone? I let my mind drift…and find myself thinking of the leak in my roof, and how I'm going to get someone to come and fix it, and how much money that might cost.

Open my eyes. Rub my forehead. Truly, this is ridiculous. Here I am, trying to invoke some power that I don't even really believe in. That I may or may not actually have. I might as well be rubbing a lamp and hoping a genie will come out and grant me three wishes. The visions I had surrounding Elizabeth Harkness's murder had come to me unbidden, when I was still scraped and raw from my recent troubles in Denver. I'm in a different place now.

So, you think you're all better?

Yeah, except for the intrusive voice of my alter ego. The one my therapist told me not to engage with, so as not to make her worse than she actually is.

#RealityCheck.

#MindYourOwnBusiness.

Since no hallucinations or psychic visions have caused me to lose track of my surroundings, I glance over to the sailboat moored next to the *Beatrice*. This is the vessel that Horne had been squatting in when he found he didn't have a job. Its sides are lower, so it's easier to climb onto than the commercial boat. It has a thin layer of grit on the boom and deck, and the sail cover is creased with dirt. The license tag displayed on the prow is out of date. Horne probably thought this would be a safe place to crash while he figured out what to do next.

The shadows lengthen, and I zip my coat against the chill. I can see why the investigating officers focused on him. Motive, means, and opportunity. He fits the bill snugly. But. Would someone really murder a man literally next door to where he was living and then simply go back to sleep?

You of all people should know how stupid criminals can be.

That's true. Habitual criminals are usually not very smart and don't weigh consequences well, hence their choice of a life of crime. But this seems way too under the bar. Horne might not be a rocket scientist but he must have at least a little street savvy. Even if this was his first offense.

Hello, assault? Drunk and disorderly? Car theft? Guy has a history.

Yeah, but not murder.

No accounting for the things people do.

Still. It just doesn't ring true. Even if Horne killed Reynolds in anger, I think he'd hightail it out of the area once he saw what he'd done. I don't have to be psychic to figure that out. What I need to do is talk to Jim Horne. See what he has to say about the night in question. Evaluate his street smarts for myself. I need to feel Horne's personal vibe before I can judge him to be guilty or innocent.

The boards of the dock rattle behind me, and a deep voice says, "What are you doing here?"

I spin on my heel. There's a man standing there, a big bearded white guy, dressed in knee-high rubber boots and tan Carhartt jacket. His knitted hat is pulled down low over his eyes. It's dark enough now that his face is just a pale smear.

And he's cut off my only line of retreat.

11

MY HEART RATCHETS up into the coronary zone. My hands are in my pockets—no way I can get to my gun quickly.

He takes a step forward. The boards creak. "I asked you what you're doing here."

"I'm just looking. Looking at the boats." My voice is higher than normal, and my palms are damp inside my pockets. I take them out, let my arms hang. "Are you—are these yours?"

I'm stalling, trying to gain time until maybe someone walks by. There's no way I can take this guy down without a weapon.

"Someone died here," he says, frowning. "We don't like people to come here and gawk."

Where is everyone? The night is silent, and I'm stuck here in this little blind alley. I didn't want someone to witness my psychic inability, and now I'm on my own, trying to parse whether his words are an implicit threat.

I inch my right hand up to my zipper pull, fiddle with it, tug it down halfway.

"Did you hear me?" The big man takes another step closer, and I see he also has a knife on his belt. They're everywhere.

"I heard you." My hand is inches from my weapon. "I'm just leaving." I take a tentative step closer, hoping he'll make way.

The man folds his arms and doesn't budge. "We don't like tourists down here."

Okay, enough. I pull the Glock and take a ready stance with a double-handed grip. "Back up, asshole. Now."

His hands come up. "Jesus, lady. What's your problem?" But he does take a few steps back, until he's on the main arm of the dock.

Do you always bring a gun to a knife fight?

"Shut up, goddamn it!"

"Okay, okay! Jesus."

I wasn't talking to him, but my outburst has the desired result. He retreats even further, and I'm able to get on the main boardwalk, away from the pinching presence of the boats. My emotions whipsaw. Terror and anger claw for dominance; my reptile brain is reared up on its hind legs, hissing. But two decades' worth of training and experience kick in, and I throttle back my feelings.

"Turn around, and walk away. Now."

"What, so you can shoot me in the back? You're crazy." His voice is outraged, upset, but underneath I can hear his fear, and his fear makes me both gleeful and ashamed.

My voice is shaking, but my gun is rock-steady. "Do it. I don't want to have to hurt you."

For a moment, he just stands there with his arms out, hands at shoulder level. Then he turns his back and walks stiffly away. After he's gone about twenty paces he breaks into a run, and his feet beat hollowly on the boards as he disappears among the moored vessels.

Slowly, I lower my weapon. My pulse throbs at my temple like a jungle drum. I head in the opposite direction, back along the dock to the parking lot, right arm hanging at my side with the weight of the Glock making a pendulum of my hand. My head is on a swivel as I reach my car, checking my surroundings. The lot is empty.

The gravel sprays from the wheels as I peel out onto the main road. Because I really don't want to be here if he's called the police.

12

I HEAD BACK to the big Fred Meyer store and merge into the sea of parked cars. Turn off the lights and the ignition. Lean back in the driver's seat with my eyes closed, until my heart rate returns to something approximating normal.

I think I might've overreacted just a tad.

Yeah, that guy was out of line, but probably pulling a gun on him wasn't the smartest thing I could've done. Still, he should know better than to corner a woman like that. Anyone would have felt threatened. I just happened to be armed.

That'll teach him to bother crazy people. Asshole.

"I am not crazy!" My voice is loud enough to startle me, and a passing shopper glances my way. I slide down a little lower in my seat, until my head is barely above the dashboard. Just enough to scan for cops cruising by on the main road. In case he called them.

I've barely settled down when my phone rings, causing me to jerk upright. It's Bernie Flowers. He's going to want to talk about ESP, and I do not want to talk to him. Especially after failing to generate anything remotely vision-like.

Retrocognition. Isn't that what the medium called it? Another double-edged gift from the Baxter Building.

I had been living with other squatters in an abandoned building in Denver as part of an operation to gather evidence against a criminal gang that sold drugs, dabbled in prostitution, and movement of stolen goods. To maintain my cover, I sometimes had to ingest mind-altering substances. I did this very seldom and only when forced by circumstances, and I cleared my system as quickly as I could.

But.

I began to see things. Visions of some of the terrible things that happened in the Baxter Building. Images of police consorting with criminals. And one day, a dealer named Sonny slipped me a roofie. Then he attacked me while I was half-conscious, stabbing me in the upper chest. I have a scar there now, a thin red line surrounded by dots where the sutures went in. Somehow, he knew I was a cop. And he timed his attack for the day of the surprise police raid. A surprise even to me.

Sonny left me in my room, bleeding from the wound. I still don't know why he didn't kill me. I dragged myself into the closet. I lost consciousness, kind of—but was caught in a hallucination of cops and criminals, while the raid was going down in the Baxter Building. Shooting. Take-downs. People running and screaming. And sometime during that chaos, while I was drugged up and dying, I killed someone.

Yeah. And that's all I know. I don't know who it was. I don't remember the face, only the body lying next to me on a grungy mattress. I don't remember doing it. The cops—my colleagues—found me in the closet, and I went to Saint Joseph's with the rest of the wounded. Took a long time to sort me out from the bad guys, and for a while I was handcuffed to my bed. Because I was so out of it, raving and seeing things that weren't there, they moved me to the psych ward until I calmed down and was able to be released back into the wild.

But in my delirium I'd said things, unforgivable accusations, against my colleagues. And my breakdown made it hard to return to work. So I didn't. I moved into my parents' basement, but after three months we all knew that wasn't a winning strategy.

My aunt died last year, and left me her house and all the contents to my mother. I'm living in that house now. I thought moving to Astoria would be a great escape hatch. As happens with many of my plans, the reality turned out to be somewhat different.

I came here, with a few sticks of furniture, my gun, and a prescription for antipsychotic meds, which I stopped taking almost the moment I arrived. I didn't like the side effects, the blunting of emotion and alertness.

And of course, the visions started again.

The phone beeps, bringing me back to the present. A new voicemail banner scrolls across the screen.

I know why he's calling. He wants to 'explore my horizons.' But really, I just want to let it go. I want to settle into my new career as a private investigator, and leave all that trauma and drama behind. Life is tricky enough without something otherworldly to complicate matters. But if I don't at least listen to Bernie's message, and send him a text or something, he'll just call again. So I set the phone to speaker and push play. A familiar gravelly voice fills the car.

"Hi Audrey, Bernie Flowers here. I'm calling to let you know I passed your phone number on to Meg Eccleston. She's a member of the seeker community, and wanted to get in touch with you. You guys connected at my little party. Just wanted to let you know. Bye."

Great, now Bernie is giving out my personal details to the local woo-woo enthusiasts. I rub my forehead. The seeker community. Ye gods.

Sounds like just what we need.

Since when are *you* a seeker, I'd like to know?

Desperately seeking sanity. And it's not like you've got friends of your own.

Ugh. Zoe's right. I'm a candidate for winning Hermit of the Year. The only people I associate with are lawyers, suspects, and my therapist. Not an incredibly healthy social diet.

It's been half an hour. There's been no sirens, no squad cars patrolling the parking lot looking for gun-toting tourists. Slowly, I get back on the highway, keeping one eye on the rear view mirror. Maybe my little misdemeanor of threatening a civilian with my weapon will fly under the radar. For now.

13

BACK AT THE house, I do a perimeter check and clear the rooms. I think about getting some furniture beyond the camp setup, but my budget doesn't run to beds and sofas. Sitting down at the card table, I make notes about my interviews and flip through the case file, adding facts and findings. The familiar ritual is soothing. Almost like being back on the force.

In your dreams. Or maybe nightmares.

The phone rings. It's Phoebe. Answer, or let it go to voicemail? If I pick up, she'll bug me about therapy. If I don't, she'll know I'm avoiding her. But right now, I'd rather avoid Zoe.

"Hi Phoebe, what's up?"

"I'm calling to confirm your appointment. Tomorrow at four, does that still sound doable?"

Ambush. "I'm working a lot."

"Glad to hear it. But Audrey, you've made so much progress, don't throw that away. Mental health is a long journey."

Don't I know it. But I just want to get on with my life. Are therapists always this pushy?

Don't worry, I'll always be here.

Zoe. How comforting.

"Audrey? Are you there?"

"Yes, I am. Just thinking." About how expensive therapy is, and how I'm going to be reduced to eating dog food if my finances don't improve. But I also don't want to be crazy again. It's a dilemma.

Phoebe says, "I'll see you tomorrow, all right?"

I say no, she'll just suggest something else. "Okay."

The call ends, and I stand, looking out the window. A huge cruise ship is making its way up the channel of the river, lights blazing as it heads toward the deep-water berths. An ocean-going freighter is heading out, its wisdom line high above the water. Lightly laden. The two ships pass, the big freighter completely eclipsed by the giant passenger craft.

A coil of fog begins to snake up the river, pale and ghostly in the moonlight. Like a tentacle.

Shivering, I try to focus on the job. It's been a productive first day, even with the confrontation at the marina. So, what next? More interviews? I'd like to know something about the incident on the marine reserve. Talk to Keith Larson and ask about the stolen crab pots. And figure out other likely suspects for the murder.

I try to imagine again how Reynolds was killed. Here comes Jim Horne, mad about being denied a job he thought he was promised. He's already had to squat in a sailboat. It's nighttime. Maybe he hears Reynolds gearing up for the next day's crabbing. The noise wakes him and he's angry all over again. Climbs out of the sailboat and down onto the walk and up into the *Beatrice*. Sneaks up behind Reynolds and conks him on the head, then reaches around and slits his throat. Drags the body across the deck to the stern, and throws it over the edge.

Right, with arterial blood splashing everywhere.

Okay, maybe Reynolds was already at the stern, maybe leaning over. Conk, cut, push. Easy.

So he's leaning over the edge for how long? And doesn't hear the murderer approaching?

Maybe Horne was on board and talking to Reynolds, trying to get him to reconsider. Reynolds says no. Turns his back, dismissing Horne. Horne flips out and kills him.

Yeah, I'd turn my back on some dude with a big knife in his hand. Not.

The thought makes me shiver involuntarily. But everyone has knives around here. For gutting fish, if nothing else. Horne might have had one on his belt. Makes sense, sleeping rough, traveling down from Alaska, that he'd have a knife for a tool and also defense.

Defense, not offense.

You sound like a basketball coach.

But Zoe's right. It just feels off. Wouldn't Horne have been more likely to throw a punch, rather than conk and kill? Maybe Reynolds insulted him somehow. What if Reynolds insinuated that Horne wasn't up to the job? That might have set Horne off in a rage. But in the moment, not hours later.

Maybe he was amped up on meth, or coke. Knife is handy.

That's an idea. I didn't see a tox screen in the case file, but maybe they'd had to lock him up to cool him off, and by the time they'd gathered the evidence he'd gotten sober. Wish I could talk to the arresting officer, get his impressions.

I shake my head. What I need is to get an impression of James Horne. See if I think he's the kind of guy who would do something like this. And that thought makes me wonder about Alicia. Because would a middle-aged mom leave her disabled son alone in the wee hours to go slit someone's throat? How would she even know he'd be there?

Maybe she looked up murder services on Dark Etsy.

Speculation without information is useless. I go down to the room in the basement where I work on my cases, my incident room. As I re-listen to the interviews, I put pins and pictures on the map for the people I've talked to today, sticky notes with pertinent data points. On the opposite wall, I've covered the whole thing with paint that mimics the surface of a white board. There, I scribble questions for further study.

1. Where did the money for Christopher's camp come from?
2. Did Alicia resent Jack enough to kill him? Have Biswas check on a possible life insurance policy and also boat loan.
3. How did Jack Reynolds get caught on the reserve?
4. What is Jim Horne's side of the story?
5. Did Keith Larson want revenge for the theft of his crab pots?

I put down my marker. It's nice to have a couple of irons in the fire. Some direction, instead of looking at the cobwebs in my cupboards and wondering whether I'll have enough money to buy food in a week.

OCTOBER 21 - DAY 3

14

After a few cups of coffee and some cold pizza for breakfast, I'm back across the bay at the Warrenton marina looking for the *Georgia Peach*, a commercial crabbing vessel, and hopefully connect with her owner, Keith Larson.

According to the case file, and corroborated by Alicia Reynolds, Larson is the man that Jack Reynolds stole crab pots from. Also according to the file but not mentioned by Alicia, is that Larson has a record, not unlike that of Jim Horne. Assault, drunk and disorderly, but no speeding tickets or other citations. He had a short stint in jail following an assault charge for what he claimed was self-defense, but the jury found otherwise.

It's a blustery day, with a chilly wind tossing the leaves and the seagulls, with clouds covering the sky like a dirty fleece. I tramp up and down the boardwalks, looking for the *Georgia Peach*. I'm worried about encountering the confrontational dude from yesterday, and find myself looking over my shoulder to make sure no one is sneaking up on me.

Back when I was a detective, I could depend on my badge to bolster authority, if someone wanted to oppose me. The badge represented the whole weight of the police department, as well as the City of Denver. Backup, if I needed it, was just a radio call away. Now, I've just got my voice, my attitude, and my sidearm.

And me.

Right, the ghost in the machine. That definitely gives me a professional edge.

I finally find the boat, and also a man I presume is Larson. He's monkeying around with the motor. Big round cages of metal mesh are stacked neatly on the deck. The smells of fish and diesel fill the damp air, as well as the omnipresent squawking of seagulls and the rumble of engines.

The man kneeling on the deck is square-built, forties, with a shadow of shaved-down hair on his scalp. His hands are gnarled and scarred. I watch as he manipulates his tools with deftness and ease. He's only got eyes for his work, which gives me a few minutes to observe before I clear my throat and say his name.

He finishes tightening something with a crescent wrench and turns his head. He's got the ruddy complexion I'm learning to associate with fishermen and others out in the weather.

"Can I help you?" He asks in a gruff voice.

"Are you Keith Larson?" I keep my voice brisk and business-like.

He nods. "That's me. And you are…?"

"My name is Audrey Lake. I'm following up on the police investigation surrounding the death of Jack Reynolds. Alicia told me where to find you."

He scowls, wipes his hand on an oil-stained rag, and puts a grimy blue ball cap on his head. When he steps down to the walkway, the dock bounces under his added weight. He extends a hand and we shake, his grip strong and controlled so as not to crush my fingers. I appreciate his care. And I notice the knife sheathed on his hip.

"I've already talked to the police," he says as he adjusts his cap. "Jack could be an asshole, but he didn't deserve to go that way. Hope they put the guy who killed him away for life. If lawyers had any guts, they'd call for the death penalty. It's right there on the books, waiting to be used."

Something tells me this isn't a great time to say I'm working for the defense, so I don't. "I understand Reynolds stole some fishing gear from you."

Larson nods. "Crab pots. Had them stacked on the deck, just like now. Bastard came and lifted them, easy as you please. That's gratitude for you."

"I know, right? How did you get involved with him in the first place?"

He snorts. "As a favor to Alicia. He wanted to learn the ropes, eventually get a boat of his own. So we went out, and I showed him how to bait the pots, attach the buoys, and work the hydraulic lift to bring them in. Then when he *does* get a boat, he goes and steals my gear." He spits on the deck between us. "Bastard. I thought I could help Alicia by giving him some skills to make a stable living. Goes to show, a rat one way is a rat all the way through."

"Ain't that the truth." I stir the pot of his vitriol, see what bobs to the surface. An old detective trick.

His voice gets louder. "Alicia's raising their kid alone, and he hasn't given a lick of support. I got no tolerance for a man who doesn't take care of his family. In fact, I told him so."

And now a little disagreement, buttressed by the family connection. "He seems to love his son. That's what Alicia said."

Larson scoffs. "You mean he likes to go over there and bring Chris a bag of cheap candy and take him out to the go-karts. That's not love, that's just fun. If he had an ounce of responsibility, he'd be out sweating it somewhere, coming up with money to support his kid. Told him that. Family ain't a game you just get into and leave when you're bored. Family is for life. That's why I pitched in to help Ali, even if I thought it'd be a waste of time." He twitches his head from side to side, eliciting loud pops from the vertebrae of his neck.

I wince at the sound. "Was Jack a good worker?"

Now he's cracking his knuckles. "Tolerable," he growls through pursed lips, as though he doesn't want to let a single positive word escape. "He went out with me a few times last winter, after the crabbing season opened in December. Miserable weather, but you can't let that be a factor. Best season is actually in the fall. Males have finished their molt, got their shells back and are feeding again. Getting bigger, with better meat."

I think of being out on the ocean in the driving winter rain, and shudder. "Why don't you just go in the fall then, and dodge winter storms altogether?"

He looks at me like I'm an idiot. "You been to a restaurant lately? People eat Dungeness crab all year long. A fair-weather crabber is never going to get rich. Plus, you got all the tourists playing fisherman in the summer. Going out with their rings and their rowboats, clogging up the bays. The state shouldn't allow it. They ought to leave it to the professionals, guys like me trying to make a living, not tourists playing at work."

This is an unproductive line of conversation. He's annoyed now, not just at me, but at those he deems to be intruding on his livelihood. I need to get him back on track, focused on his grievance with Reynolds.

"Can you show me what Jack took?"

Larson reduces his complaints to a mutter, beckons me onto the boat, and walks over to the stacks of big circular baskets made of thick, vinyl-coated wire mesh. "These are the rings. Best on the market, so of course, the most expensive. Over two hundred bucks each with the rigging."

I reach out to touch the mesh, feel how stiff it is. "What makes them so special?"

"Heavy-duty, because Dungeness are bigger and stronger than the little blue crabs you see back East. Get a Dungeness clamped on your finger, and boy, you know it. Also, it takes a sturdier pot to keep out the sea lions." He scowls. "Friggin' environmentalists won't let us take care of those pests. Port authorities can't even push them off the docks. I'd like to shoot every last one of them."

This guy doesn't seem averse to killing things that cause him grief.

Zoe's observation raises the hackles on my neck. Rather than explore his homicidal tendencies further, I try to lift one of the cages. It's heavier than it looks and I have to use both hands. Larson hefts one too, bouncing it in his grip.

"Yeah, these babies are twenty pounds, empty. You get a dozen or more crabs in there, now you're up to fifty pounds. Not easy to pull them up by hand, especially if you're at depth with a hundred feet of leaded rope. That's why I finally got the hydraulic lifts. Cheaper than back surgery. Maybe." His laugh is deep and guttural.

"Awkward, but not impossible to just pick up. Is that what Reynolds did?"

The scowl is back. "Yeah, he must've snagged 'em right off the *Peach's* deck. I never thought to secure 'em. Crabbers are competitive, but we don't steal from each other. Surprised he had the gumption to go through with it. Glad I got 'em back, though. Stupid bastard went out on the reserve and got caught, but he left the floats that had my label on the pots. I'd reported them stolen by then, so at least the cops didn't think I was part of some scheme to skim the reserve."

"Do a lot of guys do that, you think?" I'm curious about Phelps' allegation of other boats in the restricted area.

Larson spits again, this time into the water. "Just the dumb ones. Greenies got this one right—there needs to be a place where the crab stock can rebuild. Plus, that area is patrolled. Don't need to go out there and maybe lose my license. If it was me who caught him, I'd 'a cleaned his clock."

We talk for a bit longer, and I learn he doesn't have a family of his own, which is why he looks out for Alicia and Christopher. He cares about them in his own gruff way.

I say my goodbyes and leave the slip. Overall, I'm satisfied with the interview. There's no love lost for Reynolds, that's for sure. I think about Biswas's injunction to look for other suspects. Seems like losing the gear that enables you to make a living would be a good motive for offing someone, and throw in the business of Reynolds not supporting his family, and there might be a passable reason to kill. There's a suppressed violence in his willingness to destroy the people and creatures that hinder him.

I breathe a little easier when I've left him behind. I've proven to myself that I can still handle talking to difficult informants, and I didn't even need to draw my weapon.

This time.

15

I DON'T REALLY want to run into the dude I threatened with my gun yesterday, but as long as I'm here, I wonder if I can scare up a witness the police haven't interviewed. Larson was pretty forthcoming, maybe other folks will be, too.

A few berths down there's a fishing boat called the *Pot O' Gold* with a guy sluicing the deck with a hose. I straighten my jacket and walk down to him.

He's maybe in his early forties, with a dark salt and pepper stubble on his cheeks. He's wearing a red knit cap pulled down to his eyebrows, a stained blue sweatshirt and knee-high rubber boots. When I'm within shouting distance, I wave to get his attention. He stops what he's doing and I walk closer.

"Hi," I say. "I'm following up on the police report on the Jack Reynolds killing. Do you mind if I ask you some questions?"

He shakes his head. "I don't know anything about it."

"Not about the crime, maybe, but I'd like to get an idea of how the harbor works, what goes on in the area. You probably know all about that, right?" Yeah, what's he going to say, no?

His brows disappear upward beneath the edge of his cap. "Are you a cop?"

"I'm a private investigator."

He doesn't react, and I'm expecting him to tell me to mind my own business, but then surprisingly, he smiles, revealing deep creases in his cheeks and at the corners of his eyes. He clambers down onto the dock. Up close, I see there's fish scales tangled in the knit of his cap.

He extends a hand, after wiping it on the back of his pants. "Name's Tavin O'Brian. What are you trying to find out?"

We shake. "I'm Audrey Lake. Right now, I'm just trying to get a feel for what goes on here at the harbor. Looks like there's a lot of fishing boats, more than in Astoria."

"Yeah, there's no room over there, in either the East or West Mooring Basins. Big waiting list. Plus a lot of us live over here on this side of the bay. So Warrenton Marina is closer." He's got just the faintest trace of an Irish accent.

I nod. "I see. Well, I'm curious as to how someone could have come down here and killed Jack Reynolds without someone noticing. I mean, it's not like the Skipanon is very big. And there always seems to be people around. Boats going in and out."

He shoves his hands in the pockets of his worn corduroys. "People pretty much mind their business. Like I said, I don't know anything about the murder. Except they got the guy, right?"

"There's someone in custody, yes." I tilt my head. "Did you know Reynolds?"

"Knew who he was. Just like I know most of the guys on the water. But we weren't drinking buddies or nothing."

"So, what do you think about it? I mean, even if you guys weren't buddies, it's still a big thing to have someone you know murdered, right?"

"Yeah, I guess so." He looks away, adjusts his cap backward and forward. "Understand, this is a dangerous job we do. People get hurt. Boats overturn. Accidents happen. So yeah, it's too bad he's dead, but it's not strange to have someone I know bite the big one. Just his time, you know? Then you got to get on with the job."

He sounds more like a cop than I do. "What was Reynolds like?"

"I told you, I didn't really know him." O'Brian is irritated now, looking back toward his boat.

"Right. But what did people say about him? Other fishermen?"

Now O'Brian looks right at me. "They said he was a guy who didn't know how to mind his own business. You heard he stole some gear from Keith Larson? And went crabbing on the reserve? That just hurts all of us trying to make a living. Brings out the Feds and narrows the field for everyone. You won't find many guys in the industry who have a good word to say about Jack Reynolds."

"About that stolen gear." I hesitate, because it's a bit of a leading question, and I don't want to piss him off. "I've lifted one of those things. It seems like it wouldn't be easy to steal them all. It's not like you can drive a truck down here and toss them in the back. You'd have to carry them away by hand."

O'Brian glances away, and readjusts his cap. His cheek hollows as he bits the inside of his cheek.

"Mr. O'Brian? Do you have something to say about that?"

"Call me Tavin. And…yeah, I might have something to say. You said you're not a cop, right? I don't want to get someone else in trouble."

"Did you actually see Reynolds take the pots?"

"Not Jack." O'Brian glances around, and drops his voice. "That kid of his. Chris. I've seen him out on the *Peach* with Larson, and also working with his dad. They're all family, right? So, last summer, right before Jack got caught on the reserve, I saw Chris down here carrying a couple of rings. Didn't think anything of it at the time. But after the whole reserve blow-up, and Larson complaining about losing his rings, I figured I knew who did it."

My pulse quickens. "You mean, you think Jack told Chris to take the rings? Did you tell the police?"

"Nah. The cops already nabbed Jack, and I didn't figure making trouble for Chris would help."

Bingo. I've learned something new, something that wasn't in the police report. Although I don't see how it changes the case at all. I'm pretty sure Chris wouldn't have taken the rings on his own, without prompting from Jack, and even if he did, Jack must have known it was wrong.

Yeah, I agree. No sense getting Chris into trouble. Still—

My thinking is interrupted by the clop of boots behind me and I turn to see a familiar face. Big bearded white guy with a Carhartt jacket. The aggressive dude from yesterday. My gut clenches down, like it's trying to make itself a smaller target.

Beardo's mouth falls open. "Boss, this is the crazy broad I told you about. Be careful, she's got a gun!"

16

MY MUSCLES TENSE. I'm trapped between these two burly dudes. The bearded man is on one side, blocking access to the main walkway. O'Brian is on the other, between me and the end of the slip. Both of them are crowding my space. I reach halfway to my weapon before I stop myself. Take a deep breath. "You surprised me yesterday."

Unexpectedly, O'Brian laughs and takes a step back. "Chill out, Tad. It's a bad idea to sneak up on a private eye."

I'm still uncomfortable with their proximity and turn sideways, my back to the trawler, so I can see both of them equally. But there's only so much space on the narrow walk between the slips.

You are seriously paranoid.

And still alive, thanks.

Meanwhile, Tad has relaxed a bit, looks down, and tugs on the bottom of his jacket. "You surprised *me*, waving your gun around and all." He looks up, frowning. "You said last night you were just looking at boats." His voice takes on an accusing tone. "You didn't say you were a P.I."

"I didn't think what I was doing was any of your business. Since you snuck up on me, and all." Years of training take hold. Don't yield to the aggressor. Push back.

O'Brian breaks in. "She's investigating what happened to Jack Reynolds."

Now Tad looks like a goldfish, with his mouth open. Closes it. Opens it. Frowns. "I thought they caught the guy."

This feels like a bad re-run. "They did, okay? I'm just doing due diligence, making sure there's no stone left unturned."

"Seems like you should be talking to the cops, not us." O'Brian sounds puzzled; then he shrugs. "Whatever, you know your job best, I guess. It's nothing to do with us."

I keep pushing. "You know the area though. Know the locals and their habits. Did you ever see someone lurking around, or suspicious activity?"

O'Brian shakes his head. "Like I told you, no." Then he pauses, wrinkling his forehead and glancing at Tad. "Well, there was that young greenie-hippy kid. He seemed to have a beef."

"When did you see him?" I don't think the case file mentioned someone like this.

"After Jack'd been caught on the reserve. This kid was railing on him one day. Jack was like, 'shut up and leave me alone.' Remember that, Tad?"

"Um. No....?" The big man looks bewildered.

"Sure you do." O'Brian looks down at me, and I wonder if he's making this up, or if Tad is that simple. "This kid comes all the way up from Newport or something and is giving Jack a hard time about destroying the planet. Don't know if that's what you're interested in, but he seemed really upset."

"When was this in relation to the murder?"

"A day or two before. I don't remember exactly."

"What did he look like?"

"I didn't really notice. Brown hair. Young. Maybe twenties. Looked like he never worked an honest job in his life."

"Really? What does *that* look like, exactly?" I mean, come on. Less opinion and more fact.

Way to poke the nest.

O'Brian spreads his hands. "Like this. Calluses, scars. Honest dirt. These greenies are all about being one with nature, but they don't know the first thing about it."

There's an awkward silence. Me, because I don't really know what to do with this conversation, and I'm still sandwiched between these two men. Them, because in order to give me room to maneuver, one of them is going to have to back up. Something alpha types don't like to do.

But, I'm the one with the weapon. And Tad, at least, has seen me draw it.

I tug my coat zipper down a notch. His eyes widen and he takes a few steps back, then scowls. He's upset with himself for being cowed. But I take advantage, and squeeze by him onto the main boardwalk.

Nothing like a little implicit threat.

Amen, sister.

Trying to keep Tad from feeling humiliated, and thus aggressive, I say, "Thanks for letting me know about the environmentalist. If you think of anything else that might have a bearing on this case, please contact me." I hand O'Brian my card, since he's the one more or less in charge.

He scans it and says, "Who are you working for, again?"

There's an infinitesimal pause, while I wonder what to say. But really, there's no reason for him not to know. Or for me to keep it a secret.

Yeah, keeping secrets is just something you're good at.

To disprove Zoe's hypothesis, I say, "I'm on contract for the Clatsop County Public Defenders' Office." I give them a little nod, unzip my jacket all the way, and head down the boardwalk. Pretend I don't feel their eyes burning holes in my shoulder blades, or the weight of my holstered gun against my chest as I make my way back to the parking lot.

I fumble the keys out of my pocket and get into my car. A glance through the windshield reveals that no one has followed me, that the *Pot O' Gold* is actually out of view. I start the engine and crank the heat, waiting for my anxiety to ease.

Nice harvest of crumbs today.

Despite my nervousness, I have to agree. I've managed to identify another possible suspect in Keith Larson, and also come up with some things that weren't in the police report: a witness to the theft of the crab rings by Chris Reynolds, and an unknown "greenie" threatening Jack.

What this shows is that the police didn't question every possible witness, and that Chris was involved in Jack's crimes, at least to some degree. Now, whether that makes him an accessory, I'm not sure. Especially if he didn't consider what he was doing to be wrong. I can see Jack telling him that Cousin Keith is letting them borrow the rings, and would Chris help Jack carry them from the *Georgia Peach* to the *Beatrice*?

Jack was an asshole.

Yeah, he was, to involve his own special-needs child in his schemes. If Larson knew Chris was involved in the theft, he probably wouldn't have pressed charges.

If he did know, it gives him another layer of motive.

I suck in a breath. That's a dark thought. But I've seen for myself that Larson isn't averse to the idea of handing out capital punishment, and he thinks a lot of Chris.

It's only the second day of my investigation, and there's still time to turn up some more leads. But this alone should give Biswas some ammunition for the grand jury. Maybe working for the defense isn't so bad after all. It's really the same as regular police work, asking questions and digging into the past. And I've shown I've still got all my old skills, despite the beating my mind has taken.

Speaking of which, I've got to get home and meet up with my therapist.

17

I BARELY HAVE time to scrape together a lunch of cold pizza before heading next door to my therapy appointment. Phoebe has finally guilted me into coming for a session. I get it. She helped me through a rough patch, when I thought I was going insane. But now? I'm settled into my house and my job. Things are going well. Really. I'm not the loose cannon I was when I first arrived, six months ago now, jumping at shadows and imagined threats.

Except for drawing your weapon against perfect strangers.

I ignore that and take the exterior stairs that run alongside the Rutherford's house. Like mine, it's got a walkout basement. Unlike mine, their basement is finished, part of it converted into Phoebe's office. I knock on the door and she lets me in. The colors are muted, there's a desk, a loveseat, and a couple of chairs. A bookcase with reference books and a few knickknacks. Phoebe's diplomas and licenses are framed and hung on the wall above a planter with a drooping asparagus fern.

I sit in one of the armchairs while she goes to the other. It's almost like we're settling down to have a friendly chat. Delilah looks up from her bed in the corner and thumps her tail.

After the pleasantries, Phoebe says, "I'd like to try something a little different today, Audrey. You've shared about your career, and the events that occurred in the Baxter Building. Now, I'd like to talk with you about your family."

We go over that. My mother the architect, my father the cop, my older brother Dean, the soldier. It's all in the past, and it makes me a little impatient to have to talk about it. What bearing can it possibly have?

"And where are they now?" She asks.

"My folks still live in Denver."

"And your brother?"

"He's in Denver, too, in the Montview Garden Columbarium."

"I see." There's a pause. "Do you mind sharing how he died? Was he killed in action?"

"He ran his car off a bridge and into a river." I look out the window into the side yard. I can see my own house through the shaggy rhododendron. I always think rhododendrons without blooms are kind of ugly, with their big flat leaves and general untidiness.

"That must have been distressing for you and your parents. Was it an accident?"

"No, I think he did it on purpose." Some little brown birds are hopping around in the rhodie. It's a regular twitterfest out there.

"Audrey."

I hope Phoebe's cat isn't out and about, those little birdies might be in danger.

"Audrey."

I glance at the clock. Are we done yet?

"Audrey!"

"What? Why are you yelling at me?" And to think I have to give up solid food in order to pay this woman good money. Maybe I need to rethink all this.

"How do you feel about your brother's suicide?"

"I don't think about it." I don't think about the rumble of the engine as the car speeds toward the guardrail, or the crash as the car tears through the guardrail, or the splash of water as it seeps in through the vents and floorboards. I don't think about it, because the sensation is too awful. It's too awful to think my brother, the person I'd looked up to all my life, had chosen to kill himself.

Except you're thinking about it now.

I feel a cold nose against my hand, the thrust of a warm muzzle beneath my palm. My fingers automatically find Delilah's ears. It's nice to give an innocent dog some pleasure. So much easier to look at her big brown eyes, and the black spot that covers half her face, than to examine the grotesque images in my mind.

"How old were you when he died?"

Phoebe's voice is intrusive, although her tone is gentle, and I grit my teeth. "Nineteen." Over twenty years ago. More than half my life.

"And your parents? How did they deal with it?"

"The usual, I guess. Mom buried herself in work. Dad, the same. Both had pretty demanding jobs."

"And you?"

"I was in college at the time. I went back."

Phoebe is tapping her pencil on her notepad, frowning. "How old was he?"

I actually have to think about that. "Twenty-seven. Young." And with a jolt, I remember the medium at Bernie's gathering, the one who asked me if I'd had a relative or friend pass over. She couldn't have been referring to Dean, could she? But no, his death wasn't recent. And there'd been so many deaths of young men who had brushed my life. Gang killings, murders. I should have asked her for more details. What she'd really seen.

A ghost, you mean?

At the time, I'd just been trying to shield myself from delusional people.

Too bad you can't run from yourself.

I think I might need an expert opinion, so I interrupt whatever my therapist is saying. "Phoebe? Do you think people can actually communicate with the dead?"

There's a pause and I give Delilah's ears another scratch.

"Are *you* communicating with the dead, Audrey?" Phoebe asks.

I look up in surprise. "What? No, not me. Only, I met a medium the other day at a gathering at Bernie's house. So I wondered."

"Do *you* think that's possible?"

It's so annoying how she never answers a question. I feel like I'm doing all the work here. "No, I don't."

She says slowly, "I think it might be possible that someone might believe that they can hear the voice of a loved one who is dead, and it could bring them comfort."

I snort, which startles Delilah. "My voices never give me comfort."

You're such a snowflake.

Phoebe actually smiles. "How did you like the function at Bernie's? It sounds as though you met some interesting people."

"I guess. It was a bunch of other people who think they have powers." I run a hand through my hair. "Honestly, Phoebe, I'm just not sure what to do with this—this ability of mine. Most of the time I don't believe it's real. And I haven't had a vision for months, not since the Harkness murder. But I can't deny those visions were uncannily accurate. And if I accept that *my* stuff might be real, then what about the medium? What about the guy who picks lottery tickets? And all the other folks? I mean, how would *you* treat someone who came to you with that kind of story?"

"It's not up to me to make judgements. I would help them come to grips with their beliefs and experiences, just as I'm doing for you." She cocks her head. "Tell me, do other members of your family have— abilities?"

"Nope, just me. I'm the lucky outsider, as far as I know."

"Maybe you should ask them," Phoebe says. "You never know."

Maybe that's why Dean went off the bridge. Some nasty interior vision.

"I don't really want to talk about my family, if I'm honest."

Phoebe uncrosses her legs, and leans forward. "All right. Let's talk about work. You said you had a case. Do you have a new client?"

Sigh. "Yeah, the public defender's office."

"What do you think of that?"

"Well, you know. Working for lawyers. And not just lawyers, defense attorneys. It's like fraternizing with the enemy." I smile to show this is an attempt at humor.

Phoebe doesn't smile back. "How so?"

Argh. "Because I don't like helping to pick apart a police investigation. People always act like being a cop is so easy and obvious. It's not. It's putting your life on the line every time you go out on a call."

My therapist cocks her head. "And?"

"And, I don't want to be the one who undermines their work. Even if—" I shut up. But Phoebe is like a magpie, diving straight for the shiny object.

"Even if…?"

Even if I know they've got the wrong guy, I want to say, but don't. Because that means I would be aiding and abetting injustice. Even if my hallucinations in the Baxter Building, when I was under the influence of God knows what substance, were about police and gangsters working together. But I can't believe it. Most cops are good guys. Or at least, they want to be good guys, even if the stresses of the job make them jaded or over-reactionary.

Good guys who tried to kill you.

I chose to put myself in danger. They didn't know I was an undercover agent.

Phoebe presses, breaking into my thoughts. "Even if…?"

"Even if it's me that gets hurt. Because Zoe and I chose to be there. But everyone else was just an innocent bystander."

Those squatters weren't innocent. They were dealers and hustlers and thieves, every one. They made choices, too.

"But the sex workers were just trying to live," I protest. "And they had so much else beating against their psyches that they made the only choices they could. And Blue could be a nasty punk, but I don't think they deserved to die."

So, wrong place, wrong time? Come on. Blue was just another sociopathic gangster who wanted nothing more than to climb into Sonny's shoes.

"If one of them needed killing, it was Sonny. He was the one heading up a lot of the gang's criminal activity. And he tried to murder me." I touch the scar on my chest, press it hard to elicit the familiar ache. "He was evil."

Phoebe's voice is level and kind. "Are you talking to Zoe now, Audrey? Because I haven't asked you any questions about what happened in Denver."

I freeze. Because I've somehow slipped back into the funhouse. Back into the altered reality I was in when I first arrived in Astoria six months ago.

"Is Sonny the person you killed, Audrey?"

My memory hitches like a buffering error. I remember waking up on the mattress. Blood on my hands. My own and—

I remember the presence of the body next to me, the limp and cooling flesh, the face—

I shake my head. I can't bring it into focus.

"Is Blue the person you killed, Audrey?"

"I don't—I can't—"

"Or is it someone else?"

The effort to see has brought on a pounding headache. My fingers cramp from clutching the arms of the chair. I lean my head back against the cushion and swallow tears of frustration and rage. "I don't know, Phoebe. It's all such a blur. Such a foggy, blurry mess."

My therapist puts a hand on my arm. "It's all right, Audrey. I was hoping you would be able to access those memories if we came at them sideways. Just keep at it. One day you will be able to see through the fog."

Maybe the fog is there for a reason.

October 22 - Day 4

18

Today is October 22nd, so I call in to set up a meeting with the Clatsop County Public Defenders' Office to report on my progress. My gut has the same hollowness it did when I had to report a lack of progress to my Captain when I was on the DPD. Because I need this job, I need this income, and if I'm honest, I need to feel like I haven't lost my edge.

When I arrive in the lobby, I smell something scorched and bitter. As Juanita ushers me into the conference room, I ask if I need to call the fire department.

"No, that's my fault. I burned the coffee this morning. Would you like a cup?" She gives me a plastic smile.

As if.

"I'll pass, thanks."

"I made some fresh. It's not the same batch."

"In that case, sure." Actually, I could probably manage her first round. Years of terrible cop coffee have inured me to whatever extremes of bitterness Juanita can cook up. A little salt does wonders.

The glass-topped table in the conference room has been wiped clean of fingerprints, and the overhead recessed lights are reflected in six bright blazes on the surface. The pile of yellow legal pads in the center is noticeably smaller. Biswas is already here, dressed in his usual jacket and tie, and sitting near one end. As usual, the room is too warm and I take off my coat, hanging it on the back of the chair opposite him. I sit down and slide my initial report and an invoice across the table.

He pushes the paperwork aside, reaches for one of the pads, takes a pen from his shirt pocket, and begins to ask questions.

"Who all did you talk to?"

I count them off on my fingers. "The ex-wife, the deckhand Phelps who found the body, and Keith Larson, who is the guy who had his crab pots stolen by Reynolds. I figured those are the ones who most likely had axes to grind."

The lawyer nods. "Conclusions?"

"Well, Alicia—the ex—does have some reason to complain. I mean, she's got a disabled son who needs ongoing support which Reynolds hasn't been providing."

"She's also his sole beneficiary."

My cheeks heat with annoyance. "If I'd known that, I could have poked around, see what she inherited."

He takes off his glasses and polishes them with a square of cloth pulled from the inside pocket of his jacket. "The only real asset is the boat, which has a loan against it. He had a few odds and ends of personal effects, but not much actual cash." Finished, he replaces the cloth but lays his glasses on the table.

I don't try to keep the irritation from my voice. "If you want me to investigate for you, you need to give me everything you've got. Otherwise, what's the point?"

At that moment, Juanita walks in and hands me a mug emblazoned with the logo for Clatsop County. I thank her and take a sip. Not bad.

Biswas answers my question with one of his own. "Is Alicia a viable suspect?"

I shrug. "There's possible motive. I can follow up on her movements if you want me to, but that is accounted for in the initial police report. She says she was at home with her son, Christopher. No real way to confirm that, if the court doesn't accept him as a competent witness." I lean forward on my elbows. "According to you, she didn't get much from Jack but the boat, and that's probably going to be a headache to get rid of. Plus, she's had a long time—years—to kill Reynolds if she wanted to. I mean, why now? Especially because Jack gave her some money for an art camp for her son Christopher."

"When was this?"

"This summer, so maybe three months ago? Just a couple of months before the murder."

Biswas scribbles some notes. "So what was her attitude toward the deceased? Angry, frustrated?" He looks back up and meets my eyes. "Hostile?"

I think back to the conversation in Alicia's kitchen, her air of phlegmatic self-sufficiency. "Resignation, I would say. She's long ago given up expecting a fair shake from her ex. She seems to be doing okay with her craft business. I did check public records to see if she owns her trailer house. She's listed as the co-owner along with Jack. There's no mortgage, so she can probably live pretty cheaply. And now it's hers outright."

Biswas pushes his chair back and stands alongside the table, hands in his pants pockets. "That might be a reason to kill him, to get control of the property." He turns to pace in the narrow space between the table and the windows.

"But again, why now?" I resist the urge to get up and pace along my own side of the table, and instead follow his movement like I'm watching a tennis match.

"We're not trying to solve the crime, Audrey. We're trying to come up with reasonable doubt, see if someone besides Horne wanted him dead."

A gust of wind outside rattles the windows, and I take a reflexive drink of my coffee, taking pleasure in the hot swallow that warms my belly even as it causes me to break a sweat in the over-heated office.

A young ginger-haired woman with a face full of freckles pauses by the conference room and leans in the door. "Let's not ruin someone else's life trying to clear our clients."

Biswas scowls. "Madison, you are interrupting a private meeting."

She puts her hands on her hips and matches his expression. "Hey, I work here, too."

"As my employee." His voice has raised a tone.

"I work for the county, not for you." But she takes a step backward.

Feisty.

I know, right? I never had a boss I could mouth off to without repercussion. Must be nice, eh, Zoe?

I don't know what you're talking about.

Sure you don't.

Meanwhile, Biswas is dressing down his assistant, or whatever she is. "I'm the senior attorney here, and *you* are barely out of law school. Show some respect. For both me and my investigator."

She cocks her head, and a strand of red hair falls across her face. "I didn't know we had an investigator."

"She's on retainer for the Reynolds case." His voice is impatient.

In an effort to diffuse the tension, I stand and cross over to the doorway. Introduce myself and extend my hand. She nods, smiles, and after a brisk handshake and a speculative look, she leaves the conference room.

Biswas frowns and rubs his forehead. "Madison is a recent hire and idealistic to a fault. She only graduated last year, and this is her first dose of the real world." He sighs and goes back to his seat, and turns to a fresh page in the notepad. "What were we talking about?"

I sit back down as well. "Whether Alicia can be blamed for her husband's death. I honestly don't think it'll fly."

"All right, table it for now. We might want to revisit her, see if there's some reason she needed money and wanted full control of the property. Let's talk about the deckhand, Charlie Phelps."

"Okay." I think about the hard-faced young man for a moment, his reticence. "He's a dark horse. He didn't want to talk about Reynolds being caught on the reserve, for one thing. But that might be down to self-preservation if he was involved, or on the boat when it happened. He was upset that Reynolds might have hired someone without telling him, but since Horne didn't actually get the job, there shouldn't have been enough residual anger to make Phelps want to kill his boss. Phelps is actually worse off now."

"But you think there's something worth following up."

"At this point, there's not much to go on. Just his attitude."

He looks disappointed. "All right. Now, how about Larson? The man who got his rings stolen?"

I'm on surer ground here. "Larson was pretty steamed about that. He'd helped Reynolds for Alicia's sake, and then Jack goes and steals his gear. So there's a lot of resentment and anger there."

Biswas taps his lower lip with the pen, nodding slowly. "People get attached to their grievances, and don't want to let go. Reynolds wronged this man, spat in his face, basically. These types of men are hard working, have their own sense of honor and duty. They don't usually steal from each other. Compete, yes. Try to get the jump on one another, yes. But what Reynolds did was unacceptable by their standards, I'd say."

I remember Larson's anger, his protectiveness regarding Alicia. "Larson might have been looking to get even, might have thought Reynolds was trying to frame him. He seems the most likely candidate for an alternative suspect."

He nods. "You've made a good beginning, but I need more."

"I intend to find out more about what happened on the marine reserve."

"All right, that might serve. But remember, we're just looking for reasonable doubt here. Not rabbit holes."

Little does he know, rabbit holes are what constitutes most investigative work. "Listen, Mr. Biswas, I'd still like to take a look at the crime scene. Can I actually get on board the *Beatrice* and look around?" And maybe try to engage my retro-whatever.

"Until the trial is over, the police are keeping it closed off. I can't officially help you."

Sounds to me like he's giving us a bit of leeway, "don't ask, don't tell" kind of thing.

Hey Zoe, I'm the detective here. There is no "us."

'Til death do us part.

That makes me shiver.

"Are you cold, Ms. Lake? I could turn up the heat."

"No, no, I'm fine. What about Jim Horne? I'd also like to interview him, get the story from the horse's mouth."

Biswas shakes his head. "We've discussed this before."

"Come on. Maybe something will stand out to me. Maybe he'll make an admission, let something slip."

"This is exactly why I don't want you to speak to him. I don't want him to 'let something slip.' I want him to stick to his story, so we can defend him."

"Suppose I went in by myself? That way you wouldn't hear anything you didn't want to, and I could get a better picture of who he is, what he's like."

Biswas purses his lips. "Do you ever just do as you're told?"

"I'm an investigator. You have to let me investigate."

He just looks at me, forehead crinkled in what could be annoyance but maybe just means he's thinking. The seconds pass, and it feels like minutes, like he's weighing the pros and cons of keeping me on.

Finally, he says, "All right, go see him. See what you can learn."

I stand, collecting my things, trying not to let my satisfaction show. We leave the room together, but before we go our separate ways, Biswas says, "The grand jury is coming up. I need solid alternatives by then. And then we can evaluate your success in working with the public defenders' office." He nods briskly.

No pressure.

19

I DECIDE IT'S time to take the bull by the horns. Or in this case, by the Horne.

Jim Horne is still at the county jail, pending his trial. With no permanent place of abode, and a charge of murder against him, he's a flight risk. I've had some experience visiting people in jail, so I breeze through the procedures and am soon facing Jim across a table in a supervised room. The familiar smells of testosterone, sweat, and anxiety fill the space; in the distance, I hear raised voices and the metal clang of a slamming door. The whole place makes my skin crawl.

First words out of Horne's mouth are, "Who the hell are you?"

So much for pleasantries. "My name is Audrey Lake. I'm working with your lawyer, Karthik Biswas." I pull out a card, the corners slightly battered. It's just got my name and my company. Contact info is on the back, where he can't see it. Because I'm not ready to have jailbird randos come knocking at my door.

Jim's a tad on the scruffy side, with shaggy dark blond hair and patchy beard. His skin is permanently sunburned, although it's starting to acquire that jail-induced pastiness. His eyes are a kind of yellowish-brown. His hands and wrists are thick and callused, dotted with scars.

"Is that shyster going to get me out of here?" He looks around at the walls. "This place is driving me nuts."

Seriously? "That 'shyster' is your only hope, so more gratitude and less attitude, Jim-boy."

You have a bit of an attitude yourself.

Horne clenches his fists, then glances over at the guard and puts his hands in his lap. "What do you want?"

"I'm helping with your defense. I'm a private investigator. I want to hear about your version of events on the night Jack Reynolds died."

With some grumbling and eye rolls, Horne relates his story. How he was sleeping in the abandoned sailboat, down below in the stern berth. He'd been bothered by noise: boats, motors, guys yelling at each other. Then he'd heard the commotion on the vessel next door and peeked out of the cockpit to see what was going on. Charlie Phelps, who he'd seen when he'd talked to Reynolds earlier, was there with some cops. One of the officers saw Jim, and they'd called him over to ask him questions. Phelps told them about Horne's earlier argument with Reynolds, and he'd been an immediate suspect. They'd found his knife and assumed it was the murder weapon.

In other words, pretty much verbatim agreement with the case file.

"Where did they find the knife?"

"On the sailboat, down with my backpack and stuff."

I lean forward. "Okay, Jim, this is important. Did you give them permission to search?"

He blinks. "Well, yeah. I didn't have nothing to hide." He scowls and cracks his knuckles. "That goddamned Phelps. Next time I see him, I'm gonna punch his face in." Then his tone changes, and there's a pleading note in his voice when he says, "I didn't do it. You got to believe me."

And I'm starting to. Because I can't believe he'd be dumb enough to give permission to search if he'd been guilty.

Digging for background, I ask Horne how he'd first met Reynolds, and get a rambling story about Alaska. Two summers ago, both men were crewing on a commercial crabbing boat out of Kodiak, and Reynolds had bragged about how he was going to get his own boat and be his own captain. Said he'd hire Horne if the younger man could make it down to Astoria.

"What made you think the offer was still open?" I ask.

He looks at me. "Why wouldn't it be? Guy has a boat, always needs good hands. He said he'd hire me."

"You didn't think he'd already have help? I mean, it'd been over a year."

Horne's brow sets in stubborn lines. "He said he'd hire me. A man should honor his word."

I try to make my voice sound reasonable. "But what if he didn't need more crew? He might have hired you when he first got the boat, but why did you expect him to just wait until you showed up?"

He bangs a fist on the table. "He said he'd hire me." The young man is upset, angry and desperate. "If he'd just kept his promise, I wouldn't be here." Horne's voice has gone up a notch, attracting the attention of the officer supervising the visits, who puts a hand on his belt and takes a step in our direction.

"Okay, okay. I get it." I wave the officer back. He nods, but now he's paying attention. I revise my opinion about how smart Horne is. He obviously has his beliefs set and no amount of reasoning on my part is going to get him to change it. I think about the charges on his record: assault, drunk and disorderly. It's spur of the moment stuff, brought on by alcohol or emotion. Just like his outburst now.

"On the night of the murder, did you see or hear anything unusual?" I remember what he'd said earlier. "You said you heard some men yelling at each other."

"I did, but that was further away. And earlier in the evening."

"How many men?"

"Just heard one dude, but he must've been yelling at someone. Sounded like a deckhand getting a reaming."

"Could you understand what it was about?"

"No, I wasn't paying that much attention, to be honest." He slumps back in the folding chair, and the plastic creaks. "I just wanted to sleep, you know? I thought the sailboat would be more comfortable than a park bench. At least out of the goddamn rain." He lapses into a pout, his mouth like an inverted horseshoe.

"It must be a bit more comfortable here, right? A roof and three squares."

Always look on the bright side of life.

At least one of us isn't a killjoy.

At least one of us isn't a hypocritical ray of sunshine.

I snort involuntarily. Little Miss Optimist, that's me.

Horne grunts. Together we sound like a barnyard.

He says, "Three squares of cardboard, maybe." He rubs his fists into his eyes, until I half expect one to pop out on the table. "I'm not sleeping at all here. Should have gone for the park. None of this would have happened." He looks around, staring at the institutional gray with haunted eyes. "Feels like I'm going crazy."

Believe me, I know the feeling. "You don't mind sleeping rough?"

"I'd always rather be outside. Can't stand being cooped up. It's why I like fishing, just you and the air and the waves."

"What have they got on you?" If I'm honest, so far it seems pretty circumstantial. Although he's not helping himself with his attitude.

"Nothing! Just the fact that I stood up to Reynolds. And my knife. But there's nothing special about that, everybody carries one."

I don't, but that's beside the point. I don't like knives; my fingers touch the scar under my blouse. "Did they find some DNA or blood on the blade?" I actually know this, from the case file. Traces of Reynolds' blood *were* on the knife. But I want to see what Horne will say.

"No. I mean, there might be blood, like from fish or something. Or I mighta cut myself shaving."

"Any chance of Reynolds' blood?"

He looks down at his hands, picks his cuticles. "The cops probably took my knife and stuck it in the body."

"Did you actually see them do that?"

"No." His face and voice are sullen.

I struggle to hold on to my temper. "Listen, Jim. I'm working for Biswas, and he's trying to help you. But he's got a lot on his plate at the moment, so your best strategy is to level with me." I lean back, relax, try to be persuasive. "Did you threaten Reynolds with the knife, when you guys were arguing? I wouldn't blame you if you did, sounds like you had a legitimate beef. Did you pull it to scare him, did he try to grab the blade, maybe cut his hand in the process?"

Horne is silent, his forehead wrinkled, looking down at the table. He's trying to decide what to tell me: a lie, or the truth, or some combination thereof. Again, he strikes me as not particularly smart, or calculating. I'm even more convinced that, if he did attack Reynolds, it would be in the moment of anger, not hours later.

Finally, he lifts his head. "Okay, yeah, that's sort of what happened. I was mad, you know? I was just gonna scratch up his boat a little. Because he was more proud of his boat than his promise. So I went over to the side and just gouged the paint a little. And he freaked out, like I'd pissed in his beer, you know? And he tried to grab my arm but I pulled back and the blade grazed his hand. And then he started to cuss me out so I just left."

"Are you sure you just left? You didn't attack him further?"

Conk him on the head and slit his throat, for instance?

Horne is agitated, and half stands. "No way. I keep telling you. I left. Because I knew he wasn't gonna help me. Or keep his promise."

"Did you say anything about this to the police?"

"No way. Tell them I pulled a knife? That would've put my neck in the noose for sure."

"And yet, here you are."

He thumps back down in his chair and puts his head in his hands. "Jesus. This is so fucked up."

What is there to say? Up to now, I've been looking for the gap in the investigation, the possibility of reasonable doubt. But now I don't believe Horne is guilty. And if I don't find evidence to clear him, he's going to be locked away for a long time.

20

OUTSIDE THE COUNTY jail, I fill my lungs with fresh air, dampened by a recent cloudburst that must have happened while I was inside. It's a relief to get outside, away from the smells and sounds and overall vibe of criminals in confinement. I windmill my arms, stretching, trying to release some of the tension in my back and shoulders.

I want to go back to the crime scene, the *Beatrice*. I need to actually be on the boat this time, where I can assess the scene for myself. Biswas has said he can't give me permission to access the boat. Honestly, the fact that it's still cordoned off is a bunch of hooey. There's a perp in custody, so the investigation is over. Probably the cops just 'forgot' to remove the tape. Anything to stymie the defense.

But Alicia now owns the boat. Which means *she* can give me access with no worries about trespassing. So I call her, and she picks up on the second ring.

"Hello, Mrs. Reynolds. Audrey Lake here." In case she doesn't have me in her contacts.

She exhales loud enough that I can hear it. "Oh my God, please just call me Alicia. You sound like a social worker." Her voice is infused with annoyance.

"Okay, Alicia it is." A sewing machine is humming in the background. "What are you making?"

"Aprons to sell at the holiday fairs in November and December. They're fast and easy, and a popular seller. Want one? I'll give you a deal."

"Uh…maybe. Listen, I'm calling to ask you a favor. I understand that you inherited Jack's boat, is that correct?"

"Yeah, just another flaming torch to juggle. I'd like to sell it. Get some money in my pocket instead of another black mark on my credit rating."

"Really?" If she's actively trying to get rid of it, that adds a bit of a ticking clock. "When?"

"Why, are you looking for one? I could let you have it for cheap, just enough to cover the loan. A murder on board doesn't bother you, right?"

"Right." Actually, this is a perfect reason to want to see it, and for her not to say no. "I might be interested. But I'd like to check it out first. Do you mind if I go by later today and get on board?"

"Nope, but I want to be there when you do."

"That's not necessary. I don't want to put you out."

"I need to run into town, and you'll need the keys to the cabin."

I'd rather not have her hanging about while I try to induce a psychic experience, but I can't very well say that. We arrange to meet in the marina parking lot in two hours. And she assures me she'll bring a few aprons along for me to choose from.

21

ALICIA DRIVES UP into the parking lot in the same orange pickup I saw parked at her house. Christopher is in the passenger seat beside her. I'm not sure how to invoke a vision at the best of times and now there's two people to deal with. Assuming I can even muster it to happen.

Some superpower.

We walk down to the boat together, with Alicia leading and Chris lagging behind. Battered yellow crime scene tape is fluttering from the rail. Alicia pulls some stairs-on-wheels from the neighboring slip and butts them up against the side of the *Beatrice.* My heart begins to thud as we mount the steps and get on board.

The *Beatrice* isn't large as boats go. There's room for a few crab pots on deck, and there's an enclosed cabin with the controls. Alicia points things out: davits for hauling in the pots, emergency chest with life jackets, EPIRB mounted on the wall of the cabin.

She says, "We had a big tussle over the EPIRB. Jack thought he didn't need one. Didn't want to shell out the cash for it, more like."

I look at the yellow object bracketed to the bulkhead. "What is it?"

"Emergency Position-Indicating Radio Beacon. It goes off automatically when it gets submerged. Alerts the Coast Guard to a ship in distress."

"And he didn't have one before? That seems dumb." If I were on a sinking ship, I'd certainly want the Coast Guard to come.

"Yeah, that's my ex for you. Jack wanted to take Chris out on the boat, but I wouldn't let him until he had enough life jackets and the EPIRB. He was always trying to cut corners on things like that, but I put my foot down."

"Good for you."

She sticks her hands in her back pockets. "That was how Jack was for most of our marriage. Always looking for the angle, the shortcut. Whenever I raised an issue, he was always, like, 'it'll be fine.' But there is no shortcut in relationships, and I finally figured that out and got on with my life."

I follow Alicia into the cabin. There's a lot of gauges and buttons, and in the corner, a drone. I get down on one knee to examine it, ignoring the crack of my joints.

"Hey Alicia, what's this?"

"Oh, for—that's Jack's latest toy. God forbid that he pay for alimony, but he finds the money to spend on things like that."

I glance up. She's got her hands on her hips and a scowl on her face. She does her best to smooth her expression.

"If you want it, I'll throw it in with the boat. As a bonus."

Chris breaks in. "Mom, I want to keep it."

She shakes her head. "You don't know how to work it. And the last thing I need is some drone crashing into everything."

The corners of his mouth turn down. "I won't crash it."

"Why would Jack need a drone?" I ask.

"God only knows."

"Dad said, to look for fish. And see what other boats are doing."

"Spying, in other words," grumps Alicia. "Typical Jack."

Chris says, "I wouldn't use it to spy."

I stand. While Chris and Alicia argue over the drone, I walk outside and look over the stern. The water of the Skipanon River is glassy. A duck floats by serenely. The rumbling of the seafood processing plant on the opposite shore is the only sound. I lean down to look at the water. Maybe Reynolds was standing like this, oblivious to his danger. Someone came up behind him, conked him on the head, slit his throat, and tipped him over the side. I close my eyes and strain my mind for a single pixel of a vision.

I think your brain is constipated.

I ignore Zoe's intrusive presence and search the back of my eyelids for an image. Nothing. Nada. Zip. Disgusted, I open my eyes, turn around, and take a good look at the boat. The metal deck is covered with a non-slip coating, there's structural ribs supporting the sides. Remembering what Horne told me about using his knife to scratch the paint, I examine the exposed gunwales until I find a long curving gouge. Along with other nicks and dings. But the scrape looks fresh, the exposed metal hasn't had a chance to rust. And it's a lot bigger than Horne had indicated.

Anything could've done that.

But it's another indication that Horne might be telling the truth.

And something else. There's no blood. Not one measly drop. Even assuming the killer took the time to hose the boat, a slit throat results in some serious arterial spray. And it was dark. Difficult to get everything clean. Unless all the blood went into the water.

"Hey, Alicia," I call. "When was the last time you were here? On the *Beatrice*?"

She comes out of the cabin, followed by her son. "Gosh, I dunno. Maybe a week ago?"

"Did it look like this?"

"Huh?" She glances around the deck. "What do you mean?"

"I mean, was it—messy? Have you cleaned it up?"

"You mean, preparing to sell it? No, I figured guys who might be interested wouldn't care about that."

"And you didn't hire help?"

She stares at me. "Are you kidding? Do I look like I can afford a boat-tidying service? What are you complaining about? It doesn't look that bad to me."

Okay, one question down. Now, a tricky one. "Can you do me a favor?"

"What?"

"Can you try to sneak up on me?"

"What?" Her eyebrows climb up her forehead.

"I'm going to stand here at the back. I want you and Chris to get off and then come back. Try to sneak up on me."

"Are you—is this how Jack died?" She swallows. "Is this why you wanted to see the boat?"

Yeah, maybe not a good idea to involve the ex-wife. But we're here now. "I just want to see if it's possible to surprise someone."

She gives me a long look, then leads Chris away, back down the stairs and walkway.

I turn to face the stern again, resting my elbows on the rail. A seagull squawks, and then two more join him. I hear the growl of a diesel engine, the splash of a diving cormorant. I hear footsteps coming down the walkway. The cadence is slow, someone trying to be quiet. The stairway creaks underfoot. The plastic bumpers between the hull and the dock squeak as the boat rocks gently. Something clanks. I hear the rustle of cloth as someone climbs from the top of the stairs over the side of the boat.

The deck of the Beatrice is solid. But I can still hear soft footfalls. I turn to see Alicia coming up behind me.

She grimaces. "Not going to get that ninja job any time soon."

"I heard you coming long before you got on board."

"Well, the dock isn't exactly brand new. Or the stairs."

"I suppose if the engine were running, that could have covered the noise. But it seems pretty hard to sneak." And wouldn't the motor still be engaged when his body was found? Chris is walking toward us, taking long exaggerated steps like Coyote trying to creep up on Roadrunner, and grinning at the effort.

Alicia frowns and abruptly turns away. "Let's go."

I take one last look around. From here I can see the deck of the neighboring sailboat, where Jim Horne had taken shelter. The deck of that boat is cracked and flaking and covered with bird guano. I can't imagine being able to cross that expanse quietly, come down onto the dock, and then climb aboard the *Beatrice* all without making any noise.

And I can't think of a reason Reynolds would have allowed Horne on board, or turned his back on him if he had, especially if Horne was waving his knife around, angry enough to kill.

Alicia is waiting expectantly. I climb back down to the dock and she pushes the stairs away.

"No sense leaving an open invitation," she says, before heaving a sigh. "You aren't really interested in buying it, are you?"

"I'm afraid not," I confess.

"In that case, we can go look at the aprons I brought."

We return to her car, and she shows me six different ones with varying prints. I feel bad about lying to her, so I end up buying two, one with pink crabs on a blue background, and one with purple chickens holding salt shakers and spatulas. It costs me twenty bucks to assuage my guilt. Maybe I can deduct it as a business expense.

Transaction over, I ask, "What will you do with the boat?"

She pockets the cash I've given her and runs a hand through her hair. "God knows. Try to sell it, I guess. But if I can't, I really will let the bank take it back. What a pain in the neck. It's like Jack had to be a problem even after dying." But her eyes are red, and she sniffles. "All this, knowing he died here, I just—there was a lot of water under the bridge for us, and I don't miss him, but I didn't want him to die."

Yeah, that's what they all say.

22

I'M SITTING IN my car at the parking lot for the wharf. Alicia and Christopher have gone, but I'm still trying to mentally assemble the mosaic of what I've learned and overlay it onto the police report.

Where's the blood? If it didn't spill in the boat, it must have spilled in the water. And the only way that could have happened is if Reynolds was leaning way over the side. Maybe after being cold cocked with the blunt object. The killer then reached around and slit his throat, allowing the blood to fall into the water. Or just tipped him over after the cut. Either way, there might be some blood on the side of the boat.

I hadn't looked specifically for that, so I get out of the car, back into the damp and biting breeze, and tromp down the wharf to where the *Beatrice* is docked. I look at every side as well as the stern, and see no tell-tale runnels or spatters.

Now, it is possible that the killer hosed off the sides. But I know from experience that it's very difficult to completely clean up a crime scene. I'm not buying that it's been done this time, and neither is my psychic power.

It's also possible that wind and weather have scoured the evidence away. I check inside the hole where the anchor chain comes through, underneath the raised lip of the gunwale, and the ridge that circles the perimeter of the hull. Areas where a stray drop may have lodged and been protected from the elements. I find nothing but spots of rust and

103

algae and dirt. Which also tells me that there's been no recent cleanup, because the dirt is still here.

Conclusion? The *Beatrice* is not the crime scene.

Biswas hired me to find a reasonable doubt, or an investigative weakness he could exploit. And I've found a doozie. There's just no way the crime could have occurred where and how the local law enforcement have alleged.

Reynolds was found in the water beside the *Beatrice*. The derelict sailboat in the neighboring slip, where Jim Horne was squatting, comes to mind. I activate the video on my phone, in preparation for my exploration. I state the date and time, and pan to my face so there's direct evidence of who's taking the video. I'm not sure if this will actually hold up as evidence, but it feels right. I've also possibly implicated myself in criminal trespass.

The exciting life of a private eye, living on the ragged edge of the law.

Checking first to make sure no one is watching, I climb onto the derelict. Bare wood shows through the paint. A broken life preserver has a bird nest in the middle. A thin coating of green algae coats the boards. There's no sign of blood, just some bird poop. Clarify, lots of bird poop. White and everywhere.

So what? Shit happens.

I mean, there's been no cleanup on the derelict, either. None. So there's no way a bloody murder occurred on board this boat, either.

It's sad, really. At one time this craft was someone's dream, or legacy. But at some point the decision was made to abandon it to the elements. It's no wonder Horne thought he could get away with sleeping here.

The door to the living quarters is standing open on rusted-over hinges. Steps descend into what used to be the galley. The appliances are scratched and crusty. The table is scarred, and the cushions are black with mold. Birds have been in this area, too. The floor is covered with dirt and guano and feathers. And it stinks. But a doorway in the rear shows a curving scrape in the gunk on the floor. Recent use.

Behind the door is a sleeping area. It smells like rust and diesel and staleness. There's a person-sized dent on a pile of cushions. I continue taking video, with terse commentary, of the bed, the galley, the floor and all its detritus.

There's one more thing to do.

I try to relax and quiet my mind. Let the impressions come. Try to open myself to a vision. I stand there for at least ten minutes. Nothing.

I wonder if there's some statute of limitations to my ability. Because if you think about it, as old as Astoria is, there must have been violence committed all over town. I should be picking up snippets all over. A slideshow of criminal history. But that's not what happens.

When Bernie Flowers was explaining all this to me, he posited that events of extreme emotional impact are recorded in the environment. Like a hologram, only waiting for the right lens to see it. But maybe that impression fades over time, like a polaroid left in the sun.

Or maybe your lens is dirty.

Regardless of my unreliable visions, I realize I've got to approach this investigation from a different angle. Quit following the footsteps of the original investigation, and strike out on my own. Find out where Reynolds was last seen. Nail his movements. Look for the real crime scene. And find the real killer.

23

I'VE BARELY GOTTEN back to my car when my phone rings. It's the Public Defenders Office. I pick it up. "Audrey Lake speaking."

"Ms. Lake, this is Madison Jones. We met briefly this morning."

Oh right, the pushy young lawyer. "I remember. What can I do for you?"

"I'd like to engage you for some investigative work."

"Go on, I'm listening." I pace across the gravel lot, shoes crunching in the rocks. The seagulls squawk overhead. A pickup truck drives by, bass thumping, and puffs out a cloud of black exhaust. "I'm outside. Can you hear me okay?"

"Yes. Just a moment, I'm going to shut my door."

I hear a door close, and then the rustling of her clothing as she returns to her desk.

"Okay, here's the story. I'm defending a Filipino man accused of stealing some money from the Big Bridge Bar & Grill, where he was working as a dishwasher. I want you to talk to his colleagues at the restaurant, and find out if any of them is aware of his immigration status."

"Why? Is he illegal?"

She huffs. "I don't know. And the correct term is 'undocumented.' We need to get a handle on his case before ICE blows in and he disappears into some containment facility where no one can be bothered to get to the bottom of his circumstances. He doesn't have

I.D. on him, but that doesn't mean anything. I want to see what his employers know. Because if he is undocumented, and they're aware, I can use that to get them to drop the charges."

"Okay. What else?"

There's a moment of silence. Then she says, "Check in with the Filipino community, see if he has some friends or relatives here."

I cover my other ear so I can hear her above the seagulls. There's a trawler unloading over at the seafood plant, and the birds are acting like Alfred Hitchcock extras. "Why don't you ask *him* that?"

"He's not talking."

"Not even to you?"

"I don't think he understands our system. I think he's terrified of the authorities, and he doesn't realize I'm trying to help him. If he knows someone here, they can help him understand. Plus, I'm not sure he speaks English."

"What do people speak in the Philippines?" I ask, revealing my ignorance of world culture.

"Spanish. Tagalog. Other regional dialects. And English, but he isn't responding to my questions, so I don't know if that's the barrier."

"Is he in jail?"

"Yes, and I'm trying to get him out. But I can't defend him without knowing more about what he's accused of. His version of events, not the police or exploitative employers."

I shake my head over the stubborn reticence of perps, and the enthusiasm of a lawyer on crusade. "What's his name?"

"Alon Dasalon. Will you take the case?"

Honestly, it sounds a bit vague, but beggars can't be choosers. I agree to help her, although I don't have the first idea how to start looking for relatives. Maybe someone at the restaurant knows. But the very vagueness of this request means more hours on the clock, more money in the bank. And my contract with the public defenders' office doesn't specify how many hours I'm supposed to work, which is good, considering you never know how long things are going to take.

I get into my car and do a quick bit of research about the Philippines on my phone. Turns out they have a lot of languages but the main ones are, as Madison said, English and Tagalog. So chances are he understands Madison, but just isn't talking. I wonder why.

The cops told him he had the right to remain silent.

Or maybe he's hiding something.

He's probably afraid.

I don't know how tight the local law enforcement is with ICE, but there's probably not an office closer than Portland. One guy is pretty small beer when they've got the whole metro area to deal with, but eventually they'll send someone out to collect him, if he can't produce any I.D., or at least someone to vouch for him. Which is probably why Madison is having me look for connections.

I'm surprised at the theft, honestly. Statistically, first generation immigrants are more law-abiding than regular citizens. And if he's undocumented, it's another reason to keep his head down. But, it's not unheard of. Whatever, it's a job, and work is what I need right now.

When I get home, I open up the case file and review the pictures of the crime scene. There's no evidence of blood in the photos either. I shake my head. Detectives should have picked up on that immediately, but homicide is a pretty rare bird in these parts.

After a quick dinner of cheese and chips and salsa, I write up my notes from today, and open up a new case file for Alon. Juanita has sent me the contract to sign, and I finish up all my paperwork before heading upstairs to my cot. Even with the threat of an ICE incursion, this new case with Alon has a lot less pressure than the homicide with the grand jury coming up. The assurance of future work eases my anxiety, and I can embrace the sleep of the innocent, trusting that things will be all right, at least for a little while.

Yeah, keep thinking that.

OCTOBER 23 - DAY 5

24

The next morning I head out to the restaurant where Alon worked as a dishwasher before his arrest. The Big Bridge Bar & Grill is off Marine Drive on the Youngs Bay side of town. It's in a seventies-era building with only two windows, surrounded by a potholed parking lot.

I figure it's better to get right to the people of interest, so I head around back where the service entrance is, and where the kitchen is likely to be. A guy in a stained waist apron is smoking a cigarette, leaning against the building with one foot pressed to the wall. His dark hair is standing on end and he's got a full sleeve tattoo of a twining rose bramble with red blossoms, bloodstained thorns, and a skull or two.

"Hi," I say.

He nods, blows out a stream of smoke, and discards the butt on the pavement. "Hi." He turns to go back inside, and I see a wide smudge on the wall, evidence of many footprints.

"Do you work here?" I ask.

He nods, and reaches around behind his back to retie his apron.

I take a breath, and prepare for subterfuge as I attempt to find out more about Madison's client. "Do you know a man named Alon Dasalan?"

He frowns. "Dunno. Asian guy? You looking for him?"

"Sort of. Is he here?"

"You ICE?"

"Am I—? No!" I laugh. "Got enough on my plate without that. Do you think Immigration is looking for him?"

He shrugs nonchalantly, the picture of innocence. "No idea. Just thought I'd ask. You a Fed?"

"No. Why the concern? You owe some back taxes?"

He gives me a disgusted look. The feeling is mutual. "Can I talk to your boss?"

He shrugs, which isn't a 'no,' and I follow him back into the kitchen. It smells like fried fish, beer, and onions. A burly man in an apron, hairnet, and with hairy forearms speckled with burn scars spots me and says, "What do you want?"

"I'm looking for Alon Dasalan." This seems as good a way as any to get some information, pretend I'm ignorant of his whereabouts.

He wipes his hands on his apron. "Look in the county jail. Little shit worked here for two weeks, then scampered after emptying the till. You see him, tell him he's fired."

"You the boss?"

"Boss of this kitchen. Half owner, and manager to boot." He glances at Tat Boy, who is industriously peeling potatoes. "No one wants to work anymore, hold down an honest job. And meanwhile business owners who give people employment are taxed to death."

I see Tat Boy roll his eyes, and guess this is a well-honed rant.

"Tell me about it," I say. "He was supposed to mow my lawn, but he's a no show. Can't depend on anyone these days. You'd think these immigrant types would want to keep their heads down and their hands busy." I'm reaching here, trying to elicit some attitude of some kind, either agreement or defense. Get him to overcome his reticence about talking with a nosy stranger.

"You said it." He folds his arms across his ample belly.

I put a whine into my voice. "I didn't even ask him if he was licensed or legal. Offered cash. How much sweeter a deal did he want?" I have to admit, it's fun to pretend to be someone else, to be able to trick information out of people. A bit of a power rush when you do it well. The attraction of undercover work. Although duping Chef Boyardee here is low stakes compared to my work in Denver.

We had fun together, didn't we?

The cook curls his lip. "Dishwashers are a dime a dozen, or they used to be. High school students, Mexicans. Now, you can't get workers to stay on. Guys like Alon, under the radar, you'd think beggars wouldn't be choosers. But no, they want the whole American pie and single family house the first week they get here."

"Was he, really? Under the radar?" Cock my head to the side. "I wondered. I mean, he had that vibe."

"Don't ask, don't tell, that's my motto. Cash 'em out at the end of every night plus their share of the tips. But this guy's not satisfied with that, has to take the whole enchilada."

I whistle. "That sucks for the rest of the hardworking staff you got here. How much did you lose?"

"Five hundred, easy. Coulda been more."

"Coulda been a *lot* more," says Tat Boy, who's moved on to chopping cabbage.

I nod sympathetically. "How do you know he took it?"

"Are you calling me a liar?" The bossman's face twists into a frown, with deep furrows on either side of his nose.

I hold up my hands to placate. "Just wondering how you knew, that's all."

"Money disappears, guy is gone the next day. Doesn't take a rocket scientist to connect those dots."

"I see. Is that what you told the cops?"

There's a fraught moment of silence, and the atmosphere in the kitchen shifts. I hear the hum of appliances and the rhythmic clack of the knife on the cutting board.

"How'd you know about the cops?" He looks at me with suspicion.

"Stands to reason. I mean, you said yourself there was a few hundred dollars in there."

"I told them what I told you. But I didn't call them."

"You didn't?"

"Not worth the bother. That creates too much paperwork."

"So who called them?"

"Probably my partner. Dumbass. And that's the last foreigner I take on. They have no respect for hard-working Americans."

Of which there was a shortage, according to his earlier remarks. But. On with the show. "You hire him yourself? Or does the other owner get to say what goes on in the kitchen?"

"My partner is busy with the front of the house. He leaves the back of the house to me."

Except when he needs to call the police.

"Sweet, your own little domain. Well, I guess I'll find someone else to mow my lawn." I wave to Tat Boy and the cook, back out the door and wipe the congealed grease off my forehead. I've learned one thing. Alon was probably in the country illegally. The cook was cagey, but I'll bet dollars to doughnuts that he knew.

And if his business partner was the one who called the police, it stands to reason that he wasn't aware of his partner's hiring practices. Because if he was, they would just have swallowed the loss and kept quiet.

25

I GET BACK in my car and consider my next move, while watching seagulls squabble on the roof of the restaurant. This assignment from Madison, to see if Alon Dasalon has a local connection, is a bit out of my wheelhouse—my experience as a cop was confined to patrol before getting promoted to homicide, with a brief stint in narcotics when I first went undercover.

Yeah, look how that turned out.

I know, right? A permanent imaginary friend.

Who you callin' imaginary?

Now that I'm done with the obvious lead of his former place of employment, I don't have much to go on.

I suppose, technically, that Alon is a criminal. An alleged thief, and here without papers. But he's not a felon, or a killer. He appears to be more desperate than dangerous. In some ways, he's not unlike Jim Horne. Traveling a long distance to find work, currently homeless, and up to his neck in a crime.

In my internet research on the Philippines and Filipinos, I learned that Catholicism is the most prevalent religion. It seems to me that, if you're in a new country, you're going to look for folks from your own culture to socialize with, your own belief system, to sort of ease the transition. Now, I don't *know* if Alon is Catholic, but when in doubt, go with the statistics. It's the cornerstone of police investigations.

I pull out of the parking lot and head back toward downtown. I'm going to find a Catholic church and look for someone who might know who he is and can help him, or at least help Madison defend him. Maybe even get him to speak.

Ve haf vays of making you talk.

Great. Zoe is now channeling some Cold War spy movie. Or maybe it's an episode of Rocky and Bullwinkle.

We must kill moose and squirrel.

Is this actually an example of my own sense of humor? Maybe I should call Phoebe and schedule some emergency therapy.

After a quick search on my phone, I discover there's only one Catholic Church in Astoria: St. Mary Star of the Sea. It's on the corner of 14th and grand on the north side of town. The building is a lovely white clapboard church. It has a tall steeple and narrow vertical windows. This is your grandmother's church, and who wouldn't feel comforted just by its iconic shape? It's probably on the historic register —no surprise, most of Astoria predates World War II, and some is much earlier.

The patchy autumn sun is casting a warm glow on the steps and lawn. The doors are open, and I can hear organ music. I hope I haven't come during a service, because that would feel very uncomfortable. I'm basically agnostic. I just haven't seen evidence that there's some benevolent deity watching out for us all. If we want a better world, it's up to us to make it so. And most folks seem focused on piling up as much wealth as they can, never mind helping those around them.

Cynical much?

Tell me how I'm wrong, since you're the big expert.

I give Zoe a few moments, but she doesn't have a comeback. That figures. And I take a deep breath and cross the threshold.

The place is practically empty, except for a single man sitting on one of the back pews, a book open on his lap. He's dressed in black pants and a charcoal-tone sweater, with glasses and thinning sandy hair. He's focused on the book, and moves his lips silently.

I'm thinking this is the priest, but he's praying, or something, and I'm hesitant to interrupt. Just because I'm not a believer myself doesn't mean I don't respect other people's practices. But he's heard me, or divined my presence in some other way, because he turns with a ready smile.

"Can I help you?" His voice is deep and rich. "I'm the priest here, Father Mike O'Callaghan. Are you looking to worship?"

"Uh…no." For some reason I'm really embarrassed.

All your sins coming back to haunt you.

Jeez, I hope not.

"How can I help, then?" He cocks his head like an inquisitive crow. "Do I know you? Your face is familiar."

At that same moment, I realize that I recognize him, too. He's the same man who was scolding Bernie at the psychic people gathering. He didn't seem so friendly then, and I sure don't want him to send me packing as a devil-worshipper.

I smile. "I'm sorry, I don't want to interrupt your…whatever it is you're doing."

"This?" He closes the book, marking his place with a finger. "I'm praying the Liturgy of the Hours. I like to do it here sometimes, when our organist is practicing. The music elevates the spirit. But that can wait, if you need help. Sit down, make yourself comfortable. And tell me what I can do." His voice is pitched to project over the rolling music with practiced ease.

I remain standing, hands clenched in the pockets of my coat. "I know this sounds strange, but do you have many Filipinos who worship here?"

His brows go up. "There is a small community. Maybe a dozen. Why? You don't appear to be from the Philippines. If you don't mind my saying."

It's a polite way of telling me to mind my own business. Even so, I blunder on. "I'm working for the Clatsop County public defender's office. One of the lawyers is representing a Filipino man, but he won't speak to her. She's hoping to find someone who could help, maybe someone who could act as a, I don't know, as a bridge to him. Or a translator. He might even have a relation here."

Father Mike shifts, crossing his legs. "Is this man a criminal, then?"

I hesitate. I don't want to prejudice the priest. That would be two strikes, if he remembers where he saw me. But I don't want to lie to him either.

Yeah, God frowns on lying to the clergy.

Like you know anything about God.

The priest is still looking at me inquisitively, a slight wrinkle in his brow preceding a frown at my reluctance. With a sigh of defeat, I say, "He's in jail for stealing. Allegedly. But my client—Madison Jones, the public defender—hasn't been able to communicate with him."

"Your client. Are you also a lawyer?"

God forbid. "No, I'm a private investigator."

His eyes brighten. "How interesting. You'll forgive my asking, but you're not looking for a specific member here at St. Mary?"

"I don't think so." The organ music stops, and now the sanctuary echoes with my last words, my voice sounding unnaturally loud. Adjusting the volume, I repeat, "I don't think so. No. Ms. Jones just wants to find someone to help her communicate with Alon."

"Alon? Is that his name?"

"Yes. Alon Dasalan." Then I close my mouth. Was I supposed to keep that a secret? But I don't see what harm it can do. And if he does have a family connection here, maybe knowing his name will be an enticement for someone to get in touch.

The priest nods. "I'll reach out to some of my congregation. But you must understand, they may not wish to get involved with a criminal matter. If not, and if Mr. Dasalan would like, I will minister to him at the jail myself. In fact, I'll go tomorrow."

"His lawyer will probably want to be present if you talk to him."

"What passes between he and I and God is private." Father Mike is still smiling, but his voice has taken on a concrete firmness.

It's not up to me, so I don't pursue the matter. Let Madison sort that out. "She just wants to help him."

The priest nods. "How can I get in touch with you?"

I give him my card, mentioning that my number is on the back.

He slips it into his book. "Have you visited us before?"

"No." Here it comes. He's going to try to convert me. I brace myself.

"We're a tight community, and people make an effort to support each other. I'm sure at least one of my congregants will want to help."

I nod. Must be nice to have folks who have your back. A tribe of one's own. Still, that can also mean hostility toward people who aren't part of the group.

Father Mike's forehead crinkles. "I wish I could remember where I've seen you. Oh well, it'll come to me." Nodding again by way of dismissal, he turns his eyes back to the pages.

Better hope it doesn't, or he'll never want to help you.

And on that optimistic note from Zoe, I head back outside. As I leave the church, I'm both satisfied and dissatisfied. I've found a possible avenue of help for Alon, but his fate is still up in the air. Still, it's not my problem, is it?

26

THE MORNING SUN has passed quickly, and now rain is rattling down like someone is pouring it out of a bucket. There's a six-inch mist of splatter from the drops hitting the pavement. I dash for my car and jump inside, jacket already soaked with moisture.

The sudden rain darkens my mood, and I stare glumly at the runnels of water running down the windshield. I don't know what else I can do to follow up on Alon's case, so I decide to pivot back to the Jack Reynolds murder. I go home, make a hot cup of herbal tea, and get on the computer, looking for information about the marine reserve where Reynolds was crabbing.

This is what most investigative work is like. Finding stuff out. Looking stuff up. And trying to ferret out connections and causes by poking a stick into holes. Metaphorically.

When it comes to knowledge of the sea, coming as I do from land-locked Colorado, I'm starting at ground zero. I learn that Oregon has five marine reserves, the nearest being off of Cape Falcon, which is thirty miles south of Astoria. It extends offshore approximately five miles. There's actually two tiers of protection: a "reserve" area, extending for about three miles offshore, and a "protected" area beyond. Each corner of the region is defined by a particular GPS coordinate. The marine reserves are meant to be a seeding ground for commercial species to recover from being harvested, and a way to maintain healthy bioregions, as well as a place for research.

Absolutely no commercial seafood harvesting can occur in the reserve area. The protected area, on the other hand, *is* open to crabbing or salmon trolling, but nothing else. The border between this region and the reserve is clear, a line of longitude which vessels should be able to pinpoint with GPS. Given that crab pots are stationary, not drifting along like a net, there's pretty much no excuse for a crab boat to cross the line.

I sit back and consider what I've learned. Jack Reynolds wasn't really a long-term thinker. He was a hustler, looking for the next deal, the next way to turn a buck, and he wasn't above breaking a rule or two to get what he wanted. I can totally see him deciding to put a pot or three in an area where the crabbing is almost guaranteed to be good. I have the police report, but I'd like to learn more about what actually happened down there, and exactly how he was caught.

So I take a look at the marine reserve staff page and find the outreach coordinator. He's a young man named Ethan Sinclaire, probably in charge of all the social media and the website that the scientific team can't be bothered with. I call the main number and listen to the menu as it reads through the staff, and I press five for Ethan.

He picks up after a few rings, says his name, and asks how he can help me.

"Hello, Mr. Sinclaire. I'm following up on a police investigation regarding a man who was caught crabbing on the Cape Falcon Reserve. I'd like to confirm some details, just routine." Note that I don't actually say I'm a police officer. Hairsplitting? Maybe, but unless he says it himself, I haven't crossed the line. I'll correct him if he makes a mistake.

Maybe.

Before I can respond to Zoe's disparagement of my ethics, Sinclaire is talking.

"I remember that guy," he says. "We don't get many people who disrespect the boundaries. He said he had made an honest error, that he strayed into the reserve unknowingly. Except, he just happened to be working at night with gear that wasn't his own."

"That's him," I say. "Jack Reynolds was his name."

"That sounds right. Happened a few months ago."

"How'd you catch him?"

"One of our patrols found his pots and we tagged them with a GPS tracker. Then it was just a matter of waiting 'til he came back to check them."

Sinclaire tells me about the regular boat patrols going out to measure things like water salinity and oxidation. It turns out the scientific team has its own crab pots that they use to gauge population density in various areas of the reserve, after which the crabs are released. The pots are marked with floats, and the team found the illegal pots the same way, by noticing the floats and realizing they didn't belong to the study.

Ethan then launches into a diatribe, ranting about how stupid the crabbers and fisherman are who don't respect the reserve. Didn't they see how important it was to maintain the ecology, how their own livelihoods depended on it? How important it was to maintain healthy food stocks so we can eat seafood indefinitely? How can people be so short-sighted?

This kid must have grown up in Candyland.

Having had ample experience with short-sightedness in my lifetime, I note that most people are focused on the short term, living from day to day and paycheck to paycheck. Reynolds fits this vision admirably.

Sinclaire's voice gets louder. "It's that kind of thinking that's behind the climate crisis. It's the kind of thinking that's going to kill us all in the end, even those of us who are fighting to preserve the world. But at least *that* guy got what he deserved."

My ears prick up. "What do you mean?"

There's a slight pause, then Sinclaire says, "I mean he got caught, right?"

"Yes, he got caught." I wonder if he knows the full story. So I add, "and he got killed."

He snorts. "Maybe that was his karma, coming home to roost."

Interesting. "Do you think dying is an appropriate punishment for illegal crabbing?"

"Look, Detective—"

Oops. "I'm not—"

"Sorry, I don't remember your name. Look, Detective, the planet doesn't owe us a living. We're completely dependent on it, but it doesn't give a shit about us. In fact, it might just treat us like a disease and try to kill us off, before we do more damage. So we need to—" Sinclaire's voice is interrupted by some indeterminate sounds, and then another voice comes on.

"Hello? Officer? Whoever this is, I'm sorry, but Ethan isn't authorized to—"

I break in. "Listen, I'm not a cop." It takes something out of me to admit that, even as I use the investigative tools I learned in law enforcement.

"I heard Ethan call you Detective." The voice is female, authoritative, and accusing.

"He was mistaken, okay? My name is Audrey Lake, and I'm following up on the investigation regarding Jack Reynolds, the man who was caught crabbing on the reserve." In the background I hear Sinclaire saying "but she told me she was a detective…"

Except I didn't.

"Who are you then? Who are you working for?"

"I'm an investigator working for the Clatsop County Public Defender's Office."

"Wait, what? I don't understand. Are you Reynolds' lawyer?"

"No, Reynolds is dead."

"*What?*"

I pull the phone away from my ear. I guess the folks down south in Newport might not have heard about the murder. "He's dead. Killed."

"Killed? How? Did he have an accident?"

"He was stabbed."

"You mean, someone murdered him?"

"Yes." This conversation is starting to bore me. "Who am I talking to?"

"Lenore DeLibero. I'm the scientific team leader. Now, I want to know—"

"Thanks for your help. I'll be in touch. Bye." And I end the call.

These environmental types get a little overwrought.

Well, they are trying to save the world, Zoe. From their point of view, folks like Reynolds are the enemy. So I'm not surprised that Ethan is passionate about his job. But I do find it interesting that he wasn't surprised about the murder.

I think I've got another suspect.

27

I'M NO SOONER off the call with Ethan and Lenore than my phone vibrates and the name Madison Jones shows up on the lock screen.

"This is Audrey."

"Audrey, good, I'm glad you picked up. Listen, I'm setting up a bail hearing for Alon and I really need you to step up your efforts to locate Alon's family."

Huh. We've gone from a loose assumption that Dasalan has a relation here to it being a certainty. "Has some new information turned up?"

Madison sighs gustily. "No. And I'm juggling too many other cases to head down to the jail every five minutes to coax an uncooperative client. I'm disappointed that you haven't been treating this assignment seriously."

Irritation spikes through me, and I grit my teeth. The nerve. I literally just took this on yesterday. But really, this is classic. The whole 'disappointed' schtick is supposed to motivate people who are not performing up to standard without making them feel attacked. Because no one wants to disappoint others, right? In reality, I find her word choice annoying and manipulative. Especially because she is assuming I've done nothing.

So I say, "Would you like to hear what I've learned so far?"

There's an infinitesimal pause. "Please."

She shifts gears smoothly, I'll give her that. I clear my throat. "Since I was starting at ground zero, with no leads, I had to generate some." I give her a rundown on my visit to the Big Bridge Bar & Grill, and my conversation with Father Mike. "There's a small community of Filipinos here, who worship at St. Mary's. He's agreed to reach out, and see if anyone is open to helping you communicate with Alon."

"Good idea to harness the congregation's natural drive to help others with some pressure from the priest. Have you heard back from Father Mike?"

This is why I don't like lawyers. They have one lens and one only: their current case and how they can get their client off. Guilt or innocence doesn't play into it. And they don't care how they appear to others.

I clear my throat. "I haven't talked to him again. I thought I'd give him a little time to make contact. I did just meet with him this morning. Less than two hours ago, in fact."

"I want you to give him a call and rattle his cage, so he doesn't forget."

Okay, that's it. "With all due respect, Miss Jones, don't tell me how to do my job."

"Excuse me?"

"You hired me to help you with your case. You gave me no leads, just a mission statement. In other words, you left it up to me. Now you're trying to give me direction about my own tactics. That's not going to work. Don't try to dictate methodology after you chose not to give parameters in the first place."

Those are some big words.

First rule of communication is to speak the language of the natives.

Since when are you an anthropologist?

Since I decided to make my home with the human race.

I realize I'm talking to Zoe, which Phoebe told me not to do. And I also realize Madison is silent. I've surprised her, or pissed her off, or she's thinking about how best to axe my contract. Whatever. Silence is a cop's best weapon. I can wait her out.

"All right," she says.

I almost drop the phone. "What?"

"All right. I accept your statement." She exhales loudly. "I've never worked with an investigator before. Please, just be aware that we need results sooner rather than later, so I can get Alon a bail hearing. I'm trying to help him, and at the moment he's got no one else."

I thaw a little. We were all young once. "I'm working as quickly as I can. But these things only move at the speed of human communication."

"I understand. Just don't...don't let this case get lost in the shuffle." Then she hangs up.

Well, now. I didn't expect her to be cooperative. I thought she'd go all high-and-mighty lawyer, I'm-smarter-than-you. I thought we might end up screaming at each other like two jays on a birdfeeder.

Almost sounds like you were looking forward to that.

Not true. I can't work effectively if someone insists on micromanaging me. I'm newish at this private investigator gig, but the minute I let my clients start telling me how to do my job, it's over. I mean, I'm open to suggestion—everyone has their blind spots. But so much of police work, beyond the tedious ticking of boxes, is simply following your gut.

What's your stomach-sage saying now?

It's saying 'feed me.'

In the kitchen, I open a few cupboards. Settle on some peanut butter and jelly. Put my sandwich on the card table and push the case file out of the way. Look out at the river while chewing.

It's all well and good to tout my own independence, but in truth I'm floundering. I've dug up some loose ends, but nothing that definitively points the arrow of guilt away from Jim Horne. At least I've got another lead to follow—Ethan Sinclaire.

I pick up my plate to go downstairs to the incident room. As I turn, my gaze slides across the front window and I see a shadowy figure darting off the porch.

Who was that?

My heart ratchets up, and I rush to the door, sandwich plate in hand, throwing it open and running onto the porch. Look left, look right. Look up toward the street. No one in sight.

I reverse course, back into the house, engaging lock and deadbolt. Lean against the door. Go to the kitchen, put my plate on the counter, and retrieve my Glock, fitting the shoulder holster on with shaking hands. I've gotten sloppy, putting my gun down when I get home. Now I check the windows: closed and locked. Look down into the yard. There's a doe down there, laying on the grass and chewing her cud. I relax a fraction. No way would she be there if someone was lurking. Still. I descend to the basement, check the windows and the walk-out door. All secure. The incident room is full of cool white light. I forgot to shut the blinds.

I don't like the idea that someone could have seen my work.

What, you mean all this chicken scratching and maps and pictures? Looks like a rebus for a crazy person. Oh, wait…you are a crazy person.

Ye gods, don't you ever give up?

From here, I can see the deer more clearly. She's seen or heard me, and her big ears are flexed toward the house. But she's not alarmed, merely curious. Whoever the intruder is, he's gone. So, I tell myself. Chill. No one can get in.

The furnace begins to exhale a steady gust of warm air, and I go back upstairs, and sit down at my table. That's twice I've seen evidence of a stalker. Evidence, but not the actual person.

Maybe it's a ghost.

There's no such thing as ghosts. But my thought is just the default response. What if it is something…supernatural? I can't even believe I'm thinking this, but I'm the one with the unexplained psychic power. Sort of.

There's more things in heaven and earth, Horatio.

Ye gods. Now Zoe is quoting Shakespeare. If I'm being haunted, it's by something earthly. Some random dude trying to scare me, and not a spirit from the past.

That's not what the medium said.

That's right. She asked me if I had a relative die recently. The hair raises on my arms. I've seen dozens of corpses, more grisly murder scenes than I want to remember. But I refuse to believe in phantoms. It's got to be something else. What about the footprints on the porch?

They disappeared, remember?

Because of the rain, and my own stupidity of tracking over them.

Are you sure?

Are you saying I'm hallucinating?

It wouldn't be the first time.

A frisson of fear rattles my teeth. Because if I can't depend on my own senses, I'm screwed. I'd rather believe in ghosts.

28

Slowly, I gather my few dishes from the card table, where I dumped them when I ran to the door. Now what? The call from Madison is rattling around in my brain. I hate clients who nag. And I don't believe in rewarding bad behavior. But. Groceries, gas, leaky roof. Psychotherapy bills. Psychic therapy bills. All the individual snowflakes building up into a glacier of pressure. So I become the type of person I can't stand, and reach out Father Mike.

"Funny you should call just now. I did speak with someone shortly after you left," the priest says.

"That was quick."

"I had a hunch. Or perhaps a nudge from God. In any case, there was some cautious interest from one of my congregants."

Sidestepping around the reference to the almighty—after all, I'm the last one who should throw rocks at people who hear voices—I say, "In what?"

I'm glad you've decided to stop throwing rocks.

"In helping this man in jail. Alon, was it? In meeting with him and trying to communicate."

"That sounds promising." But not exactly what I'd hoped for. "Did this person say why they were interested?"

He hesitates before answering, and I can hear a tapping noise, like he's bouncing a pencil on a desk. "The person is a woman who works as a medical assistant at Columbia Memorial Hospital. Her name is Hiraya Jenson. She has lived in the U.S. for many years, and is married to a local builder. She left behind a great deal of family in the Philippines, and she thinks this man Alon may be a relative. But she isn't sure. Apparently it's a common name."

Bingo. Madison was right.

The priest continues. "When I told Mrs. Jenson that Alon is in jail, she was upset and anxious. She doesn't want to get in trouble with the authorities, if he is indeed a relation. Can you guarantee immunity, if she agrees to meet him?"

I frown. "Huh? Why would she need that?"

Father Mike's voice is wry. "There's a universal dread of ICE among the immigrant community."

"If she's here legally—"

"Oh yes, she became a citizen when she married." His voice colors with satisfaction. "I officiated at her wedding."

"Then I see no problem, as long as she hasn't aided and abetted him." I was pretty sure Madison wouldn't rat her out, even if this woman *had* been in contact with Alon, but I thought it better to err on the side of caution.

"I don't think she even knew he was here. She seemed surprised to hear his name. And he may be no relation at all. But she's willing to help. The church teaches us to aid those in need."

I don't comment. I have a prickly relationship at best with purveyors of organized religion, although it seems to come up in my cases on a regular basis. We agree that he will talk to this woman again, and I end the call.

It feels like I've been stuck in my house and on the phone all day, so I decide to go out for an evening walk. Remembering the shadow on the porch, I take my gun. There's a mist rising from the river, and the air is damp and cool. The trees are beginning to yellow and a vine maple a few houses down has turned a brilliant red.

I warm my hands in my pockets as I head down Rhododendron Street. I think about Alon. What courage it must take to cross the ocean to a new land in the hopes of a better future. His journey is a bigger version of mine, and I feel some reluctant admiration. But then what happened? He came here, got a job at the restaurant, and then stole the money. What for? That seems like a crazy thing to do. And then when he's caught, he won't speak to the person trying to help him.

As I think about it, it seems doubtful that this Filipino woman is a relation. Because if he knew someone here, why didn't he get in touch?

Maybe he didn't want to get her in trouble.

By being undocumented? We don't even know for sure if he is. But if so, he needs all the help he can get.

Maybe he was afraid she'd turn him in.

Then why come here in the first place? Why not go down to San Francisco or L.A., somewhere he could disappear in the crowd and avoid ICE forever. Plus, there'd be a lot more support, a bigger Filipino population in those larger cities.

Maybe he meant to go to Portland. Maybe he stole the money for bus fare.

That's an idea.

One of us has got to have them.

Ignoring that snide remark, I wonder whether Phoebe's advice about not talking to Zoe is wrong. Because occasionally, she's helpful. I continue my walk. Alone, as usual. There are times when I miss going down to the Portway Tavern, sitting at the bar and chatting with my friend Claire between customers. Now she's out riding her Harley around the country, and I'm holed up in this little town fending intruders off my porch. It sounds lame, but I really need to get a social life. Make some friends. Maybe even go out with some guy who doesn't know better. Start building a community.

There's always the seeker community.

I don't think I fit in.

On my return home, I call Madison and report what Father Mike has told me.

"Nice work, Audrey," she says. "I want to apologize for my attitude earlier. I don't have a lot of respect for cops. They victimize people as much as criminals."

I try not to take that personally. "That seems a pretty broad brush."

She snorts. "Don't you watch the news? Unnecessary brutality, false arrest. Shooting minorities. And that overbearing, macho attitude that so many police have."

An image of Steve Olafson flashes across my mind. "Yes, well, cops are just people. Some are heroes, some are assholes, and most are somewhere in between."

"I'll try to keep that in mind. Look, the reason I'm calling is I'm going down to the jail tomorrow to pay another visit to Alon. I'd like you to come with me."

We arrange to meet at the detention center tomorrow morning.

OCTOBER 24 - DAY 6

29

I'VE BEEN TO the Clatsop County Corrections Facility—the jail—before, when I came to talk to Horne. It's a heavy, windowless concrete building on the northeast corner of 6th and Duane Streets. Inside, it's got the depressing sameness of institutional buildings the world over. There's a room set aside for lawyer visits that smells like socks and disinfectant. We meet Alon in there.

I'm guessing he's in his mid-twenties, but he looks rough. His black hair is shaggy and unkempt. There's stubble on his cheeks and bags under his eyes. He sits like a sack of potatoes, and I'm afraid he's going to collapse sideways on the floor. On his right arm is a wide tattooed band that covers half his forearm. The design is bold and geometric, with heavy dark lines. A Filipino cultural tattoo. I've seen them before.

Madison isn't fazed by his appearance. She says, "Hello, Mr. Dasalan. How are you today?"

He doesn't answer, just looks at her. But he does seem to hear what she's saying.

She soldiers on. "I'm Madison Jones, your lawyer. Remember, I've come in to talk to you before. I'm going to be representing you at your bail hearing later this month. If the judge gives you bail, and you or your relatives can raise the money, you could get out of jail the same day."

I can tell he's listening. There's a new level of alertness. But I don't know if he understands.

Madison introduces me and explains my presence, before saying "There's a chance someone from the Filipino community may want to meet with you. Audrey here has been talking with the priest of the local Catholic Church." She turns to me and indicates I should continue.

I say, "Father Mike says there's someone who may want to help you. I haven't met this woman myself, but her name is Hiraya Jenson. She's lived here for many years." I stop speaking, because Alon is crying. He's not making a sound, but tears are running down his cheeks. He makes no move to brush them away.

Madison has noticed too. "Mr. Dasalan? Alon? Are you all right?"

His palms lay flat on the table. A drop of water falls from his chin and splats in a tiny asterisk between his hands.

I say, "Does that name mean something to you? Hiraya Jenson?"

He looks over at me. His eyes are filled with despair and pain.

He's hurting, but we need information. I keep pressing. "Do you know her?"

When he speaks, his voice is hoarse. "She is my Tita." He drags his tattooed forearm across his eyes and nose, and stands up. He walks to the door and rattles the handle. The guard comes in and escorts him away.

That was interesting.

Madison looks bemused. "Well. At least he can talk. And understand what I've been telling him. I wonder what that was all about? We've got to get this woman in to see him. Do you think she's a relation? Maybe she can assume custody, give him a place to live, be a character witness. It would really help with his hearing. Maybe she can even pay for the bail." She gets her papers together as she speaks. "This is such good news. Nice job, Audrey. I'll be sure to tell Karthik how helpful you were."

Alon looks upset enough to hurt himself.

I remember the pain on his face. "Madison—can you request that Alon be placed on suicide watch? I'm worried about him."

"What?"

"I mean it. He looked like he was staring the devil in the face. Whatever you think, this wasn't good news for him."

"He did seem upset," she says slowly. "I'll talk to the administrator."

We make our way out. What's going on with Alon? Maybe he's just afraid of being deported. But his reaction to hearing Hiraya's name seems to mean something more than that. Why didn't he contact her before he was arrested? Or after, for that matter?

Maybe he did. Maybe she told him to get lost. Take his troubles elsewhere.

Except she seems willing to see him now. And not sure whether she knows him. I don't know—I can't come up with a plausible scenario. We'll just have to wait and see.

30

AFTER LEAVING THE jail, I spend the rest of the morning doing something I should do more often. I go to the firing range. It's in Knappa, a little town about fifteen miles away, east along the Columbia River Highway. It's a nice drive, through the rural fields and deciduous forest that skirt the river. The range is outdoors, with individual stations and targets set at varying distances. I check in, don a pair of earmuffs, then take my Glock and a box of ammo and do what needs to be done. The grip is rough in my hand, and heats gradually from the energy of firing and my own blood coursing beneath the skin. I watch as ragged holes appear in the targets, some wide of the mark, but most bunching up near the center as my eye sharpens and muscle memory kicks in. The gun feels solid and strong. My hand and wrist buck a little after each shot. When I'm done, my forearm aches and my ears are ringing, despite the protection, and I've confirmed to myself that I can still hit what I aim at.

If the intruder comes again, I'm ready.

I remove the magazine from the gun, and drape the ear protectors around my neck. I can hear the boom of rifles from the long range. As I turn from the station, I see someone approaching. Another woman, which is a bit of an anomaly. Target shooting is still a male-dominated sport. Even the name of the range is the BKS Sportsmen's Club.

And then I recognize her, and my whole body stiffens. It's Detective Jane Candide from the Astoria Police Department. She has a handgun held tight in her right hand.

Well, well, well.

I'm not surprised that Zoe takes notice. My relationship with Jane is an uneasy one. We worked on opposite sides of a murder case about six months ago, and were trapped together in a burning building. But her partner, senior detective Steve Olafson, doesn't like me. He sees me as an intruder on his territory, and when I tried to get a job at the APD when I first moved to Astoria, he didn't try to disguise his attitude about big city transplants.

"Detective." I nod.

"Audrey." She plants herself in my path. "How's the P.I. business?"

None of yours, lady.

Ignoring Zoe, I wave my hand. "Fine. How about you?"

"APD is keeping me busy. We've got a couple of thefts on the docket."

Thefts. I think of Alon. "Anything interesting?"

She shrugs. "Stolen car. Some break-ins. What's going on with you? Crime in your vicinity I should know about?"

The memory of a shadowy image on my porch surfaces in my mind. "There's been an uptick in porch pirates."

Grimacing, she says, "Tell me about it. People can't keep their sticky little hands to themselves."

I make my tone light and chipper, to dispel my sudden anxiety. "If you're feeling stressed and overworked, my contract rates are reasonable."

"I doubt the chief would authorize the expenditure." A smile flickers across her mouth as she points at my gun. "I see you're keeping in practice."

"Well, you never know when you might have to shoot someone." It's meant to be a joke, but neither of us laughs. The subject is far too serious.

"Take care of yourself, Audrey." Jane nods, and continues on to the shooting station.

That was almost friendly. Maybe one day we'll be colleagues rather than adversaries.

I notice you didn't tell her you were working for the defense.

Do I look stupid to you? Wait, don't answer that.

Hee hee.

As I leave the firing range, my phone lights up with a notification that there's a new voicemail. The message is from Bernie Flowers. He wants to meet. I know he's not hitting on me—he's gay—so there's no danger of romance here. It's just that he's going to want to talk about psychic powers, and I'm still not sure how I feel about that.

31

"You've been avoiding me," says Bernie. "It's been a week since the gathering."

Yeah, I have. Good eye.

We're sitting at a table on the boardwalk next to Coffee Girl, a cafe located in the rehabilitated shell of an old cannery. It's breezy and I've got my coat on. A freighter named *Stardust Sand* rumbles by. A sea lion raises a shiny head above the chop and stares at us for a few moments before sliding back beneath the water. The barking calls of his companions echo from the docks at the neighboring East Mooring Basin.

"I've been busy," I say. "With cases."

"You found time today." He sips his latte, ruining the image of a cat which the barista sketched on the milk foam.

"Because I knew you wanted to talk."

It's not easy to decide what to do with my 'visions.' But I can't forget that it was a vision that got me involved in the murder which launched my career as a private investigator. This ability is potentially useful, if I could depend on it. Which I can't, because it is sporadic at best and imaginary at worst. I explain all this to Bernie.

To which he replies, predictably: "You're looking at this in the wrong way."

Story of my life.

"Listen," says Bernie, "Your retrocognition is just an extra sense. It's not scary. It's not evil. And it's something that, potentially, we all have. Think of sommeliers, people who sample wine for a living. We can all taste things, but a professional taster has turned this ability into something special. They've developed their palate to a higher level."

"So you're saying I should cultivate my psychic palate?"

"Exactly. And I can help you with the blocks that are keeping you from your full potential."

Alarm bells go off in my head. He wants to take me on as a client. He's a psychotherapist, as well as being an advocate for the arts of the mind. But I already have a therapist. It was hard enough to reveal all of my craziness to Phoebe, let alone someone else. But she doesn't know the full extent of my visions, and she isn't exactly a believer herself.

So maybe that means she can't really help you.

I adjust the collar of my jacket to better block the wind. "Okay, well, even if I wanted your help to expand the visions, as an investigator, I need evidence that will stand in a court of law. I can't go to a client and say I had a psychic episode and expect them to treat me seriously."

Bernie sips his coffee. "Why not take on cases that don't have such an evidentiary standard? Not all investigations are criminal, surely? Just think, if you refined your ability to see the past, you could help people with all kinds of things. Missing persons, lost objects. Even genealogy and research."

"I've only ever had visions of violence." I shiver with remembrance, and take a swallow of my coffee. Its familiar warmth and rich flavor is comforting.

"You don't have to go on being a homicide detective for hire. How many people are going to have an unsolved murder on their hands? You need to reach for new horizons."

I can see your business card now: Audrey Lake, Psychic Detective.

Yeah, no. That's not gonna happen. But for inquiries that aren't going to court, maybe the visions could be enough to provide some answers. Or at least, a direction to proceed. But I'm not going to start talking to the dead, or calling crime victims up to take advantage of their pain. No way in hell.

"How do you suggest I go about it?" I ask, more to see what he says than to follow instructions.

"Why not visit places that you know are crime scenes, and see what you can pick up. Surely you know some of those."

"A few. And they're all in Denver." And again, no way I'm going back there to be immersed in that shit show again.

"Or," Bernie said, his eyes brightening, "Maybe you could go to famous crime scenes. The grassy knoll in Dallas. Ford's Theater in D.C. Think of all the history you could uncover, the rumors you could lay to rest."

I just look at him. I am *not* going to start feeding the flames of conspiracy theorists.

He shrugs. "Well, it was just an idea."

"Seriously, Bernie. This is all new territory for me. I'm just not one hundred percent in the believer box like you."

"I understand. I think you should start a course of meditation. Learn to quiet your mind—that should help minimize imaginative intrusion. So you'll know when what you're seeing is real."

"I'm all for quieting my mind." Looking at you, Zoe.

You'd be lonely without me.

"Okay, I'll recommend some techniques. Or better yet, if you're still working with Phoebe, have her recommend some. Most therapists agree on the positive aspects of meditation. There's even phone apps."

We fall silent. A black-feathered cormorant dives down into the dark water to emerge a few seconds later with a tiny silver fish. Seagulls cry from the water, and sparrows hop among the table and chairs, looking for crumbs. I love sitting next to the river. I don't know about meditation, but watching the movement of the water, the play of sun and shadow on the surface, serves to quiet my mind.

At last Bernie stands, leaving his cup on the table. "I want you to come with me."

I follow Bernie out of the cafe and back into the old cannery building, our footsteps echoing off the concrete floor.

32

BACK IN THE day, Astoria used to be an industrial hub for the seafood business, as evidenced by all the abandoned piers that thrust into the river, fenced off and mossy and rotting. A few, like Pier 39 where we are now, have been rescued and somewhat rehabilitated. Pier 39 used to support a cannery. Thousands of workers, mostly women, stood at long assembly lines processing salmon and tuna and packing the fish into cans for the Bumble Bee Seafood Company. Part of the building houses the Rogue Public House, the home of Rogue Brewing. There's also a kayak rental shop and a small museum in addition to Coffee Girl. But a big part of the structure remains empty, and that's what Bernie and I are walking through now.

The day has darkened, making the interior of the structure gloomy. The skeleton of wooden columns and crossbeams exaggerate the perspective, and a chill wind funnels through the open space.

I shiver and hunch my shoulders inside my jacket, wondering if I'll ever get used to the cold humidity that seems to reach right into my bones. We cross the expanse, heading for the far wall. It's getting dark and hard to see. I try to blink away the shadows.

"What's going on, Bernie?" I'm uncomfortable and I want to go home, try to salvage something useful with the rest of the day. There's a dull roar in my ears, like an engine or distant machinery. Maybe a ship is out on the river. Maybe it's just the sound of the river moving beneath us.

Finally, Bernie stops. "How do you feel?"

"I'm cold, and it's dark and creepy. What do you want to show me?"

"Just look around."

Bewildered, I do as he asks. There's nothing to see, just the wooden structure and concrete floor. "What am I supposed to see?"

"Try closing your eyes."

I clench my lids together. "Now I'm really in the dark."

He sighs. "Audrey, please. I'm trying to conduct an experiment here. Do I have to spell it out?"

"Sorry, I forgot to pack my test tubes." I open my eyes to glare at him.

"Are you picking anything up?"

"Huh?"

His eyebrows come together in a frown. "Are you being deliberately obtuse?"

Probably.

Oh, now I get it. He wants me to have a vision. Like I can just twiddle my antennae and pick up a sitcom.

See if you can get an episode of Murder, She Wrote.

I make fists in my coat pockets. "Bernie, I don't have time for this."

"Just try, okay?"

Could he be more irritating? But we're here now, so I take a deep breath, and try to relax my shoulders. A gust of wind plasters my jacket to my back, and I suppress a shiver and close my eyes, although it's pretty dark already. The floor vibrates with the thrum of the nearby engine. I hear some distant voices, women laughing. A clank of metal against metal. The bark of a sea lion somewhere out on the water.

Bernie starts whistling, and I squeeze my eyes tighter. Here I am, trying to help him, and he does all he can to distract me. Plus, it's getting really cold. His whistling is tuneless, and aggravating as hell.

"Will you please be quiet?"

The sound of women laughing is getting closer. Probably some people heading toward Coffee Girl. Defeated, I open my eyes. The whistling and laughter are wiped away like a gust of wind. The only sound is my own breathing.

"Bernie?"

He's fifty yards away, standing in front of an informational placard that's been fastened to the wall.

I stomp over to him. "Look, there's nothing, okay? And it didn't help that you were making so much noise. You and those tourists."

He turns to face me. "Tourists?"

"Well, those women laughing. And your whistling. Why were you trying to distract me?"

"I wasn't whistling. And I didn't hear laughter."

"But—I heard you!" Why is he bothering to deny it?

He shakes his head. "I wasn't making noise. In fact, I came down here to give you some space."

The air is brighter now, and I've joined him in front of the picture. It's a black and white image, a reproduction of a historic photograph. There are several of these spaced around the interior of the building, showing what the cannery used to look like. This is a photo of three women, dressed in white coveralls with kerchiefs over their hair. They are sitting on the edge of the pier with open lunchboxes on their laps. The caption reads, "Cannery workers enjoy a much-needed break for lunch."

Bernie touches the picture. "This spot was an active, industrial location for a hundred years. I thought you might feel something."

"Sorry to disappoint you, but I didn't."

"Are you sure?" He shrugs. "There's no one here but us."

A chill creeps under the edge of my coat that has nothing to do with the wind.

Cue the creepy music.

I feel compelled to push back. "Why did you want to try here, of all places? Was someone killed here?"

"Part of the original building collapsed," he says. "And there was a fire back in the '90's that burned the rest. I don't know if anyone was hurt in those disasters, or died, but I thought it was worth trying."

Suddenly, I'm furious. Why can't I harness this ability? Why does everything have to be so difficult?

"Fine. Whatever. But I'm done here, okay? If you don't mind, I'm going to do something productive with the rest of my day." And I turn my back and stride through the building until I reach the parked cars clustered on the front of the pier. I've just gotten back into my car when the phone rings. It's Madison Jones. Her voice is brisk.

"I've heard from Hiraya Jenson. I want you to come with me to meet her. Now, if possible."

"Come with you where?"

"St. Mary's. We're finally getting a break. This could really help Alon."

I sigh, and pinch the bridge of my nose. "I'm on my way."

33

When I finally arrive at the church, the door is open and Father Mike beckons me inside to a small conference room just off the vestibule. He sits down on one side of the table. Seated next to him is a middle-aged Filipino woman, her hair cut short and glossy black. Her dark eyes are magnified behind thick cat's-eye glasses. A tattoo of curling ocean waves wraps around her left wrist, morphing to a series of circles and squares. Nothing as elaborate as Alon's, but the cultural resonance is there.

Madison looks up and takes a folder out of her briefcase. "Now that Audrey has finally joined us, we can begin."

I sense a rebuke in her tone. "I got caught behind a truck coming back from Coffee Girl. And honestly, I don't really know why I'm here."

Father Mike turns to the woman beside him. "This is Hiraya Jenson. She'd like to speak with you about the young man you're representing, Alon Dasalan."

Before either I or Madison can reply, Hiraya says, "Why is Alon in jail? What has he done?"

Madison clears her throat. "His employer alleges that he stole some money from the restaurant where he was working as a dishwasher."

Hiraya frowns. "How much?"

"It's unclear, because it was cash from the till. And because he can't pay for bail or provide his immigration papers, he's being held at Clatsop County Corrections."

I frown to myself. I thought the cook told me it was five hundred bucks. The restaurant should have been able to calculate how much was missing, based on receipts. I need to remember to say something to Madison about that.

"So," Madison goes on, "We're looking for someone to help us communicate with him." She digs through her briefcase and produces a booking photograph. Alon is standing in front of the height gauge, looking very sad.

Hiraya frowns. There's a pause while she looks at the picture.

I cut to the chase. "Excuse me, Mrs. Jenson, but he called you his "Tita." What does that mean?"

She goes still for a moment, and then sighs gustily. "Tita means "aunt." I have a pamangkín—a nephew—named Alon, it is true. It is a common name in the Philippines."

"Is this him?" Madison points to the photo.

Mrs. Jenson shakes her head. "I can't be sure. I haven't seen him for many years, since he was a boy."

"Has he been in touch at all?"

Again she shakes her head. "This is why I wonder whether he is really my nephew. Tita means aunt, but it is also a term of respect for an older woman, not always a relation."

"Will you come with us to the Corrections Center? To speak with him?"

Hiraya shudders, and drops the photo on the table. "Do I have to go to the jail?"

"Mrs. Jenson, I'll be blunt," says Madison. "Alon needs someone to look after him. He needs someone to post bail and vouch for his behavior afterwards. As long as he's in custody, he's vulnerable to a visitation from ICE. It would be best if he could stay with you until his trial. Assuming you choose to bail him out."

Father Mike intervenes. "Miss Jones, Mrs. Jenson isn't responsible for Alon's behavior. He is an adult, am I right?"

"Yes, he is."

"So she shouldn't be held accountable for him."

"Father, Alon needs someone to support him at this time. He's been traumatized by the incident and his arrest. Up until yesterday he wouldn't even speak. I wasn't sure whether he understood English. I can't get him released and then expect him to fend for himself."

"He's a stranger in a strange land," I say.

"Exodus 2:22," says the priest with a smile and a nod.

"Huh. I thought it was Robert Heinlein," I say. "Regardless, Alon needs some help, and family seems to be the best refuge."

Mrs. Jenson covers her mouth with a hand. "Will he be deported?"

Madison shrugs. "Probably, eventually, if he can't produce his papers. Especially if he's convicted of the theft. But, to be honest, undocumented immigrants are important to the local economy. The fish processing plants often can't get enough workers, there's dairies down south in Tillamook County, and there's farms further inland. Clatsop County probably won't bring in ICE while the trial proceeds, and maybe never if he can get a sponsor, and a work visa."

"How much is bail?" Mrs. Jenson asks.

"The hearing hasn't happened yet, but I'm guessing it will be in the neighborhood of five thousand dollars."

Mrs. Jenson looks down at her hands. "I must speak to my husband. But regardless, if it is my nephew, I will put up the money. Somehow. Alon mustn't be left in prison longer than necessary."

I glance at Madison. "Why can't she just go to a bail bondsman? So she doesn't have to pay the full amount?"

The lawyer gives me the side-eye. "There are no bondsmen in Oregon. She'll pay ten percent of the requested bail directly to the court."

Oh. I'm embarrassed that I didn't know this.

Someone didn't do their homework.

The dog ate it.

Mrs. Jenson picks up the picture again, searching the face for familiarity. "Can you tell me—was someone with him?"

Madison blinks. "What do you mean?"

"I mean, when he arrived. Who was with him?"

Madison narrows her eyes. "I don't know how he got here, or with whom. He hasn't been very forthcoming. But you're right—there must have been someone helping him. He didn't swim." She purses her lips and frowns. "That's something I hope he can tell us. Meanwhile, let's get you hooked up with Alon, and see what we can do for him."

Madison gives Mrs. Jenson details of how to visit Alon, and we take our leave. In the parking lot, I let her know that the restaurant should be able to calculate how much is missing from the register, and what the cook told me.

She runs a hand through her hair. "You're right, Audrey. We can use this at his hearing, show how his accusers can't agree on an amount, or produce evidence of their loss."

I hadn't thought of taking it that far, but she's right. It all seems pretty flimsy.

The afternoon is turning into evening. It's too late to go all the way back to Warrenton and start tracking Reynolds movements before he died. So I head home to do some more work with the case file. I want to review my findings and make sure I haven't missed anything.

34

BACK HOME, I get the case binder out and pull out the timeline I constructed by going through the police interviews and reports. Here's how Jack Reynolds spent his last day alive.

8:15 a.m.   Spoke to the manager of his apartment building to report a leaky faucet. Mentioned he was going to be out all day so if someone wanted to go in to do maintenance they'd have to have the master key.

11:28 a.m. Caught on surveillance tape at the gas station at Warrenton Fred Meyer. Purchased a full tank of gas.

12:13 p.m. Made a purchase at Home Depot, screws, paintbrush, and a gallon of black marine paint.

12:25 p.m. Made a purchase at the Dairy Queen drive-through. Hamburger and a chocolate shake.

1:17 p.m.   Seen on Warrenton Marina security camera going down the access ramp to the dock with the paint can in his hand.

4:45 p.m.   Seen leaving on Warrenton Marina security camera returning up the ramp without the paint.

5:20 p.m.   Arrives at Buoy 9, a restaurant/bar. Orders a meatloaf sandwich and a Bud Lite and sits at the counter. According to the bartender, Reynolds ate alone while looking at his phone, occasionally remarking on sports scores to the bartender, who wasn't really paying much attention.

7:00 p.m.　Reynolds gets up and leaves. Soon after there's some yelling heard in the parking lot. One of the waiters goes outside to check. Jack is yelling at a young guy with dark hair. There's some shoving but no thrown punches. Jack gets into his car and drives off. The young guy appears to be on foot, he walks east on Pacific Drive.

9:20 p.m.　Jim Horne goes down the access ramp to the dock and disappears off-camera.

3:15 a.m.　Charlie Phelps calls 911 after finding Reynolds dead in the water behind his boat.

There's almost eight hours unaccounted for. That's actually quite a long time. A whole working day. And now that I've got it laid out like this, one thing jumps out at me. Reynolds apparently wasn't seen on the wharf camera going down to the *Beatrice* after he dropped off the paint.

Interesting that Jim Horne is on the camera, but not Reynolds.

There could be lots of explanations for that. Some cameras are only active intermittently, recording, say, every thirty seconds or so. That doesn't sound like a lot, but believe me, quite a bit can happen in thirty seconds.

I check the medical examiner's report to ascertain the time of death. Lots of mitigating circumstances, immersion in water being one of them. The M.E.'s estimate is death occurred between 11:00 pm and midnight.

Okay, that narrows the window. Now we're down to four hours unaccounted for.

And Horne was already there, tucked up on the derelict boat.

Why would Reynolds have been on his boat so late at night, when he was going out early the next morning, at least according to Charlie Phelps. Seems like he would have been heading home from Buoy 9 to get some sleep in preparation for the next day. He didn't have a lot to drink, just a couple of beers with his meal. Not out-on-the-town kind of behavior.

And who is the guy in the parking lot?

Based on my own observations, and my inability to conjure up a vision on the *Beatrice*, I don't think Reynolds died there. I think he was dumped there. But that still means someone would have had to carry his body, which is even more noticeable than a man walking alone at night. However, just because he was killed around midnight doesn't mean he was dumped then.

I go back to the M.E. report. Nothing to indicate that the body was placed in any other position than the one it was found in: floating face down in the water. No discrepancy in lividity patterns, no anomalous marks on the skin caused by pressure against another object.

Could the corpse have drifted there from another location? Or been tossed off a boat? But why leave the body by the *Beatrice* in the first place? Why not just take it into the woods or something? Plenty of old logging roads and rural tracks around here. To send someone a message? As in, "this could happen to you." But then the only person likely to understand such a message would be Charlie Phelps, or maybe Alicia, Reynolds' ex-wife. The people most likely to find the body. And leaving it in such a public location pretty much guarantees that someone would find it within a few hours.

To me, that spells either panic or cool pre-thought purpose—two solutions a very great distance from each other.

Oooh, let's play Clue! Who do you think is the murderer? The ex-wife in the kitchen with the candlestick?

I dig my fingers into my hair. It *could* be Alicia. She might get a kick out of sending Jack off the deep end, plus she inherits a boat out of the deal. Or it could be Charlie Phelps. He found the body and was on the spot, and was ticked off with his boss. And what about Keith Larson? He's the one who got his crab pots stolen. He might be up for a little revenge. But the file says he has an alibi, that he was out crabbing on his boat.

Didn't those men on the dock say they saw Reynolds arguing with some dude on the day of the murder?

I flip back through my notebook. Tavin O'Brian mentioned that there had been "a greenie with a beef," yelling at Jack about crabbing on the reserve.

Sounds like Ethan Sinclaire.

Yeah, it does.

Maybe he's the dude at the Buoy 9.

Let's not jump to conclusions.

I say it was done by the idealist on the dock with the knife.

As the living room darkens, I pull the shades and go down to the basement and the incident room. On one wall I've tacked up a big aerial view of the region. The problem I want to solve is how Reynolds got in the water next to his boat.

The Skipanon River originates in Cullaby Lake, about ten miles south of Warrenton. The watercourse is barely wider than a stream, and it flows north, meandering through the fields and forests of the Clatsop Plains. After that, it gets wider and shallower, becoming the centerpiece of Skipanon River Park. From there, it passes under the bridge on Harbor Drive, into the Warrenton Marina and finally bleeds into the mighty Columbia River.

Activating my phone, I access the weather data for the night of the murder. Not much wind, and the tide was coming in, pushing ocean water into the Columbia. Tidal surge that spilled from the Columbia into the Skipanon would have pushed the body south, toward the park.

If the killer brought the corpse via boat, he was either coming from the Columbia or the park. The park feels really complicated. People use it. The killer would have to use a small craft, like a kayak, and risk being seen with the body. The other possibility is coming in from the Columbia. That would most likely mean a commercial vessel. There's numerous fishing charters, small open craft that seat eight or a dozen people. Also commercial fishers. These boats are so common no one would question their presence, or even notice, at whatever time of day.

What I need to do is find the security footage from the marina and watch it myself.

What you need to do is find the effing crime scene.

OCTOBER 25 - DAY 7

35

THE SEAGULLS ARE squawking across the Skipanon River as they cloud around the seafood packing plant. Half a dozen cormorants perch on the pilings of the dock, wings outspread to dry. They look like inkblots against the rising mist.

It's early morning, and I'm at the Warrenton Marina, hoping to find Tavin O'Brian, or even his lackey, Tad Mitchell. I want to question them again about the man they saw arguing with Jack Reynolds. My boots thunk on the boardwalk as I pass various boats in their slips, and I'm enjoying the sights and sounds of the working harbor. It's got the feel of a blue-collar community, real people exercising their livelihoods for themselves, and not just for tourists.

The sharp clink of metal on metal attracts my attention. Several slips away, on board the *Pot O' Gold,* O'Brian is kneeling on the deck next to a pile of loose fishing net. I walk toward him and he waves before standing erect and arching his back to stretch. He watches me approach, hands on his hips.

"You're out early. Still looking for clues?" His smile is sardonic, and is more a twitch of his lips.

"Actually, I'm here to talk to you." I can't help glancing over my shoulder. "Where's your deckhand? Tad, right?"

"I'm not going out today. So he's on his own."

"Great. Then you've got a few minutes to talk. Can I come up there?"

His brow creases, and he adjusts his cap. "Yeah, I guess. I'm not getting much done." He indicates a rickety staircase at the side of the boardwalk, and I climb aboard.

The *Pot O' Gold* is a lot bigger than the *Beatrice*, more professional. There's metal lockers bolted to the sides, and the complicated truss work that supports the spool which holds and deploys the net. A cabin, painted red and white, contains the helm and other electronics. It feels sturdy, like it could brave the wind and waves. There's a Zodiac with an outboard hanging off the stern.

O'Brian gives me a hand as I step over the side. "What do you want to talk to me about?"

I straighten my jacket and pull my phone out of the chest pocket. "When I saw you last, you said you saw someone, a 'greenie,' arguing with Reynolds." I open the browser, where I've got the staff page for the marine reserves ready. I show O'Brian the cluster of photos. There's a dozen staff members pictured. It's not exactly a lineup, but suits my purposes. "Do you recognize any of these people?"

"That's the guy." He points at the picture of a young man wearing a plaid flannel shirt, with a mop of shoulder-length brown hair and a tuft of whiskers beneath his lower lip. Ethan Sinclaire.

Bingo. This is the first fresh lead I've been able to find, and I can't help smiling.

O'Brian smiles back, his blue eyes twinkling. "Looks like I picked the right one. Is there a prize?"

"Not today." I look around at the deck strewn with tools and netting. "Something broken?"

"It's a fishing boat. Something is always broken." He kneels and begins applying a knife to the snarled mass of nylon filaments. "The net picked up some trash the last time I went out. I try to untangle it but sometimes it's a blade job." He meets my eyes. "Go on, tell me about your investigation. Being a lady P.I. must be exciting."

His tone is a little condescending, but I'm used to dudes not taking me seriously, so I ignore it. "There's not much to tell. I'm just trying to figure out who could have killed Jack Reynolds. And I'm working on another case now, too."

"Another murder? This is getting to be a dangerous town."

"No, this is a case of theft and a possible undocumented immigrant."

"Oh yeah? Are you working for the Feds now?" His hands pause in their task as he glances up.

"No, still the public defender."

"Are they gonna pull in ICE? Get the G-men involved?"

I shrug. "Probably not unless he's convicted."

He rotates his shoulders and resumes working on the heavy tangle. "I'm an immigrant myself. Or at least, my folks were."

"Where from?"

His eyelids crinkle. "Are ye sure ye need to be askin' that, noo?" His voice has suddenly thickened with a heavy brogue. "It's the old country, the Emerald Isle, that I be hailin' from."

I laugh, charmed despite myself. "An Irishman. When did you come over?"

He drops the assumed brogue. "I was born here. But my parents never lost their accents. It comes back when I talk to my mum on the phone." He pulls a hank of rope entwined with seaweed from the pile of net and tosses it aside. "They got their citizenship after they had me. Followed the process. But it wasn't easy. You have to live in-country for years to be eligible. And there's forms and other hoops. I say, if folks are willing to work, they should be allowed to apply as soon as they get here. None of this waiting around bullshit. I got sympathy for folks just trying to make a better life for themselves and their families. And there's nothing wrong with trying to make a buck." He throws down his knife with an oath and it clangs on the metal deck. It's a heavy weapon, with a ball on the hilt.

I feel a little frisson of awareness, and touch the scar beneath my shirt. "That's quite a knife."

He glances down at it. "Fishermen need knives, as you can see. Probably every guy down here has at least one blade like that. Go down to the Triangle Tavern some night and you'll see at least a dozen." He tugs at the folds of net. "This goddamn tangle, I don't want to cut a big hole to mend later, but—holy shit!" He jerks his hand back like it's been bitten.

"What's wrong?"

He doesn't speak, but shakes the twisted strands, and a finger falls on the deck at my feet.

"Jesus!" I jump back. "That's not yours, is it?"

O'Brian pales, and pulls off his gloves. He holds up his hands and wiggles all ten of his fingers. "No. I've got all mine." He draws a ragged breath, and laughs, with a slightly hysterical edge. "I've caught some fingerling salmon, but nothing like this."

I nudge the digit with my toe. It's pale and spongy, thick and ragged at the end where it came off the hand at the knuckle. The flesh bears deep grooves from the strands of the net. For a crazy second, I wonder if it belongs to Reynolds, but I saw no mention of a missing finger in the autopsy reports.

"Shit," he says again. "Do we need to call the cops? I mean, it's just a finger, right? Not like a whole body."

"Yeah," I say slowly. "I think we do."

"Damn. There goes the workday." But he reaches inside his jacket for his phone.

As O'Brian makes the call, I look over the water and try to settle my roiling stomach and wipe the cold sweat that has appeared on my forehead. I've seen much worse, but for some reason this thing, looking like a giant pale maggot, has shaken my equilibrium. I think of the gutted fish I saw in the water the other day, and shudder.

36

Someone from the Warrenton PD arrives within ten minutes of receiving O'Brian's call. He's maybe early to mid-thirties. His hair is black, cut close at the temples and longer on top. The collar of his navy blue jacket is turned up against his neck, and I see he isn't uniformed. He introduces himself as Detective Judd Daily, and I suck in a breath. This is the man who did the investigation of the Reynolds' case. The guy Biswas told me not to talk to. But here he is, fallen right in my lap. So to speak.

Daily is young. He probably doesn't have much experience with murder. Or finding random fingers. He asks us each for a brief statement, and gets our details down in his notebook.

"Do either of you recognize the—the body part?" he asks hesitantly.

"You're kidding, right?" says O'Brian. "I just know it isn't mine."

"Any of your crew lost one?"

It's almost laughable, except it's serious. O'Brian replies, "Tad's not here right now, but he had all his bits the last time I saw him."

We all stand around looking at the finger on the deck. Daily's a little perplexed at whether he should secure the place as a crime scene. But no one is dead, losing a finger isn't a mortal wound and it clearly didn't happen here, since everyone has all their digits. He settles for putting the finger into an evidence bag. He's a little green around the gills as he does this, but completes the grisly task without incident. The finger is easier to look at once it's in the clear plastic bag. The skin has started to slough off. The nail is almost black. There's a bit of bone sticking out of the end. The bone isn't broken, although the flesh is ragged. And it's big. Swollen by the water, maybe, but I'd guess it's from a man's hand.

I don't share my opinions with Daily and O'Brian. If I'm right, the ME will dispense that information soon enough. I do, however, make a suggestion.

"Detective Daily, I think you might want to have Mr. O'Brian cut out the section of the net the finger was tangled in. There might be other material evidence."

Tavin isn't happy about my idea. "Hey! That's gonna be a major pain in the ass for me to repair. I wanted to get out on the water tomorrow."

"Can't be helped, Mr. O'Brian," says Daily. "Why don't you cut out a piece about three feet square? From where the finger was."

Muttering under his breath, Tavin complies. There's a few green strands of seaweed in the net, but nothing else visible. As he saws through the nylon strands, Daily asks where he's been fishing recently.

"Up and down the coast. North of the Falcon Point reserve, a couple miles offshore. I unroll the trawl nets and let 'em drag along behind me, generally close to the seabed. But o' course they come up through the water when I pull 'em back aboard." Tavin's voice has taken on a faint accent. He's looking a little pale.

"See what the finger might have been attached to? Floating in the water, I mean?" asks Daily.

"Like a body?" O'Brian shakes his head. "I'd have reported that to the Coast Guard."

I pose my own question. "Heard of any drownings lately, Detective?"

He drags his eyes away from the grisly object in his hand. "No, but a corpse can drift a long ways in the ocean. And it might be an accident, some fisherman got his finger wrenched off in a net or a line, and not reported at all."

"That'd be a pretty serious injury. You could check at the hospital to see if they've treated someone."

Daily spares me a frown. "I know how to do my job." As if to prove it, he takes the net from O'Brian and wads it into another evidence bag.

I put my hands in the pockets of my jacket. "Just trying to help. I used to be in homicide, myself." I expect that to be a revelation for him and try to keep my expression from being smug. Turns out I'm mistaken.

"I thought your name was familiar," he says. "I've heard about you from Jane Candide, over in Astoria. You're not in law enforcement anymore. Now you're just a civilian."

I rock back on my heels. So Jane is spreading stories. Typical—cops like to gossip as much as the next person. Maybe more.

"Why are you even here?" Judd looks at me with narrowed eyes. He's curious, like all good cops. But I'm not in a confiding mood.

"Just looking around. Nothing related to that." I indicate his baggie with my chin. I'm sure as hell not going to tell him I'm backtracking through his murder investigation.

"All right." He glances between me and O'Brian, raises an eyebrow slightly, and drops his arms to his sides. "If there's nothing more you two can tell me, I'll take this to the Medical Examiner." He gives us a final nod, then heads back up the dock.

O'Brian glowers at his damaged net. "Now I've got a shit-ton of work to do. Thanks to you."

I shrug. "Proper procedure. He would have come up with it eventually."

"Maybe." He's still disgruntled, with no trace of his earlier friendliness.

He got off lightly, actually. "Be grateful I headed him off at the pass. Daily could have commandeered your whole net. Maybe even your boat."

O'Brian glares. "Over my dead body," he says. And then laughs grimly. "Guess I should be glad it's not *my* finger, or Tad's. All right, thank you for saving my net and my business. Now, I need to get to work."

I take the hint, and walk back to my car, boots clomping hollowly on the boardwalk.

That's one for the books.

Zoe. I'm surprised it took her this long to turn up.

Lots of dead things floating around lately.

It does make me wonder. I mean, Astoria and Warrenton are small towns. People die here, but not often by violence. Drowning's another animal, though. People fall off boats, get pulled into the ocean by riptides and sneaker waves. Maybe this finger's part of a surfer, or a tourist, or even off a passing cruise ship. Could be we'll never know.

As I approach the parking lot, I see that Detective Daily is still there, sitting in his car. And in a split second I make a decision. I don't care if Biswas told me to stay away from the cops. Now that I think Jim Horne is innocent, I need all the information I can get.

I take my hands out of my pockets and run.

37

THE GRAVEL CRUNCHES under my pounding feet. I wave my arms, and call Daily's name. When he looks up, I slow down, and stop a few feet away from the car so he doesn't get alarmed and shoot me. I drop my arms, but keep my hands where he can see them.

He lowers the window. "Why are you chasing me?"

"Detective Daily, I didn't give you all my details earlier, because it wasn't relevant, but I want you to know I'm a private investigator."

"I know that already. Jane told me. I was giving you the benefit of the doubt." A crease appears between his eyebrows, and I can practically read his mind. Cops don't always have warm and fuzzy feelings for a private eye, especially if there's no prior relationship.

I take a breath. "Can I talk with you about the Jack Reynolds murder?"

The corners of his mouth tighten. "What's your interest?"

"Hear me out, okay? You're not going to like this, but I'm working for the public defenders' office."

He draws away from the window with a look of disgust, and the glass begins to rise.

"I'm not trying to trap you." I take a couple steps closer, open my arms beseechingly. "I get it, okay? I used to be a cop. Just talk to me, so I can assure my client that everything was done right, that the investigation was copacetic."

There's still a couple of inches of air between the glass and the frame. I lean forward. "Any questions I ask you, you can bet the defense will ask you, too. Wouldn't hurt to get a little practice in, right?"

There's a pause while we look at each other.

Then he says, "All right. You can ride along while I take this finger to the M.E. But if I don't like your questions, I'm putting you out on the shoulder and you can walk back."

I nod, hoping it doesn't come to that. I circle around to the passenger side and get in. "Thanks. Listen, I've got the case file for the investigation. I just want to confirm a few things, okay?"

He nods, and peels out of the parking lot, scattering gravel. "Shoot."

"First, you guys did the scene yourselves, am I right? You didn't have the state come in to help?"

"That's right." He turns onto Harbor Drive and heads toward the highway. "You've got about ten minutes before we get to the Sheriff's office."

"I saw the crime scene pictures. There was no blood."

Daily glances over. "No. The body was in the water."

"When you arrested Horne, did you search for his belongings?"

"Why would I? The guy's homeless. It's not like he had a shopping cart or a suitcase."

"What about the knife?"

"He had it on him."

"But you didn't see blood on it."

"So? He probably dunked it in the river. And there was residual DNA and traces of Reynolds' blood. They found it at the lab."

"But you didn't know that at the time."

"I checked his paper, he's got priors. A history of violence. Domestic abuse. I got no sympathy for some dude who attacks women."

He's not getting it. He had no reason to arrest Jim Horne. No disrespect to the Warrenton P.D., but Detective Daily has obviously never worked a homicide.

We stop at the light before turning on to 101. Daily says, "Now I got a question. You say you used to be a cop. How can you stand to do business with those shysters at the public defender's office? Horne is a loser, pure and simple."

I feel a flare of anger, and a pang of guilt. Fight to keep it from my voice. "Just working to keep you guys honest."

"Maybe you're the one that needs a check-up. Ever think of that?"

"Everyone gets the right to an attorney. Everyone gets the right to a defense."

"Whatever." The social temperature in the car drops ten degrees.

We leave the highway and pass through a cluster of big box stores. Wal-Mart. Costco. A Ford dealership. A construction area. Daily slows to let a cement truck turn into the site. "That's gonna be the new county jail."

We're almost to the Sheriff's office, where the M.E. also has an outpost. I try to establish a bit of camaraderie, and also get some facts about Daily. "How long have you worked for Warrenton?"

"Four years. Was in the military for seven before that."

"My brother was in the army." An image of Dean, smiling and proud in his uniform flits through my mind, and I push it away. "What branch were you?"

"Navy. I like the ocean. When I got out, I wanted to stay by the water." We turn into the parking lot. "Stay here. I've got to take this in." He picks up the baggies with the net and the finger. I'd almost forgotten how grotesque it is. It looks like a prop for a slasher movie.

Daily doesn't have much experience. Assuming he went into the military after high school, plus a four-year criminal justice degree, plus four years of employment, and he might be thirty-three. He's probably a good enough detective for the basic crimes that happen here, but is out of his depth when it comes to murder. Biswas is going to hand him his ass in a courtroom.

While Daily is inside, I doom scroll through my news feed, and wonder if it's too late to build a bunker up in the mountains. Then I listen to an episode of a true crime podcast. I'm just learning about how some small-town cops in Arkansas arrested the wrong person when Daily returns to the car, minus the decomposing digit.

"Did they perform an autopsy?" I ask.

His mouth quirks a brief smile. "They're going to see if they can get a usable fingerprint, and send a tissue sample for DNA testing at the state crime lab. If they can get a print, I'll run it through CODIS to see if there's a match. You never know. But honestly? I think it belongs to some fisherman." He holds up a hand. "And before you get all advicey, I'm gonna check on hospital records."

I nod. "Good idea." As though I hadn't already suggested it. "The Jack Reynolds homicide was probably more exciting than giving the M.E. the finger."

He barks a laugh at the joke, and relaxes back into his seat as he drives out of the parking lot. "You can tell the lawyers that I dotted all the t's and crossed all the i's. They've got nothing to complain about."

"Charlie Phelps must have checked out okay?" Daily frowns and I add, "the deckhand. The guy who found the body."

"Oh, him. Yeah, he didn't have a weapon, or any blood on him. Plus, he was the one who called us."

Right, like the perp is never the one who calls the police. The opposite is true. Often, it's the killer who contacts the cops, hoping to make himself look innocent. Daily needs a mentor, someone to show him the ropes. Even Steve Olafson, the detective over at Astoria, would do a better job than this.

I ask him a few more questions, details I already know, things that are in the case file. Then I say, "Did you ever have another suspect?"

He scowls. "What do you mean?"

"Well, I told you, I used to work in homicide. And sometimes, you totally know who's guilty, but you can't get the evidence to prove it."

Daily smacks the steering wheel with an open palm. "I'm telling you right now, cops don't arrest innocent people. Prosecutors don't prosecute innocent people. You should know that as well as I do. The evidence is there. Horne is responsible, no one else."

What kind of fairytale is this guy living in?

For once I agree with Zoe. Mistakes happen in law enforcement, just like other human endeavors. That's why there's plenty of true crime podcasts and things like The Innocence Project. But. I lie, saying,

"I have the case file, but I haven't had time to look at it all yet. Seriously, what put you on to him so fast?"

"Read the interview. He was standing right there. He had a motive. And a knife that fit the profile of the murder weapon. No one else had reason to kill Reynolds. Case closed."

"What about Keith Larson? The crabber whose pots Reynolds stole?"

"He has an alibi. He was out on his boat at the time."

"Did you verify his location?"

"He said he went out alone. No reason not to believe him."

Yeah, except for a murder investigation. "What about the ex-wife? Seems like she'd be a likely starter."

"They were already divorced. No percentage in it for her. Plus, they were on friendly terms. Co-parenting their disabled kid."

Well, I wouldn't exactly call it friendly, but he has a point. In fact, I haven't been able to establish evidence against anyone else, either. But I'm still not buying it.

We've reached the marina parking lot, and Judd pulls in beside my car. He says, "I may need to get back in touch if something comes from that finger."

"Here's my card." I get out of the car, expecting him to pull away, but he leans across the passenger seat and lowers the window.

"Take my advice," he says. "Find a more honest way to make a living." Then he does a fast reverse and one-eighty, revving the engine as he leaves the lot.

I flinch away from the gravel spraying from Judd Daily's rear wheels as he drives away, leaving me alone.

He didn't even say goodbye.

Well, we're not exactly friends, are we?

Not like you and me.

I shudder to think that Zoe is my friend, but in reality, she's probably my bestie. After all, she was once me. Or I was once her.

Chicken. Egg. Does it really matter?

Hello. Trying not to be insane here. If you were really my friend, you'd help.

No answer. Figures.

<h1 style="text-align:center">38</h1>

DETECTIVE DAILY SEEMS very self-assured. It's been a long time since I've had that feeling of personal infallibility.

Ah, the joys of youth.

I'm not old, I'm experienced.

The more you learn, the less you know.

Is that the problem? That I've had too much experience of how things can go terribly, horribly wrong?

Shit happens.

Mistakes happen. And sometimes those mistakes are your own. Failure to check, check, and double-check. That's what separates the professional from the amateur.

Finding the finger in O'Brian's net, a dead thing located far from the scene of dismemberment, reminds me that I still need to find where Reynolds was actually killed. Since I'm in the neighborhood, I decide to investigate Skipanon River Park. It's just on the other side of the bridge from the marina. I get in my car and drive across the bridge, and wind through a neighborhood until I'm back near the water. There's a small gravel parking lot and a paved walking trail.

The river is glassy smooth. If I didn't know the current flowed ever so slowly toward the Columbia, I would think it was a landlocked lake. I walk along the shore, following the path. I'm looking for clues— bloodstains, footprints, evidence of a struggle, although it's been weeks and I'm doubtful much physical evidence would remain—but

I'm also trying to provoke a vision, to see if I get a feeling of violence done.

So far, I've only ever had them in a place where someone has been recently killed. I haven't clocked rapes, beatings, or assaults, at least not yet. For which I'm grateful, because given the sheer number of violent crimes that occur every day in this country, I'd be a basket case.

Give it time.

But. I have to try. So here I am, walking around with my eyes closed.

And, nothing.

There's also zero vessel traffic. No kayaks or rowboats or even inner tubes. Plus, there's not a boat ramp in the park, so someone transporting Reynolds' body would have to be in a small craft that they could carry down to the water by hand. Logistically, it seems too complicated, even to avoid the security cameras at the marina.

After tramping around for the better part of an hour I return to my car. I'm as sure as I can be that nothing related to Reynolds' murder has occurred here in the park. It's discouraging, but it's one more possibility I can check off my list. Although I sometimes feel like I'm spinning my wheels, even a negative result is progress. At least, this is what I tell myself.

Maybe a delivery drone dropped the body.

I think a drone carrying a corpse would be something people would notice.

You'd be surprised at what people don't notice.

According to the case file, although the video footage at the marina was checked for people coming on and off the dock, it occurs to me it might not have been checked for boats moving up and down the channel. This is a fishing community, and boats coming and going at all hours is a common occurrence. So common that ship traffic might not even have registered with whoever was assigned to go over the video evidence.

I get in my car and head back to Astoria and the Clatsop County Public Defenders' office. Seeing as how Detective Judd Daily seems prone to jump to conclusions, I'm gonna check the security footage myself. That's the only way I can be sure that nothing important has been overlooked.

39

WHEN I ARRIVE in the lobby of the Public Defender's office, there's a bit of a scene in progress. At least, I can hear an argument going on in the conference room. I raise my eyebrows at Juanita, the receptionist, and she just rolls her eyes. So I sit down in one of the uncomfortable chairs to wait.

The raised voices belong to Biswas and Madison Jones. He's berating her about spending so much time working on Alon Dasalan's case when there are plenty of other clients demanding attention.

Biswas' voice is clipped. "We have limited resources here, and Mr. Dasalan is not even a citizen of this country."

Madison's voice is loud and piercing. "Attitudes like yours are what I'm fighting against. Just because he isn't a citizen doesn't mean he doesn't have rights."

"I have no sympathy. People who want to come into this country should go through the proper process, like I did."

"It takes years. And people don't always have years. Can you blame him for wanting a better life?"

"He is not owed a 'better life' at the expense of others."

"Whose expense? He isn't hurting anyone." Sound of something being slammed against a table, probably a file. "And he was working. Not sponging off the system."

"And yet, he is accused of theft. From a business that can ill afford it." Unlike Madison, Biswas sounds cool and controlled.

"Oh, right. Property is always more important than people. And what happened to being innocent until proven guilty? It's our job to defend people, no matter what our personal positions. Are you saying I shouldn't defend him?"

"I'm saying you are spending too much time doing so, neglecting others who also need our help, others with a greater mandate."

"A mandate for you, maybe."

The door to the conference room opens, and Biswas comes out, looking over his shoulder as he does so. "I am in charge of the office. As long as you work here, you will follow my instructions." When he finally leaves the room behind, and sees me waiting, he frowns, probably unhappy I have heard the altercation.

"Audrey. Do you have something to report?"

"I came to examine the video evidence taken from the Skipanon Marina. It's not in the copy of the case file you gave me."

Biswas nods. "We have the footage on a USB drive which you can plug into your computer. But please understand, we do not have an unlimited budget for you to spend hours watching videos."

"I'm not doing it for fun. There's something I'm specifically looking for."

"All right." He turns to his receptionist. "Juanita, please give Audrey access to the security footage for the James Horne case. Now, is there anything else?"

"I'll need a laptop or a workstation to view it on. Or I can just take it home."

He shakes his head. "I'm not letting that footage out of the office. There's a laptop in the conference room that we use for presentations. You can use that." He glances at his watch. "I have a meeting in a few minutes. If you have other needs, ask Juanita." He strides back to his office.

Juanita hands me a USB drive. She points me toward the conference room. Inside, Madison Jones is gathering her papers together. Her cheeks are flushed and her eyes bright, her lips thinned in a line. She leaves without speaking.

Since this doesn't seem to be the time to talk about Alon with her, I set up the laptop, plug in the drive, and prepare to be bored.

Should have brought some popcorn and a drink.

The window of time from where Reynolds was last seen to where his body was found is eight hours. The *Beatrice* isn't visible in the camera range, but it does show the river and boats moving in and out. I fast forward through the hours where nothing is happening. In the time window, I count five different boats. I recognize two of them: Tavin O'Brian's *Pot o' Gold*, heading toward the Columbia, and later Keith Larson's *Georgia Peach* coming back in. Not long after, the *Pot o' Gold* returns. The other three are small fishing trawlers. I take note of the names for the sake of completeness, and I will contact the captains, but I'm more interested in the fact that Keith Larson, who has the strongest motive against Reynolds, is one of the people with an opportunity to dump a body. Judd Daily told me Larson had an alibi, but here he is, returning home within the critical window.

There's another folder on the drive. It's labelled SecVidBouy9. This is the footage from where Reynolds was last seen, having an argument with another unnamed patron. The folder contains two files. As long as I'm here, I might as well check these out, too.

It's like watching a silent movie, minus the plinky piano. The footage is jerky and in black and white. I see the interior of the bar, Jack Reynolds sitting at a table, eating and checking his phone. I speed through. Nothing until Jack gets up and leaves. The next video file shows Jack in the parking lot of the restaurant, arguing with a young man with longish dark hair. There is arm waving and finger pointing. At one point the young man shoves Jack. Jack shakes his head, turns, and walks away out of the frame. The young man stands there for a few seconds, and then he, too, exits the frame.

So, what is this all about? It doesn't look like the police identified the guy in the footage, only noted it was found to be unrelated. I've actually got a sneaking suspicion. I backtrack through the video until there's a profile shot of the young man. I pause the frame, and then I get online and find the webpage for the ODFW marine reserve program. I pull up the page with the staff photographs, the same page I showed to Tavin O'Brian.

The man in the parking lot looks a lot like Ethan Sinclaire.

40

It's been a long day, and I'm starving. My head is pounding from staring at hours of grainy video. I need to get away from crime fighting, get some fast food, and then head to the grocery store. Basically, I just need a break from thinking about murder and rebuffing the refrain of Zoe's remarks. So once again I head across the bridge to Warrenton. I pull off the highway into Youngs Bay Plaza for a Subway sandwich and a Killer Kupcake for dessert. The heavy frosting gives me a sugar high as I head to Fred Meyer and load my cart with cereal, canned goods, a loaf of bread, some spinach burrito wraps, and the makings for salad.

And then I notice that the store has already started putting up Christmas decorations and it's still a week before Halloween. This will be my first holiday season in Oregon, away from all my friends and family. Should I go back to Denver to celebrate, or tough it out here alone? At the thought of the big city, my heart starts to pump and my muscles tighten with anxiety. I rush through the self-checkout before a full-blown panic attack can set in. My car provides a refuge as I squeeze the steering wheel with both hands, taking deep calming breaths as perspiration prickles in my armpits despite the afternoon chill.

No need to go back there, Lake. We can manage just fine on our own.

I know I agreed to talk to Phoebe about my issues, and I know that one of them is Zoe. Phoebe thinks that re-integrating this personality shard is going to make me healthy. But if I'm honest, I kind of like her presence. She says things, and thinks things, that I stop myself from thinking or feeling. She's a safe gateway to my innermost being, one I might lose if she went away.

Glad to see I'm giving good value.

Now that I've gotten some groceries, I'm ready to do something else for my health. Get some exercise. Let the sea breeze sweep the cobwebs—and Zoe—out of my mind.

I drive through Warrenton to the dripping forest of Fort Stevens State Park, passing the World War Two-era bunkers and buildings until I reach the beach access road. I park, lock the car, and make my way down toward the ocean. It's a cool day, so I'm not worried about the groceries—it's mostly prepackaged stuff, and the veg should be able to handle a few minutes of inside car temp.

The aforementioned sea breeze has a definite bite and I shove my hands in my pockets as I head toward the remains of the *Peter Iredale*. The steel skeleton of the sailing ship juts out of the sand where it wrecked over a century ago. It's a tangible artifact of history, unlike the digital ephemera of my own time, and I love to run my hand over the barnacle-clad ribs of the prow, and peek down into the water-filled cylinder of the mast casing. I don't love the sudden thud of pain when I stub my toe on a piece of rusted metal just barely sticking up above the sand. On impulse, I kneel down and dig with my hands around the rusty stub. Maybe if it's just a fragment, I can dislodge it before it injures someone else. The sand is wet, and it keeps sliding back into the hole even as a few inches of the iron rib are revealed.

Why are you doing this?

I don't really know. But the wreck has always had an attraction for me. Who knows how deep the remnants of the ship are buried? I scrabble in the sand, revealing more of the curving rib.

Suddenly, it's dark.

The wind has risen, tearing at my jacket. I hear shouting, the scream of stressed metal and the splintering snap of wood; a thudding impact that knocks me out of the cozy niche I've found between the water barrels. A wave of terror closes my throat like a strangling hand,

and my ears are filled with the roar of the ocean, the crash and suck of the tide even as the ship lists to one side.

Faintly, I hear the captain shout. "Launch the jolly boats. We've run aground!" The footsteps of the crew thud against the deck overhead. Words are blurred with shouts and the squeal of the davits as the small boats are deployed.

An empty barrel rolls across the hold, smashing into my knee and sending pain shooting up my leg and into my hip. No one knows I'm here, no one will be looking for me. I barely notice the sour smell of the bilge water splashing between my feet as I struggle across the hold. There's only room in my head for one thought, pulsing in giant red letters. Get out, before I'm crushed by the ballast. Before the hull is breached beneath the pounding waves. Before I drown alone in the dark.

The rungs of the ladder are slick with moisture. The wooden hatch is wedged shut and the thud of running feet clatters across the deck. I push and push, getting my shoulder underneath the hatch. But my feet slip as the ship lists and I tumble backwards into the hold, sloshing bilge water covering my face.

Wake up!

I blink, and I'm back on the beach, kneeling next to the wreck, my hands buried up to the wrists in wet sand, my pant legs damp around my lower legs. The roar of wind and water recedes, and the only noise is the thunder of my heartbeat and the plaintive cry of a seagull.

Getting shakily to my feet, I dust the sand from my palms and gasp for breath. It's daylight, not night. The ocean is as calm as it ever is. The breeze blows my hair away from my face, and plasters my jacket against my chest. But it's nothing like the raw danger of the storm I've just experienced. I've had a vision—not of violence, but of the trauma and terror of a shipwreck. The long-ago wreck of the *Peter Iredale*. It must be.

Operating on instinct, I back away from the iron skeleton, fighting the shreds of terror that still cling to my thoughts. Loose sand sucks at my feet as I reach the tideline, and I turn and scramble up the face of the dune which separates me from the parking lot. My breath is wheezing in my lungs as I reach the top, and I bend over, bracing my hands on my thighs as I struggle for calm.

Easy does it, Lake. You're safe now.

Am I? Because I don't understand. I've been on this beach a hundred times, and never had an experience like this. Never lost control of my own mind.

From my place on the dune, I can see a cargo ship—tiny at this distance—heading for the Columbia River bar. Beach grass flutters on the seaward faces of the sand dunes that edge the shore. It's the same as it always is. So why—

Again the view becomes inky black, shouts rise above the wind, and lights bob on the shore. Lanterns reveal the silhouettes of running men, and the white sails flapping like shattered wings on the broken masts. I'm wet to the skin, and shivering with cold and terror. My legs and arms are scraped and bruised, and I have a long scratch on the back of my hand from a nail on the underside of the hatch. An incoming wave slides over the sand toward me, and I scramble back from the creeping surge. I'm so glad to be alive, free of the imprisoning ship. The men summoned to the rescue are concentrating on the jolly boats, and no one notices me half-stumbling, half-swimming, through the breaking waves to the safety of the shore.

Lake, wake up! Pull yourself together.

Again, the voice is Zoe's. Once more I'm myself, Audrey Lake, standing on the crest of the dune on a crisp and cloudy fall day. My heart is hammering with terror, blood throbbing in my veins. It's too much to deal with, and I sprint across the sand to the parking lot and the beckoning safety of my car.

41

ONCE MORE MY car becomes my safe space. I lean back in the seat, pressing my head against the headrest. I can feel the pulse in my neck beating, beating.

Let's get out of here.

Yeah, let's. We're still too close to the wreck, to the ocean, to the imagined night and the suck of the tide.

I navigate back through the park, occasionally wiping my sweat-dampened palms on my thighs. My pulse slows to something approximating normal as I concentrate on driving, watching for bicyclists, deer, or elk that might decide to cross the road as the evening draws in and the shadows deepen.

It takes me forty minutes to get home, and then another ten to draw my gun and clear the house before I can put my groceries away and sit down to process what has happened. The camp chair feels too uncomfortable so I sit on the foot of the staircase and rest my head on my arms. My muscles are knotted with tension. Tears sting my eyes and my sinuses flush with heat. I have to bite my lips to keep from crying.

What's the matter with me?

I need to talk to someone, a person who can help me decode my experience, who won't think I've absolutely lost it. Because I'm afraid I've crossed a threshold of sanity. A whole-body shiver causes the hair to raise on my arms. I don't ever want to go back to the psych ward. Or go back to a pill-induced fog.

Phoebe's number is on my list of favorites, and the steady ring is comforting. She'll know what to do, what to say. When I hear my therapist's voice on the line, it's like being handed a life preserver. Except then I realize it's her voicemail, inviting me to leave a message.

Shit.

"Hi, Phoebe, it's me. Audrey. Listen, something's happened, I've had a…a hallucination, or something. I need to talk to you. Please." My voice is shaking and I have to end the call before I lose it, and make her think she has to bring someone with a straitjacket.

So much for that. Just saying it aloud has brought the perspiration back to my forehead and upper lip. I don't know what to do now. Maybe I should go down to the coffee shop. Or better yet, the Portway Tavern. Someplace I can be among people while I toss back a cold one.

Drinking to escape? That's a new one for you.

So is being in a shipwreck.

You could call Bernie Flowers.

He's going to be too eager. And he doesn't have any psychic ability. He can't relate.

What about the medium?

I think about that. We spoke briefly at Bernie's gathering, exchanging small talk and business cards. She was familiar with the ability to see the past, enough to name it. She at least will take a weird experience in stride. And she's not likely to just assume I'm crazy. A slightly hysterical laugh bubbles up from my gut. Yeah, it'll be therapeutic to talk with someone who thinks she speaks with the dead. A toss-up as to which of us is the most delusional.

It takes me a few minutes to find her card. It's in a pile of mail and receipts on the kitchen counter. Meg Eccleston, Medium. It has a little purple crystal ball logo, and a phone number.

I can't believe I'm doing this. But I tap in her number and wait, part of me hoping that this call will also go to voicemail, and I can head down to the tavern.

"Hi, Audrey."

I choke in surprise. "How did you know it was me?"

"I must be psychic." She laughs, then says, "Bernie gave me your number, and I put you in my contacts."

"Oh. I thought you were going to say a spirit told you." Then I wince…maybe that was rude.

She snorts. "They're not usually that specific. It's nice to hear from you. What's up?"

I take a deep breath, shift to a more comfortable position on the stair and adjust my grip on the phone. "Listen. I know this is going to sound crazy, but—" I pause. How am I going to explain?

"You'll have to say something pretty extreme before I assume insanity, Audrey. What's going on? Did you see a ghost?" Her tone is wry but friendly, and her inquiry is without irony. Like she actually wants to know.

I feel reassured.

Just say it.

"Okay. I was down on the beach where the shipwreck is and I—" what, had a hallucination? I know that's what I said to Phoebe's voicemail, but deep in my heart I know that's not what it was.

"You what?" Meg prompts.

"I had a vision. A really strong one." I tell her what happened, how it felt, how it hijacked my whole sensory apparatus.

"Is that what normally happens?" Her tone is inquisitive, as though I haven't just uttered an impossible lie. "Do you always lose track of your immediate surroundings?"

"Yes. But honestly, this has only happened a couple of times. The vision thing. It's new to me, and I'm still getting a handle on what's normal." I laugh shakily. "If you can call any of this normal."

"Oh, Audrey," she says. "I didn't realize your ability had manifested so recently. That must have been terrifying. From the way you describe it, you were inhabiting a person who was present at the disaster, correct?"

"That's right. I guess."

"How interesting. To actually plug into another time! I would love to hear more about your experiences. But why are you calling me? How can I help? Do you want me to try to contact a spirit who was actually there? I have to warn you, it doesn't usually work that way."

Ye gods. The last thing I need is another disembodied voice. "I guess I just thought you might be able to throw some light on this for me. I'm really at sea. I don't know how to manage these visions, or how to work with this ability. I thought you might have more experience with the—the paranormal." I can't believe I actually uttered those words.

She laughs again. "Okay, well, I'll do my best. It sounds like your ability is always tied to an actual place, right? Have you ever had a vision on the beach before?"

"Never. And I've been down there a hundred times."

"So there must be something that sparked it this time, yes? Any ideas?"

"I was hoping you might have one." What was so special about this morning? Or is it something to do with me, my PTSI?

Meg says, "Let me check something out, okay? Hang on, I'm going to put you on speaker while I get on my laptop."

I hear her put the phone down, followed by the clack of keys. Then she says, "What do you know about the shipwreck?"

"Nothing, really. Just that it happened more than a century ago." The hard wooden stairs are starting to make my backside sore, so I get up and walk to the rear windows and look out over the river. The sun is setting in a painter's splash of orange and yellow, gleaming through the barren branches of the tree in my downhill neighbor's backyard. I shift the phone to my other hand.

When Meg speaks again, her voice seems thoughtful. "Audrey, you said in your vision you were trapped in the hold. How did 'you' get out of the ship?"

I bite my lip. It feels so weird to discuss this. "I'm not sure. I think I swam to shore. I mean, the ship was aground on the beach, so I didn't have to go very far." I shiver again, thinking of the pounding waves and biting wind. "It was stormy, though. And scary."

"I'm looking at the Wikipedia page for the *Peter Iredale*. Did you know there were two stowaways on board?"

"What? No." I think of where I was in the vision, a space between barrels. Would a crew member have been down there normally? Was I seeing through the eyes of a stowaway?

"And here's something else that's really interesting," she says. "The shipwreck occurred in 1906. On October 25th."

My heart skips a beat. Today is October 25th.

Happy anniversary!

"Do you think that's why I had the vision? Because of the coincidence of dates?"

"Very possibly. And that explains why you haven't had one there before now. Anniversaries are often intertwined with events in the spirit world. It's like a psychic echo. Things like violent death or trauma can leave the spirits of the departed confused, unable to comprehend that their bodies are dead. Which means they don't pass over, they remain stuck on the physical plane, and they sometimes get agitated and angry, because of their confusion."

Overwhelmed by the sudden need for a cup of tea, I go into the kitchen and turn on the electric kettle. "Are you saying you think I saw a ghost?" The image of the ship, the men on the beach comes back to mind. "Multiple ghosts?"

"Nooo." She hesitates. "It doesn't sound like that, and it isn't at all like my own experiences of interacting with the departed. I've never known anyone with retrocognition, but I know it's a rare thing. Maybe you're tapping into the time stream, descending into a particular vessel who, for whatever reason, is open to your presence. Like a walk-in spirit."

I set a mug on the counter and get a bag of rooibos tea, tucking my phone between my cheek and shoulder. My head is spinning. I don't know what to make of all this talk of spirits. Bernie thinks my ability is being able to see events that have been recorded in the environment, like a hologram, or a movie. He never mentioned possessing other people. The hair on the back of my neck prickles with the thought.

"Audrey, are you there?"

I swallow to loosen my throat. "Yes, sorry. This is a lot to take in. I need some time to think about everything you've told me."

"I totally get that. I hope I've been of some help. I know it was scary for me when I first became a vessel for the dead. You just have to trust yourself, and the process. Just remember to walk in the light. You're stronger than you think."

We say our goodbyes, and I put my phone down. A vessel for the dead. How could she voluntarily let herself be taken over by a ghost? It sounds terrifying. And also like some crazy, made-up shit.

But. There's my own experience. Which I'm *not* making up. Which means, I have to accept that *all* of this stuff could be real.

Never too late for an old dog to learn a new trick.

You know what? I'm just going to make myself some dinner and stream a movie on my laptop, maybe do some laundry, and stop worrying about all this.

Good luck with that.

As I putter around the house, my fears of ghostly invasion recede, and I realize how, well, *nice* it was to just talk to a regular person. Even if I'm on the fence about her profession. She genuinely seemed to want to help. And there's some relief to being able to confide in someone who isn't being paid for the privilege.

Do I need can invitation to join this pity party?

Ugh. I need to get some actual friends, people to distract me from all this internal jabber. People who can help me feel normal, instead of assuming I need to be fixed.

I wish I hadn't left that voicemail for Phoebe.

OCTOBER 26 - DAY 8

42

THE NEXT MORNING, I'm up and about, having regained my emotional equilibrium. Unburdening myself to Meg Eccleston has had a rejuvenating effect. There's no sense stressing about something I can't control. Better to focus on what I can actually do, and I'm ready to hit the ground running.

Trusting the process, are we?

Yes, as a matter of fact, we are. Walking in the light.

Phoebe sends me a text, concerned after listening to the voicemail. I assure her I'm fine, and we set up an appointment for this evening.

Now, back to business. I've been working on this case for a week, and I've finally dug up a new direction. According to Tavin O'Brian's eyewitness testimony, Ethan Sinclaire was seen arguing with Jack Reynolds on the dock of the Warrenton marina.

Once again, I call the Oregon Department of Fish and Wildlife Marine Reserve Program office, and this time I punch in the extension for Lenore DeLibero, the scientific team leader.

"This is Lenore."

Quoth the raven, "Nevermore."

"Ms. DeLibero, hi. This is Audrey Lake. We spoke a few days ago regarding the apprehension of an illegal crabber on the reserve."

"The Reynolds affair. I remember." Her voice is cautious, controlled.

"I'm sorry, I had to get off the phone in a hurry last time we spoke. Do you have time now to answer a few questions?"

"Who are you, again?"

"I'm an investigator working for the Clatsop County Public Defenders' Office."

"Reynolds was murdered, you said."

"Yes. There's a man in custody. I'm just trying to put together a timeline of Reynold's movements. Can you help me?"

"It's hard to believe someone killed him. You don't think it was connected to his crabbing, do you?"

"Do you?"

She laughs nervously. "No, not really. I mean, the reserve is sacrosanct to us, of course, but I don't think anyone else would get that worked up."

"Ethan sounded pretty worked up when we spoke last."

"Oh, Ethan!" She scoffs. "He's young, and it upsets him when someone puts their own interests ahead of the environment. He even wanted to go up to Warrenton and find Reynolds and explain why illegal crabbing and fishing are so detrimental, teach him a lesson. I told him it wouldn't work."

I think about the young man on the bar video, haranguing Reynolds in the parking lot. If that was Sinclaire, then he's been seen twice. "Did he actually come up here? Ethan, I mean?"

"I think I dissuaded him. Explained that he'd never get Reynolds to agree with the principles of sustainable sea harvest. It's all about money to them."

"Them?"

"You know, commercial fishermen. It's a dangerous profession, they're manly men, and they don't like to be told what to do."

"Yeah, there's a lot of that going around." I get her to repeat the story of how Reynolds was caught. It tallies with Ethan's account of how reserve scientists discovered the illegal pots, called the State Troopers and lay in wait for the crabbers to come back. The arrest occurred at night, and the *Beatrice* wasn't using her onboard lights, which was also a safety violation. But of course, they didn't want to be seen. The troopers had waited until Reynolds was actually pulling in the pots and removing the crabs before making their arrest.

"And then they just let him walk free, with a fine and a warning. It's so maddening. I mean, there *were* a lot of crabs in the area—my team and I had noted a dense population about half a mile out from the shore—but that's the purpose of the reserve, to shelter the breeding population. Eventually they will migrate into the commercial area, and everybody wins. It just takes a little time."

"Can I speak to Ethan again? Just to make sure I've got his information correct."

Pause. "I'm afraid I can't allow you to do that. He's not a spokesperson for the reserve. He shouldn't have discussed it with you in the first place."

"I thought he handled outreach. That's what his staff profile says."

"He does our social media and writes up press releases. He's not the voice of the program."

"Did Jack Reynolds know that?"

"What's that supposed to mean?"

I sigh. People are so obtuse. "Look, Ms. DeLibero. I'm investigating a murder here. I understand your reserve is important, but a man is dead. If your employee went up and threatened him, then this just got a whole lot more complicated. Now, let me speak to Ethan."

"He's not here. He's taken some time off."

"And you just let him go?"

"I can't deny him his vacation. He's earned it. And he's not a criminal, whatever you may think."

We end the call. I'm even more convinced that he's the man on the video. He was never identified by the police, so my next step will be to go over to the restaurant to confirm. I access Sinclaire's staff photo and bookmark it on my phone. Then I make a carafe of coffee and pour myself a cup. I savor the heat and the gentle jolt of caffeine, scribbling a few notes to myself about my conversation with Lenore, and prepare for an interview at Buoy 9. Until the silence is broken by three hard raps on the front door.

43

My blood pressure, which was sloshing along so peacefully, leaps into the hypertension zone.

Intruder alert! Intruder alert!

I put my cup down on the card table with a clatter and walk to the front of the house. There's no peephole, or sidelight, so I can't see who's there. I touch the butt of the Glock in my shoulder holster. The weight of the weapon over my heart is comforting, and I put my back to the wall beside the door. Easing the gun out of the holster, I hold it down by my thigh.

Bam! Bam! Bam!

I flinch at the noise. The knocks are loud, and the vibration trembles through the wall. My hand tightens on the grip of my gun, until the scoring imprints itself on my palm.

I clear my throat. "Who is it?"

"Police. Let me in, Lake."

The voice pings in my memory, and I open the door to Detective Jane Candide. She's dressed in dark pants and a blazer, hair pulled back in a bun at the nape of her neck.

She doesn't smile when I let her in. Her gaze passes over the empty spaces, the sparse furniture, and pauses at the view. Then she turns back to me. "Homey."

"I'm a minimalist," I retort.

She glances down at my sidearm, still clutched by my side, and puts her hands on her hips. "Jesus, Lake. Were you going to shoot me?"

The thought has its attractions.

Embarrassed, I holster my weapon. "I've had a trespasser."

"You should call the police."

"Looks like I'm already getting personalized service."

"I like to check up on persons of interest."

Her terminology doesn't escape me. This isn't a social visit. "Why are you here, Detective?"

"I want to know why you are digging around in the Reynolds investigation." Up to now, Candide's voice has been flat and businesslike, but in these words, a red thread of anger surfaces.

"I'm working with Karthik Biswas. He's hired me to look into the case."

"The defense attorney." She folds her arms across her chest.

"I see that you know him."

"Oh, I know him all right." She strides past me, through the empty front room, turning when she reaches the card table and camp chair. "I don't admire you for trying to undermine a police investigation."

"Why, is there something to hide?"

Candide's face is like a thundercloud. "You won't find anything wrong with the work."

"Then you shouldn't be worried. Besides, it's the Warrenton cops' work, not yours."

She glares at me, and I put on the stone face I reserve for talking to criminals.

She looks away, puts her hands in her pockets in a more relaxed stance. "So. What have you found?"

I hesitate. "I'm not sure we should be having this conversation."

"Oh, so now you're all about following the rules? Please." She scoffs.

"Listen, Jane," I start. And then I stop, because I don't really know what to say. I have too much sympathy for her as a fellow police officer, and too much self-doubt, to rake her over the coals, or to assume some self-righteous stance. So I opt for honesty. "I wanted to work with you guys, but you didn't want me. At least Olafson didn't. I'm just trying to make a living."

"By working for the enemy."

"Biswas isn't the enemy. He's just the other side of the coin. I know you don't like defense lawyers. Hell, I don't like them either. I know what it feels like to have your work, your professionalism, questioned." I search for the right words. "As long as the Warrenton P.D. has done their investigation well, there shouldn't be a problem. But it's Biswas's job to defend his client. So he'll use whatever he can. It's not personal."

We stand there looking at each other for what seems like a long time. Finally, I say, "I've made some coffee. Would you like some?"

Jane shakes her head.

"Sure? I know it must be better than what your department provides."

"I wouldn't know what to do with Joe that was actually drinkable." She offers a ghost of a smile. "I suppose you wouldn't tell me if you found something wrong with the investigation?"

This is hard to answer. "I haven't found anything wrong, exactly. But—"

"But?"

"There are some holes. And I don't think the perp is guilty."

She goes on high alert, like a retriever watching a duck fall from the sky. "Why not?"

I shrug. "Just a feeling."

Again she just looks at me. Candide and I have some shared history. She was there when I worked a missing-person-turned-murder case, when my 'feelings' led me to a solution opposed to the scenario worked out by the police.

"Evidence?"

"Not yet."

I honestly don't know why I've told her this much. It's a huge breach of confidentiality, even if I haven't given out facts or details. But it's hard to walk away from the 'thin blue line.' The camaraderie, the knowledge that these are the folks who get why you've got insomnia, or a drinking problem, or PTSI, because they've been in the front line themselves.

Not because you have something to prove to Jane Doe here. Not at all.

Not. At. All. But I have to know why she's here. So I ask her.

Candide nods. Her mouth is stiff. "I came because the investigating detective told me you were asking questions yesterday. He learned you'd talked to other people, too. Some of them believed you were a cop. Did you tell them that?"

"No. I did not."

"Did you tell them you were working for the defense?"

"Not always."

"What did you tell them?"

"That I was following up on the investigation."

"So you let them believe you were a cop."

"What a person believes is their own choice. If they don't ask me who I am, or who I represent, I'm not duty-bound to tell them."

"If I find out you're impersonating a member of the police, I'll throw your ass in jail quicker than you can blink."

My feelings of camaraderie have vanished. "Don't threaten me. I'm a private citizen performing a legitimate job." I try to swallow my annoyance, turn the tables. "Why don't you tell me why Judd Daily would call you for a case that's out of your jurisdiction? Why are you acting as his goon squad?"

Maybe they're sleeping together.

"Are you sleeping together?" My tone is sarcastic, but the blood rushes to her face. I can't believe it. It's like some bygone soap opera. "Shit. You *are*, aren't you?"

"It's none of your business," she snaps.

I lean forward, until we're almost nose to nose. "Threatening me, an investigator who is working for the defense, is far more damning than anything I've done. Or will do."

Candide is the first one to blink. "Just watch your step. I'll see myself out." She breaks eye contact and walks away, her boot heels clacking on the bare wood floor. The door clicks shut behind her.

I wonder if she's been stalking me. I wonder if it's her footprints I've seen on the porch, her that I chased down the hillside the other day. And I wonder what would have happened if I caught her.

44

My ENCOUNTER WITH Candide has left me shaking with a mix of anxiety and anger. But would I be so angry if there wasn't a kernel of truth in her accusation of impersonating law enforcement?

A little deception never hurt anyone.

But it was deception that caused my psychosis, wasn't it? Living undercover in all the layers of lies until, in the end, I didn't know who I was.

Maybe you never knew in the first place.

All the criminals I consorted with never had a problem with lying. When they were caught in one, they just came up with another, massaging their own memories until they couldn't tell truth from fiction.

Unlike yourself, is that it?

You were at the center of every one of those lies. In fact, *you're* the one who told them. All of that mess happened when I was you.

Nothing like a little compartmentalization.

My phone rings, and I see that it's Madison Jones. I'm of two minds whether to take her call, since I'm having a little psychotic break. But, she's a paying client. And I want to keep getting work from the Clatsop County Public Defenders Office, so I pick up.

"Audrey, I have great news! I just got back from Alon's bail hearing, and he's been released to the custody of his aunt. I couldn't have found her without your help."

Finally, a concrete result of my efforts. "That was fast. What happens next?"

"As long as the Big Bridge Bar & Grill continues to press charges, he'll have to appear in court. But his aunt is going to have her husband sponsor a work visa for Alon, so he'll have a legal basis to be here. He can help her husband with his building projects."

"Wait, her husband?"

"He's a contractor, remember? Mrs. Jenson told us at the meeting."

"What kind of a contractor?"

"He has a small residential building company." Her voice is impatient. "What does that matter? The important thing is that Alon will have employment and a place to live."

"Can you give me Mr. Jenson's contact details?" I've been blown off by so many contractors, I'm willing to use a little of my influence with Alon's aunt to get her husband to come and look at my roof.

"I'll send you a link, okay? Can we get back to the main point?"

"Yes, sorry. Shiny object and all. You were saying about Alon?"

"Hiraya's husband can sponsor him, get him a work visa and eventually a green card. We can get him into the system, do it legally so he doesn't have to hide."

"Will that work if he's been in jail? I thought the Feds were picky about things like criminal records."

"I'm going to exert some pressure on the restaurant. The evidence is very thin. In fact, if he wasn't undocumented, the police probably wouldn't even be holding him. I'm sure the owners won't really want to go to court, especially since their own role in hiring workers under the table will get some serious scrutiny. And they still haven't come forward with the amount he allegedly stole. Without that, there isn't a solid basis to charge him."

"I wondered about that." I go back into the kitchen to refresh my cup of coffee, and shake cereal into a bowl.

"Something fishy is going on there, definitely. I want you to check that place out again. See if you can find evidence that they knew he was undocumented."

"Will do. Don't forget to send me Jenson's details."

Madison sighs noisily, but texts me the information. I end the call with her and immediately punch in the contractor's number.

"Jenson's Building and Construction, can I help you?" The voice is accented, a woman. And one I think I recognize.

"Excuse me, is this Hiraya Jenson?"

Her tone shades with suspicion. "Yes?"

"Mrs. Jenson, this is Audrey Lake, the private investigator who is helping Madison Jones with your nephew."

"Has something happened?" Suspicion has changed to anxiety. "I thought we could keep Alon at home. Does he have to go back to jail? I thought—"

Way to go, Lake.

I hasten to reassure her. "No, no, everything's fine. Listen, I just wanted to find out if your husband's company could do some roofing work for me."

Her voice is cautious. "We do things like large remodels, or whole house builds."

My heart sinks. "I think I just need some new shingles."

There's a long pause. "He would have to charge you."

I'm confused. "What?"

"Perhaps…there could be a discount, because you helped, but…"

Oh my God, she thinks I'm shaking her down. "No, no, I don't want a discount. Please. I just want someone to fix my roof. No one ever calls me back."

She takes my details down, and promises that someone will come to take a look. After the call ends, I feel a mix of elation that I've finally, maybe, got a roofer, and bewilderment that she thought I was blackmailing her.

What's up with that? Is it because she's now sheltering an undocumented family member, and she's afraid that will land her in trouble with the police?

Duh. Of course that's the problem.

I would never extort favors, or money. Ever.

Why should she trust you?

I've been helping Alon. Why would I turn on them now?

Ever watch the news?

Not if I can help it.

I bang my coffee cup down on the counter and run a hand through my hair. I get it. I know. It's just hard to realize that someone you've been helping now sees you as a possible enemy.

I wish illegal immigration wasn't such an issue. I wish there wasn't so much misinformation flying around. I wish no one ever smuggled guns, or drugs, or people. That no one ever felt they had to leave their birth nation in order to have a better life.

I wish I had a pony.

Oh, shut up.

<h1 style="text-align:center">45</h1>

THE REST OF my morning is taken up by running errands, grocery shopping and dropping by the credit union to argue about my overdraft. By the time I get done I'm cranky and hungry and looking for some lunch.

So I head back across the New Youngs Bay Bridge to the town of Hammond, which is really just the north end of Warrenton. Buoy 9 is right on the main drag. I've never been inside, but I've driven past plenty of times on my way to the state park and the beach.

The exterior is single story, with vertical wood siding and a roof covered with green corrugated metal. The interior is dark wood, the bar fronted with more corrugated metal. One gray-haired guy is sitting at the bar with a bottle of Miller Lite, watching a football game on the TV perched above a shelf of liquor bottles. A few tables are scattered about, and various domestic beer posters are tacked around for decoration. The scent of cooking wafts from the kitchen. I take a seat at the bar, a couple spaces down from Miller Man, and order the fish and chips with a pint of Widmer Hefeweizen. The plate comes with a nice bowl of coleslaw, a generous serving of tartar sauce, and three pieces of golden brown cod resting on a pile of potato wedges.

I take a big swallow of my beer and pull out my phone, navigating to the image of Ethan Sinclaire. Turning it face down, I beckon the bartender over. Start off with some small talk, then give him my spiel about following up on the police report, and getting his version of the disagreement in the parking lot between Jack Reynolds and the unidentified young man.

The bartender rolls his eyes, gripes about already talking to the cops and a reporter for the *Astorian*. I nod and smile, commiserating about what a pain in the neck it is to answer questions. He reiterates what I've already seen in the police report and security video, adding that the young man, who he refers to as a 'kid,' came into the bar after Jack had arrived, and then hung out at a corner table drinking Bud Lights until Jack finished his meal and got up to leave.

"So the kid didn't order a meal?" Interesting. That could mean his whole purpose in coming to the restaurant was to confront Reynolds.

"Nah. Just milked a couple of bottles and played with his phone."

"Typical kid," Miller Man interjects as a commercial breaks into the game. "Would rather look at his text messages than talk to a real person."

"Were you here at the time?" I ask politely.

The bartender snorts. "He's always here."

"Hey, I gotta keep you guys open," Miller Man says.

"Yeah, we'd miss that one-bottle-a-day order if you bugged out."

"Can I help it if your poker machines never pay out?"

I wait for their banter to be over, taking bites of the tender cod surrounded by crispy beer batter. When they finish, I turn over my phone and bring up the picture of Ethan, turning it toward the bartender. "Was this the guy you saw?"

The bartender takes a long look, wiping the taps as he does. "Maybe. Hard to say. Hair color looks right."

"Lemme see," says Miller Man. He grabs the phone. "Looks like him to me."

I glance at the bartender, who shrugs.

Miller Man enlarges the photo. "So the cops finally figured out who he was. Little late though, right? I thought they got the guy who did it."

"Gotta nail down all the loose ends," I say, putting out a hand for my phone.

Miller Man fingers the screen, getting back to the page where the staff photos are shown. "Hey, these are the folks who manage that science zone down south of here."

Annoyed, I try to grab my phone but Miller Man swivels his chair, half-turning his back.

"Can I have my phone back, please?" There's an edge to my voice I can't smother.

Let's just shoot him.

Nope. I'm walking in the light.

"I'm sure this is the kid. He was hooting and hollering about fish being more important than people. Gotta be him. What do you think, Hardy?" This comment is directed to the bartender.

Hardy slaps the bar with his towel. "Give the lady back her phone, Reg."

"Just hold your horses." Miller Man—whose name, apparently, is Reg—has the photo app open on my phone.

The bartender grabs Reg's beer bottle by the neck and pulls it over to his side of the counter. "I'm serious, Reg. I let you sit here all afternoon without spending more than five bucks, but when you start bothering the paying customers, it's time for you to leave."

"Sir, I'm asking you to give me back my phone. Now." I lean forward, my jacket gapes, and Hardy catches sight of the Glock in the shoulder holster. His eyes widen.

"Better do what the lady says, man."

Reg scrolls through my photos of the marina. "Look at this picture. This looks like the *Pot o' Gold*. What're you doing taking photos of people's boats for?"

Hardy glances at me. "She's a cop, Reg. For God's sake, stop screwing around."

"Okay, okay. Jeez, don't get your shorts in a wad." He shoves the phone down the wooden bar top toward me, through the ring of moisture left from his bottle. "Are you really a cop? I thought it was all over. Got yer man and all."

I wipe my phone on my pant leg. "For the record, I'm not a police officer."

"FBI! I knew it!"

"Sorry, not FBI either."

"Aw, but you'd say that, wouldn't she, Hardy? What happened? Did the guy they caught turn out not to be right after all?"

"I can't comment on an ongoing investigation. But I am interested in what you heard this young man say to Captain Reynolds."

"See, she is a cop. You are, aren't you? But I won't tell anyone. Gimme another beer, Hardy."

The bartender replaces the half-empty bottle he removed earlier. His eyebrows ask a question of me, like whether he needs to kick this guy to the curb. I shake my head no.

"Did you follow these two men out to the parking lot, Reg?" I ask.

"Not right away, just was going out to my car for something. Left my beer on the bar to hold my place, didn't I, Hardy?"

"You did." The bartender's voice is weary.

"What were they saying?"

"Oh, the kid was angry about overfishing, or some such. Captain tried to walk away, but the kid got in his face. Finally he'd had it and pushed him out of his way."

"You mean Reynolds pushed the kid, or the other way around?"

"Captain pushed the kid. Got in his truck and took off down the street.

"Did the kid look mad?"

"Looked like someone pissed in his ice cream." Reg guffaws and slaps the table. "Kids today, don't know how to work, don't know where their food comes from, don't have the first idea of what it takes to earn a living. He's lucky the captain didn't rearrange his face for him."

"What direction did they go?"

"Oh, back toward the highway." He waves a vague hand. "Wouldn't you say, Hardy?"

The bartender heaves a sigh. "I wasn't out there. Because I work for a living."

"Thank God I'm retired. Life is my own now." Reg finishes up his beer, searches his pockets with a jingle of keys. "You wouldn't want to spot me ten for the poker machine, would you?"

"Go home, Reg." The bartender claims the empty. "Your wife is wondering where you are."

The old man snorts, but picks up his hat and heads out the door.

Hardy watches him leave, then wipes the counter where Reg was sitting. "Sorry about that, ma'am. Reg is kind of a pest but he wouldn't hurt a fly."

I finish up my fish and chips, savoring the salt of the potatoes and the sharp bite of the tartar sauce. "Is he reliable?"

"I'd say so. I mean, he probably didn't understand whatever the kid was saying to Reynolds, but he never buys enough beer to get drunk."

"Thanks." I pocket my phone, pay the bill, and stand to leave. "Just so you know," I say as I walk to the door, "I'm not a cop."

46

I'M ENERGIZED TO be moving forward with the Reynolds murder investigation. Ethan is definitely looking more plausible, and after viewing the security footage, and seeing Keith Larson's boat arriving earlier than he said he did, I'm interested in nailing down this discrepancy in his statement.

Larson is the guy who taught Reynolds how to crab, and who Reynolds stole pots from when he made his illegal foray out onto the reserve. So not only did Reynolds betray someone who was helping him, he also set him up for possible prosecution if law enforcement had traced the gear back to Larson. And Larson is Alicia Reynolds' cousin, which makes it personal. Yeah, there's a lot to like about him as a suspect.

You fancy him as a body dumper?

Yeah, I do. Glad to see your instincts are still working.

Mine were never in question.

The only trouble is, he's a crabber, and likely to be out on the water. I drive back into Warrenton and go down to the docks. My luck is in—Larson's boat, the *Georgia Peach*, is moored at its berth.

Biswas has told me that we don't need proof of another killer, we just need reasonable doubt that it was Horne. But that goes against every grain I have. If Jim Horne isn't guilty, then I want to know who is. Suspicion of murder is a life-wrecker; it leaves a long shadow. I don't want to implicate someone else without pretty meaningful evidence, even with as strong a motive as Larson has.

I walk down the gently bobbing boardwalks to Larson's boat. Larson himself is tinkering with something on the deck. As I get closer, I see he's pulled some of the electronics from the out and has pieces spread out on a cloth. I watch him for a few minutes, taking in the lines and details of the *Peach*. I don't know much about such things, but it looks neat and trim, the pots stacked in a tidy pile, the paint touched up, and the brightwork, well, bright. It's cleaner than the neighboring boats. Despite that, it's still battered and dinged along the waterline, with spots of rust. A pair of seagulls perch on the gunwale.

When Larson notices me, he frowns, then puffs out an exasperated sigh. Standing, he arches his back in a stretch. He's dressed in sweats stained with oil and other mysterious fluids. Probably different varieties of fish gunk.

Waving, I approach the access stairs. He doesn't seem to object to my presence, even as I clamber gracelessly onto the deck, but stands with his hands on his hips.

"To what do I owe the pleasure?" He asks.

"Oh, following up," I say vaguely. "You know how it is."

"Listen." He rubs his stubbled jaw with an oily hand, leaving a black streak across one cheek like a scar. "I know you've got a job to do, but they've got the guy. I'd rather not dig into this whole thing again."

"But see, my boss doesn't think they have the *right* guy," I say virtuously, in an 'I'm just the messenger' tone. "Want to tell me where you were on the day they found Jack's body?"

"Probably catching crabs. It's what I do." He nods in the direction of the piled pots. "I already gave the police my alibi. You should ask them."

"I've got the case file, thanks. You're on video arriving back at the harbor at around three in the morning the same day Reynolds' body was found."

His frown deepens. "So?"

"So, you said in your statement that you didn't get back until later, *after* the body had been found. Since your alibi is now in question, I'd like to know why you lied."

Larson's face reddens, either in embarrassment or anger, but seeing his fists clench makes me think it's the latter. Reflexively, I take a step back.

He makes a visible effort to calm down, relaxing his fingers and taking a deep breath. "Why's it important?"

"Because you passed right by the *Beatrice,* which is where the body was."

He freezes. Just for a second, but it's noticeable. His Adam's apple bobs in his throat. "So?"

I wait him out. He doesn't have to answer, of course, but it'll be interesting to see what he says.

He turns and goes into the cabin, comes back out with a spiral-bound notebook, slightly tattered around the edges, with one end of the spiral bent and twisted. He thumbs through it

"I was down toward Tillamook Bay. Had to set the pots, so that's why I was out so early."

"Anyone with you? To confirm?"

"Yeah," he says after a long pause. "Alicia's boy was with me."

"You mean Chris?" I try to contain my surprise. "Do you often take him crabbing with you?"

"He likes it."

"Do you pay him?"

He slaps the notebook against his thigh. "No, I don't pay him. And I don't have to, he's family."

"Why did you lie to the police?"

"Because I didn't want him to get in trouble. Since I didn't do anything wrong, I didn't think it mattered."

I'm bewildered. "Why would Chris get in trouble with the cops?"

"Not the cops, with his mom. She doesn't like Chris being out on the boat. She's afraid he'll get hurt. But he likes it, and he's a pretty good hand with the pots. He's strong, likes to crank them in and see all the crabs."

I'm still not clear on his reasoning. "Let me get this straight. You told the police you got back later than you actually did, in order to protect Chris from his mom?" I shake my head. "I'm not understanding."

"Look, Chris was staying the weekend with me. He likes to hang with other men sometimes, you know? And he likes to be out on the water. He likes to be working, not just doing chores or painting pictures and watching Alicia make stuff for Etsy. So when he knew I was going out, he begged me to take him with me. So I did. Because whatever his issues, Chris isn't a child. He's twenty-three. He's a good worker when you give him the chance. Shit, he used to haul in Jack's pots by hand, with ropes. At least with me he gets to use the hydraulic lifts."

I raise a hand to stop the flow. "Okay, I get it. But I still don't see what that has to do with lying about when you got back."

"I didn't want the police to go out and question Chris and Alicia. We didn't see Jack or anyone else on the dock that night. And I didn't want Chris to be upset about his father's death, or by the cops asking him questions."

"But you didn't know about the death at the time."

"The police were clear about why they were asking people questions. I was cleaning the boat, when all the hoopla happened. Chris had already gone home, and I saw no reason to involve him. I knew we were innocent, so why put up with the hassle?"

I think back to the security footage I viewed in Biswas's office. "What about the other boat?"

"What other boat?"

"There was a fishing boat that came back shortly after you got in. The *Pot O' Gold*. Did you see it out on the Columbia?"

He runs a hand through his hair. "I don't remember. But it wouldn't surprise me, lots of guys go out early."

I feel like there's something else here that I should be thinking about, some squiggle in the back of my mind. But it won't come forward. So I head back to my car.

You didn't ask him if he dumped Reynolds' body over the side.

Chris was with him. How likely is it that he could lift a corpse over the rail without Chris seeing it? In fact, none of these guys are ever alone on their boats. O'Brian has that Tad guy. Reynolds had Charlie Phelps. It takes more than one person to operate the vessel and the equipment. Body dumping from a working boat would be a conspiracy, not a lone gunman. So that's a dead end.

Unless we're looking for a conspiracy.

You mean, more than one person? People working together?

It happens.

I don't really know what to think about that. It's not impossible, but it seems farfetched. And why would a bunch of people want to kill Jack Reynolds? This isn't *Murder on the Orient Express.*

I start the car and roll over the gravel, filling the car with a crunching sound. If only there were audio files associated with the harbor security video. I'd be able to hear if someone drove into the lot, even if no one appeared on the screen. I'd hear if someone dropped a body in the water, even if I didn't actually see it happen.

Technology. It falls short in so many ways.

47

AFTER DRIVING ALL over the county, I'm back home, standing around in my sock feet, watching a big fog bank advance over the bar and inch toward my house. I'm starting to get hungry, but I've got one more thing to do before I call it a day. Well, two things. First, I call Alon's aunt's husband, the contractor. He doesn't pick up so I leave a voicemail, which feels exactly like throwing a message in a bottle into the Pacific and hoping it arrives in Fiji.

Which leads me to my second task. Once again I call the Oregon Marine Reserve, and drum my fingers as I listen through the automated menu options, until it reaches the extension for Lenore DeLibero, program manager.

My earlier conversations with her have been neutral with a chance of negative. I rehearse in my head the things I want to ask her as I pace around the living room while the ringtone pulses in my ear.

"Lenore speaking. Who am I talking to?"

My preparatory remarks go out the window. "Hi. This is Audrey Lake. We spoke this morning."

"Yes. I remember." No indication whether this is a pleasant memory, or otherwise.

"Great. Listen, Ms. DeLibero, if you recall, I'm following up on the investigation of the circumstances surrounding the death of Jack Reynolds. His body was found on September sixth."

"Uh-huh."

"Well, here's my issue. On September fifth, your employee, Ethan Sinclaire, was seen on a security camera, talking to Mr. Reynolds. But you know how these things are. The footage isn't great, and the identification may be wrong. What I want to verify with you is whether he was working in Newport that day, in which case the I.D. is mistaken, and I'll stop bothering you."

There's a silence in which I can hear her breathing. Honestly, she doesn't *have* to do anything, or answer my questions. I don't have a warrant, there's no subpoena. But. It's better for everyone if she cooperates. No bad publicity for Fish and Wildlife. Plus, they are a tax-funded organization. Cooperating with law enforcement should be a given.

I hear the click-clack of a keyboard. A muttered curse as she struggles with some technical issue. Then more silence, and a muted sigh.

Time for a prompt. "Ms. DeLibero? Are you still there?"

"I'm here." Another sigh. "It looks like Ethan took a couple of vacation days at that time. He wasn't working on the day in question. Now, if there's nothing else, I've got work to do."

Stalling while my mind races for further questions, I say, "Busy day at the reserve?"

"Establishing a base population for commercial fish species. We're trying to get a count before winter weather sets in. I've got to get these numbers into the database so we can establish how successful we've been in growing the fish and crab stocks."

"I'm glad you guys are out there," I say. And I am. It seems like a viable enterprise, a no-brainer when it comes to something as basic as sustaining an important food source.

"Thanks." She thaws a little. "Everyone on staff is dedicated to the health of the reserves, and the ocean at large. That's why it feels so personal when someone disrespects the rules. We're working for the fishing community, and big picture, the whole human race."

"It's good work. Do you know where Ethan went on his vacation?"

She gets distant again. "I don't give out personal information about my employees."

"I get it. Thanks. Have a good evening." And I end the call.

So, the young Sinclaire was out and about when Reynolds was killed. Between the bartender's identification and Lenore's confirmation, I've got no doubt that he was the guy in the footage from Buoy 9.

I check the clock on my phone, and realize it's time for my appointment with Phoebe. She's going to want to hear about the incident at the shipwreck, and I'm going to have to keep her from committing me. With a sigh, I put my shoes back on and silence my phone. As I leave the house, a slow drizzle begins, peppering the pavement with spots of darkness.

48

I ALWAYS THINK of Phoebe's office as being restful and clean. The asparagus fern in the corner is quietly shedding slender yellowed leaves onto the carpet. The light through the window is cold and gray, with a view into my side-yard where I so recently slipped while running after the intruder. Was that just three days ago? Seems almost like a dream. Or a nightmare. Anyway, that experience has been eclipsed by yesterday's vision.

I settle into the armchair. We exchange greetings and small talk. Then Phoebe says casually, "How's Zoe these days?"

The unexpected question throws me, and I lean forward. "Much as always. Maybe one day she'll go away."

In your dreams, sister.

I groan aloud.

Phoebe doesn't ask me to elucidate. Instead, she asks me about my hallucination.

Here we go. I try to deflect, say it wasn't as bad as all that, and I've gotten over being upset about it. But my therapist isn't having it.

"I'm glad to hear that you've regained your equilibrium. But Audrey, I'm concerned. We've been operating on the principle that your psychosis isn't manifesting at present, but if you're having hallucinations, especially ones that upset you so much in the moment, we've got to consider putting you back on your medication."

"No, Phoebe. No. I don't like how the pills make me feel, like I'm walking around in the fog." I get up and pace to the window, looking at the rain falling outside.

She sighs. "Why don't you tell me what happened?"

"I was down on the beach, where the *Peter Iredale* is. I had a vision, like I was experiencing the original shipwreck." I describe how it felt to be in among the barrels as the ship rolled and tossed, the footsteps overhead, the cold of the wind and the rain. Just remembering it makes me shiver. And then I go on, tell her about my conversation with Meg, omitting the fact that she speaks with spirits. Just relay the historical facts Meg shared with me.

Phoebe is silent for so long I turn from the window to look at her. Her expression is...odd. Almost blank.

"Phoebe? What do you think about what I saw?"

Phoebe says slowly, "Your friend is correct. It's a fact that anniversaries of traumatic events can affect people psychologically. Trigger them."

"I'm not sure I understand. I mean, I wasn't actually in the wreck. It was a hundred years ago. So there's nothing to trigger."

"Do you think you may have learned about the facts surrounding the event in some other way, and then forgotten?"

"How can I say what I might have known, and might have forgotten? But if that's the case, even hearing about it again didn't jog my memory. It's nothing I've ever looked into myself."

Phoebe's voice has a bit of a tremor. It makes me nervous. "Dr. Flowers has linked your ability to the environment. And environment can also trigger trauma in people with PTSI." She shakes her head. "I don't know what to think. But if your visions are, indeed, linked to past events, then I'd say the combination of the wreck and the anniversary would be enough. More than enough to trigger a flashback."

"But..." I can't even articulate my objections. Or even if I have an objection. I didn't expect her to corroborate what Meg told me. "Do you think that it's my own PTSI that is...enabling this process?"

"I can't say, it's really beyond me. But some cases of PTSI have been linked to physical changes—damage—in the brain. I suppose it's possible that you've also sustained damage, and that altered condition is what allows your… ability… to function."

La la la la la, weird science.

Great. Zoe is hooked into an '80's radio station.

But. Brain damage? I feel a little stab of fear. I haven't had a concussion, or other head trauma. But God knows what kind of drug mix Sonny was peddling in the Baxter Building, and I'm sure he couldn't have cared less about a safe dosage.

I clear my throat. "What about drugs? Can those cause brain damage?"

"Yes, with prolonged use. Some are worse than others." Phoebe frowns. "Have you ever experimented with psychedelics?"

I lick my lips. "Not voluntarily."

"There's some therapeutic use for them, in a controlled environment." She shrugs. "I'm very wary of them, myself. I'm sure you've heard about LSD-induced flashbacks, sometimes years after intensive use. But maybe—and I'm just hypothesizing here—some combination of trauma and substance may have triggered the emergence of your ability. Especially since you didn't have it growing up." She cocks her head. "That's correct, right? You didn't have a psychic childhood?"

"No. Nothing like that."

We've moved so far beyond conventional therapy that I'm not sure how to get us back to shore.

Phoebe and I are quiet. Outside, there's a patter of rainfall as it strikes the broad leaves of the rhododendron outside the window.

Eventually, my therapist says, "What else you want to talk about?"

I pull on a lock of my hair. "I know you're skeptical, but the trouble is, I'm on this case where it would be useful to have my 'psychic powers' click in," I say, making air quotes, "because I'm honestly pretty stumped. I don't think the guy they've arrested is the criminal. And if I could find the crime scene, then I could try to induce a vision, but since I can't find the crime scene, I've got nothing."

There's another long pause, and I glance over to where Phoebe is sitting silently. She takes off her glasses and rubs the bridge of her nose.

"Help me understand. You're trying to induce a hallucination? And you're unhappy that you can't? Even though the spontaneous one you had at the shipwreck was upsetting?"

"Right." I pace back to the armchair and plop down into it. "And I wouldn't say the vision was upsetting. It's hard for me to parse the emotions that are part of the experience, versus what I personally feel about having it."

"How did you feel about it?"

"I dunno. Afraid, yeah. But also relieved, in a way, to know that this ability is still there."

"I thought you wanted to get rid of the hallucinations."

"Well, I do. I did."

"I thought they frightened you."

I fidget, tucking my hands under my thighs. "They do. But..."

"But?"

"They've also been helpful. In the past. You know they have."

"So you've decided you trust them?"

I shuffle my feet on the carpet. "I mean, they don't take the place of hard evidence, but they have pointed me in the right direction in the past."

Phoebe sighs. "I know I introduced you to Bernie Flowers, and his beliefs about the paranormal. I thought it would help you, if you believed someone might have an explanation for your hallucinations that didn't indicate mental illness. But now it sounds like you're using a psychotic episode as a tool, and I'm not sure we should be comfortable with that."

"Wait a minute, Phoebe. I thought you accepted Bernie's explanation."

"To a point. Because there are things about your experiences that defy rational explanation. But the emergence of your visions coincides with your mental health issues. I don't want the exercise of this... ability...to be detrimental to the progress you're trying to make here."

"Are you saying that you think trying to use my ability is going to make my problems worse?"

"I'm afraid so. Because this whole thing with Zoe, for instance. Zoe is a sliver of your personality that has fragmented from your psyche.

These visions are also a split from standard, everyday awareness. I don't want to encourage more fragmentation."

She acts like I'm the one that's not real. Huh.

I find Zoe's comment chilling. "Fragmentation. You think I'm going to blow my mind to pieces."

"I would use the term 'disassociate'."

Does this mean I'm going to get some roommates?

"Ye gods." Here I am, struggling with my own unbelief, my own skepticism, but still trying to make sense of my ability. I'm already afraid my PTSI is going to crop up and kneecap me at a crucial moment. And now she's telling me I'm going to pieces.

"You've told me that your initial trauma, the one that resulted in your first psychotic episode, was the series of events in Denver. Until you can resolve those events, figure out what happened and why and move on from there, I'm afraid there won't be meaningful progress. I can give you tools, exercises, and listen to your troubles, but you have to make the commitment."

"I'm trying. But my job—"

"The fact that you're not avoiding me completely is a good sign. You have to see the value of therapy yourself and make it a priority. Otherwise, I can't help you. No one can. If Bernie is a better fit for you, well and good. I'll just be your neighbor."

"Phoebe—" The truth is, I'm not sold on Phoebe's brand of therapy. Bernie wants me to 'expand and embrace my gift,' Phoebe wants me to eradicate it. And I'm somewhere in the middle. Maybe there is no kind of therapy that can help me with my problems. "Can we talk about the intruder?"

"What intruder?"

I tell her about my scare of a few days ago, and the incident of the footprints on the porch and my chasing a shadow around the house. Explain how not knowing who it is or what they want or even if anyone is really there is creeping me out.

"You said not knowing his intentions is what frightens you. The testing of your boundaries is what angers you. The last time someone ignored your boundaries, back in Denver, you got hurt. And you were powerless to enforce those boundaries. What can you do in this situation?"

"I was planning to get some security cameras. So I can see who the intruder is and what they're doing. And so I can have a record of it."

She nods. "I think that's a good idea. But why do you want a record?"

"So if I need to, I'll have something to show the police, so they'll believe me."

"Do you have a history of the police not believing you?"

My heart is pounding. "Maybe. It's always good to have evidence."

"What would happen if you didn't have evidence?"

There's a roaring in my ears. For some reason it's hard to think. "They'll think I'm being emotional and overwrought. They won't take me seriously." In my mind's eye, I see the apartment squat, the roaming gang members. Margie, smiling through her ruby lipstick, with a cigarette in her hand.

"Did you try to tell the police about Sonny before he hurt you? Did no one take you seriously in Denver?"

I'm confused. What are we talking about? "I couldn't put cameras in my apartment. There wasn't any way to actually show them."

"Show them what?"

My own voice sounds like it's a great distance away. "The threats. How Sonny acted."

"Did you know he was going to harm you?"

I saw the knife. How he flashed it, how he kept it sharp, how he looked at it, constantly honing the edge. "He wanted to use his knife."

"On you?"

"Yes. On me."

"Why?"

"Because he knew all along I was a cop." Not just near the end, when I thought someone had picked up the law enforcement vibe. He knew the whole time I was there. I saw his broken smile, his glittering black eyes, full of malice. He'd been pushing my boundaries all along.

"And what does that mean?"

I speak slowly, dredging up the words. "It means somebody told him."

I succeeded in pivoting away from my visions, but this realization is just as frightening.

OCTOBER 27 - DAY 9

49

A LASER LIKE sunbeam across my face wakes me in the morning. My sleeping bag is warm and cozy, but my back is aching, probably because my cot doesn't have any support. After twisting about to find a more comfortable position, I give up and go downstairs to make some coffee.

I've got to get some better furniture. A bed, a chair, a table that doesn't fold up. Otherwise, I'm going to do permanent damage to my back. There's just so much to do. Plus, money.

Not to mention deciding you're here to stay.

That, too.

I wonder if my mother kept the house contents. She inherited those at the same time I got the house, and she had it all shipped back to Denver and put in storage. Maybe she'd like to donate some of the furniture back to me. But that means I would have to call her, and I'm not ready for that. I'm just struggling with too much, and she would ask questions, and have input. I've got a therapist. I don't need more input.

Maybe you should get your own furniture. You know, like an adult.

I'm saved from the morning criticism by my cell phone ringing. It's Madison Jones. I glance at the time to see if she's violating the pre-eight-o'clock rule, and see that it's actually 9:12. So I pick up the call with a sigh.

"Hello."

"I need you to get down to the office ASAP. Something bad has happened."

"Good morning, Madison. How are you today?" I take a long slow sip of coffee.

"What? Fine. Whatever. Listen, can you get down here now? I've got Alon's aunt and her husband here. Alon has been attacked. We need to get to the bottom of it."

"Wait, what? He's only been out of jail for one day." It's the crisis du jour.

"Just come down to the office, okay? We'll get all the information from the Jensons together."

"Okay. I'm on my way."

Which is why I'm back in the Clatsop County Public Defenders' Office before I have a chance to shower or do more than throw on yesterday's clothes. Juanita glances at my rumpled appearance and raises an eyebrow. But all she says is, "Madison is waiting for you in the conference room."

The young lawyer is sitting at the long, glass-topped table, along with Hiraya Jenson and a man I don't know. I'm still struggling to process what happened on the beach, and my discussions with Meg and Phoebe, but now I really have to push it to the back of my mind and concentrate on the job.

"Good, Audrey, I'm glad you could come on such short notice," Madison says. "You already know Mrs. Jenson. This is her husband, Randall. Mr. Jenson, this is our staff investigator, Audrey Lake."

Oooh, staff investigator.

I reach out a hand to Randall, and he takes it in a very firm handshake, squeezing my fingers into a painful lump. I don't think he's being a jerk, I think he's just strong.

The two are not mutually exclusive.

"Audrey Lake…that sounds familiar." He laughs, the guffaw filling the room. "Have you been investigating me?"

I flex my fingers behind my back to make sure nothing's broken. "I called the other day about getting my roof fixed."

He snaps his fingers. "That's right. I meant to have my wife call you back. I'm afraid we're booked out with builds. Most guys are going to be busy. You'll have to get on someone's waiting list."

Madison clears her throat. "If we can get down to business, please."

"Yeah, sure. Sorry," I say. "It's just that I've been having a hard time getting a contractor." And if I'm honest, I'm kind of annoyed at having to come down here at a moment's notice.

"We're here to discuss what happened to Alon. Mrs. Jenson, would you repeat what you told me?"

Hiraya looks down at her hands and laces her fingers together. Randall puts a protective arm around her.

"Go ahead, honey," he says.

For some reason, that feels really patronizing to me, and I clench my teeth.

She takes a breath. "Last night, Alon did not come home. I asked Randy to go out and look for him—"

"Excuse me, Mrs. Jenson," I break in. "Did Alon tell you where he was going?"

"He said he was going down to the waterfront to take a walk on the trail down there."

"When did he leave?"

She closes her eyes briefly. "Maybe four o'clock? It was his first day out of prison, and he wanted to feel his freedom. We are still working on his visa paperwork."

"Thank you. Please, go on. You asked your husband to look for him?" I may have interrupted her train of thought, but it's important to get the details right. I grab a notebook and begin taking notes.

"Yes. Randy drove all around—"

Randall interrupts. "I went down to the south waterfront where the walking trail begins. When I got to the area behind Fort George Brewing, where there's all those warehouses, I saw someone lying in the shadow of one of the buildings. Thought it was a drunk, but went over to check and it was Alon." He glances at his wife and takes her hand. She is looking down at the table.

"What did you do then?" I ask, scribbling.

"Well, the boy was pretty beat up, but conscious. Someone had done a number on his face. Nose was all swole up. Blood all over his shirt."

"What time was this?" I ask.

At the same moment, Madison says, "What did he say to you?"

Randall glances at me and then her. "I found him this morning, about six. I usually get up at five to get to the jobsite early, but Yaya wanted me to look for him." He shrugs, and tightens his grip on his wife's hand. She wriggles her fingers in protest. "As for what he said, it was just a bunch of gibberish. I asked him who attacked him, and he clammed right up. Wouldn't answer."

That sounds like Alon. He'd done the same thing to us.

"Do you think it was a hate crime?" Madison asks.

I glance at Randall. By his expression, this has never entered his head.

"Uhhh…I don't really know. I mean, it's not like he was Black. Or Jewish. He speaks good English."

Oy.

I wonder if Randall is as clueless as he seems. Madison seems to have a bit of tunnel vision herself. Maybe she's just looking for a legal angle to the thing. But not everything is political. This could be revenge-based, or simply bad luck—wrong place, wrong time. I ask the classic question. "Did he have any enemies?"

"Enemies? How? I mean, he just got here." Randall rolls his shoulders. "Doesn't seem like he'd make either friends *or* enemies in that short of time."

This guy seems to think that Alon's life in Astoria began when he walked into their house. I shift my gaze to his wife. "Mrs. Jenson? What do you think?"

She pulls her hand free of her husband's paw. "There were the people he worked with at the restaurant."

I nod. That's the obvious answer.

Madison says, "Have you ever had racist experiences, Mrs. Jenson? Anyone with a grudge against Filipinos?"

Hiraya brushes a tear from her cheek. "Please, I have never experienced anything like you are describing. Sometimes, sure, people look at me strangely. But many people are welcoming. The church has made a place for us. I don't like to think someone would hurt Alon just because he is from another land."

Boy, does this lady have a lot to learn.

I ask, "Where is your nephew now?"

Randall answers. "He's at home in bed. We didn't want to take him to the hospital because he's not insured."

Hiraya frowns at her husband. "I was worried the hospital would notify ICE."

"That was probably smart, especially these days," says Madison. "I'd like to talk to him myself. See if he can remember enough details to press charges, especially if it was someone from the restaurant. That might convince them to drop their own case."

Bringing in the cops and the justice system, while Alon's status is so precarious, seems to me like a bad idea. Why draw more attention to him? If the cops think he's a troublemaker, they just may call in ICE to get him off their hands.

After the Jensons leave for the hospital, I express my views to Madison.

"You think we should drop it?" She looks at me incredulously.

"Why make a bad situation worse?"

"He deserves some protection. He's had a terrible time ever since he got here."

"At least the Jensons are looking after him now."

"One of them is, anyway." Madison scoffs. "It's not like Portland, where there's a bigger Filipino community and they have lots of mutual support. Out here on the coast, it's mostly women like Hiraya who come to do minimum wage labor like cleaning hotels, and then get trapped in a relationship with some bro who wants a submissive wife."

Not that I disagree with her, but. "I get that you are all fired up for justice, believe me, I do. But let's think about what's best for Alon, the man, not Alon, the poster child."

She fumes. "People need to be held accountable."

"Shall I do some nosing around the restaurant again? See what I can discover about the attack?"

Madison chews on her pen for a moment. "Karthik would say no, there's no more resources available. But I'm saying yes, take a couple of hours and go talk to his old boss and workmates. See if one of them knows something. I'll authorize the expenditure."

Lawyer Jones is going to authorize herself out of a job.

I close my notebook. "Yes ma'am, If there's something to get, I'll get it." And work will keep my brain occupied, so I don't have to think about other things. Things like visions and shipwrecks and ghosts.

50

I LEAVE THE county offices and I head back to the Big Bridge Bar & Grill, where Alon worked before he was jailed. My thoughts are a mishmash of the attack on Alon, and my experience on the beach two days ago.

I mean, what the heck is going on?

Yeah, the whole thing's a shipwreck.

One thing I've gained here is that I know my ability is alive and well.

Too bad it's not well enough to find the crime scene.

In this business, we take what we can get.

The last time I was at the Big Bridge, I didn't get farther than the back door and the kitchen. This time I'm using the front door, like a paying customer. It seems like a dive, if I'm honest. For one thing, it's really dark inside. The only light comes through the flyspecked north-facing windows. The threadbare carpet is so covered with stains that it's hard to determine the original pattern. The bar is wood with about an inch of sticky lacquer. There's so many dried drink rings across the top that it looks like everyone on the north coast was here.

I order a bottle of Budweiser which I have no intention of drinking. The bartender brings it to me sans glass, and helpfully pops off the top before sliding it across the bar.

"Haven't seen you in here before," he says, and winks.

Seriously? As pick-up lines go, it could use some work. "Are you the owner?"

"I am. Ben Yost, at your service." No mention of a co-owner, the lovely guy in the kitchen. But now he looks a little more alert.

I push a business card across the bar top. Its progress is arrested by a sticky spot. "I'm following up on an investigation regarding a former employee of yours. Alon Dasalan, who was working here as a dishwasher. I'd like to ask you a few questions."

He glances at the card. "Are you a cop?"

"I'm an investigator working for his lawyer."

"Lawyers. Jay-zus." He cracks his neck by bending it first to the right, then to the left. It's a thick neck.

"I understand he allegedly stole some money from you."

"No allegedly about it. Money was gone, and so was our dishwasher. Case closed."

"Who made the report? You?"

"Damn right. Can't have employees stealing the cash on hand."

That answers one of my questions. "Who discovered the theft?"

"I did, when I balanced the register after closing. Every bill was gone. Little bastard even nicked the quarters."

I take a fake sip of my beer. "How do you know it was Alon?"

"Practically saw him do it, didn't I?"

"Did you?" This is news to me.

"Good as. He was the last one in the kitchen that night." Yost wipes the beer taps with a cloth that hasn't been laundered recently, if ever. I'm suddenly glad my beer came in the bottle.

"That doesn't mean he took the money."

"All the other employees were gone. That's what I told the cops. They waited for him to come in for his next shift, but he was a no-show."

"Maybe he saw the police cars and was afraid."

"Honest folks aren't afraid of cops."

But undocumented people are. This guy is really starting to irritate me. "How'd they find him then, if he didn't come to work?"

"We have employee addresses on file. We know where they live."

"So you just handed it over to the police."

"Well, yeah."

"Did you know Mr. Dasalan was assaulted recently and badly beaten?"

He scowls. "Why would I know—or care—about that? Maybe he stiffed someone else. Maybe the little rat deserved it. What's it to you?"

"I told you, I'm working for his lawyer."

He's fuming now, his mouth twisted into a snarl. But he doesn't quite have the backbone to push back against the magic word: lawyer.

I smile gently. "Do you know who might have wanted to hurt Mr. Dasalan? Other than yourself or your employees?"

"No one here laid a hand on him." His teeth are almost audibly grinding.

"Oh, really? Are you with your employees twenty-four-seven? How about your business partner, the cook? Are you aware of everything he does?"

"What are you implying? Alvin's on the level."

"Who is in charge of hiring people? You or him?"

"We both do. Alvin hires for the kitchen, I hire the waitstaff."

That seems complicated. "But you were the one who wanted to prosecute your dishwasher, who is as back of house as it gets. Why is that?"

"Alvin wanted to let it go, but I said no way. We need to show an example."

"Did he, now." That's interesting. I rotate the beer bottle in my hands. I still haven't taken a real drink. "Are you aware of Mr. Dasalan's immigration status?"

"His what?"

"His immigration status. Did you fill out an I-9 form, and require a federally recognized I.D. when you hired him?"

For a moment he looks like the proverbial deer in the headlights. Then he blinks, and slaps the bar top with the flat of his hand. "I told you, I didn't hire him. Alvin did. But I'm sure he followed the rules." Despite his words, a worry line wrinkles his forehead.

"Do you know it's a federal crime to employ undocumented workers?"

"Are you saying Dasalan is a wetback?"

This guy is a real charmer.

"Did he have a green card?" I ask.

The bartender chews his lip, his eyes shifting to the left. "I'm sure the paperwork is in his file."

"*I'm* sure that if you help me figure out who assaulted him, there won't be a need for me to ask you for his paperwork." Not that someone else won't ask for it down the line.

He leans heavily on the bar. "Listen, lady, I don't know who attacked him. I didn't even know he was attacked. I haven't seen him for weeks, not since his last day of work." He runs a hand through his hair. "Listen, there was a guy that came in earlier that day. Fisherman. Ordered a beer. Dasalan came out to pick up the bussing tub with the dirty dishes, saw this guy, turned white and dropped the tub. Broke three plates. Alvin reamed him out for that."

Enter the mysterious stranger.

"How do you know he was a fisherman?"

"He said it was a bad time to be out on his boat."

"So you're saying this fisherman might have been the person who beat up your dishwasher?"

"I'm just giving you what information I have. Didn't seem to mean anything at the time, but what do I know?"

"Nothing, apparently. But I suggest you should question your partner, see what's going on in the 'back of house.' I'm sure you don't want to have a federal case on your hands. It's definitely not worth whatever you think Alon took out of the register."

"Christalmighty." The bartender rubs his jowls.

I nod and smile, and slide off my barstool. As I leave the premises, I glimpse him pick up my untouched bottle of beer and take a healthy swig.

That was fun, I think smugly as I cross the parking lot to my car.

That was a bunch of bullshit, and you know it.

What?

Whether or not Alon's undocumented doesn't have anything to do with the theft.

Maybe Alvin's buddy in there will drop the charges now. I dig in my pocket for my keys, which have gotten hung up on a loose thread or something.

Shaking down the witnesses, are we?

Alon didn't steal the money. He'd be long gone if he did.

Who did it, then?

My bet's on the tattooed kitchen boy I encountered the first time I was here.

I finally get my keys out and get in the car, and think about what to do next.

What, you think Tat Boy saw Alon on the waterfront and decided to pound on him for fun?

I don't know who did it, but I doubt it was some random fisherman. I'm hoping that a little brush with federal law will motivate the owner of the Big Bridge to withdraw the theft charge. I'll bet Alvin wasn't paying Alon minimum wage, certainly not paying taxes or social security or insurance for him.

Truthfully, I'm starting to agree with Biswas, that this case is a waste of resources. It's so low-stakes, and I don't understand why these dudes want to even press charges. It only hurts them, in the long run, especially if they are convicted of employing undocumented migrants.

No one's going to waste their time going after these guys and they know it. They're small fish.

Maybe, maybe not. ICE is a lot more aggressive these days.

I've used up my two hours that Madison authorized. Time to do something I can bill to the Reynolds case. See if I can squeeze some more value from the search for justice. Which kind of makes me feel like a hypocrite, rather than the lone gunman trying to push back the darkness. Sometimes I wonder why I do what I do.

Food. Shelter. Utilities. The trifecta of modern life.

I've decided on my next course of action, and rev the car engine to drown out Zoe's depressing assessment of existence.

51

Heading out to Alicia Reynold's place, I think about her relationships. Keith is her first cousin, so her son Christopher is Keith's second cousin. Or is that first cousin twice removed? I can never remember. Jack wasn't a blood relative to Keith, but still. The interaction between them is bound to have the added layer of familial obligation. And when that obligation isn't honored, look out.

Soon enough I'm outside Alicia's manufactured home. As I rumble into the driveway, I see her stand up in the garden and shade her eyes with her hand. She's wearing overalls and rubber boots, heavy gloves and clutching a trowel.

"Hi," I say, as I get out of the car.

"Hello, Audrey. What brings you back all the way out here?" She wipes her cheek on her shoulder, leaving a damp blot.

She's not exactly unfriendly, but not overflowing with welcome, either.

"I was just talking yesterday to your cousin Keith."

"Oh, yes?"

"He said Christopher was out with him on his boat the day Jack's body was found."

Alicia bends down and begins to dig at the base of a leggy hydrangea. "This plant isn't doing so well. I'm going to move it to another location."

"Alicia? Did Chris go out on Keith's boat?"

She stabs her trowel deep into the earth. "Keith knows I don't like Christopher out on the boats, his *or* Jack's. It's too dangerous."

"He says Chris was with him. Did you know?"

"Goddamn it! Yes, I knew! But not until afterward. Christopher let it slip. He's not very good at lying."

"Why didn't you tell me that the last time I was here?"

"You didn't ask. Why, is it important?" She tugs on the stems of the hydrangea, wiggling the shrub to loosen the grip of the roots.

I try to hold on to my temper. I can't ever decide if people are deliberately obstructive, or just obtuse. "I'd like to talk to Chris about that night."

She stands, trowel dangling from her hand. "Why?"

"I'd like to know if Keith dropped something overboard."

"Overboard? What kind of thing?"

"I don't want to tell you, because I don't want Chris to feel prompted to say any particular thing. It's a simple question, really."

"I don't like Chris being questioned. He gets confused."

"Look, you can be with him the whole time, and listen while I ask the question."

"Are you trying to pin Jack's murder on Keith? Because you're wrong. Keith wouldn't hurt anyone."

It's interesting that she jumped to that assumption. "If that's true, you've got nothing to worry about."

She's reluctant, staring down at the trowel in her hand. "If I allow this, will you leave us alone? I just want to move on, and have Chris move on. It's not good for him to keep remembering Jack, and wondering why he doesn't come."

"I can promise I won't come back to talk to Chris. I may still have to talk to you." I'm reluctant to promise even this much, but it's clear she's very protective of her son. Maybe too much so. All things considered, Chris seems pretty able to me. Her attitude is infantilizing him, when what he really needs is support to build his own life. Not my call, though.

She frowns, then lets out a breath that blows the bangs away from her face. "Come on, then."

Alicia leads me up the steps and into the house. I hear the television. Christopher is playing a video game, piloting a helicopter as animated bombs explode around him.

"Sweetheart," calls Alicia, "can you come talk to me, please?"

He doesn't look up. "I'm busy, Mom."

"I know, Boo. It'll only take a second." She flashes me a warning look.

Christopher sighs. "Okay." He pauses his game and rotates on his backside until he faces us. "I remember you," he says to me.

"Hi Chris, I remember you, too. Looks like you're pretty good at that game."

He grins. "I've had a lot of practice flying."

Alicia breaks in. "Ask your question, Audrey."

I ignore her and keep my attention on her son. "Hey Chris, do you remember going out on your cousin's boat? The *Georgia Peach*?"

He nods several times. "I like to go crabbing."

"The last time you went, did Keith drop anything overboard?"

He cocks his head. "We put the rings out when we get to the ocean."

"Not the rings. I mean, when you were still in the marina. Did Keith drop something over the side?"

The young man's forehead crinkles. "Like a cigarette?" He shakes his head. "Keith doesn't smoke very much. And he won't ever let me."

Alicia interrupts. "Are you *smoking*?" Her voice is shrill. "Where did you get them? Who gave them to you?"

"Not Keith." Chris hangs his head. "Dad would sometimes let me smoke on his boat."

"Oh. My. God. Jack!" Alicia's voice is disgusted. "It isn't enough that he goes and gets *himself* killed, he has to endanger my son's health. How long was this going on? What else haven't you told me?"

"Dad said you'd be mad. I don't like it when you're mad." His shoulders hunch, and he draws his head in.

I strive to rescue the conversation from Alicia's derailment. If she upsets Chris, he might not answer. I repeat my question about whether Keith dumped something overboard. At the risk of leading my witness, I tell Chris it would be larger than a cigarette, or even a rock.

He sits quietly, lost in thought. "I don't remember anything like that."

I glance warily at Alicia. She has her arms folded across her chest. Crouching down so I'm on a level with Christopher, I say, "what *do* you remember about that night, Chris?"

Alicia inhales. She's getting ready to object.

Chris smiles. "Cousin Keith let me drive the boat! All the way out of the harbor and into the Columbia."

Alicia says, "I don't think—"

I interrupt her. "So you were in the cabin the whole time? Was Keith with you, helping?"

He nods rapidly. "He stood beside me, but I did it all myself." His face falls. "He wouldn't let me drive in the big river. But Dad does. Mom, where's Dad?"

"He's not coming back, Chris. I've told you that before." Alicia turns to me. "That's enough. You've asked your question. And more besides."

I ignore her. "Did you drive both times, going out and coming back?"

"I did. It's fun!"

I stand. "Thanks, Chris. You can go back to your game."

He smiles and turns around, relaunching the helicopter flight. The sound of explosions and gunfire resumes. We go back outside.

"Satisfied?" Alicia asks.

"I learned what I wanted to know."

"Then off you go. I've got work to do." She strides determinedly back to the hydrangea bush, grumbling. I take the hint and get in my car, backing out of the driveway and onto the highway. Just then, it begins to rain, fat droplets splattering across the windshield. In the rear view mirror, I see Alicia sprinting for the front door.

I flick on the windshield wipers, and they begin to squeak across the glass, smearing water and insect corpses into foggy streaks. Another task to add to my to-do list, washing the car. But I found out what I wanted, that is, that Keith didn't dump a corpse into the river as he passed by the *Beatrice.* I also learned that Chris keeps things back from his mother. I wonder what else he knows about what Reynolds got up to. And if so, how I can find out.

52

By the time I get home, most of the bug smears have been washed away, so I decide not to make a special trip to the car wash. Let Mother Nature do the hard work for me. After parking in front of the house, I sit a moment to nerve myself up to dash out into the squall. Maybe it'll let up if I give it a few minutes. The naked treetops are twisting in the wind, and dead leaves are tumbling across the sidewalk. The clouds overhead are the color of old bruises, a kind of purplish green. Dang. I think it's going to hail.

Something moves on the porch.

I squint my eyes, trying to see past the driving rain. And then I honk the horn, a pathetic little beep. But the figure on the porch is now running. Whoever it is jumps over the railing and runs downhill, disappearing around the corner of the house.

Pushing the car door open, I grab the Glock from my shoulder holster. Rain is splashing on the street and sidewalk. I jump to the curb and hurry down the steps to the house. Check the front door and flanking windows. No glass broken, and the door is still locked. So I follow in the intruder's footsteps, around the house and down the hillside. Rain has made the grass and underlying clay as slick as a hockey rink. My feet go out from under me and I land on my backside, gun hand waving wildly for balance.

Scramble to my feet, turn sideways and edge down the slope. No sign of the intruder. From the back yard he could do any number of things, go right onto Phoebe's property; go left into the other neighbor's yard, or run through the break in the hedge that separates me from the downhill neighbor. I stop to listen, but hear nothing. No heavy breathing other than my own, no footsteps running away. Just the sound of rain, bucketing down, and the whip of the wind.

The windows on the back side of my house are above my head, thanks to the slope of the lot, so I can't see inside, but nothing looks broken. I complete the circuit, going up the other side of the house. I check the walk-out basement door. It's locked, as always. Head up the broken concrete steps which scale the hill on this side, open the gate at the top of the steps, and circle back to the front door, keeping my eyes open for tracks or other signs of passage. Nothing. The only footprints on the porch are my own damp smears. I feel a frisson of deja vu.

Keeping the gun in my hand, I unlock the door and back inside, making sure no one is lurking to follow me in. Slam the door and send the deadbolt home, deep into the frame. Pause in the hallway to listen for any sound above the rain. Without taking my coat off, I clear the main floor, then the basement, making sure none of the ground level windows have been breached. Then I go upstairs, each tread creaking ominously as I ascend. At the top of the flight I listen again.

Plink.

Plink.

Son of a bitch. My roof is still leaking, and I still haven't gotten anyone to fix it. Quickly I clear the two upstairs bedrooms. There's no one here, and as far as I can tell, the house is still secure.

Plink.

Bending down, I access the tiny door which leads to the attic. The leak is in here, and the bowl I'd set here earlier is almost full. And now I'm dripping on the floor, as my raincoat sheds its load of water.

Plink.

Back downstairs, hang up my coat in the hall, get my biggest pot, go back upstairs, and switch the vessels out. One more trip downstairs to empty the bowl in the kitchen sink. Put the electric kettle on in preparation for tea, and sit down, with my head in my hands. My hair is damp, and so is my backside from my tumble on the hill. My pants are wet from the mid-thigh down where rain sluiced off my jacket, and even my socks are moist. And now that I'm not dashing around, I'm starting to get cold.

Screw the electric bill. I crank the furnace to seventy-five and am gratified by the gust of warm air that blasts from the old-fashioned wrought iron grill. When my tea is ready, I pad back upstairs, snagging my socks on the treads that need refinishing.

Old houses. There's always something to fix.

I shuck my clothes while standing over the heating vent and pull on some sweats and dry socks. Pull the pillow off my cot and sit down on the floor, leaning against the wall with the pillow at my back. Watch the rain make abstract patterns on the window pane, and try to ignore the plinks from the attic.

Tea tastes good, makes a column of heat from my neck to my belly.

And then the phone rings. Caller I.D. says Phoebe Rutherford. I sigh, and thumb the talk button. "This is Audrey."

"I'm glad you're home. Someone has been in your yard. I saw them just now, circling the house. Are you safe?"

"Yes. I think that was me you saw. I was chasing someone off the front porch. This isn't the first time."

"I didn't see anyone else."

Maybe it's all in your head.

Oh, now you show up. I could have used a little help earlier.

You don't like it when I take control.

Newsflash: you've never had control.

Except that one time, remember?

Right, when you threatened a guy I was trying to question.

Hey, my methods were successful, if you recall.

I strive to ignore Zoe and concentrate on what Phoebe is saying.

There's a pause, where the only thing I can hear is the soothing patter of rain on the roof.

Phoebe's voice is kind. "How are you doing? Is Zoe still bothering you?"

Tell the old broad to take a hike.

Ye gods, it's like I'm being haunted by a persistent ghost. And that's what Zoe is, a ghost of the person I was, not the person I am now.

You can't drive me off, because I'm part of you. I AM you.

Oh, yeah? We'll see about that.

"Audrey, are you there?"

"I'm here. I'm fine. Everything is fine."

"Are you going to call the police? About the intruder?"

Yeah, that's what I want, is for Jane Candide to hear and decide she wants to make another personal visit.

"No."

Another long pause. "What are you going to do, then?"

"I'm gonna get some security cameras, and catch the guy in the act."

"You said that in our last session. I gather you haven't been to the store yet?"

"No, I haven't." I can't be spending money on every last thing. "But I will. Soon."

"Well, at least that's something. Take care of yourself, okay?"

"I am. I will."

"And try to limit your interactions with Zoe."

"…I hear you."

"Please, Audrey. It's for your own good."

We'll see about that.

53

I END THE call, feeling irritated with Phoebe's intrusion.

Is therapy really necessary? I'm sure I can live my life as a high-functioning adult without all that digging around in the past. Because nothing will change, will it? However much I know, or learn, the past will still be irrevocable. I'm sure that's supported in the scientific literature somewhere.

This is partly what's been dogging me about my current caseload. It all seems so pointless, working for lawyers, looking for loopholes. Where's the justice in all this? But even when I was a cop, actual honest-to-God justice was elusive. So I usually try not to think about it.

Avoiding the truth is actually dysfunctional. *Just sayin'.*

Life advice from Zoe. But this time she's right.

What do you mean 'this time?' I'm right pretty much all the time.

And that's another thing, Phoebe's opposition to Zoe, wanting to 'cure' me of her presence. I didn't push back today, because of all the other stuff, but I'm actually learning to live with her. At least my empty house isn't so lonely with her here.

Aw. That's the nicest thing you've ever said to me.

Don't get used to it.

I look around the great room, which takes up most of the main floor of the house. I notice that I've tracked in some leaves, and fetch a broom from the kitchen to sweep them up. Outside, the rain continues to beat against the windows. The air is damp and chill, despite the hum of the furnace.

My earlier conversation with Jack's family has rekindled my drive to solve his murder. I go down to the room in the basement I use as an incident room. I spend time staring at the big area map and various pictures I've got tacked up on the wall. My suspicions have hardened against Keith Larson, and also Ethan Sinclaire. To my way of thinking, both these men had a motive to harm Jack Reynolds. Both were on location. Larson seems more likely to be the type to strike out in aggression. The method of the murder, a blow to the head and slitting the throat, is a particularly brutal and messy way to kill. I have a hard time envisioning Sinclaire committing that kind of violence. But Larson? Yeah, I can see it.

And Alon? There doesn't seem any more to do on that score. Maybe he'll have more to say when he recovers from his beating. Hopefully this will turn into the happy ending that Madison is clearly looking for. Me, I figure his troubles are just beginning.

I go upstairs and finish the afternoon by writing up a report with all my findings, and send it off to Biswas with an invoice for services rendered. I've done what he wanted, even if my cop instincts aren't completely satisfied. I still have questions.

Yeah, like, where the hell is the crime scene?

No kidding. If only we had omnipresent CCTV cameras on every corner like they do in the movies.

And that reminds me of what I said to Phoebe, about installing some security cameras. So once again I put on my still-damp jacket and go outside, hunching into the pelting rain, and drive across the bay to Costco and buy two cameras, once again bumping up against the limit on my card. The squall has let up by the time I get back home, with the lowering sun sending shafts of light through rents in the clouds, turning the droplets that spangle the trees into swaths of diamonds.

The cameras are easy to install, and I put one on the underside of the porch roof and one directly over the walk-out basement door. The associated app on my phone lets me see what's going on realtime, and also has controls to turn the cameras on and off or to set up a schedule. They are motion activated, and will record whatever is in the vicinity.

It takes me some time and fiddling to get the field of view that I want. I expect to get some animals and folks up on the sidewalk, but this should allow me to collect evidence of someone wandering around the property or trying to break in.

I'm doing a final check of the controls when my phone vibrates in my hand. I close the camera app and check the caller ID, half-expecting another call from Phoebe, but this time, it's Madison Jones.

"There's been a development in Alon Dasalan's case." Her voice sounds tired, lacking the acerbic edge I've come to expect.

What now, I wonder. "How is he? Did he end up going to the hospital after all?"

There's a pause, and I hear another voice in the background, probably Juanita.

Then Madison says, "Mrs. Jenson called me. He's stable, for now, and still at home. But he wants to talk to us, tell us what happened. Maybe he knows who attacked him. I want you to meet me at the Jenson house at nine tomorrow morning. I'll text you the address."

"Right. Okay. I'll be there."

I finish up the evening by summarizing all my recent findings in a report for Biswas, and sending it off in an email. Maybe he'll have some additional instructions. Maybe I won't have to be at Madison's beck and call.

But it's all money in the bank. I can't complain even if there is a garnish of entitlement attached.

OCTOBER 28 - DAY 10

54

OCTOBER 28TH IS typical fall, complete with clouds as gray as the back of a whale and a chilling breeze straight off the ocean. I open the upstairs windows and let the fresh air clear out the stale atmosphere of the night. Then I go downstairs and fix myself a quick breakfast of peanut butter on toast. I'm just finishing it up when a text from Madison appears on my lock screen, urging me to hurry up for our morning appointment. I plug the Jenson's address into my map app and head out.

The instructions lead me to a house on the edge of town, big and soulless with a view of Youngs Bay. I knock on the door and Mrs. Jenson admits me to a living room with a black leather sectional and giant TV. The house is infused with the aroma of baking bread and—I sniff appreciatively—toasted coconut. Madison is already there, seated on the edge of an armchair with a clipboard on her lap. Alon is lying down on one end of the L-shaped sofa under a blanket and propped on a pillow.

I've seen the results of fights before, but even I am taken aback and grimace in sympathy. His face is a mess. There's a patch of hair missing from his temple, and one eye is still swollen shut. Both eyes are ringed with bruises, and a cut has scabbed over on his chin. He looks pale, his unkempt hair and rust-red scabs give his face a Frankenstein look. His hands are lying on top of the blanket and the knuckles are red and scraped, swollen enough to look like someone has inflated them with air.

At least he got in a few licks of his own.

Mrs. Jenson brings us mugs of coffee and a plate of round buns dusted with strings of toasted coconut. She leaves, returning with a short stack of smaller plates.

"Please, eat." She hands us each a small plate and waves a hand to the pile of buns. "This is pan de coco, a traditional breakfast pastry from the Philippines. I made them for my pamangkín, but he cannot eat anything right now, so now I share it with you."

I reach for a bun and park myself on the other end of the couch. The coffee is rich and hot, and when I bite into the pastry, a warm filling of brown sugar and coconut oozes across my tongue, mixing with the sweetened bread. It's so good my eyes close momentarily. Much better than peanut butter toast.

"Mrs. Jenson," I say, "this is fantastic. Thank you."

Her mouth curves in a small smile. "You are welcome. Randy—my husband—likes these, too."

Madison ignores the buns and the coffee, and becomes brisk and businesslike, flipping to a fresh sheet on her notepad.

Rude.

More for us. I surreptitiously wipe my fingers on my pant leg and take another bun.

Madison says, "Alon, can you tell us what happened on the night of October 26th, in your own words?"

He glances at his aunt, who nods encouragingly before sitting in the near the bend of the sectional, where she can rest a hand on his feet.

Alon closes his eyes, then describes what he can remember. He'd been walking down on the waterfront, enjoying his freedom, whistling on and off. A man came out of the shadows and attacked him, beat him unmercifully, and left him bleeding on the ground.

Madison scribbles some notes on her pad.

I ask, "Was it one of your coworkers from the bar?"

He shakes his head, and meets my gaze. "No."

I remember what the owner of the Big Bridge told me. "Was it the fisherman who came into the restaurant on the day you left?"

Alon shrugs, grimacing slightly at the pain from his bruises, and looks away without answering.

Madison looks up from her paper. "Were you robbed?"

"Of what?" Alon spreads his hands. "I have nothing."

"Did he call you names? Make racial slurs?" she presses, the pen poised in her fingers.

"No."

I ask, "Did he threaten you?"

He flinches, but says "No."

I don't believe him. "Why do you think he attacked you?" I ask.

There's a long silence. Then Mrs. Jenson breaks in. "It was a trafficker."

"What do you mean?" Madison's voice is sharp. "Alon, is this true?"

He closes his eyes again, but his aunt is relentless. "It was one of them. I know it. And you know it, too." The last remark was addressed to her nephew. "You will never be safe while those men are free. None of us will."

I raise a hand. "Wait, who exactly are you talking about?"

"The people who brought him here from the Philippines," says Mrs. Jenson. "The men who profit off those who are trying to get a better life."

"Okay, but why?"

"Because he knows who they are," says Madison, as though this should be obvious.

"But so would all the migrants," I object. "They can't go around assaulting everyone they traffic, right?"

Alon's voice is hoarse. "But I *don't* know who they are. I didn't see their faces."

"Alon," says Madison, "you need to tell us how you came to this country. Please. It's the only way to bring these men to justice."

Alon shakes his head, gripping the edge of the blanket.

"You don't understand," Mrs. Jenson says to Madison. "Trafficking is not the crime."

"Of course it's a crime," Madison says, her voice sharp.

Mrs. Jenson shakes her head. "To us, it is not an injustice to help those who wish to come to this country. Yes, these men are often harsh. Outlaws, even. But for many, they are the gateway to a better life." She gives her nephew's foot a gentle shake. "But in this case, people were killed." Her eyes gleam with moisture, but her voice is steady.

"Wait, what?" Madison asks, bewildered. "Killed? Who? Who was killed?"

I can't say I'm surprised—human trafficking is a dirty, violent business.

Mrs. Jenson shakes her nephew's foot again. "If you do not tell them, Alon, then I will."

He leans back on his pillow. "Tita Hiraya, please—"

"No. I must speak." She focuses her gaze on Madison. "Ten years ago, I came to this country, to Astoria, as a guest worker for a fish processing plant. While I was here, I met Randy. We got married, and I became a citizen. Because I was here already, my nephew Alon, and my brother Angelo, contacted someone they believed would help them get into the United States."

"Your brother?" Madison's eyebrows go up.

"Angelo is Alon's father. They made a deal with a freighter captain who said he could bring them to Astoria. I did not know they were coming." And she spares a frown for Alon. "If I had, I would have told them not to do it. It is too dangerous. But they didn't want to wait for visas."

"They're lucky they weren't caught." Madison shakes her head. "Even so, Alon is going to be classed as an undocumented immigrant. There's no way around that."

And the murders?

"I feel like we're missing the point." It's aggravating when Zoe is right. "I still don't know who was killed."

Mrs. Jenson raises a hand. "Please, let me finish. Alon and Angelo paid the captain of a freighter for a place inside a shipping container with several other men. They had to bring their own food and water. The container was shut for ten days. Some of the men didn't have enough supplies, and my brother shared what they had. But this meant everyone suffered. The men were very weak and some were sick when finally the container was opened."

"Where was this?" Madison is looking down at her legal pad, scribbling away.

"Still on the ship, on the ocean. Alon and the others were forced to climb down the side of the ship to a smaller open boat with a motor on the back. One man was unconscious and Angelo had to carry him down the ladder. It was very dark and foggy."

Mrs. Jenson glances at Alon, who remains silent. She folds her hands in her lap. "They thought they were being taken to America, but instead they went to another boat, a fishing vessel."

A fishing boat? My ears prick up.

What about the murders?

Cool your jets, and let her finish.

I polish off my second bun and take another long drink of coffee.

Mrs. Jenson looks down at her hands, and twists her wedding ring. "The men from the crate had to climb up into the fishing boat. The man who was unconscious couldn't climb, and Angelo couldn't carry him farther. So the freighter captain dropped him into the sea."

Madison gasps. "That's murder! What was the name of the freighter?"

Alon whispers, "I do not know, I only ever saw the container. It was loaded on the ship after we were inside."

"Did you see a flag, or some indication of nationality? What language were they speaking? We need to track this vessel down."

Alon spreads his hands. "I don't know," he says miserably. "We spoke to them in English."

I don't want us to digress away from the point, so I say, "Let's let Mrs. Jenson finish her story, unless Alon wants to continue?"

Aunt and nephew exchange a meaningful glance. Her expression says 'well?' The lines on his face deepen in discomfort. He touches the cuts on his face with ginger fingers, then covers his eyes as he speaks.

"There were two men on the fishing boat," Alon begins. "They had masks that covered their faces, except for eyes and nose. Like what you wear in the winter. Once we were on board, the captain of the freighter came on, too. He gave the captain of the fishing boat some money.

Then they argued. The other fisherman told us to go down into the hold."

I glance at Madison, who is scribbling away. "What were they arguing about? Could you tell?"

"The fisherman wanted more money. It was because of the man who was put in the sea. He had also paid to come and the fisherman wanted a share of that payment. The freighter captain said he was paying for those of us on the boat only. The dead man no longer counted."

Jeez, that's cold.

"I see," I say. "Then what happened?"

"The men from the freighter went back to their ship, I think. It was very foggy. I could not see it, but I heard the big ship's engines."

Madison asks, "Did you go down into the hold? What do you remember about that?"

He hesitates. "Yes. It smelled like fish, and made me a little sick." He wrinkled his nose. "But my father didn't want to go down there. He wanted to know where we were going, what was happening, when we would get to America. He wanted to stay on deck." He looks up at Mrs. Jenson. "You see, he had been ill in the container. I think he just wanted to be in the fresh air."

Hiraya nods, and leans over to take his hand. Her eyes glitter with unshed tears, and her voice is husky as she says, "Go on."

"So then," Alon continues, "the boat captain took out a gun, and said he will *make* us go below. So everyone climbed down into the hold. I was last, except for my father. He was still asking to stay on top. The captain was angry, and I thought he was going to shoot us. But he just pushed my father down the ladder and slammed the hatch. It landed on his hand. He screamed."

Mrs. Jenson's face contorts in helpless rage, and tears run down her cheeks, unchecked.

55

THE LIVING ROOM is silent except for sniffles from Mrs. Jenson. After a moment, I scoot over beside her and put a hand on her shoulder.

"Are you okay?"

"No!" She hiccups. "Please. I know my nephew and Angelo made the wrong decision to come to this country illegally. But please, Alon is still a person. Please help him."

"We will help him," Madison assures her. "This is my job. But he must tell us the truth, and help us identify the traffickers if he can. Now, what happened after Angelo got hurt?"

I get that it's important to get all the information you can. There's always a balance between that and not making the victim's trauma worse, and it's a line that all cops have to learn to walk. And I think Madison could use some lessons in that, because she's treating Alon more like a cause than an actual guy who's been through—and is continuing to go through—a rough experience. So I ask him if he wants to take a break.

He shakes his head. "I just want this all to end. I want to start work, do all the things. But it is hard." He wipes a hand across his eyes, then winces from the pain. He closes his eyes and takes a breath. "My father screamed, as I said. I climbed back up to help him, but his hand was crushed under the hatch. I banged on it for help. The captain pulled it open. He yelled at us, told us to be quiet. I said, 'my father is hurt' and the captain said, 'it's his own fault.' Then he yanked Father back onto the deck. His hand was bleeding everywhere, some got on the ground. I climbed partway out, and saw—" Alon stops speaking. His breathing is now shallow and panting.

"Take your time," says Madison, glancing at me. "It's all right."

Alon nods. "I saw…a finger. My father's finger. The hatch chopped it off."

Mrs. Jenson covers her mouth with both hands. Tears leak down her cheeks.

I feel a hitch in my breathing. Because I remember where I have seen a loose finger. On Tavin O'Brian's boat. We'd even talked about immigration, him being second generation Irish and all.

Alon is saying, "They kept shoving him, telling him to shut up. And he kept screaming. So the captain—" Alon glances at Mrs. Jenson, and reaches a hand toward her.

"So the captain…?" Madison prompts.

His voice is a whisper. "The captain shot my father. He killed him. And then…and then the fishermen threw him overboard." A sob bubbles up from his chest, and he sinks back onto the pillow. His face is ashen.

These guys are serious criminals.

Yeah. It's gone from human trafficking to assault to murder.

We sit in silence. Mrs. Jenson's face is wet with tears, but she doesn't make a sound. Her hand, where it is linked with Alon's, is white and trembling. The wordlessness stretches across the room, tight as a drum skin. The HVAC system hums to itself, and in the kitchen, the refrigerator emits a metallic clank.

"Alon, I'm so sorry. I know this is hard." I keep my voice low, suitable for a traumatized witness. "But can you keep going? Can you describe these men?"

He shakes his head, without opening his eyes. "They wore masks over their heads."

"Skin color? Eye color?" I think of Tad Mitchell's beard. "Visible facial hair?"

He opens one eye. "They were white. And spoke English."

Which is about ninety percent of the local population. "What about the boat? You said it was a fishing boat. Was it a trawler, or a seiner?"

"What is that? I don't understand." His voice is barely above a whisper.

"Did it have a big spool of net on the back, or arms sticking up?"

"A spool? Is that like a wheel?" I nod, and he thinks. "It had a big spool. And a cabin on the front."

I lean back in my chair. It's a loose description, sure, but it easily fits the *Pot o' Gold.*

And half the other boats on the river.

"If we drove down to the harbor, could you point out the vessel?"

He shakes his head in denial. "No. I want nothing further to do with these men. I have told you what I remember. For my father's sake. But I am trying to start a new life. I don't want them to see me again. Or they may kill me like they did him."

I wonder if that's why he was attacked, because he witnessed a murder. Two, if you count the man who died in the shipping crate. I have to take his fear of the consequences seriously. And I'm still grappling with the idea that Tavin O'Brian might be involved. That I was alone on the docks with a human trafficker and his henchman.

A murdering trafficker.

I don't blame Alon for not wanting to go back.

Then I remember I have pictures. Images from the marina in Warrenton. I flip backwards through the photos on my phone until I find them. Show them to Alon, and ask him to see if he sees the boat. There's a lot of vessels in the pictures, including the *Pot o' Gold.* He scrolls through, going back and forth through the images. He pauses, looking at one photo, then he scrolls through a few more, before backing up. He looks at it for a few moments, then turns the phone back around to me.

"I can not be sure, but the boat I was on looked a lot like this one."

It's Tavin O'Brian's boat. The *Pot o' Gold.* Berthed just a few slips down from the *Beatrice.*

My brain scrabbles with possibilities and unanswered questions and all the loose ends that need to be tied up. The emotion in the room is suffocating. My heart is pounding, and my palms feel clammy. What's the matter with me? Why am I reacting this way?

Just a little PTSD. Being alone with a killer will do that to you.

My mind flashes back to the scene on the dock. The mournful cry of seagulls, the scent of water and diesel. The two men, O'Brian and Tad, boxing me in on the boardwalk. What if they had decided I knew too much? What if they had decided to kill me?

But they didn't, did they?

Right. I take a deep breath, and bring my focus back to the room with the others. Madison is staring at me strangely.

"Are you all right?" Her voice is infused with doubt and concern.

"Yeah, I was just thinking."

Ask about the theft.

"Alon," I say, "did you steal money from the till at the Big Bridge Bar & Grill, where you were working?"

"No, no, I never did." He shakes his head with vehemence, then raises a hand to his temple. "That would be stupid, to draw the attention of the police. And to bring trouble to the men who were kind enough to give me work."

I'm not sure I'd use the word "kind" to describe the owners of the Big Bridge—more like "exploitive" or something even nastier—but what he says makes sense.

Madison throws me a glance. I can't tell if she's annoyed, confused, or grateful that I've brought the subject up. But she adds, "Why did you leave your job, then?"

"One morning when I went to work, there were police cars there. I did not want to get caught, so I went back home."

Yeah, that's pretty much what I suggested to Ben Yost.

"But later a policeman came to the room I was renting. He yelled at me, kept asking where was the money. I thought he wanted a bribe. I only had a few dollars but I tried to give it to him. Then he was shouting so loud and fast that I could not understand and was afraid to answer." Alon looks away from us, his chin trembling. "I did not know what to do, or what to say, I was afraid to do the wrong thing. So I kept quiet. And that is when they took me to jail."

We've come full circle, with almost all the pieces in place.

56

I LEAVE THE Jenson home with a bag filled with the leftover coconut buns, their aroma dispersing into my car's interior. I've said nothing to Madison or the others about the fact that I know the boat's owner, only that it was one of several vessels moored at the Skipanon Harbor where I had been investigating another case. Madison, who knows about the Reynolds investigation, takes my remark at face value.

Now, what to do? I don't think Alon will testify, because his immigration status is still in limbo. Plus, he's been traumatized by the attack. Meanwhile, O'Brian—or someone—continues to traffic and more people are hurt. I've got to find some way to catch him that doesn't involve Alon.

In some ways, I can relate to Alon. I, too, came to Astoria to look for a different life. A better life, one that got me away from the memories and trauma and hostility of my former colleagues. I, too, was willing and able to work, but met with opposition wherever I turned. It's why I became a private investigator. I don't blame Alon for what he's done, but he should have done it differently.

I don't feel like going home just yet, so I go get the oil in my car changed and then drive south to Seaside to talk to a roofing company about fixing the leak. They're expensive, but they say they can do it sometime next month, if there's a break in the weather. November isn't known for sunny days, but I sign on the dotted line and hope I will have been able to clear a space on my credit card when the time comes.

Mrs. Jenson's coconut buns hold me over through lunch and several more errands. The blue light of evening is settling in as I arrive back in Astoria. Once inside my house, I shuck my jacket and my gun before steeling myself to head down to the basement. It's cold down here, and I click on the space heater in the incident room. Once again I scan the big area map, photos of the boats in the marina, blurry headshots of the people I've questioned. What the hell am I missing? Every time I look at the incident wall, I feel the weight of failure.

You've done your job, given Biswas what he wants.

But I still don't know who really killed Jack Reynolds, or even where it happened.

The bright colors of Christopher's painting catch my eye. It's partially covered by a yellow sheet of paper from a notepad, listing things I wanted to look into. Almost everything has been crossed off. I pull the list off the wall, drop it to the floor, and lean closer to the picture. It's a bird's eye view of a crab boat, presumably the *Beatrice*. Circles on the deck and in the water must be the crab rings. Two stick people are on the deck, one with yellow hair: Christopher and his father, Jack.

There's another boat in the image. This one is less detailed, just an outline on the page. But on the deck of this vessel are several people. The background is blue ocean, but there's a stripe of black at the top of the paper. Does that mean it's nighttime?

The rest of the paintings at Alicia's house were more or less front-on views of boats and simple landscapes. This is the only one I remember being from the air. It reminds me of the game he was playing, piloting a helicopter. And that makes me think of the drone on board the *Beatrice*.

Chris said he had a lot of practice flying.

You think he meant the drone?

It's possible.

I take the picture from the wall. Next to the second boat, almost obscured by a splash of blue paint, is another person. In the water. My heart begins to pound in my ears.

I pull my notebook out of my jacket pocket, and flip through my notes. In reviewing my first interview with Alica Reynolds, I realize I never learned where the money to send Christopher Reynolds to art camp came from.

The boards of the staircase rattle beneath my feet as I run upstairs to get my phone. Then I call Alicia. It rings several times before she picks up.

"Hello?" Her voice sounds tired.

"Hi Alicia, it's Audrey Lake."

"Are you stalking me?"

Since she sounds grumpy, I decide to cut to the chase. "You told me your ex-husband paid for Christopher to go to an arts camp, remember?"

"I remember. So what?"

"So, do you know where he got the money?" I bite my lip and cross my fingers for luck.

Her answer is an exasperated sigh. "If I tell you, will you leave me alone?"

"No promises, but if this gives me something to follow up on, I'll get out of your hair."

"Look, Jack always had a side hustle, okay? Lately he'd got this notion that people would pay for ideas, or information, or...or silence, if they didn't want a story spread around town. Or wanted a counter-story spread. I'm sure you know what that's like. Everyone knows everyone else's business in this place."

"That sounds pretty vague. Can you give me an example?"

"Well, he'd dangle some bit of information, say a place where the crabs were heavy, or some tip about some sports team, and offer to share for a few bucks. Or he'd say something like, 'is that story I heard about you and so-and-so true?' And then he'd get a retainer not to spread it around. It didn't work all the time, or most of the time, in fact. People would just tell him to go to hell. But then he got onto something. He told me he knew something no one else knew, and it would be worth a lot of squeeze money. His words, not mine."

"Do you know what he was talking about?" I hold my breath.

"No. And I didn't want to know. Didn't want to be a part of his sleazy games. He just said he knew where some skeletons were buried."

My jaw drops. "Skeletons? What skeletons?"

She scoffs. "Not literally. It was just an expression, meaning he'd got the goods on someone."

I let my breath out in a whoosh, and rub my forehead with my free hand. "Alicia, you realize that is blackmail, right? Getting someone to pay you for not telling what you know."

"I guess. Whatever, it meant Jack had a few dollars to spare. It didn't have anything to do with me and Chris."

"Does the blackmail victim know that? Listen, Alicia, you've got to be careful. Both you and Chris."

"What? Why?"

This woman is dense like granite.

"Because blackmailers have been killed by their victims."

"But I'm not—"

"Don't you see? Jack Reynolds is dead. And blackmail is a very strong motive."

"But I thought Jim Horne—"

"Horne isn't guilty," I say recklessly, trying to get her to see the danger. "And that means the killer is still out there, and if they think you know what Reynolds knew, they might try to finish the job they already started with Jack."

There's silence while she considers what I've said. So I keep pressing. "Do you *know* who Jack was blackmailing?" If she can answer this, it could either confirm my suspicions about O'Brian, or lay them to rest.

More silence.

"Mrs. Reynolds? Alicia? Do you know who paid Jack to keep quiet?"

"Well...I don't *know* know. I don't—didn't—want anything to do with Jack and his schemes. It's just something Christopher said once, before Jack was killed."

"What did Christopher say?" I'm biting my lips, my cheeks, everything to keep from yelling at her.

She sniffles. "It was when Jack took him out on the boat, and they went on the reserve. Which, I might add, I didn't know he was doing, and when I found out he was crabbing illegally, I told him he could never have Chris on the boat again."

I flex my fingers, because I really just want to strangle her. "Okay, I exonerate you of all wrongdoing regarding Jack's activities on the reserve. Now, what did Chris say?"

"Don't be nasty," she huffs. "He just said they weren't the only ones out there, the night Jack was setting crab pots."

"You mean, someone else was also crabbing, or fishing, on the reserve?"

"I guess." I hear the rustle of fabric through the speaker, and imagine her seated at the sewing machine. "I mean, I don't know this was the person Jack was putting the screws to. But it's something he knew about, and I could see him asking for a little hush money."

I drum my fingers on the table. It's a lot vaguer than I was hoping for. "But Jack himself was crabbing illegally."

"Maybe the other person didn't know he was there, until later."

"But who? I haven't heard of someone else being active out there."

"Whatever, you're the one trying to rescue Horne. You make it work. I'm just trying to get on with my life here." And she ends the call.

I pace across the empty living room. Did any of this matter? Suppose there was someone else on the reserve, and Reynolds knew about it. Whoever it was might lose their fishing license, their livelihood, if they got caught. Big stakes. But how could it be proven? Reynolds himself was ambushed by the reserve staff and law enforcement when he came back to check his pots. That's the nature of crabbing, setting traps and leaving them behind. But fishing is capture in the moment. If the other person was fishing, would there be evidence? I didn't see how. And you need evidence if you're going to blackmail someone.

Could he have seen something on the reserve while using the drone? And if he did, where was that footage now?

57

Ye gods. Could things be more confusing? Here I thought I might have a link to O'Brian, and now Alicia has introduced a whole new possible player.

The trouble is, I have too many plot threads to untangle. And I can't seem to stick to the directive just to find reasonable doubt. Looked at that way, I have more than fulfilled Biswas's brief. If the Warrenton cops had uncovered half this mess, it was no wonder they'd decided to connect the obvious dots of Reynolds' murder and Jim Horne's serendipitous presence on the neighboring boat.

In fact, if I succeed in eliminating the other suspects—Ethan Sinclaire, Keith Larson, or even Alicia—it actually weakens the case for the defense. Horne would be better served if I left it just a cloud of possibilities. Because then Biswas could argue it could be any of these other people.

So, leave it alone.

But that goes against all my instincts as an investigator.

Horne as the perp makes sense in some ways. He was the anomalous factor. Alicia and Keith Larson especially could have killed Reynolds any old time in the past ten years, if they'd wanted to. Granted, the theft of the crab pots was a thing, but Larson had gotten them back and Reynolds had been caught and was facing punishment. What was the point in further revenge? Alicia got the boat, and whatever money she could sell it for, but again, that was a bigger headache than just letting Reynolds go to jail and get out of her hair.

That leaves Ethan Sinclaire, whose violence had been precipitated by the invasion of his precious marine reserve. But would he really have come up to do more than confront Reynolds? I tried to imagine it. The two men arguing, Sinclaire all het up and righteous, Reynolds shaking his head at the young man's idealism and naiveté, his inability to see how a working man has to provide for his family. Not that Jack had been stellar at that, but I couldn't see him admitting that to Ethan. Meanwhile, Ethan tries to bring the fate of the planet into it, make Jack see the bigger picture. Reynolds turns his back, refusing to engage. Sinclaire, enraged, pulls a k-bar knife, conks Jack on the head and slits his throat.

Yeah, no. That just doesn't play. Ethan isn't some Rambo wannabe. Would he even carry a blade bigger than a pocket knife? What for?

Rewind. Reynolds turns his back. Ethan grabs a pipe or a piece of wood from the dock and takes a swing at the back of his head. Reynolds falls. Ethan finishes him off with his pocket knife, waving the bloody weapon and howling with glee.

That image actually makes me want to laugh, it seems so unlikely.

Nice going. You've talked yourself out of all your suspects. Way to work for the defense.

That's what the prosecutor is going to do, too.

The burden of proof is on the prosecutor.

But the jury will see Horne as a bird in the hand, and without a compelling argument for someone else he'll go down. Especially since he was a stranger and Reynolds was one of their own.

Just do what you were hired for. It's Biswas's job to defend his client.

Damn it. Horne is innocent. I'm missing something.

Maybe you're wrong. About all of this.

Nothing happened on that derelict boat. Nothing happened on the *Beatrice*. I know it.

Eventually, I decide to get up and go upstairs. I've barely gotten to my feet with all the associated cracks and creaks of my inner architecture, when I hear a noise. The walk-out door rattles, and something pushes against it. I reach for the comforting butt of my

Glock, but my fingers find only the folds of my shirt. The gun and its holster are upstairs where I left them. My hands clench and unclench uselessly as I step into the open basement. It's freezing outside the incident room, and I hold my arms tight to my chest.

The door rattles again.

Someone is out there. The intruder, trying to breach my walls.

Maybe it's the wind. Or an animal.

Maybe it's Bigfoot.

I glance back into the incident room, where the overhead light is still burning. I can see from here that the window is down and locked. But I didn't do a perimeter check. I was too focused on Alon's story.

Did I lock the door behind me when I came home? I must have, it's my ritual, but I don't remember specifically whether I did this time or not.

Just one minute of carelessness, that's all it takes. That's all someone like Sonny needs.

My heart is hammering, and a cold sweat starts in my armpits. Whoever the intruder might be, it's not some gangster out of my past. None of them knows where I am. It's probably a deer, or a raccoon.

Maybe it's whoever went after Alon.

Now I definitely want my gun.

I back away from the basement door, until my heels bang against the stair riser on the opposite wall. I could check the other windows down here, but I never open them. Ever. So I'm going with the assumption they're still closed and locked.

Assumption. Ass, you, me.

Shut up. I'm a rational person. Those windows are secure.

The floor above me creaks. Once. Twice.

Is someone up there? Shit, shit, shit. My gun is on the kitchen counter upstairs.

I start climbing the stairs, glancing back to keep my eyes on the walk-out door. When I reach the door at the top of the flight, I stop to listen. Hearing nothing but the roar of blood in my ears, I turn the metal knob slowly, but can't muffle the rattle of the ancient hardware, or the squeak of the hinges when it opens.

I dart into the kitchen. Grab my Glock from the counter. Check to see the front door and all the windows are closed and locked. I settle with my back against the wall next to one of the windows that overlooks the sloping side yard above the walk-out door. The narrow space between me and the neighboring house is empty, but if someone is pressed against the house, I wouldn't be able to see them.

The floor above me creaks.

Is someone on the second story? My heart tries to crawl into my esophagus before falling to cower somewhere in my belly.

There can't be anyone up there. I'd have heard them going up the stairs, which squeak like a family of mice. It's got to be just the old house settling.

Unless they've been up there all along.

With the gun clenched in my fist, I barrel up the stairway, feet clattering on the wooden treads. A movement catches the corner of my eye, and I raise my weapon, shouting "Stop!" I surge into the street-side bedroom, my off hand fumbling for the light switch even as I clock the shadow moving in front of the window.

My fingers slip on the switch before it finally clicks to life and light fills the room. It's empty, and the window overlooking the porch roof is open, with the curtains blowing in the wind.

58

THE WINDOW IS a black square, and I'm a visible target in a room full of light. Scrabbling my free hand along the door jamb, I turn off the switch before crossing the room to put my back against the wall next to the window. I'm half-blind in the sudden darkness, and I can barely see through the glass. A cool breeze whispers against my skin. I peer down onto the porch roof and the front yard, and scan the street and sidewalk. As far as I can tell, there's no one out there. But the world is dark beneath the heavy overcast, and the nearest streetlight is far away.

I push the sash down until it hits the sill, and twist the latch to lock it. I clear the other two rooms upstairs, even peering into the attic before I go back down to the main floor. I move to the windows overlooking the back yard, see nothing. Ditto the side yards. But when I peek out the front window to survey the porch, I notice that the gate which allows access to the side yard is ajar.

Has someone gone through? Did I leave it unlatched myself? Or is it only the wind?

Hello, security cameras?

What does it say about me that Zoe keeps track of things better than I do? I retrieve my phone from where it's been charging and fumble through the app. There's an earlier video from the side yard camera showing a cat ambling up the outside stairs, looking back at the camera with glowing eyes, but nothing recent. I check the camera mounted on the porch. If a person was on the porch, or the steps that lead to the street, this camera should have caught them. But the only thing I see in the feed is a moth fluttering in front of the lens.

I sit down at the foot of the staircase, put the Glock down beside me, and rest my head in my hands.

I could have sworn someone was in the house. But the cameras say otherwise.

Too bad they're all outside.

No. They're motion sensitive. If someone broke in, the system should have caught them. Should have alerted me through my phone, in fact. There was no one here except for myself and my imaginary friend.

And the ghosts of your psychotic past.

Shut up. There's no such thing as ghosts.

Oh, and by the way, I'm not your 'imaginary friend.'

You *are* imaginary. Phoebe says so.

I mean, I'm not your friend.

My spine prickles. Yeah, that's what I need, threats from inside *and* out. I sit on the step for a long time, listening to the wind moaning around the eaves. Eventually, I stand up and fetch the shoulder holster, returning the Glock to its home. I'm not going to carry a gun in my own, demonstrably empty, house. But I do put the weapon in one of my kitchen drawers. No sense leaving it out in plain view. Then I sit down at my card table, looking out into the darkness, and think through the events of the evening.

What the hell just happened?

Okay, focus on the lack of video evidence. All it really means is that what or whoever was at the basement door didn't use the outside stairs, which means they came and left through the back yard, hugging the side of the house to keep out of the camera's field of view. So I need another camera that shows the back yard.

But what about the upstairs? If someone was there, they must have gone out the bedroom window, dropped onto the porch roof, then jumped down onto the hillside and ran away. But the porch camera shows nothing.

That means you're seeing things, Lake. And hearing things, too.

A shudder ripples through my body. Because if I'm hallucinating again, that means I'm getting worse, not better. Or is this somehow tied to my retrocognition?

But maybe I'm just blowing things out of proportion. I mean, the house is over a hundred years old. It makes noises all the time. And there's all kinds of animals that live in town—deer, raccoons, rats. Not to mention random cats and dogs. The outside noises could have easily been an animal.

And the shadowy figures?

"I don't know, all right? That's all it's been, is shadows. Never an actual person. Just movement, and footprints that one time, which I stupidly mucked up."

Almost like they were never there.

"I walked over them, okay?"

Sick of the conversation, I stand up, bumping the card table with my knee. The binder of the case file slides toward me, and I reach for it reflexively. And I suddenly realize I've been speaking aloud to a voice in my head.

It's good to talk.

"No, no, no. I'm not that crazy. I just need some sleep. That's all."

But I can't relax until I've retrieved the gun and peered into every cupboard and closet. Only then am I ready to go to bed.

Tucking the binder under my arm, I head upstairs to my cot. The forms and notes of the case file act as a soporific, and an hour later I turn out the light. When I lie down, I put the Glock beneath my bed. Just in case.

OCTOBER 29 - DAY 11

59

After a rough night with the wind rattling the shingles and the windows in their frames, not to mention my heightened anxiety, I finally roll out of my cot as the mid-morning sun sticks its fingers through the blinds. My back is killing me, and I check my phone for email. There's one from Biswas thanking me for my good work, and letting me know he's going to court with what he has now, as he thinks there's enough for reasonable doubt. I'm officially off the case.

Well.

I should be glad, right? First assignment, a success. On one hand, I'm happy *he's* satisfied. On the other, I wish *I* was. I can't let go of the feeling that innocent people are still in the line of fire. Even if Horne gets off, people are still going to think he did it. Or suspicion is going to fall on someone else, who may be equally innocent. That doesn't feel like a good exchange.

Oh please. No one's innocent these days.

I rub my forehead. Here in the light of day, this whole thing with Zoe, and the maybe-intruder, has me questioning my sanity. Again.

I check the camera feed, but there's nothing to show. Last night was quiet. But I still go outside and walk around the house, looking for some sign of an intruder. There's no footprints, no marks around the doors. No track through the dew-laden grass.

Maybe I did hallucinate the whole thing.

I don't want to go to Phoebe with this, because she might decide it's enough to put me back on the meds. And I don't like the way they make me feel, like I'm watching the world through a cloudy window. Plus, something tells me that once I'm taking drugs again, my chance of exploring my retrocognition goes down the tubes.

Maybe you're just scared of your own shadow.

"Maybe you should stop being a smart ass and be helpful for once."

Give a girl a chance.

The last time I opened myself to Zoe's influence, she took control and roughed up a potential witness. No way I'm giving her the opportunity to hijack my brain again.

Stop being so paranoid.

"Okay, fine, I'm ready for your great insight." And I tap my foot for effect.

Your ability is seeing nasty things in the past, right?

"I think so. I mean, I don't know all the parameters. Because 99% of the time it doesn't work."

Because you're afraid of it. So it's creeping in through the corners.

"What are you saying?"

That if you just admit you're one of those psychics you can't stand, you won't have all this backwash.

My hackles go up. Where does she get off? "You mean, just exercise my power? But I've tried that. I've been trying all along."

Correction. You've been in denial all along.

Could my subconscious really be twisting the fear of my ability into shadowy, half-seen threats? Or maybe there's so much psychic residue floating around that it's leaking into my waking moments. Ghosts from Astoria's tumultuous past.

Meg might know something about that.

I try to shake all the anxiety and confusion out of my brain. At least now I can focus on my other case, the one for Madison Jones. With Alon's story and the presence of the severed finger, it seems obvious. But if Alon won't testify and give it context, the finger is pretty circumstantial. What I really need to do is re-examine the *Pot o' Gold,* and see if there's evidence of human trafficking.

A glance out the window tells me the day is going to be overcast, the sky heavily blanketed with interlocking clouds, as impenetrable and unforgiving as the hull of a battleship. If the atmosphere retains its armor, tonight will be very dark, the moon and stars obscured and lightless. The perfect time to go nosing around the moorage.

I spend the morning reseating the side yard camera so it points directly over the walk-out door, making it impossible to evade the field of view by standing up against the house. Then I walk down Rhododendron Avenue to where it meets up at a T-junction with Alameda Street, and I turn right, hugging the narrow gravel shoulder. To my left is a precipice, and I walk facing the traffic so I can see oncoming cars. There was a landslip last spring, a big scallop of hillside loosened and oozed down into a dead-end street below. No houses were damaged, but since then, the roadbed feels a lot more precarious.

I've been told that the whole peninsula where Astoria is built is actually a prehistoric landslide. Basically, a big pile of mud. The soil is very unstable, and there've been instances of houses sliding downhill and into another street or structure below. My mother, the architect, would be appalled at the fact of so many dwellings constructed on such unpromising ground, but hey, most of the community is still in place, and some of the houses date from the 1800's, and my own bungalow is over a century old. Which is probably why it makes so much random noise.

One day you're going to wake up and your house will be down by the river.

That'll be a win. Waterfront property has a high value.

The informal pedestrian trail that cuts down across the hillside down to Marine Drive is blocked off with yellow tape, probably until the city gets the slope a little more stabilized. But it's not raining, so the longer walk along Alameda isn't discouraging. I pass the mildewed bungalows and sagging Queen Annes, circling around the cars which overlap the curb and reduce the sidewalk to a few navigable inches.

When I reach Marine Drive, on impulse I decide to turn up the street and go to the Pig 'N' Pancake. It's only a couple more blocks, and I haven't had breakfast, or lunch for that matter. As usual, the parking lot is full of cars, and the hostess asks if I mind sitting at the counter instead of a table. I order coffee and inhale the enticing aromas of bacon and maple syrup.

As I'm scanning the menu, I hear a familiar voice. Or rather, two voices. I spin my stool around, and see Alicia and Christopher sitting in one of the booths. Alicia is digging in her purse, and then she gets up and heads for the bathroom, admonishing her son to stay put.

He looks around and meets my eyes, breaking into a smile. I wave. And think, this is the only chance I'll ever have to speak to him without Alicia around.

Before I can change my mind, I hop off my stool and walk over to his table. "Hi, Christopher."

"Hi, Audrey." His grin is wide and contagious, his blond hair slicked to his head with styling gel.

"Enjoying your meal?" I glance over my shoulder toward the restrooms.

"I love the Pig 'N' Pancake!"

"Me too. Hey, listen, remember when we were talking about you being out on your dad's boat?"

He nods, looking past me toward the short hallway where Alicia disappeared.

"Did you ever see anyone else fishing? When you went crabbing with your dad, down south along the coast?" I think of Christopher's picture, of the stick person in the water, and suddenly my blood runs cold. It couldn't be. I swallow past the new tightness in my throat. "Or did you ever see a freighter? A big ship? Like the ones that anchor in the Columbia?"

He nods. "Sure." Then his face falls, and his voice drops to a whisper. "But Dad told me not to tell."

"It's all right, Chris," I whisper back. "You're not in trouble. I promise not to tell your mom." I feel like a monster, pumping this young man who probably wouldn't be deemed competent by a court of law. But I have to know. "Did your dad fly a drone and see something?"

"I flew the drone," he says proudly. "Dad let me."

"What did you see when you flew the drone?"

Chris looks toward the restrooms, then down at his plate. He fiddles with his napkin.

I struggle to keep the impatience from my voice. "Please, Chris. It might be important."

"I saw a big ship. And a group of people going from the big ship to a fishing boat."

"And what else?" My mouth feels suddenly dry, and I take a swig out of Alicia's water glass.

"Dad took the controls away from me when the engine backfired. So I didn't see any more."

"Huh?" I grapple with his words in confusion. "The drone backfired?"

Not backfire. Gunfire.

A server with a loaded tray edges around me as I continue to whisper urgently. "Okay, so you heard a backfire. Then what did you do?"

"We waited, then we followed them."

"You did what?" My voice comes out as a squeak.

"We followed the boat. The fishing boat, not the freighter."

"Followed it? To where?"

"Up along the coast. Almost to the Columbia. But then it stopped. And dad sent out the drone again. He didn't let me do it, but he said I could man the helm while he played with the drone. I kept the *Beatrice* really steady." He nods proudly.

"I'm sure you did. But how did the people in the fishing boat not see you?"

"It was dark. And kind of foggy. But the drone sees in the dark."

Infrared. Got to be.

Chris is whispering now, too. "We didn't have our lights on. Mom says that's really bad. Another boat could crash into you."

"Your mom is right." My mind is racing, trying to pull all this new information together. "Chris—"

"What's going on here?" The voice is loud and strident, and it's right behind me.

60

I whirl around, bumping my hip against the sharp corner of the table. Wouldn't you know it. Alicia has returned from the bathroom. And she looks unhappy.

Zoe, why the hell didn't you warn me?

I can't see through the back of your thick skull.

Alicia clutches her purse to her side. "What's going on here? Are you talking to Chris without my permission?"

Oopsie.

I paste a smile to my face. "Hi Alicia. I was just sitting down for a meal, and saw Chris here, and we were chatting while I was waiting for you to come back."

Chris presses himself into the far corner of the booth. He starts rearranging the cluster of condiments without looking at either his mother or me.

"Well, I'm here now, so what do you want?" Her voice is thick with suspicion. She throws her handbag onto the bench seat but doesn't sit; instead, she folds her arms and glares at me. "I don't mind telling you, I'm pretty sick of your prying."

"Umm…" I do a quick brain scrabble, searching for a good reason. "We were just discussing the drone on the *Beatrice*."

Her brows go up and her voice lilts into confusion. "Yeah. What about it?"

"Do you know if there was a recorded video feed?"

She throws up her hands. "How on earth am I supposed to know?"

Chris breaks in. "There was, Mom. It uses those little card things."

Alicia glances down at him. "And how would you know that, Boo?"

He looks down at the table, and re-centers the salt and pepper shakers. "I saw Dad using them."

She turns back to me. "Then they're probably in the shed at home, with all the other junk he left us. Or maybe on board the *Beatrice*."

I've already decided Alicia isn't a serious murder suspect. So it's better to protect her than leave her hanging in the breeze as a possible target. "If you find them, keep them close. They might contain some evidence."

"Evidence? Of what?" She picks up her water glass, looks at it and frowns at the depleted level, then puts it back on the table. "Did you drink some of my water, Boo?"

"No," mutters Chris, and gives me a side-eye.

I wave a hand to attract her attention. "Remember what I said about the blackmail? It might be a good idea for you to know whatever Jack knew. You'd better start looking."

"Looking for what? A little plastic card the size of a quarter? You must be joking." Her voice is loud, and several other diners glance over. An elderly woman at the neighboring table raises her index finger in front of her mouth in a shushing motion. I notice that the restaurant is quieter than usual, and glance around. Everyone is looking at us.

Alicia grimaces, but lowers her voice. "It will take me forever to go through all Jack's crap."

"I'm not kidding. It might be important. You and Chris might be in danger."

"Chris? In danger? I don't understand." She sinks into the booth and reaches over to grab his hand.

"Because," I hiss, leaning over the table, "whoever killed Jack, if it's the blackmailer, will want to destroy the evidence Jack had. And if he killed Jack, why wouldn't he go after you two? What does he have to lose?"

"I can't believe you're just telling me this now."

Chris pulls his fingers away from hers and scrunches down in his seat, ducking his head and putting both hands in his lap.

Alicia's denial is beyond irritating. I slap the table top. "I tried to tell you yesterday, but you were too stubborn to listen."

"Well, no one has been at the house except for you. No one has called me, except for you. We were fine until you started nosing around again." She grips the edge of the table. "Just leave us alone. Don't come by, don't call, and don't speak to my son again. Ever. Or I'll take out a restraining order." Her glare is fierce enough to scorch my jacket.

That went south pretty quick.

I back away from the table, and decide I don't want to eat here after all. "I've only ever tried to find out who really killed your ex-husband. But never mind. I'm gonna take off now, Alicia. Bye, Chris." I give them a wave before I head for the exit.

61

In a hurry to put the P'N'P behind me, I cross the street and walk south, back down Marine Drive. Traffic is backed up and I get a nose-full of car exhaust as I walk past the Holiday Inn. Behind this hotel is where I had my first retrocognitive event, back in March of this year. I thought it was a hallucination, but it led me to a murder. My first case as a private investigator here in Astoria.

How can Alicia be so oblivious to the danger? Chris witnessed a crime, and even if she doesn't know that, you'd think she'd be more protective. But I can't give her more details without betraying her son's confidence.

A rumble burbles up from my stomach—I still haven't eaten. So I head to the Portway Tavern, located on the edge of the waterfront. This is my go-to place for burgers and beer. It's a bit of a hike from the Pig, and by the time I arrive I'm pretty much starving. The door bell tinkles as I enter, and I pause for a moment as my eyes struggle to adjust to the dimness of the taproom. The place smells deliciously like grilled meat and deep-fried fish.

"Well, well. If it isn't Audrey Lake."

I recognize the voice, and my shoulders tense. It belongs to Steve Olafson, senior detective on the Astoria Police Department and my own personal nemesis. What's he doing here in my favorite bar?

As my eyes grow accustomed to the dimness, I see he's not alone. Sitting across the table from him is Detective Jane Candide. Olafson is smiling; Candide is not.

Steve says, "I hear the grand jury for the Reynolds murder is going ahead today." His voice is jovial, but I'm not fooled.

"Was there some danger that it wouldn't?" I pass their table and put my elbows on the bar. There's only one other person in the small taproom, an old man seated three stools down. He's scrolling on his phone with his other hand locked around a glass of dark beer. I order a pint of Alaska Amber and turn back to face the detectives. They're both still looking at me. Olafson's legs are spread wide beneath the table. Taking up space. Mansprawling.

"Were either of you involved in that investigation?" I ask. It was handled by the Warrenton P.D., but these are small towns, and close together. They cooperate.

Olafson chuckles. "Not officially, no, but Jane here is what you might call 'involved.'" He makes air quotes with thick fingers. And I'm annoyed on Jane's behalf.

Candide scowls. "Just lending some expertise, is all."

The senior detective shakes his head. "Never thought I'd see the day when a cop went over to the other side. Even a former cop." He's referring to me, of course, and resentment starts to burn.

"Just lending some expertise to the defense, is all." My voice is only slightly sarcastic. I'd wanted to work for the Astoria P.D. when I first moved here, but Olafson pretty much scotched that idea from the get-go. It doesn't help for him to jab a fork in that wound.

"Find anything?" Candide's voice is casual, and she doesn't look at me. But the hand that circles her glass is tight, and the rim clicks against her teeth as she raises it to drink.

"I'm afraid I can't talk about an open case." I nod at the bartender as he delivers my beer. "But Biswas believes he has enough evidence to convince the grand jury to drop it."

Olafson snorts. "Juries."

It's a moment where I could build some rapport, scoff about soft-hearted or soft-headed juries and shake my head over 'the ones that got away.' But I let it slide by. I tried to break into their little club when

I moved here, and got shown the door. I'll be damned before I try that again.

"That new detective in Warrenton, Judd Daily, is showing real promise," Olafson continues. "Especially since he's got Jane to hold his hand." He winks.

Candide flushes, and I recall my own confrontation with her when she came to my house, and my own deductions about the relationship between her and Daily. But I wonder why Olafson is needling her. I take a drink. The malty brew floods my mouth and throat, and I feel my chest relax as the cool draught hits my empty stomach.

Olafson takes a long swallow of his water, and the bartender delivers two plates of burgers and fries to the table. "Be a shame if Daily lost his first real case." He picks up his burger and takes a big bite, then daubs the juice from his chin. It's like chum in the water, and it's all I can do not to snatch it out of his hand.

Candide twirls a French fry in a pool of ketchup. "Cops should help each other. Assuming we're all on the same side." She raises her eyes and gives me a gimlet glance.

I'm nettled by her tone. "I think we all want to make sure justice is done. And if a case has been investigated properly, there shouldn't be a problem." I take another drink. My glass is now half empty.

Olafson snorts. "Properly! You mean, by the big-city book? There's a lot you don't know about working in a small town, Audrey."

I've had this conversation before. "Yeah, I get it, Steve. You all are the experts, and I'm the interloper. And if that means I do things by the book, and you cut corners, well then, I guess we'll just have to agree to disagree."

Jane interjects. "It's not cutting corners to support each other!"

I feel my forehead getting hot. "You guys didn't want my help when I offered it. Besides, why are you bothered? The Reynolds murder wasn't your case."

Steve speaks up around a mouthful of burger. "Jane here has taken a personal interest in young Detective Daily's success."

Jane's voice is tight, and her eyes flash. "It's important to mentor the young guns."

Yeah, by sleeping with them.

"But I guess working for the defense means you don't have to actually solve cases, just pick holes in them."

Resentment flares like a white hot iron, and it takes all the control I have not to respond. Because that's what he wants. He's baiting me. He wants me to react. I take a gulp of beer to keep myself from shouting.

I'm so done with this. I'll never be one of them. I'll never be the recipient of anyone's mentorship, let alone any so-called support. I'll never be a law enforcement officer again.

Because you're different now.

Yeah, different. Shattered by the past, psychosis creeping in through the cracks, living alone in an empty house. Bitterness washes through me like a sneaker wave, and my throat tightens painfully. I drain my glass to the dregs.

Done with your pity party?

"Just shut up for once, okay?" The old man glances at me, and to my horror, I realize that I've spoken aloud. Again.

Olafson puts his burger down. "Did you just tell me to shut up?" His voice is low and dangerous.

Oh, crap.

I slam my glass on the bar top. The beer on an empty stomach has made me reckless. "I'm sick of you two harassing me for doing my job. And there might come a time when you need an extra pair of hands, or an extra pair of eyes. There might come a time when you need the help of an investigator who isn't constrained by the same rules."

"Don't think you can go around breaking the rules, Audrey, or the law. Not in *my* town." Olafson shoves his chair back and stands.

My head is spinning a little from the alcohol and hunger. "This is my town too, *Steve*, so you just back off before I come after you for harassment. In case you don't remember, I've got a friend who's a lawyer."

He scoffs, then signals the waiter. "We've decided to leave. Can we get some to-go boxes?"

Candide objects. "We just got here."

He curls his lip. "I don't like the clientele."

As the detectives leave, Candide throws a glance back over her shoulder. Her expression is unreadable, and I do my best to quell the anger, resentment, and humiliation that are welling up behind my eyes.

Are you finished?

I don't answer. Instead, I order a plate of fish and chips and another beer. I've got to fortify myself if I'm going out tonight. Because there's answers awaiting at the Warrenton Marina. On the *Pot o' Gold*. And this time, I'm going to strike it rich.

62

Hours later, my gut is still churning with resentment from the clash with Olafson at the Portway. I've been replaying the exchange in my head, continuing the argument until I have him groveling at my feet.

A victim of your rapier wit.

So he doesn't think I can solve my cases, does he? I'll show him. He'll come begging on his knees to put me on the force.

The tires of my car crunch the gravel, and cool damp air wafts in the window as I lower the glass to ease the stuffiness. Darkness presses against the windshield, pierced by the dazzling globes of the high-mast security lights. A drizzle has begun to patter the ground and stipple the hood of the car with moisture.

There's a couple of other cars in the parking lot of the marina, but I don't see any people, and I don't hear anything besides the occasional hum of vehicles on Harbor Drive as they rattle over the bridge. I put the window up and get out, zipping up my coat halfway so I can still reach my gun at need. It just takes a few minutes for me to traverse the now-familiar boardwalk ramp down to the berths. I know exactly where the *Pot o' Gold* is moored, and walk unerringly to where the bulk of the fishing boat looms over the water in a complicated silhouette. On one end is the wheelhouse jutting up above the deck; on the other is the net on its spool and the surrounding armature.

There's no other way to get on board except the portable stairs. Grimacing, I shove them over against the hull of the boat as the boardwalk shifts minutely beneath my feet. The steps creak and crack as I climb, but no one else appears and I get up to the rail and scramble aboard. The gentle rock of the vessel makes me feel unsteady, and I look around as I gain my sea legs. All seems normal. The net is wound on its spool instead of piled on the deck, and the lockers are shut and snugged against the gunwale.

I've had second and third thoughts about checking out O'Brian's boat. But after my little run-in with Olafson and Candide at the Portway, I've decided to go ahead. My feelings about it aren't clear, but I don't stop to think about all the tangled reasoning. I just go with my gut. And after I finish with the *Pot o' Gold*, I can move on to the *Beatrice*. These boats are central to my cases, and at least one must hold some answers. I don't care that Biswas went to the grand jury hearing today. I'm going to find some evidence to solve Reynolds' murder, and stop the trafficking, so more innocent people aren't harmed.

Or die trying?

Hopefully it won't come to that.

I stand and breathe deeply, trying to quiet my monkey brain and just feel. I hear a distant motor, a dog barking far away, a small splash out on the water. The squeak of the hull rubbing against the bumpers on the dock. I can smell diesel, fish, and dampness. But nothing else comes to my senses: no vision, no intrusive emotion, only an undertow of melancholy, which is probably my own as I face another dead end. Just like the exercise with Bernie at Pier 39.

Damn.

Alon said he and the other migrants were kept down in the fish hold. I don't love the thought of getting down there, but I've got to see if I can find something to corroborate his story.

And then what? He's still undocumented.

Maybe Madison can cut a deal with the state, allow him to stay while he gets his green card in exchange for his testimony. Hell, I don't know. I'm not a lawyer, or an immigration expert. I just need answers.

The hatch is a raised square on the deck, and I kneel, feeling for the bolts. They pull out of their sleeves with a grating protest that brings my heart to my mouth as I freeze in position, knees cold and wet against the deck, waiting to see if the noise attracts attention.

After a couple of minutes which feel like hours, I open the hatch and activate the light on my phone. The glowing beam reveals the top of a ladder, descending down into the black. I stuff the phone in my jacket pocket and grab the edge of the hatch, feeling for the rungs with my feet. Descend into the darkness, murky with the smell of fish. Cold and clammy and the faint slosh of water. My boots splash into the inch or two of water that has collected in the bottom of the hold, but I don't let go of the ladder. It's really dark down here, and I feel like Jonah in the belly of the whale. Breathing through my mouth because the smell of fish is gag-worthy, I shine my light around. It seems dim, getting dimmer, as the darkness swirls like a fog.

Here it comes.

My vision doubles. Spots of color dance across my eyes. I'm still gripping the ladder in a cold fist, standing on the bottom of the hold, but I'm also climbing down, the rungs pressing against the soles of my feet. A male voice above me says, "Watch your step." I recognize the tone, the trace of accent. It's Tavin O'Brian.

My throat vibrates, and the voice that emerges is deep and tinged with self-satisfaction. "You better have the money. Be too bad if someone found out what you've been up to on the reserve." Bravado helps to cover the fear that constricts my chest.

O'Brian replies, "I'll give you what you asked for. But this has to be the last time."

"We'll see." I've reached the bottom, and I step away to make room for the other man, whose boots are ringing on the metal rungs.

He says, "I've got a cash stash in the salt box. It's over against the hull."

I spot the metal box and walk towards it. O'Brian's feet hit the deck as though he's jumped down, and as I turn to look, something smashes into the back of my head. My knees hit the floor with a jolt of pain, and the cold kiss of a knife arcs across my neck. A warm tide sluices over my chest, and a rich coppery taste coats my tongue. Emotions scribble across the screen of my mind: fear, anger, surprise, and a terrible loss.

"Christopher!" The desperate utterance reverberates in the empty hold.

The last thing I hear is O'Brian's voice, vicious and victorious. "Goodbye, Reynolds. You always were a dumbass."

My vision clears. I'm gasping, blinking away the fog and darkness, squeezing the ladder rail like a life preserver with the edge biting into my palm. Struggling to make sense of the vision, the same kind of immersive event which I felt at the remains of the *Peter Iredale*. But this time, instead of experiencing a shipwreck, I've witnessed the murder of Jack Reynolds. Here. On board the *Pot o' Gold*.

I've finally found the crime scene.

Better late than never.

A twisted plait of relief and repugnance fills me. Tavin O'Brian is the killer. Not Alicia, or Keith Larson, or Ethan Sinclair. Or poor Jim Horne. It was O'Brian all along. And I'm suddenly very, very afraid.

63

THE RANK ODOR of dead fish permeates my lungs and my gorge rises. Terror makes me clumsy as my boots scrabble on the ladder, my hands plucking at the rungs. At last I scramble up and out of the hatch to lie, gasping, on the deck, rocked with confusion and deep anxiety. But the tendrils of violence have followed me.

Here she goes again.

The hatch slams down, severing my finger, and I feel an excruciating agony in my hand. Another wave of terror causes my heart to stutter, and I curl up in ball, moaning, cradling my wounded hand as shouted curses fill my ears. Someone kicks me in the back, pain thuds into my kidney. Tears fill my eyes and I scream in agony.

Wake up, Lake!

What? Zoe? What's happening?

For chrissakes, pull yourself together. Open your eyes.

The pain and terror recede like a wave slipping back to the ocean. The skim of rainwater on the deck has soaked through my pants, and my cheek is rasping against the grit embedded in the deck coating. Finally, I'm able to roll to my knees and stare at my palms. I still have all my fingers. With shaking hands, I close the hatch, ramming the bolts home.

Crouched on all fours, I shudder with anxiety. This boat is a casket of horror. I can't sort out which emotions are my own, and which are echoes of the fearsome events that happened here. Zoe's right, I have to pull myself together. Get out of the rain. The wheelhouse promises shelter and I stumble inside. Red and green LEDs glow with the wakefulness of technology, illuminating the cabin with a faint radiance. I lean against one of the swivel chairs, and feel a trail of rainwater drip across my forehead.

Okay, okay, okay, I tell myself. Breathe. You aren't hurt, you aren't dead. Figure out what you've just experienced. Get it clear in your mind.

Reynolds was asking for money. That squares with my suspicion of blackmail. O'Brian was taking him down to the hold. When they got there, O'Brian killed him.

The memory of the knife, cold on my neck, makes me shudder, and I reach up to touch the place where a scar lies beneath my jacket.

No. It's not *my* memory, it's Reynolds' last experience.

But what about the rest of the vision? My hand throbs with remembered pain. This is also where Alon's father lost a finger, which later became caught in O'Brian's fishing net. It's all here, the murder, the human smuggling. This boat is the Venn diagram overlap of both my criminal cases.

I'd assumed Reynolds was milking someone for fishing on the reserve. But if he'd discovered O'Brian trafficking migrants, it made more sense. And didn't Alon say one of the migrants had been shot once they'd transferred over from the freighter? And Chris said they'd heard a noise while he was piloting the drone, which he had assumed was an engine backfire. Had Reynolds seen that killing, too? If so, no wonder O'Brian wanted to kill him. What's a little more murder, after you've done it once? And to think I'd actually sort of liked the guy.

Too bad you're here without a warrant.

Ye gods. I shake my head to clear the final cobwebs, and stand up straight. How am I going to bring this place into evidence? Maybe Madison can authorize a search, based on Alon's testimony. There must be traces of Reynolds' blood down in the hold. Traces of DNA on the hatch that match the finger. I've just got to—

"Did you leave the stairs here? Christ almighty, Tad, do I have to do everything?" Tavin O'Brian's voice cuts testily through my scattered thoughts. For a moment I think it's a recurrence of the vision, then I realize I'm actually hearing it. My head goes up and I freeze in place, ears straining. O'Brian and his deckhand, Tad Mitchell. They must be down on the boardwalk.

At the steps I left by the side of the boat.

"I thought I put them back. But maybe I forgot." Tad sounds apologetic.

"Be more careful, okay? It just takes one little mistake. And we don't want some tourist thinking they can just get on board."

"Sorry. "

"Never mind." O'Brian says impatiently. "Let's go get some big fish. Untie the mooring lines." And I hear the sound of heavy feet coming up the wooden steps.

I can't let him find me here. He'd never let me get off alive.

Looking desperately around the inside of the wheelhouse, I see a narrow ship's ladder slanting down beneath the deck. I descend, nearly losing my footing in my haste, even as I try not to make a noise. Once down, I have to risk a light. I'm in a small galley, with a hallway beyond. I pause for a split second, but I know I can't stay here—anyone in the wheelhouse above might see or hear me.

I dart into the hallway. It's short, more of a vestibule, with two doors, a tall metal cabinet, and a trapdoor in the floor. One door leads to a tiny bunk room with space for two people. A dead end. The other door is that of the bathroom. The cabinet is stuffed full of wet-weather gear.

O'Brian shouts something indistinct, and I hear him cross the deck.

In desperation I lift the trapdoor. A cloud of diesel and grease assaults my nose. Another ladder leads down to the engine compartment.

This is it. I've got to hide. So I duck down inside and close the trapdoor as quietly as I can.

The place stinks like an industrial mechanic's shop times ten. I can't stand upright. It's also going to be noisy as hell when they start the engine, but at least if I make any sounds myself, no one will hear me.

In space, no one can hear you scream.

We're not in space, FYI, and there won't be occasion for screaming.

I crack the trapdoor open a sliver. O'Brian's voice is louder, maybe in the wheelhouse above, yelling orders at Tad. Something is being dragged across the deck. The engine revs to life, and it's as loud as I feared. The boat rocks gently as it pulls away from the dock. The sense of motion continues for about ten minutes, and I imagine we're heading for the Columbia. When we get into the bigger river, I can feel the additional surge and speed. There's some chop in the water and the wave-strikes make the metal structure gong.

I can't risk O'Brian noticing the additional noise so I drop the hatch and get down to floor level. The engine has taken on a louder tone and is starting to generate some heat. I unzip my jacket. I'm guessing we're headed downstream, toward the Pacific Ocean.

You could be in for a long ride.

The smell of diesel is making me feel queasy, and runnels of sweat start to trickle down my sides. My ears are ringing from the noise of the engine. I activate the light on my phone. It's a tight squeeze, and I'm not looking forward to being trapped down here for hours.

So let's get out of here, before we die of carbon monoxide poisoning.

There's nowhere else to hide.

To take my mind off my discomfort, I think about what I've learned.

The *Pot o' Gold* is definitely the scene of the crime. Both of them.

And after O'Brian killed Reynolds, what could be easier than dropping the body over the side where it would drift near the *Beatrice*, and then calmly hosing off the deck and hold? He'd been doing that the first time I saw him. And even if a little blood was missed, well, there's always blood on a fishing vessel. From the bait, from the fish, and even from the crew, who handle hooks and knives and other sharp objects all the time, on a rocking boat which might make any man clumsy.

And I'd seen the *Pot o' Gold* on the security footage, cruising on the Skipanon the night Reynolds was found. It all fits.

If you're so smart, why didn't they just drop the body at sea?

Maybe because then he'd be reported missing, with a greater search and a wider net and a chance that all the boats in the marina would be examined. Or maybe they wanted to send a warning, in case someone else knew what O'Brian was doing and was thinking of interfering. Or engaging in blackmail like Jack.

What I don't fully understand is how the attack on Alon fits in. Was O'Brian the man who'd come into the bar where he'd been working, the same day Alon had run away from his job? Had O'Brian realized who Alon was, that he'd remained in town instead of heading inland to a farm, that he'd been a witness to the killing of Alon's father? Or had it just been bad luck, an encounter on the waterfront with a white supremacist?

Suddenly, the trawler rears and bucks like a rodeo bronc. I'm thrown against the motor and the skin of my wrist burns before I can pull away. The synthetic material of my jacket scorches, adding another layer to the pervading smell. My nausea is worse, and my head is starting to pound from the noise. The increased turbulence must mean we're crossing the river bar. The breaking waves are visible from my house, distant white crests marking the zone where the mighty Columbia hits the churning ocean. Why incoming ships are required to take on a river pilot to guide them safely through, because so many vessels have been wrecked. Like the *Peter Iredale*.

The graveyard of the Pacific.

And I realize, the reason the migrants had to be transferred from the foreign freighter to the trawler was because of the risk imposed by having to take on a pilot. As a local fisherman, in a smaller craft, O'Brian would be exempt from that requirement. And where better to make the transfer than at nighttime on the marine reserve, a place no other vessels should be? Except for lawbreakers like Jack Reynolds.

My belly roils in time to the roll of the boat, and the bitter taste of bile floods my mouth even as I feel a tightening anxiety. I tell myself that Tavin O'Brian has probably navigated these waves thousands of times. We're not going to sink. Or capsize.

You hope.

Finally, the ride smooths out. The engine continues to roar and throb. The heat in the engine compartment is rising. I take off my jacket and roll up my sleeves. I hope O'Brian isn't planning on heading too far offshore, because sooner or later I'm going to have to pee. But for now, I have to sit tight and wait until we get back to port.

64

With a sudden lurch, the boat rolls sideways. Again I'm thrown against the engine, and my forearm burns before I can push myself away. I struggle to the foot of the ladder and hold on tight. Just in time, because now we're rolling the other way. We must be turning to parallel the coast, and the ocean swells are hitting us broadside. My stomach heaves. The unexpected movement along with the reek of diesel is the last straw. Without letting go of the ladder, I empty my belly onto the floor of the engine room. The sharp smell of half-digested beer and fish acts as an accelerant, and I retch until I half-expect to see my socks and shoes coming out of my mouth.

Finally, the trawler comes back to level, more or less. I hope nothing has happened. I hope we're not sinking. I have a vision of being trapped in the engine room as the ship capsizes and plummets beneath the waves. My heart ratchets up another notch, and perspiration slicks my face. My finger-joints ache from their grip on the ladder.

Wow. Paranoid much?

Shut up. I'm terrified.

If boats tipped over that easy, there'd be a shipwreck every day.

Maybe there *is* a shipwreck every day. A sour taste fills my mouth. I glance down at my forearm. There's a painful, angry red crescent.

Shouldn't have taken your jacket off.

Is that my choice here? Steamed or fried?

The boat rolls again. This time it's on more of a diagonal. My gut twists again, and I feel another wave of nausea. I may have to get out of here before I'm completely immobilized by seasickness. But even my uneasy belly can't keep Zoe from intruding on my thoughts.

You always seem to put yourself in compromising positions.

This is the safest room on the ship.

Pretty sure stowing away is against the law.

I'm not a stowaway. I got stuck here by accident.

Just like you got stuck by accident in the Baxter Building?

There is no comparison.

Isn't there? Undercover assignment? Trespassing?

That's not what I'm doing.

Then what are you doing? What's the endgame?

What *is* my endgame? I came here to investigate Alon's accusation. Now, I've finally discovered the scene of the Reynolds murder, but no evidence to support it. Even if I go to Biswas and tell him, what can he do? The grand jury hearing was today. He doesn't have the resources to send a team to the boat to look for forensic evidence, especially without probable cause. I have to find something concrete, some evidence that Biswas can present in court. Something like a murder weapon.

And all at once I remember, clear as crystal, the knife O'Brian used to cut the tangled nets on the day we found the finger. It had a heavy knob on the end and a long blade. If I can get the knife away from O'Brian, Biswas can test it for DNA.

You're going to take his knife? How's that going to work?

I don't know yet. Maybe there'll be a time while he's fishing, or something. I'll just have to keep an eye out. Which really means I need to get out of the engine room. Plus, if I don't, I'm going to be sick. Again.

Clambering up the ladder, I listen at the trapdoor. But there's nothing to hear over the growl of the engine. Ever so slowly, I raise the hatch an inch, two inches, so I can see out.

The vestibule is deserted.

A roll costs me my balance, I lose my grip and my sweaty palms slip from the ladder. My knee bangs painfully on the metal floor of the engine compartment, and for a moment I have to pause as the pain washes through me. But at least I didn't fall in the vomit.

The momentum of the trawler slows. And the rolling increases.

I tuck my coat under my arm, jam my phone into my pants pocket, and climb back up. Check the surroundings as much as I'm able, then drag myself through the trapdoor and up into the vestibule. There's the standing cabinet secured with a hook and eye. Inside is rain gear and bright orange insulated survival suits, designed to keep someone alive in the water. I pray we won't need them anytime soon, and squeeze into the cabinet. I can't latch the door behind me, so I hold onto a coat hook at the top of the interior side to keep it closed and hope no one notices the catch is loose. It's hard to hear past the snare-drum rattle of my heart.

Remember the last time we hid in a closet? That didn't work out so well, did it?

Amid the roll and toss of the ship and the smell of rubber, I remember a similar hiding place in the Baxter Building. The disgusting mattress. The darkness punctuated by shots. The reeling mosaic of my own mind, a mix of drugs and what I now think was my emerging psychic ability. A hallucination, or a vision. Cops. Dealers. Money changing hands. Traffickers and victims allowed to operate with impunity. I see myself from above, a huddled figure on the mattress while the hallways of the Baxter Building teem with chaos. The door opens, a blade of light slices across my body. The silhouette of an arm, a head, a shoulder. Reaching down to me. I see myself jerk, roll to my knees, grab the attacker and…

And what? Jeez, you're pretty good at hiding what you don't want to see.

Zoe's sardonic tone breaks into the vision. Or memory. Whatever it is, it's left me shaking and damp with sweat. My fingers are cramped from hanging onto the coat hook, and I desperately want some air. The trawler heels to the side, and I lose my balance and hit the cabinet wall with a thump, tangled in the gear. What if the boat sinks while we're out here, the water rushing in to the forward rooms? No one knows I'm here. And no one would be looking for me in the water.

Sinking again? Talk about glass half empty.

65

I'M STILL TRYING to untangle myself from the rain gear while keeping the cabinet door closed, when the timbre of the engine changes. The trawler is slowing down. Maybe we've arrived wherever it is we're going. Maybe they're going to deploy the nets, giving me a chance to catch my breath.

The boat stops moving, and the engine shuts down. I hear the rattle of metal—a chain?—and it goes on for several minutes. I don't know if we're dropping anchor, or deploying the net, or what.

With the engine off, the wash of the waves is clearly audible. The metallic noise is done, and except for the sound of the water, the boat is silent and rolls gently.

Should have gotten yourself together while there was still noise to cover it.

Yeah, yeah. Whatever.

I ease the locker open a crack. I don't hear voices or people moving around, so I open the door wider. The vestibule is dark and empty. Beyond the vestibule is the bunk room, the bathroom, and the galley. I consider my options.

Bunk room? Possibly safer, but further from the action.

Galley? Feels like someone might go in there at any time to rustle up a sandwich.

Engine room? Already tried that, and it's uncomfortable, stinky, and deafening.

Really, this cabinet seems to be the safest place, as long as no one needs rain gear. But I want to know what's happening.

Curiosity killed the cat. Better stay safe.

Like I'm ever going to be safe by taking your advice.

I ease out of the cabinet and take a couple of steps until I'm just inside the galley. I glance up the ship's ladder to the wheelhouse, but it's dark up there, too. And then I hear the engine.

It's not our engine—the trawler is still at a dead stop. And this is different, louder and deeper, even though it's still at some distance. I hear voices, O'Brian and Tad Mitchell talking, and then other, more distant voices, and the approach of another motor. An outboard?

I slip my coat back on and creep up the stairs to the wheelhouse. The door to the outside deck is closed, so I peek out of a window. At first I can't see anything. There's no lights on deck. But the moon is washing the sea with silver through a rent in the clouds, and in a few moments I can see the glistening water, and a dark shadowy bulk towering up against the sky. It's hard to judge the distance, but I estimate there's a big ship about a hundred yards away. Big like a container ship.

But that's not all. As my vision adapts, I can see a smaller boat in the water. It's full of people, and the wake from its motor leaves a white trail on the swells. O'Brian and Mitchell are standing at the stern of the *Pot o' Gold*, watching this small boat and facing away from me. Whatever is happening, it's not fishing.

Migrant trafficking. Got to be.

The small boat, the dinghy or whatever, is jam-packed. It's so dark, I can't make out details of the passengers, and when the dinghy gets close, I lose sight of it beyond the stern rail. But a few minutes later, O'Brian throws a coiling ladder over the side of the trawler. Mitchell steps back and opens the hatch to the fish hold. And then he draws a gun.

My stomach drops. I hadn't noticed he had a weapon. And with that gun, the situation has escalated a thousandfold.

The first man is coming up and over the side. He's dark-skinned, with black hair. His clothes are dirty and ragged. O'Brian barks an order, and the man puts his hands behind his head and proceeds to the open hatch, lowering his hands only to climb down into the hold.

Another person follows the first, and then another. The group clusters together at the mouth of the hold. One calls out, in accented English.

"What is happening? We are supposed to be in America! Why do we go down inside this boat?"

"You are in America, or almost," barks O'Brian. "Now get down there."

"No. Not until you tell us what is going on. I have already paid my money, thousands of dollars, to this man." He points to the last figure to climb aboard. "Why now are we on another boat? I have no more money!"

The others grumble, their complaints echoing the outspoken leader.

"I'll show you what's going on," growls Mitchell. Without warning, he slaps the complainer across the face with the barrel of his pistol. "Now get down in the hold, and no more backtalk."

The man he hit reels and almost falls, his hands going to his face, blood oozing between his fingers. The others looked stunned as Mitchell points his weapon at them. "Start climbing."

One by one they descend, the injured man leaving streaks of blood on the deck. Mitchell slams the hatch closed.

The last one aboard doesn't go down the hatch. He's got a roll of money, and he hands it to O'Brian. Then he crawls back over the rail and presumably back to the dinghy. I hear an engine growl, and the dinghy appears atop a swell, headed back to the container ship.

I think of Alon. Are these men also Filipino? Or are they from other countries? In any case, I've seen protesting, I've seen money change hands and people arrive from a foreign ship. I've seen menacing with a deadly weapon. A multitude of charges. I look over the water to the container vessel. The moonlight gleams on the stacks of containers. One is standing by itself on the edge of the deck, and some sailors appear to be working around it, jacking up one side until it overbalances and falls into the sea with a loud splash.

66

I DUCK DOWN beneath the edge of the window, and try to figure out what to do next.

Hello, this is people smuggling. Not much doubt about that.

I check my phone. Of course, there's no signal. So I can't just call the cops, or the coast guard, or whoever. Plus, I don't know where I am. The presence of the container ship argues for deep water, but that's about all.

And Tad has a gun.

I touch my own weapon, the Glock in my shoulder holster. I can defend myself if need be, but I don't like my chances on a rolling boat with two strong guys.

Discretion is the better part of valor, and all that.

If I wait until we get back to port, there's a good chance the migrants will be let go before anyone can respond. Plus, I'm increasing my own exposure. I can try to keep hidden, but I might get caught before we get to shore.

And what about the container ship? Don't they need to be apprehended, too? I need the Coast Guard. But how do I call them? I can't just get on the radio, either O'Brian or Mitchell would see me and kill me.

How about the emergency rescue thingy? Didn't Alicia say all commercial boats are supposed to have them?

The EPIRB? I remember Alicia telling me that they automatically deploy when the boat sinks or capsizes. If I could throw it overboard, that might bring the Coasties without alerting the crew.

I'm not sure where the thing is. I know what it looks like, thanks to Alicia, but finding it is another matter. Still, it should be right out in the open, right? I mean, the whole purpose is to float clear and bring help. You wouldn't stick it in a drawer. It's got to be outside. But O'Brian has shown he's willing to kill. I know he murdered Jack Reynolds. And Tad has a gun.

Are we gonna do this or what?

Zoe's right. I peek outside. O'Brian and Mitchell are still at the stern. They still haven't turned on any lights, so I risk slipping outside and onto the deck, my legs feeling like coiled springs. No one yells out, so I sidle alongside the wheelhouse, looking for the EPIRB. There's a narrow walkway between the wheelhouse and the gunwales. I creep along, keeping below the windows of the bridge. No sign of anything that might be an EPIRB. I round the bow and continue along the other side. Nothing.

Okay. Now where? Attached to the rail? I squat between the wheelhouse and the rail and scan the deck, trying to find something that looks like what I want, but there's stuff everywhere. The trawler arms, the big net spools. Ropes. Other things I can't identify. There's not actually a ton of open space.

Voices drift from the stern, and O'Brian and Tad cross the deck to the wheelhouse. I feel like we're in a deadly game of cat and mouse, chasing each other around the boat. At least they're both in there at the same time. And then I hear the anchor chain begin to grind.

Shit. They're getting ready to leave. It's now or never. I dart along the rail, squeezing between the vertical truss of the trawler arm and the gunwale. Please, let them be looking ahead, through the front windows, and not out at the deck. I follow the edge of the boat, trying not to trip, keeping an eye out for the EPIRB. But there's nothing.

Damn, damn, damn. Maybe the *Pot o' Gold* doesn't have one. I crane my neck, looking up on the trawler arms. As my gaze sweeps past the wheelhouse, I see it: mounted next to the doorway between the jamb and a ladder going to the roof. I was so intent on getting to cover, I didn't see it when I left the cabin.

A cold ocean breeze knifes through my coat; my shirt is damp where I sweat through the fabric in the engine room. I shiver in the draft and a splat of spray. There's no way I can get to the EPIRB now. They'll see me.

Stop being such a drama queen. Remember the fire escape? That was way scarier.

And I'm suddenly there, engulfed by the memory, crouched on the Baxter Building fire escape in the winter wind. I'd been working undercover, posing as Zoe, an ex-prostitute and drug user, squatting in the building with other transients. I'd been trying to see what the Junkyard Dogs gang had hoarded on the upper floors. But I'd gotten trapped on the fire escape, unable to get back into the building without alerting the gang.

Now, as then, every choice is dangerous. But I'd rather do something than nothing. So I cross the deck, trusting to the darkness to hide me, and the grind of the anchor windlass to cover my footsteps. Make it to the wheelhouse and hook my forearm over the ladder to gain a little leverage. Then I wrest the EPIRB from its cage and throw it. Watch as it arcs over the rail and into the sea with a small splash.

My chest loosens. I've called for the cavalry and now all I can do is hope they get here soon. Meanwhile, I've got to find somewhere else to hide. So I put my foot on the lowest rung of the ladder that goes to the roof of the wheelhouse, and start to climb. It's a bit of a scramble against the roll of the boat, but I make it to the top of the cabin. On my hands and knees, limbs splayed against the movement of the ocean, I glance around. The container ship is moving off. I pull my phone from my pocket and try to get a few pictures of the freighter, operating the camera one-handed.

It's a mistake. I lose my balance and land on my side, thudding against the roof. Shove my phone back into my pocket. Wait an agonizing few seconds before deciding it's better to get off this slippery surface before I fall and alert everyone. On hands and knees again, I back up and get my foot on the top rung. Look over my shoulder as I grope for the next one.

The door to the wheelhouse bursts open. My eyes meet those of Tavin O'Brian. For an instant we're both paralyzed with surprise. Then he yells for Mitchell and swings onto the ladder, blocking my path of escape.

67

I barely recognize O'Brian. His face is distorted with rage, and in an instant I understand how this man could have killed Jack Reynolds.

He reaches up to grab my ankle, but I kick his hand away and aim a stomp to his forehead. He jerks back, swearing.

Mitchell comes barreling out of the wheelhouse and gapes up at me.

O'Brian's voice is shaking with anger. "Don't just stand there, you idiot. Shoot her!"

Mitchell fumbles for his weapon. I scramble back across the roof. The ship pitches, and I lose my balance and fall again. O'Brian's face comes up over the edge as he climbs the ladder. The ship yaws, and I roll off the side of the roof and onto the deck, in the narrow space between the wheelhouse and the gunwale.

A coil of rope breaks my fall, but I'm still bruised and winded. On all fours I scuttle across the slippery deck, trying to regain my feet. O'Brian is standing on the roof of the wheelhouse, riding the swells like a surfer.

"Mitchell!" He shouts. "Get to starboard! She's over there!"

I don't want to be trapped in this narrow walkway. I dash out onto the main deck, sideswiping Mitchell as he comes around to trap me. I hear him curse as he hits the floor and I duck behind one of the big net spools and draw my gun.

"O'Brian!" I shout. "I know you killed Jack Reynolds! Tell your mate to lay down his weapon."

O'Brian yells something I don't hear and starts to descend the wheelhouse ladder. Mitchell has regained his balance and has his pistol out, waving it in one hand. My own arms are braced against the armature surrounding the spool, my gun as steady as I can make it against the rocking of the boat.

O'Brian is down on the deck now. He yells, "You don't know anything, Audrey. But you're guilty of trespassing, and attempted murder."

He can't buffalo me. "The only thing I'm guilty of is not realizing it was you for so long."

"You've got nothing, Audrey." He approaches slowly, hands spread wide. "Be reasonable. Put your gun away."

"You killed Reynolds. I couldn't figure out why, but your mistake was when you attacked Alon. No one had a reason to hurt him except to hide all this." I gesture with one hand. "Your people-smuggling operation."

He grimaces. "That wasn't me. Tad got a little ambitious and thought he'd make a point. You may have noticed he's not the sharpest hook on the line." Behind him, Mitchell frowns.

"Yeah, like you're some kind of genius. Reynolds saw your whole operation."

"Jack was an idiot. Just dumb luck he was on the reserve when we made the pickup."

"Is that why you murdered him?"

"The fool was trying to blackmail me. He threatened me. I'm the injured party here." O'Brian has halved the distance between us. He takes the gun from Mitchell, who doesn't seem to know what to do with it.

"Whenever you have to kill someone to hide your activities, you should rethink your choices." I barely know what I'm saying, don't let my eyes stray from his weapon. My own gun is now trained squarely on his center body mass.

"I was helping those people. These people." He waves a hand at the hatch to the hold. "They're just immigrants, trying to start a new life. My parents were immigrants, too. And believe me, they worked harder than most of the natural-born citizens who are too lazy to appreciate what they've got."

"Back off, O'Brian. Now." My arms are starting to tire, and my aim wavers with the rocking of the boat.

A smile tugs at the corner of his mouth. He takes another step forward. Now he's only about ten feet away. "See, Audrey, I don't believe you've got what it takes to actually shoot me."

"That's where you're wrong, *Tavin*. I *have* done it before." I can't wait any longer. I have to let them know I mean business. I pull the trigger.

The bullet skims by his ear and lodges itself in the wood of the wheelhouse. Mitchell looks shocked, with his mouth hanging open. The deck hatch pops up. I had assumed the hold was locked, and it's the last thing I expect. One of the migrants looks out, and shouts when he sees what's going on. Mitchell yells at him to get back in the hold. The hatch falls back down, and Mitchell kicks at the latch.

In my moment of distraction, O'Brian lunges forward and grabs my arm. I yank it back reflexively, but it's no good. His grip is like a manacle. I try to kick him but miss, smashing my toes into steel structure supporting the net windlass. His fingers dig into the bones of my wrist, and pain shoots up my arm as my hand opens. He pulls my weapon from my numb fingers, and I take a swing with my left hand. It's my non-dominant, weaker side, but my fist lands on his cheekbone with a satisfying smack.

But. He's stronger than me, by far. He palms my gun and twists my right arm behind my back, forcing me to my knees.

"Tad," he calls. "Get a rope."

"Tavin, you can't tie her up. She's a cop!"

"No, she isn't. She's a P. I., no one we need to worry about." O'Brian's voice is cold and matter-of-fact. "She's poked her nose in where it ain't wanted."

"A private eye? That's worse. She's—"

"Just get the rope, all right?" He presses the gun against my temple. My awareness spirals down to that cold little circle against my skin. "What are we going to do with you, eh, Audrey? You should never have gotten on the boat."

I tried to tell her.

I force some bravado between my chattering teeth. "Other people know where I am, you know."

"Do they? Do they really? Because I doubt that. You're trespassing, and working for a lawyer, I doubt he'd be okay with your breaking the law. So I bet you didn't tell him." He shakes his head. "In fact, I can't have you telling anyone anything."

By this time Mitchell is back with a rope. He pulls my wrists together, crossing them in front of me and looping the cord around and around before securing it with a sailor's knot. He does the same with my ankles. The cords bite into my skin. Despite the chill of the air, I'm pouring sweat.

"You don't have to do this, Tavin."

"I do. I really do." He turns to Mitchell. "We need something heavy. I don't want to risk another shot and get the cargo unruly."

Mitchell frowns. "Something heavy? What do you mean?"

O'Brian rolls his eyes. "Something we can tie to her feet that will sink her when we drop her overboard."

A cold fist of fear squeezes my heart. A shard of my vision on the shipwreck flickers by, the roar of the wind and the sea. I swallow hard. "Tavin, don't. This isn't who you are."

He glares at me. "You don't know me. You think you've got righteousness on your side. Well, let me tell you. There's no justice, there's no gifts from on high. There's only hard work, and looking out for yourself." He waves a hand toward the hold hatch. "Those poor suckers are all just looking for a better life. God help them when they discover America isn't the land of milk and honey they think it is, but that's their lookout, not mine."

Mitchell is digging around in a metal locker alongside the rail. I can hear the rattle of chain and tools, metal against metal.

"Just shoot me, okay?" My voice is surprisingly level. "Don't drown me." Because my brother drowned, when he ran his car off the bridge and into the river below. Accident, suicide, the verdict doesn't matter. But he didn't die in the crash, he drowned, the water filling his chest, his lungs.

O'Brian sits back on his heels. "I can't shoot you. If your body turns up, I don't want there to be a wound, or a bullet, they can trace. Drowning is better."

"It'll still obviously be murder, if I'm found with an anchor tied to my leg."

He scowls. "Your body will sink. No one will find you, unless your legs come off and you wash up on the beach." He leans closer. "By the time that happens, you'll be rotten clear through. Fish food."

Mitchell looks over his shoulder. "I can't find anything, Tav."

"Oh, for…" O'Brian gets up and goes to where Mitchell is kneeling by the locker. "Go below. Maybe there's something in the bunk room."

At that moment, the radio in the wheelhouse squawks to life.

"Attention, *Pot o' Gold*. This is the U.S. Coast Guard. We've intercepted the emergency beacon from your EPIRB. Do you require assistance? Over."

O'Brian and Mitchell are frozen in surprise. The captain snarls a curse and runs to the cabin, staring at the empty bracket, before he turns back to me, face ugly with anger. "You fucking bitch! What have you done?"

"*Pot o' Gold*, this is the U.S. Coast Guard. We have launched a helicopter in response to your signal. ETA in twenty minutes. Respond if you are able. Over."

He darts into the wheelhouse, followed by Mitchell. Their silhouettes are fuzzy outlines through the windows. I hear O'Brian's voice, ragged and breathless. *"Pot o' Gold* to Coast Guard, Captain O'Brian speaking, it's a mistake, we're—"

I take the opportunity to yell as loudly as I can. "Help! I'm a prisoner! I need help!"

"Shut up! Mitchell, keep her quiet."

A staticky voice inquires, "What's that, Captain? I didn't copy. Over."

"Nothing, Coast Guard, no help needed…"

I scream bloody murder, omitting words in the quest for volume. Mitchell reaches me and covers my mouth with his hand. I twist my head, trying to bite him, but he backhands me so hard my ears ring.

"Captain, we are hearing sounds of distress. Helicopter ETA in fifteen minutes."

"Son of a bitch!" O'Brian throws down the mic.

In the center of the deck, the hatch to the fish hold opens, and a man emerges. One of the migrants. I thrash and moan, trying to dislodge Mitchell's grip.

"What is happening? I heard a woman scream." The man climbs out onto the deck, and sees me lying down and tied, twisting like a landed fish. "What are you doing to her?"

O'Brian emerges from the cabin. "She's called the authorities, and ICE is coming. Get back inside! Tell everyone to keep quiet."

"ICE?" The man pales, but makes no move toward the hatch.

"Immigrations and Customs Enforcement! She wants to turn you over to the Feds, so you'll get deported. Probably to some nasty place in El Salvador."

I manage to dislodge Mitchell's grip. "He's lying! Help me! Please!"

"Shut up," Mitchell says, slapping me again.

My vision tunnels, and I fall on my side, straining against the tautness of the ropes.

"Stop hitting her," says the man.

"Do you want to get arrested? Tortured? Then get below! I have to get us out of here." O'Brian is now shouting in the man's face.

The man is frightened, but he stands his ground. "Stop hitting her."

"Oh, for…the Feds are coming! I don't have time to argue with you." O'Brian shoves the man in the chest. He steps back, his foot descending into the empty space of the open hatchway. With a cry, he topples backwards, hitting his head on the edge of the opening as he falls.

"Now, stay down there!" O'Brian grabs the edge of the hatch and slams it closed, shoving the bolt across so no one can get out. My last hope dies with that echoing scrape of metal against metal. Because I know I'm going over the side.

68

There's a brief reprieve while Mitchell dashes back inside the wheelhouse. O'Brian crosses the deck to stand over me. Neither of us says a word. His eyes are glacier cold.

Mitchell emerges, dragging a rusty tool chest. He says, "I found this in the engine compartment. There's also a big puddle of upchuck down there." He looks at me with an expression I can't read. "This is the only thing loose I can find. But it should be heavy enough."

O'Brian grimaces. "Dammit, I'll have to replace that. But okay, we've already lost too much time." He begins fastening the box to my feet with a trailing length of rope.

Oh, hell no.

O'Brian had to let go of my feet to fasten the tool chest, and I take advantage of his distraction. My hands and feet are tied, but I thrash my body like a fish on a line. Kick out with my legs. My knee connects with O'Brian's chin. A trickle of blood shows between his lips, and he curses.

"Tad! Hold her down."

The crewman pins me to the deck. The metal is cold against my skin, the ropes tight and terrifying. Tad's weight makes it hard to breathe.

"Don't," I wheeze, swallowing past the tremor in my throat. "Don't do this."

"It's your own fault, for snooping around." For the first time O'Brian looks directly at me. "I'm sorry, Audrey. I admire your persistence. But this is where it's gotten you. You chose to trespass on my boat. You've got only yourself to blame." He turns to Mitchell. "We've got to get rid of her before the Coasties get here."

Tad rolls back into a crouch. The tool chest is attached with a sailor's knot. I strain against my bonds to no avail.

O'Brian turns away to check the bolt on the cargo hatch, and glances up to scan the night sky, no doubt looking for the helicopter. Mitchell's eyes are wide and white, and he presses something into my palm, glancing over his shoulder at his boss.

I feel the familiar contours of a folding knife. I clamp my fingers around it.

O'Brian comes back. "Okay, let's do this."

Ignoring my protests, the two men pull me to the rail. The toolbox grates against the deck as it drags behind me.

"No," I say, and because I see the cold determination in O'Brian's eyes, the fear in Mitchell's, I yell, as loud as I can, hoping one of the passengers below will break out. "Help! Help me! They're killing me!"

"Shut up!" O'Brian slugs me in the jaw. I can't dodge, and my head explodes with pain.

The men don't say anything more as they heave me and the toolbox over the side.

The boat rolls, my arms scrape against the hull, and I take a breath a split second before I hit the water. The cold is shocking. The weight of the toolbox yanks my feet toward the bottom. Salt stings my eyes and my fingers cramp as I struggle to open the knife. I'm terrified of dropping it. The box is pulling me down. My nose pulses with pain as salt water floods my nasal cavity, and I exhale precious air. The blade comes open, and I curl into a ball, trying to reach the rope around my ankles. I'm somersaulting through the waves as I saw at the cord connecting me to the box. The rope parts, and the box drops away into the black depths. My legs flail like a loose pair of scissors.

Lungs burning. Colored lights dancing across the backs of my eyelids. I've lost track of my bearings. I can see my brother's face, his arms are floating as the car fills with water. He turns to face me, his expression bleak, as he mouths my name.

I can't help reaching for him with my bound hands. Calling, Dean! Please, don't do it.

He already did. But you don't have to. Use the knife.

Reversing the grip of the knife in my hand, I push the blade through the rope around my wrists. The narrow strands fall away, and the sudden release of tension drives the metal edge into my palm.

Blood in the water.

Focus, Lake. Get going. Onward and upward.

Sense of direction is completely wrecked. I exhale a tiny bit of air, watching the bubbles stream what looks like sideways but what must be up. I follow them as the sea heaves around me, the cold ocean sucking away what body heat remains as I kick like a wounded frog. My arms are exhausted, my legs leaden as I try to get into a rhythm instead of just thrashing.

One, two, three four, now you can do four more.

Zoe's count helps me to focus. My eyes sting and I squeeze them shut.

Do four more.

Through my eyelids, I see a bright, flickering light. Is this it, then? The last final journey into the light? I strain to see if Dean is there, waiting for me. The light slides away, and I feel a terrible sense of loss. Abandoned. Again.

Four more. Kick hard!

And then I break the surface with a choking gasp, rising with a swell that enables me to see the *Pot o' Gold*, a bright light above it in the sky, and the sound of helicopter rotors as the downdraft turns the sea to foam. It's the Coast Guard, and I've never been so glad to see anyone in my life.

But if I yell for them, O'Brian will know I'm alive. And then he'll try to kill me. Again.

But if you don't, you're done for.

69

A MAN LEANS from the orange rescue helicopter with a bullhorn. "Attention, *Pot o' Gold*! Are you in distress?"

"No!" O'Brian shouts back. "We're all okay. Just lost the EPIRB."

I sink down into the trough of the following wave. I shout as loud as I can, wave my arms. They feel like two anchors. I'm shivering, and my voice is a squeak.

The spotlight sweeps the water, blinding me with a white-hot flare. The voice is distorted, booming. "You've got a man overboard! We are deploying a swimmer. Stand by." The helicopter moves away and descends, until it is barely above the waves. I can't see what happens as I drop down into another trough. But as I rise, I see the splash from a man in an orange drysuit hitting the water.

I wish I had a drysuit. I try to tread water, try to stay above the surface, but it's hard. I'm so tired, and beyond cold. The swimmer is coming toward me, like an orange seal. He's moving impossibly fast, and I glimpse the long fins on his feet as he propels himself like a dolphin through the waves. I close my eyes—it takes too much effort to keep them open. My arms stop their weary circling, and I float, rising and falling with the toss of the ocean.

Keep your chin up, Lake. Help is on the way.

I tip my head back to keep my nose above the surface. It seems like too much work. I'm just so tired.

"Ma'am, are you injured? Can you speak?" The voice is crisp, with military directness.

I open my eyes, see the rescue swimmer treading water beside me. He's wearing a yellow helmet and his face is obscured by a scuba mask, but I can see his eyes. They look friendly.

"Ma'am? Can you speak?"

There's so many important things to tell him. "I'm—I'm—he has a gun. People. In the hold."

His eyes widen behind his mask. "What? No, don't explain. Are you injured?"

"No." My teeth chatter together and a wave splashes over my face. I feel a supporting arm beneath my shoulders.

"Okay, just relax. I'm going to tow you back over to the *Pot o' Gold.*"

Panic stiffens my spine. "No! Guh-gun! There's puh-people—"

He frowns. "Someone has a weapon on the boat?"

I spit out a mouthful of water. "Yes! Threw me over. Tied me up. Tried to kill me." I'm afraid he can't understand my words, chopped to bits by my chattering teeth. So I lift my hands and their trailing ropes.

His arm tightens around me. I can feel his legs kicking. "Okay, ma'am, we won't go to the boat. I'm going to tow you over to the copter, and they'll drop a basket." His voice is steady and reassuring. "My name is Ross. Just relax, let me do the work."

He gets behind me, crosses one arm over my chest. "Lean back, ma'am. I've got you."

Too tired to struggle further, I relax back against him, feel the movement of his body as he sidestrokes away from the *Pot O' Gold,* back toward the hovering helicopter. Seawater splashes over my face as a swell crests, and I tense and struggle weakly as we slip down the back side of the wave.

His arm tightens. "Relax, ma'am. Don't fight. It's gonna be fine."

Chill out, Lake. You're not drowning now, okay?

I want to believe him. And Zoe. And I'm so tired, and cold. I can feel the weight of his arm as he pulls me through the water. The helicopter shines its spotlight at us, blinding me again. The wind from its rotors makes the skin on my cheeks flutter and corrugates the surface of the water. The swimmer is signaling, waving his other arm. The copter rises and the turbulence lessens.

A basket made of metal tubes with two cylindrical orange floats splashes into the sea. A long tether connects it to the helicopter. I hear spoken words, but the whup-whup of the rotors and the roar of the engine drowns them out. Ross gives me a shake.

"Ma'am, I said, can you get into the basket?"

"Don't think so." My words sound slurred. At least my teeth have stopped chattering. A distant part of my mind thinks that's not a good sign.

Stay with us, Lake.

The swimmer says, "I'll help you, okay? It's right here. Easy does it."

He opens a gate in the side. I watch with clinical detachment. The ocean cold has become a part of me, the chill is touching my heart.

Ross pulls us both into the basket. He has to drag my legs inside, because I don't have the strength to move them. "We're just going to hang on and they'll pull us up, okay? Hold onto the rail, right here." He wraps my hands around the edge of the basket, and loops his arms around my shoulders, bracing his feet against the side. He motions the crew to pull us up.

I want to stay this way forever, nothing to do except be, with his arms around me to hold me steady. We rise into the air, and I feel a thousand times heavier outside the buoyancy of the water. My body gives a convulsive shiver, and I try to speak.

"Just relax, okay? You're safe."

"There's people."

"What people?"

"Prisoners. In the hold."

"There's *prisoners* in the hold? Not the crew?"

"Yes—" The basket swings at the end of its tether, and I feel the backwash of the rotors. "Prisoners. Lots of them."

We've risen to the helicopter, and another man leans out and pulls me into the cabin. He wraps a blanket around me as Ross follows me on board.

He pulls off his mask and says, "Lieutenant, I think we've got a situation on the *Pot o' Gold.*"

70

THE PILOT HALF-turns in the seat, and I realize it's a woman. She shouts over her shoulder. "What are you talking about? What situation?"

Ross shucks off his fins. Bellows to the others, "Weapons and possible prisoners on board the *Pot o' Gold*. What's the ETA for the response boat?"

The co-pilot's voice rings through the compartment. "Fifteen minutes."

Another voice chimes in. "The trawler is gunning her engines. She's making a run for it."

I say, weakly, "Don't let them get away. The captain is a murderer."

"Damn," says Ross. "Lieutenant, are we going to pursue?"

The pilot nods. "Take care of our passenger first."

Ross turns back to me. "What was your name again, ma'am?"

"Audrey."

"Okay, Audrey, you're in danger of hypothermia, and we have to get you stabilized before we go after the bad guys. First, you need to get out of those wet clothes, okay?"

I nod shakily. If I have to get naked to stop O'Brian, so be it.

Ross smiles. "Me and Kent here are going to help you undress, okay?" He gestures to the man who helped me out of the basket.

They remove my waterlogged jacket and Ross does a double-take at my empty holster, but unfastens it with practiced ease. Kent gives me a gray hooded sweatshirt with the Coast Guard logo emblazoned on the chest. I pull off my shirt and bra and yank the hoodie over my head. Immediately, I feel warmer. Peeling out of my jeans is harder, and Kent and Ross have to help me. My pants end up inside out on the floor of the helicopter, my underpants caught inside. The chopper banks, and I land on my naked butt, feet still encased in soggy wool socks and every muscle trembling.

Good thing you put on clean underwear.

Ross hands me a pair of sweatpants. I tug them on over my wet skin, the cut on my hand pulsing with pain and oozing blood. I have to draw the string tight to get them to fit. But the dry clothes make a difference, as does the blanket and Ross's arm wrapped around my shoulders. Kent bandages my palm, and gives me a set of headphones with a mic. My hands are shaking too badly to put it on myself, and he has to help me. I glance out through the windshield. The *Pot o' Gold* is heading away.

Kent leans over and shuts the door, cutting off the noise of the rotors. Then he reaches into a bag and gives me two chemical hand warmers, which I activate and stuff into my pockets, along with my hands.

Kent straps into his seat, Ross buckles me into another, and pulls down a jump seat for himself.

"Victim secure," he says.

I refuse to be a victim. "They're getting away! We've got to stop them."

"No ma'am, no one's getting away," says Lt. Braddock, the pilot. "We're on it. Everyone secure?"

Ross nods. "That's affirmative. Let's go get some bad guys."

The nose of the copter dips, the engines roar, and we bear off into the night.

Without looking away from the windshield, Braddock says, "Ma'am, can you tell us who you are and what's going on aboard that vessel?"

I adjust the mic. "My name is Audrey Lake. I'm a detective working out of Astoria. I was hired to investigate the murder of Jack Reynolds, and was on the *Pot o' Gold* in the course of that assignment. While I was on board, the captain—Tavin O'Brian—and his mate, Tad

Mitchell, got on and started the engines. I didn't want him to find me, so I hid in a closet."

Leaving out the bit about puking in the engine room, are we?

"I thought I knew all the Astoria cops," says Ross. "I don't recognize you."

"I just moved here six months ago." I'm not going to let my lack of law enforcement status jeopardize the pursuit, or let them see me as a civilian victim.

The light from the escaping fishing boat is getting larger, as are the waves.

Braddock says, "Just to confirm, you say they definitely have a weapon?"

"Yes. Mitchell—the crewman—has a handgun. And the captain has my Glock." I go on to relate, in as few words as possible, the trafficking I witnessed, the transfer of migrants from a freighter. "There's a dozen people in the hold, more or less."

"Ma'am, can you tell us the name of the freighter? Or its nationality?"

I shake my head. "I couldn't see either the name or the flag."

The co-pilot is on the radio, relaying information to the response boat—which I gather was launched in tandem with the helicopter— and calls for an additional cutter to intercept a container ship in the vicinity of the marine reserve.

The reserve. I hadn't realized where we were. The crime has come full circle.

The *Pot o' Gold* is now below us, illuminated by the helicopter's spotlight. Ross grabs the bullhorn as the helicopter follows in the fishing boat's wake. He opens the door, and a cold tumult of wind plasters my wet hair to my head. A shiver shakes my frame, which I try to suppress.

His voice booms over the water. "Attention, *Pot o' Gold*! Stop where you are and kill your engines."

The trawler does the opposite, surging forward until it shudders to an abrupt halt. Even over the sound of the rotors, I can hear the crash.

The *Pot o' Gold* lists heavily to one side. The waves are foam-flecked, and spray scatters across the deck.

"What the hell?" Ross leans forward to get a better look and calls through the bullhorn. "Attention, *Pot o' Gold*. Captain O'Brian. What just happened?"

"They've hit something," says the co-pilot. "A drift log, or something. They're going down."

The co-pilot switches to another channel. "Intercept craft, what's your ETA?"

Another voice crackles over the headphones. "We can see your light. Five minutes."

"Look!" I shout, and point. O'Brian and Mitchell have exited the wheelhouse in their survival suits. The *Pot o' Gold* is definitely lower in the water.

"What's down there? What did they hit?" The co-pilot cranes in his seat, playing the spotlight over the prow of the damaged boat. The helicopter dips and banks, circling the scene. The light beam lasers across the water, illuminating a big yellow rectangle just under the surface.

Confusion grips me, and then I remember the freighter, and the busy crew pushing it overboard. "They've hit the container!"

"What container?" barks the pilot, her voice sharp. "Explain."

"The one the migrants came in. They were in a shipping container before they transferred to the *Pot o' Gold*." The listing vessel is drifting broadside to the waves. I grab for Ross's arm. "There's people in the fish hold. We need to save them."

He begins pulling on his flippers.

Kent sets up the winch and hook in preparation.

"Be careful," I say. "Remember, he's got a gun. At least one." My voice is shaking, but I can't help it. I don't want my heroic rescuer to get shot, especially with my own gun.

On the trawler, O'Brian and Mitchell run to the stern and release the Zodiac dinghy from its mounting davits. I can't tell which is which, but one of them jumps off the heaving deck and clambers aboard the Zodiac. He releases the line attaching it to the trawler, pushing away just as the second man hits the water.

I tear my attention from the small boat to the listing deck of the *Pot o' Gold*. They've left the hatch to the hold battened down.

They are going to let the migrants die rather than be caught by the Coast Guard.

The helicopter circles, the rotor wash stirring up spindrift.

The second man in the water—I can see he has a beard so I know it's Mitchell—is having trouble. He keeps getting washed away from the Zodiac by the waves. And O'Brian isn't helping him.

"That guy's in trouble," exclaims Ross. "I'm going in." And he jumps feet first into the surf.

The helicopter pulls up to reduce the rotor wash. In the water, Ross begins to swim toward the flailing Mitchell. The *Pot o' Gold* rises on the crest of a swell, and I can see torn metal in the bow.

71

THE CRUSHED METAL has compromised the structure. The hold will fill with water, if it hasn't already. I'm screaming. "We have to get the people out! Put me down on the deck! We can't wait for the intercept boat!"

Kent yells, "No way! You're a civilian."

"Let me go down. I'm law enforcement. I've been on board. I know what to do."

The pilot swears as the *Pot o' Gold* lists to starboard, settling further.

Kent calls to the pilot. "Lieutenant Braddock? It's your call."

I unbuckle my seat belt. "You've got to let me go. We're wasting time. People are going to die."

The headset hisses. "Goddamn it! All right, Kent, get her into harness."

"You sure, Lieutenant?"

"We're search and rescue, saving people is our priority," barks Braddock without turning her head.

Kent straps me up, shows me how to disengage the skyhook. The helicopter circles once, I see the Zodiac hovering nearby while Ross struggles with Mitchell in the water. Then I'm out the door and dangling on the end of a cable, and the deck of the fishing boat is rushing up to meet me.

I so did not sign up for this.

I hit the deck, and the vibration goes all the way up to my hips. Then I feel the lift of the tether and feel nearly weightless, then heavy again as the line slackens and the boat rolls, and I lose my balance and fall painfully to my knees. A sharp pain shoots through my left shin.

We're getting a little too old for acrobatics, Lake.

I disengage the skyhook in order to move more freely. I hear shouting, look back up to the helicopter, where Kent is making hand gestures which I don't understand. I wave so he knows I'm okay, and begin to crawl toward the hatch that covers the fish hold. Even from here, I can hear the yells and banging from the men trapped below.

The *Pot O' Gold* is low in the water, moving sluggishly with the waves.

The hatch is fastened with a sliding bar. I try to slide it back, but the pressure from the men below has jammed it in place.

"Hello!" I shout. "I'm trying to help you, but you need to stop pushing on the hatch."

There's a slice of a second of silence, then the noise redoubles, the banging intensifies, the pressure on the hatch increases. The latching bar now has a very slight bend.

If it bends too far, I won't be able to get it loose.

"Stop!" I bang on the metal with my fist. "Stop! Everyone back away!" But I don't think they understand me.

I can't save them. Why can't I ever save them?

A wave crashes against the side of the ship. The spume splatters me with briny cold, and the craft heels over until I'm afraid we're going to capsize. I have to grab the latching bar to keep from slipping down across the deck, and my feet paw helplessly against the slickened steel. Cries and curses come from below, and the hatch settles back into its frame. I can see a tiny sliver of space between the bar and the housing.

The boat rolls back to horizontal. I look up to see another wave coming. The helicopter is circling, and the spotlight sears my retinas, blinding me.

Fucking hell.

I reach for the latch, get my hands around the cold and angular metal, pull it back with all my strength. It slides a few inches, until the bend catches in the housing.

No. No. No. I bang my fist on the latch, trying uselessly to flatten the curve. The deck pitches, and I'm drenched anew.

A dark figure crawls over the side. It's O'Brian, come back to kill me. No—it's Sonny, with a long knife in his hand. The mattress is cold and hard, but I won't let him kill us. I won't. The hatch slams closed on my hand and I scream in pain. I flail an arm to fend off my attacker.

Not now, Lake! Focus!

"Audrey, stop! Let me help!"

I blink. It's Ross, and he's holding a crowbar.

I roll off the hatch to give him access, point out the upward bend in the latch. His face is grim. He slides the bar back into place, erasing my progress.

"No!" I croak. "We need to save the people."

"We will," he says, and smashes the crowbar down on the latch, right where it's bent. Again, and again, ignoring the answering bangs and cries from below.

"Where's Mitchell?" I croak. "The crewman in the water."

"He wouldn't stop fighting. I had to let him go before he drowned us both. Then the other guy came back in the Zodiac and pulled him in, and they took off."

A bullhorn cry from the helicopter: "We've deployed a life raft. The intercept craft is almost here."

The words are meaningless, punctuated by the clang of metal on metal as Ross swings the crowbar until the latch is almost straight.

"Come on," says Ross. "Let's do it." Together we pull on the locking bar. It squeals as it scrapes through the housings, but it's moving, and moving, and suddenly the hatch springs open with an explosive waft of fish and brine, and I'm staring at a man with panicked eyes and dripping black hair. Beneath him are other men, clustered on the access ladder, and below them is the dark slosh of seawater.

72

Ross and I extend our hands. The prisoners scramble out onto the deck. Some are crying. Some are bleeding from cuts and scrapes. Their number seems fewer as I count them. Eight. One man looks wildly at the shivering cluster of men, then darts back to the ladder, peering down into the hold.

"Ramón! Ramón!" His voice is anguished. Then he stretches a foot to the first rung.

Ross grabs his shoulder. "Let me do it. How many are missing?"

The stricken man holds up two fingers. Ross nods, and slides down the ladder and splashes into the hold. The water level looks higher to me. I count the number of rungs I can see. Seven.

Another wave hits the hull, staggering us. One of the men grabs my elbow. "We must get away. The boat, it sinks!"

I nod, look for the circling helicopter. The spotlight illuminates an inflatable raft, floating on the sea.

Kent leans out with the bullhorn. "You'll have to swim, Audrey. Get everyone to the raft!"

Oh, hell no. This can't be on me. I'm so tired, and cold. And terrified. But. Who else?

I turn to the man standing beside me. He looks terrified, too. And determined.

I glance around the deck, see circular life preservers on the rails. Were there life jackets in the gear closet? I can't remember, and there just isn't time.

"Come on," I say, staggering to the side like a reeling drunk, trying to ignore the pain in my shin. "Everyone get a life ring. And then," I pause to swallow hard, "we must swim to the raft."

About half the group complies. The rest seem too dazed to understand. The man who wanted to go back to the hold is lying on his belly, staring down into the darkness below.

There's only four life preservers.

The boat lists. And suddenly I'm terrified that Ross will be trapped below. But. The prisoners.

"Listen," I say to the man who seems to be the leader. "What's your name?"

"I am Marco Avelino." His voice is remarkably calm, all things considered, and I feel steadier just hearing it.

"Okay, Marco. Everyone needs to get to the raft. You'll have to jump in the water and share the rings. You can swim, I hope?"

He nods briefly, and calls to the others, relaying instructions in a language I don't recognize. I can't stay to supervise, trusting in his resilience. I have to get back to the hold. Urge the others to get to the raft. Tug on the arm of the prone man.

"You have to leave!"

He jerks away. "No! Ramón! My brother!" We both grab the edge of the hatch as a deep roll threatens to dislodge us.

What fresh hell is this?

The *Pot O' Gold* is turned broadside to the waves. The next big swell could cause us to capsize.

"Ross will find your brother." But there's no sign of anyone in the black water below. I shout Ross's name. Turn back to the man beside me and shake his shoulder. "Please, get to the raft with the others."

There's only five rungs visible.

"Not without my brother."

Goddamn stubborn man. "Ross! Where are you?" The fishing boat rocks sluggishly, weighted down by the water in the hold.

Four rungs.

"Ross!"

"Ramón!"

And then I see him, Ross, sidestroking and towing a dark-haired man behind him. My heart surges like the water in the hold. Because Ross is exhausted, I see it in his eyes and the slower movement of his arms. He reaches the ladder and locks a hand around a rung, pulling the other man toward him. "C'mon buddy, time to climb."

The man is unresponsive. Ross meets my eyes and gives a slight shake of his head, and my heart constricts.

Nevertheless, Ross hooks an arm around the prisoner's chest, hauls himself up the ladder one-handed. I reach down to help, grab his burden, the other prisoner also helping. We pull the motionless figure onto the deck and roll him over on his back.

"Ramón! Wake up!" His brother slaps the face of the unresponsive body. The lids are open, but the eyes are lifeless.

I pull on Ross's arm as he heaves himself onto the deck.

He cracks a grim smile. "Can't climb a ladder in these bloody flippers." He leans over the prone figure and begins chest compressions, addressing the man beneath his hands. "Come on, buddy. Don't give up."

The bullhorn blares. "Ross! Audrey! Get off the ship! You're about to sink!"

There's only one rung left.

73

Ross and I look at each other. I glance out over the ocean, see the lifeboat bobbing on the waves. Three men are inside, and helping the others over the air-fattened sides. The water is dotted with life rings.

Ross makes a trumpet of his hands, aims his voice at the helicopter. "Drop the cage!"

"We're pulling you in!"

"Drop the cage! For these two! I'll be fine!"

"No, wait," I protest.

He drops his hands. "I'll head for the raft. You'll be okay. We'll get you in the cage with this other guy."

"But what about—" I point to the man lying on the deck. Ramón. His brother is still trying to wake him up.

Ross shakes his head. "He's gone."

"And the other missing man?"

"I couldn't find anyone else. If he's down there, he's dead."

I hear the growl of the winch, feel the downdraft of the rotors, as the rescue basket drops beside us with a clang. Together we get the struggling brother into the basket. I lock my arms around him to keep him from jumping out. It jerks and sways as we lift off the deck. I look down to see Ramón's body still lying next to the open hatch. Not a single rung is visible. Ross lifts a hand, salutes, and then vaults overboard into the heaving sea.

I want to close my eyes, but I wait until he breaks the surface, arrowing toward the raft. The man in my arms strains and struggles but at last falls limp as he wails the name of his brother. Below us, Ramón's body is shifting as the waters begin to wash against him.

Kent pulls us through the open door of the helicopter.

Another light splits the darkness. A small motorized vessel packed with men speeds into view. The intercept craft has arrived at last.

There's no sign of the Zodiac. I kneel on the floor of the chopper, feeling the vibration of its engines against my bones. My cage mate is huddled in a blanket, sobbing quietly.

Braddock's voice shouts over the engine. "You up for a bit more flight time?"

I nod, give her a thumbs up.

Let's get the bastards who caused all this.

The co-pilot turns his head. "Kent, how's our newest passenger?"

Kent has been talking quietly with Ramón's brother. Now he says, "Not great. But not dying, either."

Braddock nods. "All right, then."

The co-pilot speaks. "I called the cutter. It was already at sea, and she's headed in our direction. If you're up for it, we're going to find our rogue captain."

"I'm up for it." I try to disguise my shivers and the pain in my leg. "What about the men in the raft?"

"Intercept will pull them in. They'll also tag the container for retrieval."

I dearly want to watch, to make sure Marco and the rest of the migrants and Ross are safe. But time's a-wasting, and I know it. "Okay then, let's go."

The pilot nods, and we head toward the horizon, chasing our prey.

74

The helicopter turns south, paralleling the coast, using its spotlight to scan the waves. There's nothing but dark water.

"Where do you think they're going?" My throat is raw from shouting, my mind still half on the rescued migrants. And Ross.

Kent shakes his head. "Nearest dock is in the Nehalem River. Or they could just run the Zodiac up on shore somewhere. That would be easiest for us, because we could land on a beach. Or they might just intend to go offshore and sit tight. We can't stay out here too much longer. Not enough fuel."

"What then?"

"A cutter is out there looking, too." He shrugs. "It's a big ocean, and hard to find a tiny boat in the middle of it. But they don't have unlimited fuel, either. I doubt they can get farther than five or ten miles."

The thought of losing O'Brian makes me almost physically sick. This guy has murdered people, imprisoned people. And what about the assault on Alon? O'Brian blamed Mitchell for that, but was it true? Tad had a gun on the boat, but he isn't really that aggressive. He gave me the tool I needed to survive.

Yeah, but he also helped throw you over the side.

I clench my fists in frustration, causing the cut on my hand to flare with pain.

It takes the better part of thirty minutes to find the fleeing men, but we do. The beam of the spotlight reveals the Zodiac cresting a wave, and O'Brian's face is white as he looks over his shoulder at the helicopter. Kent gets on the bullhorn and orders him to stop. The co-pilot is on the radio to the cutter, relaying our position and calling for assistance. The lights from the small town of Manzanita shine in the east, and behind us is the bulk of Neakahnie Mountain where it juts into the ocean. We're a good forty miles from Astoria.

O'Brian turns his back on us and looks resolutely ahead. And then he reaches inside his survival suit and pulls a gun. Smoke spurts from the barrel, and a split second later I hear the shot. Mitchell's arms go up and out, his mouth a dark O of surprise. The crewman falls overboard. O'Brian fires again, the bullet spurting into the water a few inches from Mitchell's head. O'Brian stuffs the weapon back into his suit, guns the motor and speeds away.

"Son of a bitch!" The co-pilot swears. "We can't leave that guy to die."

"But O'Brian'll get away!" I protest. But even as I say it, I know we have to let him go.

It takes us twenty minutes to drop the basket down to the stricken Mitchell and get him in the helicopter. He's in a survival suit, so better off than I was when I landed in the drink, but we don't have Ross to help. By the time he gets hauled in, the pilot makes the decision to head back to Astoria. We don't have the fuel to continue the chase, and the helicopter is full of people who need medical attention. Mitchell is bleeding heavily from a wound to the shoulder, not fatal but serious enough to warrant a hospital.

His face is a mask of surprise. "He shot at me. Why? I don't understand."

"You were the distraction he needed so he could get away." I shrug. "Maybe you knew too much."

"But I never would have told. That's my captain." His eyes close against the pain.

I have to make a real effort to keep from throttling him. "I think your loyalty was misplaced." And I turn my back on his bewildered face.

As the adrenaline wears off, I become aware of my own state, cold and exhausted, covered with bruises. Everything hurts. My eyelids droop and I have to jerk myself awake on the flight back home. The call to the hospital goes out, and the promise of law enforcement and an ambulance for Mitchell comes through.

Maybe he'll tell the cops everything he knows, after being nearly killed by O'Brien.

I just hope it'll be enough to prosecute.

Maybe O'Brian didn't set out to be a mass murderer, but he was able to step over the line without too much trouble. At some point, other people's lives just stopped mattering to him. Was it the trafficking, when humans became just another commodity, like crabs and fish? Or had he always been this way?

Why, in the end, had he chosen evil? And did he even realize he had done so?

OCTOBER 30 - DAY 12

75

We arrive back in Astoria and head straight to Columbia Memorial Hospital. It's a small facility, only twenty-five beds, but they apparently have a helipad for life flights to Portland, and Lieutenant Braddock takes advantage of it. We are met by a medical team. The migrant we picked up in the basket and Tad Mitchell can both walk, although Mitchell looks pale and sick and his survival suit is stained with blood. As for me, I'm not feeling wonderful either. The adrenaline has worn off, my leg is throbbing with pain, the cut on my hand hurts, and I can't stop shivering. The EMTs put me on a stretcher and carry me to the ER.

Once there, the medical staff diagnose me with mild hypothermia and a cracked tibia, as well as assorted minor injuries. They put me in a room and hook up an IV drip, immobilize my leg, stitch up the cut on my hand, bandage the engine burns on my wrist and forearm, and cover me with blankets. Whatever drug they inject into my port puts me out like a sledgehammer to the head. At some point I'm transferred to a regular hospital room. When I finally wake up, I'm dressed in a hospital gown, there's a splint on my leg, and a visitor is waiting in the guest chair. It's Ross, the rescue swimmer. For an instant, I think I'm hallucinating again.

Those are some good drugs.

Then he smiles, and I'm so relieved to see him that it feels like a candle lighting up in my heart, and I sternly tell myself to put it out.

But I can't stop staring. He's dressed in his uniform, blue pants and long-sleeved shirt, with U.S. Coast Guard embroidered above one pocket and R. Jordan above the other. He's got shadows beneath his eyes but seems otherwise unscathed.

"Hi," I manage. My voice is a dry croak and I wonder what I must look like.

"Hi," he says. "How are you?"

High up in the sky in my beautiful balloon.

I clear my throat, sounding like a three-pack-a-day smoker. "It feels like someone has been beating me with a stick."

We smile at each other. I'm having a hard time focusing. The thin hospital gown is bunched up behind my shoulders and the neckline is tight against my throat.

I'm too sexy for my nightie, too sexy, yeah…

I ignore my headmate and ask what happened to him while I was flying around chasing bad guys.

He tells me they got the migrants into the intercept craft, and brought them back to Astoria, along with himself. Many are suffering from minor injuries, malnutrition, and exposure, and they are being kept under observation in this very hospital. As far as he can tell, they are all from Southeast Asia.

He says the shipping container the *Pot O' Gold* smashed into, the one pushed off the freighter, has been marked with dye and a salvage vessel will be dispatched to retrieve it. They hope the container will yield proof of the trafficking operation, which will help in O'Brian's prosecution. There might also be evidence that can be used to identify the cargo ship, and that information will be sent up the chain for ICE to deal with, along with the migrants after they have recovered.

I can't imagine what it must feel like to come all this way, crossing an ocean inside a box, survive being shot or drowned, and then to be stuck in a detention center for who knows how long. It's depressing. But I keep all this to myself.

Ross continues bringing me up to date. He says O'Brian was picked up by the Coast Guard cutter. The Zodiac had run out of gas, and he was drifting off the coast. He didn't resist, and is now being held in the Clatsop County Jail, waiting to be charged.

Ross stops talking, and we look at each other for a few moments. I don't want him to leave, but for the life of me I can't think of anything to say. So I fall back on an old standard.

"Thanks for saving my life."

"It's my pleasure." He cracks a smile, and I notice he has a dimple in his chin.

I wave a hand. Actually, it's more like a twitch of the wrist. "How can you just, you know, dive into the ocean like that? With waves and things." What I'm really asking is, how can he endanger himself to help a stranger, and a stupid one at that.

There's a mystery every moment.

He shrugs, but his voice is serious. "Saving people is my job. That's what we do, whenever it's needed. Semper paratus. Always ready."

I can tell he means it. The echo of an old oath comes back to me: selfless devotion to duty, to protect and to serve, to take action in the face of danger. There's more, but I've forgotten the words. We look at each other for an endless moment. Until I break it by saying, "Maybe I can buy you a drink sometime, when I'm back up to room temperature."

For some reason, that makes him laugh. "I'd like that." There's another pause before he says, "Take care of yourself, Audrey. I'll be seeing you."

When he leaves, the room seems a few degrees colder. And a whole lot lonelier.

Couldn't you, for once in your life, be a little more approachable?

Is that Zoe, or my mother? I close my eyes. I'm just not the warm and fuzzy type. All the years of being a cop, of keeping the emotional tides locked down in order to do my job, has made me what I am, for better or for worse.

Oh, please. Drama much?

I'm too old for him.

Forty is the new thirty.

The nurse arrives to check my vitals, splint, and bandages. She disconnects the IV and brings me some crutches so I can use the bathroom. When I return, she helps me settle more comfortably in the bed before hanging a new bag and hooking me up again.

"Are you going to give me more drugs?" I ask.

Yay.

"Not this time, I'm afraid. Just some saline to keep you hydrated."

Boo.

I grimace. Zoe was a drug user as well as being a sex worker. I've never been either, but apparently I buried myself in the part.

The nurse must have noticed my expression, because she says, "What's your pain level, on a scale of one to ten? If it's too bad, I can bring you something to help."

Yes, please.

"No thanks, I'm okay, for now." Despite Zoe's enthusiasm, I have an aversion to drugs.

"I'm sure the doctor can send a prescription to your pharmacy. She'll be here in a little while to look you over, and give you the okay before you can be discharged. Do you have someone to drive you home?"

"I'll have to think about that." Who can I call? Phoebe? I glance at the phone on the bedside table. And I realize, my own phone is probably inoperable, having been immersed in seawater. If I even still have it. I look around, but can't spot it. "Where's my stuff?"

"Everything you had with you is in there." The nurse points to a cabinet by the door. "But it's probably still damp. I've got to go, but you can buzz the nurses' station if you need anything."

Great. No clothes, either. I hope my keys are still in my jacket pocket, because that's going to be a problem if they're not.

The nurse leaves, and I settle in for the duration, watching the minutes tick by on the wall clock. I wonder how much this stay in the hospital is going to set me back, and whether my insurance will cover it. Maybe I can expense it out to Biswas.

You were operating on your own recognizance.

That remark depresses me again. Where the heck is the doctor? How much longer will I have to wait, especially since each minute I spend here probably costs as much as a new car? I look down at the port in my hand, into which the IV tube disappears. In the movies, people yank these out all the time. I wonder if it hurts when you do that. Maybe I can get out of here right now.

Broken leg, remember?

Grumpily, I try to find a watchable show on television when someone else taps on the door. I'm astonished to see Meg Eccleston, the medium. Her hair is caught up in a pony tail and she's wearing jeans and a green cable-knit sweater.

"Meg. This is a surprise." I search for the bed control in the blankets so I can sit up properly.

"Hi, Audrey. I heard you've been having some adventures."

"Did the spirits tell you?"

We weren't that *close to death.*

She laughs. "I have an emergency services scanner app on my phone. I like to know what's going on. I heard them talk about this big migrant bust, and taking people to the hospital, and I had a feeling you might be involved. And when I got here, the admittance staff were all chattering about it." She brings the visitor's chair to the edge of the bed. "How are you doing?"

I don't know what to say about her "feeling", especially since it turned out to be right, so I just say, "Good, all things considered." I fill her in on the night's activities.

Her eyes grow round. "Wow, getting thrown into the ocean, jumping out of helicopters. You're like a female James Bond."

I scoff. "A lot of it was involuntary. And I broke my leg. That never happens to James Bond."

"Still." She leans forward. "What were you doing on that boat in the first place?"

So I tell her about Alon's case, and the vision. I don't reveal particulars about the people involved, but I do share what I felt and experienced. Because there's no one else I can tell, and she's had a dose of my surreal ability already. It feels good to not have to watch my words, or worry that she's going to think I'm insane.

Almost like having a friend.

"So your ability came through in the end. That's wonderful." She puts one hand on the bed rail. "We should totally work together, Audrey. We could really help people."

This doesn't put me off as badly as before, but only because I've learned to like Meg. Still. "There's one small problem."

"What's that?"

"I don't believe in ghosts." I say it with a smile so she doesn't think I'm insulting her personally.

"I'll take care of the spirits. You just take care of the past." She stands up. "I'm glad to hear that everything has come together for you, and that you're doing okay. Is there anything you need?"

I hesitate, but she did ask. "I need a lift home later today, when they discharge me. And maybe…could you bring me some clothes?"

"Of course. Do you want me to go to your house, or buy something?"

I can't be in debt to her, I'm going to have to hock all my possessions as it is. "My coat is in that cabinet. See if my keys are still in the pocket of my jacket." I mentally cross my fingers.

To my relief, she retrieves the keys, jingling them in her hand. I give her some directions to my place, and where to find some fresh clothes—folded up in piles on the floor upstairs.

"I'll go grab some things, and put them in my car. Call me as soon as the doctor lets you go."

I explain about my phone being inoperable, and thus all contacts lost, and she gives me another card. We chat for a few more minutes before she takes her leave.

"Take care of yourself, Audrey. I'll see you soon."

If Meg is a standard example of the seeker community, I misjudged both her and them. She's been nothing but supportive. I wonder what she's going to think about my empty house.

Maybe she can talk to the intruder.

Only if the intruder is a ghost. And there's no such thing, remember?

Nothing on the vids, remember?

Then I probably hallucinated it.

Your crazy is showing. Better tuck that back in.

Better a hallucination than a vengeful phantom or some random burglar. I really hope the only thing Meg finds in the house are my clothes.

76

AFTER ZOE'S DIRE predictions, I feel even more antsy. It's already after noon. Maybe I can squeeze some billable time out of my enforced stay. I ping the nurse call button, and fidget until someone comes. She insists on checking my vitals and the level of the saline bag before she asks what I need.

"Can you look up the number for the Clatsop County Public Defenders' Office?"

I'm sure that's not a request she gets every day, but she pulls out her own phone and does a little tap dance with her thumbs and reads off the number.

I ask her to repeat it as I punch the buttons of the bedside phone.

"Is there anything else?" She asks, with a tinge of sarcasm.

"No thanks," I mouth, giving her a thumb's up just as Juanita answers. I ask for Biswas and he picks up on the second ring.

His cultured accent has an overlay of concern "Audrey, Juanita said you were calling from the hospital. What's happened?"

I fill him in on everything I've discovered: O'Brian's confession, the connection with Alon Dasalon, the possibility of video evidence on Jack Reynolds' drone. We talk for a long time, him asking questions, me answering.

Finally he says, "I have some news. The grand jury gave the go-ahead for Horne's trial, but I've had a discussion with the DA, and shared all the material you provided about other possible culprits.

That, as well as the generally poor quality of the police investigation, has made him decide to drop all charges except trespassing. Horne will be released."

"That's great," I say. "Will they go after O'Brian now?"

"He'll undoubtedly be indicted for his role in migrant trafficking, and probably for his assault on Tad Mitchell, but no one heard his confession to Reynold's murder except for you, and you were working for us at the time, even though I did NOT authorize you to trespass on his vessel. If he were my client, I would say your testimony is no better than hearsay, and possibly biased. Without physical evidence, there's nothing to connect him to that killing."

My irritation rises at his dismissal of the evidentiary potential of my experience. "Maybe Mitchell would testify."

"Was he an eyewitness?"

Mitchell wasn't present in my vision of Reynolds' murder. It was just O'Brian and Reynolds down in the hold. Maybe Mitchell helped dump the body, or maybe not. "I don't know."

"There's a lot that needs to happen before this case is ready to go to trial. They'll probably want to concentrate on what they can prove, and not muddy the water. You should know that better than I."

I sigh, lean back on my pillows and close my eyes. I'm glad they got O'Brian on something, but if Horne is released and no one else is charged, the murder of Jack Reynolds will remain officially unsolved. And meanwhile, the family gets no closure.

But I can help the Jenson's. "Will you tell Madison what I've told you? She'll want to know the trafficker has been caught, and she can pass that on to her client."

"I will." There's a pause, and then Biswas says, "I had my doubts about hiring a private investigator, but our association has been fruitful. You can count on more work from the public defenders' office."

Great. I'm going to need it when the bills start rolling in. And I don't mind the idea of working for the defense like I used to. We saved an innocent man from going to prison for a crime he didn't commit, and that's good work.

My experience on the *Pot o' Gold* solidifies what I've already begun to accept, that my visions of violence are something more than coincidental, more than just hallucinations. In some way I don't understand, they are reflective of reality. I don't know how I feel about that. Kind of terrified, and a little bit sick, if I'm honest. Because if I know for sure that something bad has occurred, aren't I bound to do something about it?

As my conversation with Ross reminded me, I swore an oath to serve and protect. And just because I'm no longer a cop, I don't feel released from that oath. At the end of the day, as flawed as the police sometimes are, we fight for the victims and their families. People like Christoper, and Alicia. And Alon.

Even if I'm no longer in law enforcement, that motivation is still in play.

I press the redial button on the phone, and when Juanita answers, I ask her to give me Alicia Reynolds' number. Then, before I can change my mind, I call Alicia. It rings a few times, and I wonder if she's out in the garden. But she finally picks up, her voice sounding panicked.

"Hello? Hello? What's wrong?"

I'm a little taken aback. "Nothing. I'm just calling to tell you—"

She makes a sound of disgust. "Audrey Lake. I should have known. Why are you calling from the hospital? You almost gave me a heart attack. I thought something had happened to Keith."

"Oh. Sorry. No, I'm the one in the hospital." And because I don't want to go into everything with her, I say, "I broke my leg."

"Did you get hit by a car?"

She sounds hopeful.

"I jumped out of a helicopter. But the reason I'm calling—"

"Wait, you did *what?*"

"It's not important, okay? Just listen. Please." In a few words, I tell her about Horne being released, but that the real killer confessed to me. That he's going down for other crimes, but probably not the murder of her ex-husband, due to lack of evidence.

There's a long silence on her end. Then she says, "He'll be in prison? For a long time?"

"Yes. Eventually." Because I can't imagine that O'Brian won't be found guilty.

He'll probably cut a deal.

Mitchell will turn. I know it.

Alicia's voice is strained. "Can you tell me who it was?"

My gown is bunching up again and I squirm against the bed pillows. "I can't. I'm sorry. But I imagine his crime is going to be big news."

"You're saying I might be able to guess."

"Yes."

"And Christopher and I will be safe."

I take a deep breath. "Yes." I hope. As safe as any of us ever are in this world.

"All right then."

She ends the call without saying goodbye, and I hang up the phone, still feeling unsatisfied. But I've done what I can. I don't believe in ghosts, or spirits, or that some magic sky-man is gonna reach down and save us. It's up to us to save ourselves, and to help each other. Because if it's all just dog eat dog, if we're all alone in the wilderness, what's the point?

At least you'll always have me.

Is that a threat, or a promise?

Author's Note

I hope you enjoyed your sojourn in Astoria with private investigator Audrey Lake. I'd be eternally grateful if you'd take a few minutes to leave some stars and/or a review at Amazon, Goodreads, and/or Library Thing. Writers need readers, and reviews are a great way to show your support and spread the word to other folks who might enjoy this story. And please, tell your friends!

Most of the places referenced in this book are real. Astoria and Warrenton are real towns in northwestern Oregon. The remains of the shipwreck on the beach at Warrenton where Audrey has her vision actually exists. The only place that isn't real is the Big Bridge Bar & Grill.

If you're interested in hearing about Audrey's next adventure, sign up for my free newsletter. You'll get a free Audrey Lake story exclusive to subscribers, plus early notice of the next book and other tidbits.

Thanks for reading and sharing. For more information visit my website at https://nichelleseely.com

If you'd like to contact me directly about this book, I'd love to hear from you. Drop me a line at nichelle@nichelleseely.com, with this book's title in the subject line.

All the words of this story and the cover were created by me. I do not use AI in any form, unless you count the spellchecker on my writing software.

Acknowledgments

If you regularly read acknowledgments, you know it takes a village to complete a book. With that in mind, I'd like to thank the following people.

John Kreske, rescue swimmer for the U.S. Coast Guard, for answering my questions about his profession and how the Coast Guard operates when aiding a vessel in distress. Any mistakes in my portrayal of the procedure and personnel are my own.

Once again, my husband Aaron deserves a trophy of his own for his unfaltering support, his cooking ability, and his willingness to read and comment. I choose you.

My sister Elia Seely is my alpha reader, digesting the rough draft and spitting out suggestions, and always willing to provide a soundboard for book talk. She's a mystery writer, too. Check out her stuff on Amazon.

My mother Norma Seely, for her support and writing advice. She, too, is a writer, with books available on Amazon.

In addition, I have to thank the members of my critique group: Kathy Mendt, Anne Hunsinger, and Jack Matthews. These folks kept me on my toes and offered nuanced and intelligent commentary. This book is a hundred times better because of them.

The beta readers who read the revised manuscript and offered suggestions and advice: Anne Hunsinger; Norma Seely, Aaron Hall, and Jodi Janz.

Lastly, thank you, the reader, for your time and attention. I hope you enjoyed meeting Audrey Lake and immersing yourself in the mossy streets of Astoria and Warrenton. To hear about Audrey's next case, sign up for my newsletter from my website at https://nichelleseely.com

www.ingramcontent.com/pod-product-compliance
Lightning Source LLC
Chambersburg PA
CBHW030523190726
48283CB00006B/1749